Praise for Keith McCafferty

Crazy Mountain Kiss

"This is a must for fans of eclectic mysteries in which the setting is just as important as the characters." —*Publishers Weekly* (starred review)

"A believable, thought-provoking, and rewarding mystery. In a genre brimming with hyper-stylized action and slick narrative devices, McCafferty defies convention and delivers a straight-ahead story based on authentic characters and honest emotion." —*Arizona Republic*

Dead Man's Fancy

"McCafferty knows his country and his characters, who have a comfortable, lived-in feel and yet shine as individuals. . . . [His] understated prose deserves to be savored." —*Kirkus Reviews*

"McCafferty's beautifully written third mystery . . . The complex, multilayered story smoothly switches from one character to another." —*Publishers Weekly* (starred review)

"[*Dead Man's Fancy*] delivers a carefully plotted western procedural. . . . Good reading for fans of [C. J.] Box, Craig Johnson, Nevada Barr, and Paul Doiron, although McCafferty has his own distinctive voice." —*Booklist*

"McCafferty's third series entry lassos up a range of topics—wolf reintroduction, wilderness living and survival, animal rights—that are uncovered through his protagonists' meticulous sleuthing." —*Library Journal*

The Gray Ghost Murders

"This is a truly wonderful read. In an old and crowded field, Keith has created characters fresh, quirky and yet utterly believable, then stirred them into a mystery that unfolds with grace and humor against a setting of stunning beauty and danger. Stranahan, the fisherman sleuth, breaks free of the old clichés and delights with his humanity, vulnerability, and love of cats. Yes, cats. Keith has written a book that speaks to women and men regardless of color or background. The only downside of this book is that we must wait a year for the next one."

—Nevada Barr, *New York Times* bestselling author of
the Anna Pigeon Mysteries

"McCafferty skillfully weaves Big Sky color, humor, and even romance (in the form of Sean's stunning new girlfriend, Martinique, who's bankrolling veterinary school by working as a bikini barista) into the suspenseful plot as it gallops toward a white-knuckle . . . climax."

—*Publishers Weekly*

"Think big-city CSI teams have it tough? Their examinations of crime scenes are hardly ever interrupted by a grizzly bear like the one that sends Deputy Harold Little Feather to the hospital. . . . Irresistible."

—*Kirkus Reviews*

"You'll find yourself obsessed with the story . . . due to McCafferty's hilarious, spot-on depiction of rural politics (starring a female sheriff, a latte-making love interest, and a fishing buddy), which proves that small western towns are as rich . . . as any world capital."

—Oprah's Book Club 2.0 (5 Addictive New Mysteries
We Can't Put Down)

The Royal Wulff Murders

"Keith McCafferty has pulled off a small miracle with *The Royal Wulff Murders*—a compelling Montana-based novel that will please both mystery readers *and* discerning fly-fishers."

—C. J. Box, *New York Times* bestselling author of
Back of Beyond and *Force of Nature*

"Keith McCafferty hits a bull's eye with Sean's story in his debut novel, *The Royal Wulff Murders*. . . . Like bacon and brownies—Stranahan's odd mix of painter, P.I., and fly fisher *works*. . . . Add the backwoodsy feminism of Sheriff Martha Ettinger, and the mystery is a good fit for enthusiasts of Nevada Barr who have read through all the Anna Pigeon novels. Packed with wilderness action and starring a band of stalwart individualists, *The Royal Wulff Murders* will have readers begging McCafferty for more."

—Tom Lavoie, ShelfAwareness.com for Readers

that make this novel so enjoyable: it's the rich characters, the robust sense of humor, a sadly topical plot, and a writing style that is as gin-clear as a Montana trout stream."

—Paul Doiron, author of *Trespasser* and *The Poacher's Son*

"*Wulff* is fun . . . with sharp dialogue between characters . . . [and] fishing scenes that read right. . . . [McCafferty is] *Field & Stream*'s survival editor, and that savvy shows in subtle and satisfying ways."

—*Fly Rod and Reel* (online)

"[A] muscular, original first novel. McCafferty is one of the country's most convincing writers on survival and life in the wilderness, and this mystery is an impressive foray into fiction—taut, often highly amusing, filled with memorable characters like the lady sheriff and the former private eye who paints and fly fishes—and it's a real page turner."

—Nick Lyons, author of *My Secret Fishing Life*

"The last time I fished the Madison River it was high, fast, and dirty—words that come to mind for parts of McCafferty's tangy debut mystery. But there are also episodes of angling wonder and Montana beauty, rendered in prose so gorgeous they make this book a truly rare catch, the page-turner that doubles as a poetic meditation."

—Mark Kingwell, author of *Catch and Release: Trout Fishing and the Meaning of Life*

CRAZY MOUNTAIN KISS

Keith McCafferty

—A SEAN STRANAHAN MYSTERY—

PENGUIN BOOKS

PENGUIN BOOKS
An imprint of Penguin Random House LLC
375 Hudson Street
New York, New York 10014
penguin.com

First published in the United States of America by Viking Penguin, an imprint of Penguin Publishing Group, a division of Penguin Random House LLC, 2015
Published in Penguin Books 2016

THE LIBRARY OF CONGRESS HAS CATALOGED THE HARDCOVER EDITION AS FOLLOWS:
McCafferty, Keith.
Crazy mountain kiss : a Sean Stranahan mystery / Keith McCafferty.
pages ; cm
ISBN 9780670014705 (hc.)
ISBN 9780143109051 (pbk.)
I. Title.
PS3613.C334C73 2015
813'.6—dc23
2015006858

Printed in the United States of America
3 5 7 9 10 8 6 4 2

For Gail,
a thousand Crazy Mountain kisses

One crow sorrow
Two crows mirth
Three crows a wedding
Four crows a birth
Five crows silver
Six crows gold
Seven crows a secret, ne'er to be told

—*Traditional*

Acknowledgments

Rarely can a writer say this is the moment the seed was sown. Not so, *Crazy Mountain Kiss*. I know exactly where I was when the novel began to take shape in my mind. I was sitting in a booth at Ted's Montana Grill in Bozeman, Montana, with my wife, Gail, and an old colleague from our days as newspaper reporters in California, Steve Swenson, and his wife, Mary. Though Steve was battling cancer, his spirit was undimmed, and I marveled, as I had before, at the skill with which he told a story. One story he told that day is the inspiration for this book, and to Steve I owe a debt of gratitude.

I started writing *Crazy Mountain Kiss* in the Old Faithful Inn in Yellowstone National Park, where I have penned at least a chapter of each of the Sean Stranahan novels. My wife and I spend a couple nights at the Inn to celebrate our wedding anniversary every May, and my tradition is to wander down the long hall into the lobby at three or four in the morning, when the cathedral-like inn is wood dark and deserted. I can lift my eyes to the platform four stories up, and imagine the bands that used to play there for dances after the Inn was built in 1904, when tourists were drawn there by horse and wagon. That morning, the desk I sat at on the second floor was illuminated through a stained glass lamp shade, and with a window cracked in the hopes of hearing a wolf, I opened the novel by writing "It was a dark and stormy night," just to break the ice.

Before rising from the chair I had the scene as well as the weather, and for once it actually was a dark and stormy night on the page, or at least one of brooding sky and portentous nature. So began the sojourn into the unknown that is the author's peculiar province. For me writing a novel is akin to setting sail, in that you can see only as far as the horizon, after which you are lost at sea until a bird perches on the mast, and you know that you will finally again come within sight of land. That is to say, the beginning is easiest, the end doable, and the open ocean of the middle chapters fraught with shark teeth and other perils. The trick is to resist the temptation to jump, and it is the readers who keep me onboard as much as anyone else. Specifically, I want to thank those of you who have reached out to me through email and letters. Your kind words bolster my spirits during the more perilous hours.

I owe a debt to the law enforcement officers who indulged my questions over the years, starting with my uncle, the late Bob Bailie, who was a game warden in the Appalachian foothills; my cousin Bill McCafferty, who is the police chief of Steubenville, Ohio; former Gallatin County, Montana, sheriff Jim Cashell; Lieutenant Jason Jarrett; search and rescue incident commander Chris Kent; search dog handler Bonnie Whitman Gafney; Chaplin Warren Hiebert; and old friend and former Park County sheriff's deputy Doug Wonder. Any matter of error in their fields of expertise is entirely my own.

Kathryn Court, the president and publisher of Penguin Books, deserves more thanks than I can give, for without Kathryn there would be no novels. I also want to thank my literary agent, Dominick Abel, for the same reason. Penguin editor Scott Cohen keeps me abreast of developments, the incomparable Beena Kamlani brings the book home, and my special thanks to editor Tara Singh, whose insights help me improve and shape the novels. Artist Jim Tierney designs the striking covers. Rick Holmes lends his rich, nuanced voice to the narration for Recorded Books. Copy editors are often overlooked in the process, but Roland Ottewell's light, intelligent touch makes me look better.

Then there are those who make a morning's work less lonely, including Ron Gompertz, the owner of Wild Joe's Coffee Spot, and baristas and regulars Sarah Grigg, Kezia Manlove, Carson Taylor, Jim

Devitt, Bill MacDonald, Brian Best, Patrick Topel, Emily Suemitsu, Sam Val Daele, Marty Sanders, Marta Plante, Matt Olsen, Kat Knisely, Julie Tate, Roger Robichaud, Mollie Eckman, Natalie Van Dusen, Corina Croaker, Denver Bryan, and Clair Langerak.

Last, never least, are my wife Gail, my daughter, Jessie, and my son, Tom, without whom I would surely drown in that deep and wine-dark sea.

CRAZY
MOUNTAIN
KISS

Prologue

As he reached for the bottle of George T. Stagg fifteen-year-old bourbon, Max Gallagher thought wryly of his oft-quoted principle of writing, the first of "Max's maxims," which he'd once confided to an editor of *American Crime* magazine—"Always write on the level." When he was working on *A Nose for Trouble*, the first book in his mystery series featuring a sleuth who was a "nose" for a perfume company, writing on the level meant a speedball, the cocaine slamming into his bloodstream seconds before heroin slowed the train to a more manageable speed. By the time he penned *A Nose for Romance*, his fifth novel and only best seller, he'd kicked his habit and was balancing the high provided by prescription Adderall with vodka and maintenance tokes of marijuana. By then his protagonist had gone through changes of his own. Having lost his wife in a car crash, he was bedding a Parisian film star who smelled of Dior J'Adore in a hotel room in Cassis, on the French Riviera. Gallagher was in fact writing a page from his own life, for he had traveled to Provence to research the setting, booked himself into a waterfront hotel, and carried on his own affair, the difference being that the woman between the sheets was not the French lovely of his imagination but his all too real Argentine mistress, who, having just come from a swim, smelled like kelp.

The mistress cost him his second wife and half his money; investing in a winery run by her uncles in Mendoza lost him the rest. His sixth and seventh books hadn't sold, his publisher dropped him when the eighth failed to materialize, and now, halfway through the rewrite of his comeback attempt, *A Nose for Tea,* which his agent refused to shop until he'd made drastic revisions, he was alone in a Forest Service rental cabin in Montana's Crazy Mountains, chickadees outside a frosted windowpane for company, chewing nicotine gum for the buzz and tamping it down with the whiskey.

"How the mighty have fallen," he said aloud. He lifted his fingers from the typewriter keys and swished the bourbon in his mouth. At this rate, financially speaking—he permitted himself a smile—his next book would be written on Red Bull and beer. He laughed silently—his sense of humor would be the last of his qualities to desert him—then let out a sigh. Plot had never been his strong suit, and this one was particularly flimsy, revolving around an Indian mountain goat called a ghooral, which was being poached to extinction because its scent glands were valued by perfume mixers. The setting was Darjeeling, hence the title, and it didn't help that, one, there were no ghooral in Darjeeling; two, the scent glands from an actual ghooral would make perfume smell like goat gonads; and, three, with no advance and residuals claimed by his vices, research consisted of scanning maps on Google Earth. Max Gallagher had never been to India. He didn't even like tea.

He drained the glass. Though the cabin was chill with a clammy odor, he hadn't bothered to build a fire after snowshoeing from the trailhead. The exertion had warmed him and he was in too much hurry to flesh out the thoughts of his road trip, which he'd scratched down on the backs of envelopes while driving with his elbows. Now he sat back in the rough wood chair, rubbed his sore fingertips—it had been twenty years since he'd worked on a manual typewriter—and declared himself satisfied by pouring another shot of the George T. Stagg. The clammy scent he'd noted when coming in the door had a moldy taint, earthy and with an unplaceable metallic tang that made his nostrils flare. He'd chosen a nose for his protagonist because his own sense of smell was acute, and the odor bothered him. Though the drive had long since caught up to him, he thought he'd better open the cabin's windows, build a fire in the open fireplace that faced into the bunkhouse, and air the place out good before going to bed. He threw on a buffalo plaid stag jacket that made him look like a cigarette model—he'd been that model once and it was a look he cultivated—walked outside, and rendered several blocks of firewood into splits.

Breathing heavily in the altitude, he let his eyes wander to the pond below the cabin. The shoreline was rimmed with ice, the windless surface reflecting muted smears of lilac and magenta that made a drama of the evening skyline. It was the beautiful gloom that is April in Montana: the red wine ribbon of the Shields River far below, puzzle pieces of old snow on the mountainsides, subdued skies through which the sun shone only in the gilded edges of the clouds. Gorgeous if you were an artist, but in an unrelenting way that made the native want to bring an elk rifle to his forehead.

Gallagher stacked the wood and carried it inside, where he crumpled up newspaper and built a tepee of the splits. He looked for the chain or lever that worked the damper and, not finding it, lit the fire. In seconds the cabin had filled with smoke. Something had to be clogging the flue. He picked up an iron poker and stuck it up the chimney. It jammed against something solid, and as he withdrew the iron, a piece of red cloth dropped onto the firebox. He lifted it with the fireplace tongs, narrowing his eyes as he held it at arm's length. The look on his face was one of perplexion, his frown deepening as he saw that the cloth was a Santa hat, complete with a tassel and a band of fake white fur.

A pack rat's cache? Part of a bird's nest? At the clubhouse he co-owned on the Madison River with three other fishermen, there had been problems with birds building nests in the flue, clogging the length of the passage with sticks. Well, he wasn't going to sleep until he found out. He fished a flashlight from his jacket pocket and walked outside.

He looked up at the roof. No chimney cap. Might as well have handed out invitations to every feather in heaven. Against the eaves was a wooden ladder. Snow had thawed and frozen around the feet of the ladder, and the rungs were solid as a marble staircase as Gallagher ascended to the roof. Edging to the southern exposure where the snow had burnt off the shingles, he climbed on all fours until reaching the chimney. Built of river stones chinked with hundred-year-old mortar, it was the centerpiece of the cabin, much bigger than a modern chimney, with a wide, squarish opening.

As he got to his feet, hugging the chimney to maintain his balance, a great racketing sounded from within. He ducked as a crow burst out of the chimney, so close to his head that he saw the pebble of its eye and felt the air beating from its wings. The bird, an arrow of black, flew low into the gloom, cawing.

Gallagher watched it out of sight. "One crow sorrow," he said under his breath.

It was the first line of the "Counting Crows" nursery rhyme his Irish grandmother had recited when he was a child. He tried to think of the second line, knowing that he was stalling. Something was bothering him, a conversation, no, an argument, the details lost to the alcoholic haze in which the memory had been made. *Just do it,* he told himself. Shielding his eyes in case there was another bird—*Two crows mirth,* that was the next line—he raised his head and shone the flashlight into the mouth of the chimney. A crosshatch of sticks woven around the broken tip of a graphite fly rod obscured his view. The crow had been building a nest.

Gallagher felt the tension flood out of his body. He let out a long breath. Now it was just work, and he started pulling up the sticks, tossing them onto the roof. He paused with the tip of the rod in his hand. The crow must have flown with it all the way from the river. Gallagher had pocketed the flashlight while dismantling the nest and switched it back on. There were still sticks too far down to reach and he pushed them aside with the rod tip until he could see into the flue. What stared back at him, from about ten feet down where the smoke chamber narrowed, were empty eye sockets that were as dead black as the wings of the crow.

PART ONE

ONE CROW
SORROW

Three Degrees of Sean Stranahan

The way I see it," Undersheriff Walter Hess said, "is we can go through the side of the chimney with a jackhammer, which would make a Judy of a mess, or we could drop a lasso around her neck and see if we could pull her up. Harold says he's got a lariat in his pickup."

"Humpff. And hope her head doesn't come off?"

Martha Ettinger rested her chin on steepled fingers. Martha the thinker, the latest in a sequence of postures she'd run through since hiking in ten minutes earlier—hands on hips while looking at the chimney, fingers searching for her carotid, then rubbing her badge as if it was Aladdin's lamp.

She popped a Chiclet into her mouth and drummed her thumb against the grips of her revolver.

"No," she said, "we're going to wait for light. Meantime I want to talk to the guy who found the body."

They were standing outside, looking at the roof where Harold Little Feather was shining a six-cell flashlight.

"Warren's babysitting him inside," Hess said. "Named Gallagher. Says he schlepped back to his car and drove down to Wilsall before he got a bar of reception. I figured you'd want to do an informal before anybody took his statement."

Ettinger nodded. "Harold, get on down here," she said. She and Walt unnecessarily braced the ladder as he climbed down.

"It isn't pretty" were the first words out of his mouth. "She backed down the chimney with her arms extended, so it seems like she's reaching up at you. Her eyes are gone. The ancients would tell you the birds took them up to the gods, so they could reconstruct her soul."

"Is that Blackfeet folklore?"

"No, I think it goes back farther than the people."

"So how do we get her out?"

"I'm thinking we could drop ropes over her hands, cinch the loops on her arms, tug her out that way."

"I was just saying maybe her head," Walt said.

Harold frowned. "You might pull it off, she's really stuck."

Ettinger's hands went to her hips. "When I fed the chickens this morning, this isn't a conversation I thought I'd be having."

"Maybe we could try fairy dust," Walt said. "My mother told me that's how Santa gets down the chimney."

"Fairy dust is in somewhat short supply." Martha was in no mood for Walt's deadpan. "No, that body's been there a while. It isn't going anywhere, not until we can see what we're doing."

"What I'm wondering about is what she thought she was doing?" Harold hugged his jean jacket about him. "No one more than a year off the breast can get all the way down a chimney. Even if they made it as far as the smoke chamber, then you got your angle space to the damper, and the damper, door open, you're talking six inches of passage, ten tops."

Walt shook his head. "There wasn't no damper, that's what the fella said. It's a straight shot to the firebox. Maybe she figured she could worm on down."

"But how would she know it didn't have a damper?" Martha said. "It makes me wonder if she isn't from the area."

Walt climbed the steps onto the rough-hewn floorboards of the porch and shone his flashlight on a piece of wood nailed above the door. Letters had been burned into the wood. "Mile and a Half High Cabin," he read out loud. "Three X's. I'd say somebody has a sense of humor."

Ettinger jutted her chin toward Harold and they sidled to the edge of the porch.

"What makes you say that, her not being from the area?" Harold said in a quiet voice.

"Most people who deal with an eight-month winter know how a chimney works."

"What about the Huntington girl?" Walt said. "You were the detective on that case, Harold. They never found her or the boy." He'd been listening, after all.

"Could be. Bar-4's the next drainage up. If it turns out, I don't want to be the one tells the puma on the painted horse."

"That what they call Loretta Huntington?"

"Among other things. Woman like her has a lot of names."

"Tomorrow's April Fool's," Walt said, apropos of nothing.

"April Fool's the first day of the month, not the last." Martha kneaded her chin, thinking about how long the girl had been in the chimney before dying, wondering if she was still alive when the crow carried her eyes to heaven.

———

Martha Ettinger's first impression of the man who stood to shake her hand was that he was Rhett Butler's ghost, risen from the mists of Tara. Wavy black hair, something in it to keep it that way, a squared-off chin with a dimple and heavy five o'clock shadow. He even had a pencil mustache.

"At last we meet," he said. "I was beginning to wonder if Stranahan made you up." The voice came from his diaphragm, the eyebrows lifting in self-amusement. But fatigue behind the gray-blue irises. The sweat sheen of man who'd been up for forty hours.

"How do you know Sean Stranahan?" Ettinger drew a notebook from her breast pocket.

"He's a member of the Madison River Liars and Fly Tiers Club. I own the clubhouse with Pat Willoughby and Ken Winston."

"I feel like I should recognize your name, but I don't."

"That's because it used to be Smither, Jon Smither."

"Uh-huh." Ettinger clicked her pen. "We're going to get back to that, but answer a question for me first. If you own property on the Madison River, what are you doing up here in the Crazies?"

"It's a long story."

Ettinger glanced at Sheriff's Sergeant Warren Jarrett. "Warren, do you have any coffee in that thermos?"

She took a chair at the cabin's battered pine table, which was caked with swirls of wax that had dripped from candles stuck in wine bottles. She kicked out the chair opposite and nodded to Gallagher.

"Take me through what happened."

"I'm a writer. I was writing."

"Your car has California plates. Let's back up a couple thousand miles."

"One thousand and sixty-seven, door to door," he said, and began to recount the steps leading to his grisly discovery, starting with a conversation he'd had in a bar that had inspired him to drive to his home in Marin County, throw his computer bag into his Lexus, and hit the highway. A night and a day had passed since he'd seen the Bay glitter under the lights of the Richmond Bridge. Certainly, he'd intended to stay in the clubhouse, but when he contacted the property manager from the road, asking to have the electricity hooked up and the antifreeze drained from the pipes, the manager had bad news. Getting the clubhouse up and running was an all-day job and it would be at least three days before a plumber was available. However, he knew the Forest Service supervisor and might be able to pull a string. Would Gallagher be interested in staying in one of the backcountry rental cabins? He was thinking of one on the west side of the Crazy Mountains, at the northern extreme of Hyalite County. The season had closed at the end of February, so it would need some airing out and he'd have to dispose of the mice in the traps, but there was a woodstove and he could tote water from the creek. Or melt snow. At seven thousand feet, winter waved a long goodbye. He called back in five minutes, having got the okay, said he'd leave a pair of snowshoes at the road end for the trudge in. He'd tape the combination to the door lock on one of the bindings.

As Gallagher talked, Ettinger watched the way he wrinkled up his eyes recalling details, how, when he leaned across the table to face her, his smile drew commas of irony through his cheeks. *The insolent bastard's trying to charm me,* she thought.

"I'm still having trouble understanding the why," she said. "Leave like that in the middle of the night. You'd think this big of a trip, you'd do some planning. Leave word where you were going."

"Not really. My fishing gear is at the clubhouse. Groceries I can buy in Ennis. Do you live alone, Sheriff Ettinger?"

She looked at him without expression.

"Does anyone care what time you make it back to the house or whether you drink too much?"

"Why, do you drink too much, Max?"

"Sometimes. I did tonight. You would have, too. But that's not my point. When you lay your head on the pillow knowing if you don't wake up, nobody's going to come looking until they notice the smell, it isn't such a big deal."

"What isn't?"

"Anything."

"Just up and take off, huh?"

"Why not?"

"But if the point of the trip was to write this book and there's no electricity . . ."

He shrugged. "I didn't know I'd be staying here when I left. When I heard, I stopped off in Elko and bought a typewriter at a thrift store." He reached under the table for the battered blue manual, which he'd zipped back into its case. "This is a Lettera 32 Olivetti, the same model that Cormac McCarthy used to write *No Country for Old Men*. It was made into a movie, the one where the killer uses a cattle gun to blow holes in people's heads."

"I'm familiar with it. Up here we're old-fashioned. Murderers use bullets; it's a time-honored tradition."

"I thought pounding these keys, some of the maestro's magic might rub off on my fingers."

"Has it?"

"That remains to be seen. Look, Sheriff, I'll level with you. I went through a hard breakup a few months ago. Ever since, I seem to be gripped by inertia. And financially I'm not in tip-top shape. I tell people I changed my name to Gallagher because it starts with one of the first seven letters of the alphabet, and that's better for book sales because it's closer to the top of the bookshelf. Which is true enough. I've used Gallagher as a pen name for years, and half my friends have called me Max for just as long. But that's not the real reason I petitioned to have it changed. The real reason is when you go bankrupt, you change your name to throw creditors off the trail. I had a good thing going and let it slide south. Now I'm trying to make amends."

Ettinger wasn't going to let it go. "You said you'd been talking to a bartender, a woman. What did she say that made you decide to go?"

"It's what she didn't. She was an acquaintance, a friend with benefits." He scrolled quote marks with his fingers. "I was lonely and she was . . . well, not lonely enough." He shrugged. "I walked out the door feeling sorry for myself, then thought, what the hell, why not go to Montana and finish the book? Do something right." He sat back and gave her the right side of his face to admire.

"What were you before you were a writer?"

"I was a crime reporter for the *San Francisco Herald*."

"You don't say?"

"Ten years."

"Why did you quit?"

"I burned out."

"Were you drinking then?"

Gallagher folded his hands on the table. "Look, I'm just doing my civic duty."

"Yes, you are." Martha exhaled. "It's late. I'm going to have Warren here take your statement and we're going to call it a night. Then you can go crash in a motel."

"I'd rather not. Is Sean Stranahan living in his tipi?"

"He's in Florida."

"Sam Meslik's in the club. I suppose I could bunk with him. I was going to look him up and see if he wanted to fish some evening anyway."

Ettinger scratched the back of her head with her pen. "They're both in Florida."

"Oh." Gallagher nodded. "Yeah, I heard something about that. Sean's helping Sam set up a guide business there for the off season. Key West, right?"

Ettinger kneaded her chin. "I know where Sam hides his key. I'm sure he wouldn't mind."

Gallagher smiled, drawing the commas in his cheeks. He was, Martha had to admit, very good-looking.

"It's funny, isn't it?" he said. "How we know each other. I mean, I know Stranahan because the club hired him to find those trout flies that were stolen, and I met Sam because Sean knows Sam. If I did that in my books, connected everybody up, my editor would say it was too convenient. She'd accuse me of cheating."

"Your editor doesn't live in Montana."

"Six degrees of Sean Stranahan."

"More like three degrees, and he's a newcomer. Spot me an old-timer and I can link up the whole damned valley. Are you sober enough to drive? I don't want you pulling a *Signal 30* halfway up the valley."

"After what I saw? I'm too sober."

CHAPTER TWO

Love on Four Continents

It was midnight before Martha turned onto Cottonwood Road and lowered the window, hoping to hear the great gray owl who was the shaman of wilderness, whose voice, she'd often thought, was the lament of all women who lay in bed alone, sisters of a certain silence.

She let Goldie, her Australian shepherd, out for a quick tour of the property while she fed chopped-up elk venison to Sheba, her brittle-whiskered Siamese. She stood in the doorway and whistled to Goldie—she didn't like to let her roam after dark, as there was a tom lion whose beat extended up and down the canyon. She whistled again and shut the door after Goldie bounded in.

Goddamn degrees of separation. It was bad enough to pass the silhouette of the tipi on her drive home every night, but why couldn't a week go by without Stranahan's name crossing someone's lips other than her own?

I won't hate him, she told herself. *I won't hate him for the wall I built to keep him out of my life. I have only myself to blame for the night I turned out the light.*

For the light had been their understanding. On nights when she turned the porch light on, the signal that she was done with the workload she'd carried home from the office, he was free to drop by, to have tea, iced or hot as the season dictated, while they sat before the varnished tree stump that served as her desk, and on which she always had a partially completed jigsaw puzzle. They would work the puzzle and talk about their days—Sean was a fishing guide so his were spent on the river, but he also was a watercolorist, specializing in angling art, and a now-and-then private detective, which was how they'd met several years before. They'd stir the surface of life while the tension built underneath. At a certain point, it could be ten minutes, it could be thirty, Sean would carry his glass to the kitchen and come back—she'd hear the footsteps on the floorboards and shut her eyes—and he'd bend down behind her chair and wrap his arms around her, cupping her breasts while she let out a sigh.

"Take off your gun," he'd whisper against the side of her neck, and she'd feel the tickling in the soft down of her hair. And she'd set down the puzzle piece in her fingers and stand up, lean back against him for a long minute, both of them feeling the other's arousal, and she'd take him by the hand to the bedroom.

The first time they'd made love, she actually had been wearing her gun when he'd told her to take it off, and the puzzle on the stump had been elephants against the backdrop of Kilimanjaro. Since then they had shared each other's desire after working other puzzles—the Spanish Steps, Machu Picchu, a box of gaudy steelhead flies called Dead Man's Fancy, and a pride of lions in the Okavango Delta. They'd made love on four continents without ever leaving the log walls of her hundred-year-old farmhouse. Or so she had liked to think of it.

And then the day she didn't like to think about, when she had walked to the door to switch on the porch light and hadn't. She'd told herself it wasn't any one thing, although it had happened the same night she'd had a call from her youngest son, David, who was a sophomore at the University of Arizona in Tucson. David, who, like his older brother, Derek, had chosen to live with his father after the divorce. David who made her heart jump when he said he'd like to visit her this June, do some fishing and hang out with her before earning credits toward his geology degree by spending six weeks in the Montana badlands on a dinosaur dig sponsored by the Museum of the Rockies. Martha hadn't even known he'd applied for the position, and the prospect both thrilled and terrified her. Immediately she'd thought of Sean, what a good mentor he could be for her son, not only on the river. But how would David react, her dating a man in his midthirties when she had seen forty flow under the bridge last October? Of course, that wasn't it at all, not if she was really being honest. She was simply, utterly terrified of being hurt when it ended. Because it was going to end, like every relationship in her life had ended, and how much it hurt was a function of how long it lasted. And so she had made the excuses, she had built the wall, and the light stayed out.

Stranahan had called her on it. "You cut your happiness to cut your losses later, that's not a very courageous way of living your life."

"That's just it, though. It's my life."

Her porch had been dark now through the heart of the winter and into the thaw, four months during which they'd barely spoken. Now, because Sean knew Max Gallagher, she'd have to call him about the body in the chimney. She got into bed and opened her book, the Franklin Library illustrated edition of *Gone with the Wind* with a cracked spine that she'd glued and reglued, and yellowed pages that she had read and reread since she was a girl. Though she hid it under a dour smile and acerbic wit, what Doc Hanson, the medical examiner, called her "warts and graces," Martha was a tragic romantic, her doomed love affairs the ever-present minor key of her life. The saga of Rhett Butler and Scarlett O'Hara, with its deceptions and revenges, its cross-purposes and earthly passions, was the most tragic romance of all.

She propped the book on her chest, thinking about Gallagher, who had the blackguard's insolence and devilish looks, and wondered at the color of his heart. He had showed her one side of his face. What did the other conceal? In her line of work, people changed their names either to hide something or hide from something. Gallagher's explanations sounded logical enough, yet it bothered her. She looked over the book to regard Goldie, who was looking up with her amber eyes, her head resting on Martha's thigh.

"I'll take Scarlett's advice," she said to Goldie. "I'll think about it tomorrow."

CHAPTER THREE

Entertainment, Romance, and Live Bait

Key West, Florida, is the end of the road in the way that the darkest bar is the end of the day. It's a place where shattered lives exhaust their final hours, where fortune-tellers manufacture hope for the hopeless for a ten-dollar bill, where men who can't recall when it all went wrong lean in 2 a.m. shadows among six-toed cats that are scarcely more than shadows themselves.

In Key West, people who would pause to consider if they were farther up U.S. 1, or farther up the ladder, don't. And those who don't smoke might just light one up.

When Sean Stranahan hopped onto his bicycle at five in the morning, the town was at slack tide, the only sound the hiss of the tires. A liquid trail of Spanish beckoned him toward the deli at the M&M Laundry, where he stopped for Cuban mix sandwiches to go and a shot of sweetened espresso.

"If you need sandwiches tomorrow morning," the counter man said, "try the *Ernesto*." He jabbed his chin toward a feral rooster pecking up scraps behind the kitchen. "It will be tough, but good."

Ten minutes later he was at the dock, Sam Meslik waiting for him, fistfuls of fly rods bending over the pulsing jellyfish that floated in the oil-slicked water. The big man racked the rods under the boat's gunwales and they were idling past the sign for the Harbor Lights Restaurant—ENTERTAINMENT, ROMANCE AND LIVE BAIT—then the skiff was up on a plane, shearing the moonstone surface.

Ten minutes later, Sam cut the motor inside a necklace of mangrove islands and Stranahan stepped onto the bow, feeling the way a fighter feels when he dances into the ring to face a better man. Tarpon fishing had proved to be the most masochistic experience Sean had ever had holding a fly rod, not because tarpon were so difficult to catch, but because after the first few jumps it was just your muscles against theirs, and then after a half hour or so it was your heart against theirs and a sober question as to whose would give out first. Men paid $650 a day for the pleasure.

Sixty feet away, the reptilian-looking back of a tarpon arched out of the water as the fish gulped air into its rudimentary lungs, its scales reflecting the fire of the sunrise. Stranahan pulled the fly once, he pulled it again . . . the line stopped. There was a point early on when he was looking up at five feet of fish coming down, and another, seemingly moments later, when the tarpon was so far away that, jumping, it looked like a tangerine minnow imprinted against the mangroves.

"Tell me that wasn't more fun than eating a ham sandwich," Sam said a half hour later, when the tarpon wrenched its head to spit out the fly. He smiled, showing the grooves in his front teeth.

Stranahan rubbed the muscles where the rod's fighting butt had ground into his gut. He'd wear the bruise as a badge of honor. But that first cast was the extent of his luck; after that it was just one mistake following another.

"The tarpon doesn't eat from that end," Sam said, when Stranahan cast behind a cruising fish. "Not that left, your other left," he'd said, when he tried to point out a fish at ten o'clock and Stranahan faced the wrong way. When Sean finally got another of the beasts to eat the fly, he forgot to bow to create slack line when the fish jumped. The leader snapped with the tarpon in midair, its gill rakers rattling like a diamondback rattlesnake. "You set that hook like you were in diapers," Sam said.

At midmorning they anchored off Sawyer Key to wait out a tide change. "You're getting better with your insults," Sean said, removing his sandwich from its tinfoil wrapper.

"Thank you," Sam said. "I'm thinking about putting a shock collar on my clients, give 'em a zap when they make a bad cast. Say twenty volts casting too short, fifty if they line one and it spooks. Anybody forgets to bow when the fish jumps, I juice him to his knees."

"That will get you bookings."

"They'll be lining up." Sam shook his mane of graying copper hair. "These guys are all type A's, they've been 'yes sir'ed all their life and they're tired of it. They want to be cuffed and spanked. 'Course what they really need is a dominatrix with a whip. A flats guide with a bad-ass tongue is the next best thing."

"Sam, you're full of shit." Stranahan looked off toward the Gulf, marveling at the palette of colors as the depths changed—white grading to tan over the flats, a rind of lemon beyond, then one of lemon-lime, and cutting through the flat, a zigzag channel of deepest emerald.

The phone vibrated in his pocket.

"Don't you dare answer that fucking thing," Sam said.

Stranahan flipped the phone open and listened. "I wouldn't call us friends," he said. And after a minute: "No, I can't see that. He used to do a little blow . . . okay, maybe more. Max had this thing about writing on the level, balancing uppers and downers . . . I fly out tomorrow, I thought you knew."

Sam extended a tube of sunscreen. Stranahan clamped the phone to his ear with his shoulder and rubbed the cream onto his nose. "If you can't pull her up, maybe you can push her down into the fireplace . . . I know that could make things worse, but you asked . . . You, too. Bye."

"That was—"

Sam made a cross of his forefingers, as if to ward off a vampire. "I know who it was. She who must not be named. Not on my boat."

Stranahan told him about the body in the chimney as Sam shook his head. "I don't know Jon all that well, I didn't even know he changed his name to Max, but I feel for him. Be hell to get an image like that out of your head."

Stranahan removed the push pole from its chocks and stepped up onto the poling platform over the transom. "Your turn. I'll see if I can come up with some creative insults."

"That be Sam's pleasure," Sam said. He reached for the fly rod.

CHAPTER FOUR

Cinderella

Ettinger parked behind Harold Little Feather's truck at the road end and unscrewed her thermos cap. She looked back down the valley, her eyes following the switchbacks to the bridge across the river. The Shields was smothered in mist. Beyond it, low cloud cover lopped the top off Sacagawea Peak. A phrase came to her lips. "Into the gloaming." Who had said that? Tennyson? Robert Burns? Someone from somewhere that saw a lot of rain. She sipped the coffee.

"Martha, my dear."

Harold's voice came from the depths of his sleeping bag, which was spread across the bed of his pickup and carried a sparkle of frost.

"Thrange thing happened lass nigh."

"Unzip so I can hear what you're saying," Martha said.

Harold's head squirmed halfway out of the sleeping bag. "A woman tells me to unzip . . . ouch."

"What's wrong?"

"Got my braid caught in the zipper."

"Here, let me." Martha set her coffee on the hood of the Jeep and climbed into the pickup bed. She frowned at the coarse black hair peeking out of the zipper threads. "I'm going to have to cut it. Goddamn it, stay still." She wielded the scissors of her Swiss Army knife. "You move, I'll cut out your heart instead of your hair."

"You already did that once," came the muffled voice.

"Yeah, tell yourself that. There, I think I got it." She forced the zipper down and Harold's head reemerged. He shook out his hair and saw her looking at him. "What?"

Martha shook her head. "Never mind." She *had* cut his heart out once, at the same time he'd cut out hers and claimed it for his own. Then he'd taken back up with his ex-wife, who lived on the Blackfeet Reservation, and at some point Martha had given up waiting for it to fail. Two office romances, if you counted Stranahan, who had contracted for the county as an independent investigator on several occasions. It was strict violation of her own policy. But where else was she going to meet anyone?

She sat back and hugged her knees. "As you were saying," she said.

Harold struggled into a sitting position. "Had a visitor last night," he said. "Mr. Gallagher drove in, 'bout four in the morning. Seemed a little taken aback to find me blocking the road."

"What did he want?"

"Said he forgot his computer. Wanted to hike in and get it because he could plug it in at Meslik's place."

"So much for magic."

Harold raised his eyebrows.

"Something he said about working on a manual typewriter. I'm just talking to myself."

"You shouldn't do that, Martha. It's a bad habit."

"So I've been informed. What did you tell him?"

"I told him to come back this morning. If he was looking to take anything away from the cabin, it's still in there."

"Good. I got the impression he was hiding something. All that antebellum charm, he doesn't fool me."

"Well." Harold was examining the damage done by Ettinger's scissors. "The man hadn't slept in two days, so sure as hell something was bothering him to come all the way back here."

Martha nodded. "I just got off the phone with Stranahan down in Florida. He said Gallagher powders his nose. Maybe he left some blow in the cabin."

"That would be an illegal search, Martha."

"I don't think so. But he can put a Canada goose up his nose for all I care. I'm wondering if there's something else he left behind, something that could tie him to the girl."

"You're really thinking along those lines?"

"No. But he's the only person of interest we have."

"So how's the morning shape up?"

"Kent's driving in. He's going to chain up and bust through the ruts, so we can caravan to the cabin. Walt's coming, so is Wilkerson; that way we cover our asses. This looks like an accident, but if it turns out the victim died somewhere else and was placed in the chimney, I want Gigi to conduct the evidence search before the place gets mucked up. Then, by God, we're going to get that poor girl out. I don't want to bust up the stonework, but if that's what it takes . . ."

"Any fairy dust?"

"Don't go Walt on me today, not even a little bit." She blew a strand of hair out of her eye and felt the cold of the metal pickup bed working into her bottom. Far below, they could hear Jason Kent's four-by-four diesel grinding in third.

"This place gives me the willies, Harold."

"You mean the legend of the crazy woman."

"No, I think that's a myth. I don't mean it couldn't happen. Indians pincushioned their share of settlers, I just doubt that a woman whose husband and children were slain by the Blackfeet would go on living here by herself, or they would let her. Never mind that her spirit would haunt the place ever since."

"Glad you're on our side."

"No, it's these mountains. You go to other ranges, the Madison, the Absaroka, they have a soft side, meadows, flowers, they show you their beauty. You can feel the breeze, hear them breathe. But the Crazies are just a jumble of peaks. They're nothing but hard edges and cold winds. There's a remoteness factor, a godlessness. You aren't welcome here. You can feel it."

"Rock has no heart."

"Is that what your people say?"

"No, but aren't you the poet this morning?"

Martha shook her head. It wasn't like her to show a feminine side, to shed the insulation that hid her from the male half of the world.

"This one bothers me," she said quietly. "Whether she's the Huntington girl or isn't, she was somebody's daughter. I woke up last night thinking about that crow mincing down the chimney and cocking his eye, wanting dibs. What must go through a person's mind at a time like that?"

"Nature might have given her a little mercy there, Martha. You figure she'd have been hypothermic in a few hours. You get dreamy. They say it isn't a bad way to go."

"I hope you're right. Here's Jase."

———

Montana was a country of three-fingered men. It was hard to find a bar where at least one of the regulars didn't shoot pool off a bridge made of knuckle stumps, and the sheriff's department's contribution to the count was Jason Kent. Kent powered down the driver's side window of his truck. He draped his big left arm out the window and drummed his pinkie, ring finger, and thumb on the door panel. The middle and first fingers he'd lost in a farm machinery accident and kept in spirits in a Mason jar in his bathroom. In the passenger seat, huddled in a puff jacket that made her look like a hand grenade, sat Georgeanne Wilkerson. She was eating a carrot.

"What's up, doc?" she said brightly.

"Good morning, Gigi," Ettinger said.

Kent slowly nodded, moving his eyes from Martha to Harold. "You think you can move that truck for me, chief? Or are we on Indian time today?"

"No, I'll move it. I know white men can't walk."

Martha looked from one to the other. Kent was a "just the facts, ma'am" man, as deliberate in his manner as a mudslide. Here he was trading insults with Harold at seven in the morning, an hour when Martha had scarcely ever merited more than a grunt out of him.

"You're getting to be downright garrulous in your middle age," Martha said.

Kent seemed to think about it. "Just naturally talkative, I suppose. Now, who wants to lie down on the snow and help with these chains?"

———

Harold's perimeter search was perfunctory. It had snowed and melted several times in the past couple weeks and any tracks the girl had made were long obliterated. What first caught his eye was a tag of animal skin sticking above the snow under the eave of the cabin's west wall. Upon excavation this proved to be an elkskin jacket that fastened with bits of bone. The jacket was stained to a dark color and had been crudely hand-sewn. Harold knocked the ice and snow off it and brought it under the porch. He continued his search, finding a link of chain that was attached to a metal contraption. He frowned, then, realizing it was a chimney cap, uttered a low whistle that brought Ettinger to his side. The cap was not a simple cover to keep rain out, but part of a top-mounted damper system that fitted flush with the chimney opening. The assembly was old and warped, the screws that had attached it rusted through, the gasket rotted away, but the link chain that dropped down the chimney so the occupant could open or close the damper was still attached. Harold thought it was possible that the girl had been strong enough to have pried the assembly off the chimney before climbing in. It threw a little water on Martha's suspicion that the victim didn't understand chimneys and might be from somewhere south, and he said so.

"If she had a flashlight, once she removed the damper she'd have seen it was a straight shot down into the firebox. She took off the jacket so she could fit. Maybe we need to give her more credit."

"But she still managed to get herself stuck, didn't she?" Ettinger said.

Harold canted his head.

"You don't think so?"

"Just reserving judgment, like I was taught."

Ettinger left Harold reserving his judgment and turned her attention to the cabin. Briefly she looked for the computer, but that was a waste of time. Gallagher had been lying, she was sure of that much. She noted that the floor had been swept by the last renter, the comb marks of the straw broom a pattern of whorls in the corners. She sat down at the table and began to leaf through the guest logbook, occasionally glancing at Wilkerson, who wore knee pads as she collected fiber and hair evidence.

"A lot of traffic," Martha offered.

"I've got hair samples from at least a dozen individuals. Mostly Caucasian, a few strands of Latino or Native American. By the way, the Santa hat you bagged had samples from two people on it. Without doing the lab work I can tell you one is dark blonde, which Harold says is the color of the victim's hair, but there's also some curly hairs in a much darker brown. A lot of dogs have been in and out. Malamutes, huskies, longhair dogs. You'd think people came in here with sled teams."

"At least one party did," Martha said. "Here, look at this entry." She pushed over the log. The entry was dated January 3.

Wilkerson read aloud, "Something was prowling around last night. The sled dogs set up a racket and Bill had to go out and calm them down, especially Molly. We found tracks this morning that were three lengths of a dollar bill. Bigfoot?"

The entry was signed, "Yikes! Carolyn."

———

The electric line camera Harold lowered into the flue was scarcely bigger than a fountain pen. It offered a low-lux color recording that Ettinger, Wilkerson, and Jason Kent could view on the screen of Ettinger's battery-powered laptop. As well as manual focus and zoom, the camera had remote-control pan and tilt, and it quickly became apparent how the girl had become fixed. It was not, as Ettinger had surmised, because the flue grew progressively smaller, but because she had brought one knee up to her chest, after which she could neither descend nor climb without dislocating her hip and was effectively trapped.

"Wouldn't that be more likely to happen if she was climbing up, not going down?" Ettinger's question was to the room.

Wilkerson nodded. "It could happen either direction. It's the kind of mistake you'd make if you were trying to hurry. Looks like somebody's going to have to go spelunking."

Martha raised her eyes.

"We have to check the upper part of the flue before we pull her out. If we pull her up first, then the flue will be contaminated by fibers scraped off her clothes. The only way we'll know that she got stuck in the process of going down is by finding fibers scraped off on the descent." Wilkerson held up a bag containing a clear plastic jumpsuit. "That's why I brought a condom. Do I go, or does anyone want to volunteer?"

It was a facetious remark. Wilkerson was the only one who would have any shot of descending the chimney, or, having done so, know what to look for. Ettinger was a strong, solid woman who stood eye to eye with many men. Walt was her size, add an inch. Harold was six foot two or more, and Kent, in his birthday suit, had to weigh 240 pounds.

"I'd volunteer," Walt said, "but my package would get stuck. That's luck for the ladies, but the downside of an endeavor like this one."

Everybody laughed, even Martha. "You wish, Walt." She cocked a finger at Wilkerson. "If you get stuck . . ."

"I won't. I brought my Under Armours, just in case."

Under Armour was compression underwear, and Wilkerson, dressed head to toe in stretch polyester with the plastic jumpsuit fitted over it, a neoprene cap to cover her hair, a face mask, safety goggles with a magnifying bifocal, and a headlamp clamped to her forehead, looked like a deep-sea diver as she climbed the ladder a half hour later. Martha had to hand it her. She wouldn't have gone head-first down that chimney for anything. The thought of coming face-to-face with a face with no eyes made her shiver.

"This is like something you'd see at a Salem witch trial," she muttered, standing at the base of the ladder beside Kent, as Walt and Harold stood on opposite sides of the chimney, holding Wilkerson by her feet as they lowered her into the opening.

Half an hour after her head disappeared down the flue, Martha heard Walt say that he could see her toes wiggling. It was the signal that she wanted out.

A tense minute later, at least for Ettinger, who had a bad habit of envisioning the next day's headlines—*"Crime Investigator Suffocates in Chimney, Hyalite County Sheriff Mum"*—they'd hauled Wilkerson up and she was sitting on the roof ridge. When she regained equilibrium, she rather shakily descended the ladder and took off her cap.

"Gigi, you look like a Kentucky coal miner," Ettinger said. "That was . . . way beyond the call."

"I'll put today in my back pocket for the next time we negotiate a raise," Wilkerson said. "But it was sort of cool, really. I'd rather get a little dirt on my face than sit in a lab any day."

"So what's the verdict?"

"She was going down. I bagged threads that look like poly. I'll take some fibers from her clothing once we get her out."

"Gigi, I wish we had some water here so you could clean up."

"Just give me a minute to breathe clean air. I think if they lower me on a rope this time I can get far enough down to get a harness on her."

Martha nodded. Beyond the call didn't begin to describe it. "How does she . . . look?"

"Dead at least a week or the crow wouldn't have had time to build a nest. Birds pecked her eyes and ate away her lips. Her gums are receding. Too bad it's so cold up here or the Calliphoridae would make timing a cinch."

"You mean blow flies," Ettinger said.

Wilkerson nodded. "As it is, we'll have to rely on decomposition rate. This time of year the initial process is largely from inside out, from bacteria and protozoa in the body. Her stage falls somewhere along the time line from initial decay to putrefaction. So the odor isn't too bad. If that guy who found the body had got here a couple weeks from now, the stink would have dropped him flat on the floor."

"This falls under the category of too much information. Let's get her out and then you can work your magic."

"I'm just trying to prepare you. A lot of law enforcement personnel think they've seen it all and can handle it, but their experience is usually limited to fresh kills and desiccated remains. It's the in-between vics, the black putrefaction and butyric fermentation cadavers, that give you nightmares."

"I'll take your word for it."

———

They couldn't get her out. The body rocked when they pulled on the harness, but the offending knee wouldn't budge. Wilkerson offered to crawl up from the firebox and see if she could get a harness around the foot belonging to that knee. If they could pull it down until the leg was straight, there was a decent chance the body would follow. Ettinger agreed to the strategy.

Wriggling on her back into the firebox and elbowing up several feet, Wilkerson managed to get the harness over the shoe on the drawn-up foot. When she climbed down, Harold tucked his braid into his jacket and took her place in the firebox, looking none too happy about it.

The first heave yielded a half foot of progress and a sickening crunching sound as the hip dislocated. A shower of ash fell into the firebox. One more heave and Harold was able to reach up and place a hand on either ankle. Both legs were extended now and he wrestled the body down the flue a few inches at a time.

"Her torso reaches the smoke chamber she'll come down all—"

He never finished the sentence, but started choking as a curtain of ash rained down into the firebox. A second's hesitation, then the body cascaded through the ash, falling loose limbed into Harold's arms. For a moment he cradled it, the way a fireman cradles a body from a burning house. Then he scrambled out from under the weight and backed crablike across the room until coming up against the wall.

"I haven't seen anybody move that fast since Walt stepped on the rattlesnake in Yankee Jim Canyon," Martha would later say.

But that was later. To a man and two women they just stared at the body, the legs sticking out from the hips in an obscene spread, and the chin resting on the chest so that the hair, matted with soot, fell forward in a wing across the face. Then, as gravity asserted its imperative, the body collapsed sideways, the head and neck coming to rest against the side of the firebox in that awkward position that airline passengers fall asleep against a stranger's shoulder. She stared at them then, from the blackened holes where her eyes had been.

Nobody spoke. Finally Walt asked Harold if it was the Huntington girl. The question was absurd. What they were looking at was recognizable as having once been a human being, but only to the extent of a ballpark age and probable gender.

"I just had pictures and some video," he said. He shook his head. "Be a hell of a thing if it was."

"Why do you say that?" Martha asked.

"Because her name was Cinderella."

Martha knew the name but hadn't made the association with the chimney. She could see the headline, and hated herself for it.

"God have mercy on all of us," she said.

CHAPTER FIVE

The Monster of Montana

Stranahan spotted the familiar figure standing beside the bronze grizzly bear sculpture at the baggage claim and strode over.

"Martha, fancy seeing you here." He pinched the brim of his cap. It was their way of late, keeping it light while reestablishing a relationship under a new set of rules. "Peachy Morris is picking me up. Who are you here for?"

Martha tapped her badge. "I'm your ride. Plans have changed."

"Did you think it was time for us to be friends, or are you interested in my services?" That too was their way, the dig, not so subtle.

"The first," she said. "For Choti's sake." Martha had boarded Sean's Sheltie while he was in Florida, and the little dog had become fast friends with Goldie. "I figure if they can get along, we can, too. No luggage?"

"Just the carry-on."

"Here, I'll be your ghillie and tote the rod case." They'd walked halfway to the Cherokee with HYALITE COUNTY SHERIFF'S DEPARTMENT stenciled on the door when the other shoe dropped. "Maybe a little of that second thing you mentioned."

Stranahan smiled. He'd known Martha hadn't picked him up to bury a wounded heart. "Is this about the girl in the chimney?"

She nodded, jangling the keys in her pocket. "We got her out yesterday. It's the Huntington girl who disappeared last November, ninety percent chance. She was wearing a rodeo belt buckle her mother identified, and Doc Hanson contacted Deaconess to send over X-rays taken when the girl broke a forearm bone barrel racing. The autopsy's this afternoon."

"Bad, huh?"

"The birds had been at her. We think a crow dug out her eyes."

Stranahan let this sink in. "Is there any reason to believe it isn't an accident?"

"No, but there's a larger question here. Wilkerson put the time of death at two weeks, give or take, which means she was alive for at least five months after the disappearance. So where was she? Not the cabin. Renters come in and out all winter long. Still, you'll want to see it. I thought we could swing by on the way back to the canyon."

"That's a big swing out of the way and I don't see where I fit in. You said it was Harold's case."

"It is."

Stranahan waited.

"Well, the thing is, there's no evidence of a crime. Her dying this way is sensational, so there's going to be press, but unless Hanson determines a cause other than exposure, or forensics comes through with a surprise, our scope of involvement will be limited. Harold's canvassing the valley, but he's knocking on the same doors he knocked on five months ago, and if he doesn't get any traction, it will go on a back burner sooner rather than later."

Stranahan thought he saw where Martha was going. "And that's not going to wash with the family."

"In particular, the mother. Loretta Huntington is a formidable woman. She made her name as a rodeo champion, then parlayed her looks into a job modeling ranch wear. That got her a minor television career. But nobody knew her name until she did those Chevy Absaroka commercials. You don't know what I'm talking about, do you?"

Stranahan shook his head. "I live in a tipi, Martha."

"Google her," Ettinger said. "The husband's a treat. We picked him up on a DUI a week after the girl disappeared and you could say he isn't a big fan of law enforcement. They're using the video as a teaching tool at the academy—how to deal with an asshole. Pled the whole bereaved bit. Skated because the Breathalyzer hadn't been re-calibrated in a timely fashion. Anyway, when the sand ran out on the initial investigation, Loretta hired a private investigator. He didn't get any farther than Harold, but my guess is she'll go that route again."

"What makes you think she'd hire me? I don't advertise."

"Because I'm going to tell her to."

That made Stranahan sit back in his seat.

"Thinking about it, aren't you?"

He nodded to himself. "You don't want a loose cannon, someone you don't know."

"No, Sean. Because I don't have the resources to hire you myself."

"Oh."

"I knew the Huntington girl. Back when I made the mistake of rec-onciling with Burt, we rented a place up Thread Creek, that's the next drainage over from the old Huntington spread, over by Pony. Four or five years ago now. Cinderella showed up on her horse one day, asking if my son could go riding. I think she was lonely. Her mother had just remarried, they were off honeymooning somewhere. So Cinderella was staying at the ranch manager's house for a couple months. She would have been about twelve. David was starting high school, so she wasn't exactly on his radar. But she looked at him with those hydran-gea eyes of hers. You know how girls get around twelve, they start cultivating the dead look. But she had this earnest inquisitiveness that was refreshing. And a beautiful smile. You just wanted to bottle her and carry her around in your pocket. She got a big crush on David and they became thick as thieves. I let myself daydream they might get married someday."

Martha looked at Sean and lifted one shoulder. *What can you do?*

She reached a manila folder from between the seats. "This is a summary of Harold's investigation. The second report's about the groomsman who worked the horses at the ranch; he went missing at the same time."

"They ran off together?"

"That's one possibility. He was two years older than the girl, eighteen to her sixteen."

"I remembered reading something in the newspaper," Sean said. He opened the folder and gleaned the bare bones of the teenagers' disappearances as the skeletons of juniper trees marched past the side window, blackened reminders of last summer's burn up the Bridger Canyon.

Cinderella Huntington had been reported missing from the Bar-4 Ranch at 8:47 a.m. on Tuesday, November 7, about an hour and a half after she had failed to come downstairs for breakfast. Not finding her in the kitchen, her mother had checked her room, then the lot where the ranch vehicles were parked, thinking that her daughter had skipped breakfast and gone straight to school. Like many ranch kids, Cinderella drove a pickup to the gate at the county road, about a mile and half away, where she caught a bus to take her to school in Clyde Park. She'd been driving since she was eight and her mother had to tape boards to the clutch, brake, and gas pedals so her shoes could reach. But her pickup was still in the lot.

Not overly worried, Huntington thought to check the stall where her daughter's horse was stabled. The girl often retreated there after dinner to do homework and usually checked in on Snapdragon before going to school. The horse was asleep with her foot lifted; the electric oil heater Cinderella switched on during cold evenings was unplugged.

While in the stables, Huntington met the horse trainer, Charles Watt, who did not live on the ranch but had a house a dozen miles away up the Brackett Creek Road. He told Huntington that he'd seen Cinderella the previous afternoon, after she'd returned from school and was mucking out Snapdragon's stall. They had said hi to each other and he'd left the ranch to drive home shortly thereafter.

Huntington then roused her husband from bed. Jasper Fey, the girl's stepfather—it was a second marriage for both of them—had driven in to Bridger the evening before, Tuesday being poker night at the Cottonwood Inn. He'd seen Cinderella briefly before leaving the house, told her dinner was in the refrigerator. Six p.m., give or take.

He didn't get home until after midnight and had gone straight to bed. The couple had separate bedrooms, his on the ground floor. Loretta's was upstairs, down the hall from the room where Cinderella slept. Fey told his wife not to worry—wasn't she just saying how unpredictable her daughter had become?

"Teenagers are like terrorists," Huntington recalled him saying during her interview with Harold. "They live among us and we don't know what they're thinking." She told Harold they'd had a row over Fey's insensitivity, repeating a remark he'd heard somewhere, probably on the set of the television western he was a technical expert for and that was shot in eastern Montana. The row was just a short exchange of remarks. Fey had grasped the seriousness of the situation and joined in the search, riding the property lines behind the house in his ATV.

Stranahan looked up. "There's no mention of the last time the mother saw the daughter."

"That's Harold for you," Martha said. "He likes to bury the lede. It's in there, you'll get to it, but she hadn't seen Cinderella since the previous morning. She left early Tuesday to drive up to Helena to conduct a horsemanship school. She decided to eat dinner there, then waited out a snow squall and didn't get back to the ranch till around eleven. The house was dark. She figured Cinderella was asleep and didn't want to disturb her."

Stranahan turned his eyes back to the report.

By eight in the morning, Loretta Huntington was thoroughly alarmed. Only one other person who lived on the sixteen hundred-acre property might have seen Cinderella, and that was the ranch manager, Earl Hightower. The girl was friendly with Hightower, who Huntington said was teaching her guitar. Huntington tried to raise him on the VHF handset. Although you could use a cell phone from the main ranch house, which was set on a bench above the river, Hightower's house was tucked back into a cottonwood grove at a lower elevation and didn't get reception. Hightower didn't pick up, so she drove to the house, which was out near the main gate, and found him in his barn. He reminded Huntington that he'd been out of town the day before to pick up a brood mare from a ranch out of Big Timber. So no, he hadn't seen Cinderella. Questioned more closely about the previous afternoon, he said he'd driven back to the Bar-4 at 5 p.m., turned the horse over to Watt, and then had driven back out the ranch road to his house and had dinner with his wife. Afterward, maybe seven-thirty or so, he took his dog on a walk out to the main gate and back, like he did every night, and spotted headlights turning onto the ranch access. He recognized the truck as belonging to the groomsman, Landon Anker. Anker idled down and they had acknowledged each other by each cocking a forefinger, the ubiquitous Montana salute. Anker came in to do chores once or twice a week after school and again on weekends. Sometimes he'd worked till nine or ten at night. Hightower thought nothing of the brief encounter and no words were exchanged.

They were standing on Hightower's porch during the conversation, when Loretta Huntington saw the ranch manager's face change. Hightower had extended his arm toward the county road, where the low-angle sun glinted off a metallic speck in the distance. The glint was from U.S. 89, in the direction of Wilsall. A car parked at the roadside? Anker's car? His family was from Wilsall. Hightower got binoculars from his house and confirmed that it was a dark-colored truck. Anker's GMC was dark blue. They investigated, found that it was in fact the young man's truck, parked behind a berm in the road, maybe twenty yards off the pavement. The truck was unlocked and the key was in the ignition. The right rear tire was flat. Hightower squatted down and found what looked like the head of a roofing nail flattened against the tread. There was a spare in the bed of the pickup. Hightower climbed into the bed and stood on it. The spare was flat also.

At this point, a logical solution presented itself. Huntington said that on two previous occasions, Anker had picked up her daughter from the ranch early in the morning and they had gone into Wilsall to his parents' house to eat a pancake breakfast prepared by his mother. That would explain why her truck was still parked in the lot, rather than at the gate. Then, while driving to town they had got the flat and, unable to fix it, had probably walked the last two miles to his house. There were holes in the theory, starting with the fact that if Landon Anker had pulled up to the ranch house at six-thirty or seven that morning, Loretta probably would have heard the motor, or at least the dogs barking, and she hadn't. Then, too, it was unlike her daughter to fail to mention the change of schedule to her. As she confessed to Harold, she was trying to talk herself into believing the best-case scenario. Upon first seeing the truck, she had feared that her daughter had been involved in an accident, or that the two had driven off to go neck somewhere during the night, and as it was cold, had run the motor and asphyxiated on the fumes. She told Harold that Cinderella had a crush on the young man, but that she really didn't know if he returned her affections.

Not wasting time, Huntington and Hightower drove to the Anker homestead, where they found the boy's parents sitting down to break-fast. They hadn't seen their son for twenty-four hours and thought he was at the Bar-4, that he had gone straight from school to work and then had slept in the stables. He'd told them that he was going to give lying in wait for the horsehair thief one more try and they assumed last night was that.

Horsehair thief? Stranahan put the question to Ettinger.

"It's a separate file," she said. "Last fall someone cut the tails off a dozen or so horses at the Bar-4. You know, for violin bows."

"Violin bows?"

"I keep forgetting you're a pilgrim. Belts, horsehair jewelry, violin bows, hair extensions for show horses, a lot of stuff. There's money in it."

"How much is the tail of a horse worth?"

"I think you can get up to a couple hundred dollars a pound. White's the most valuable. The thefts occurred about a month before Cinderella disappeared. They paid Anker to spend a few nights in the stables after it happened, but no one returned to steal any more hair."

"Why didn't Loretta Huntington think of Anker right off the bat?"

"Because it was the boy's initiative to spend the night. Neither the trainer or ranch manager had asked him to. After getting over the shock of seeing their horses shorn, they'd realized that horsehair thieves probably wouldn't hit the same ranch twice. Even meth heads aren't that dumb."

"So, drug addicts looking to score?"

"Smash and grab, or in this case snip and run."

Stranahan turned to the report on Anker's disappearance, but Martha stopped him by placing two fingers on his arm.

"You've read all there is to know. Etta Huntington made the call and Harold caught it. He ended up interviewing everyone the report mentions, all the kid's friends at school and probably half of Wilsall and Clyde Park, plus the boy's relatives up in Ringling, where the Anker clan is from."

"Isn't that where you grew up?"

"No, our place was out of Roundup."

"Ringling, Roundup, same bit of nowhere."

"Tell that to your gas tank. You've been here three years. Learn your geography."

"I know where all the best trout streams are."

"*Anyway,*" she said, drawing out the word, "nobody contradicted what Huntington told Harold. Nobody reported seeing the kids after they disappeared or ever heard from them. Neither set of parents envisioned the two of them running off, and even if they had, you'd think they would have surfaced. There were rumors Landon Anker was gay, but his parents denied it. They described the relationship between Landon and Cinderella as more like brother and sister than boyfriend-girlfriend."

The road rose abruptly and there were the Crazy Mountains, the ridges puzzled with snow, but green showing in the lower elevations. Maybe summer would come, after all. In Montana, you held your breath.

"How much farther?" Stranahan said.

Martha frowned. He sounded bored to her, maybe indifferent was the better word. "Do you see that bald ridge running north and south? The cabin is tucked under it."

She slowed for a doe whitetail deer to cross the road. Heavy with fawn, her winter coat was already patchy, the gray shedding in clumps to reveal the rich reddish coat underneath.

Martha nodded toward the folder. "What's your take on this?"

Stranahan seemed to shake himself awake. "What did Harold think?"

"I'm asking you."

"If I didn't know about the chimney? I'd say the most likely scenario was they drove off in the Anker kid's truck, maybe he had a place they could go and be alone, and then they broke down and somebody came by, a drifter, and said he'd give them a lift into town. He killed them, maybe the boy first so he could have his way with the girl. He disposed of the bodies down the road. Like those long-haul truckers who prey on prostitutes in the rest areas. The bodies turn up two states away. I read a book called *The Monster of Florence* about a serial killer in Italy who preyed on young couples making love in cars in the countryside. This reminds me of it."

"The Monster of Montana," Ettinger said.

"It happens."

"How do you explain her living through the winter and ending up here?"

"Well, that makes the drifter theory less plausible. It makes me think if she was abducted, the perpetrator lived nearby, either knew her or knew of her. It could be like one of those cases you hear about, where the girl escapes after months in a cellar."

"But isn't a cabin in the mountains out of the way for anyone running for her life to wind up at? And she was wearing an elkskin jacket that was homemade. It seems odd."

"You're right, I could be way off."

"Maybe not. The scenario you painted is pretty much the same conclusion Harold drew. Frankly, if either of you had come to me with that fifteen years ago, I'd have said you watched too much TV. When we got a 187 you never had to look farther than the husband. Now we have murder for no reason. Do you know what happened while you were getting a sunburn? A housepainter in Miles City with no criminal record told his buddy he wanted to kill somebody, anyone would do. The friend went along, to use his words, 'for giggles.' They killed a young man with a sledge hammer." She shrugged. "It's a disease, like hantavirus. You never think it will reach the border and then someone breathes in mouse feces in some hunting shack and winds up dead."

"What's Montana coming to, huh?"

"It's no joking matter."

"No, it isn't."

Martha pushed the four-wheel-drive button as they turned onto the access road. Heading east toward the ridge Martha had pointed out earlier, the road rose, yellow snow packed into the ruts. Stranahan spoke over the growling of the gears. "So did you ever meet her, the lady Huntington?"

"A couple of times. She had a feral quality, an aloofness. I can't say I got to know her. Look, Stranny, are you okay? I'm having a hard time reading you."

"I'm just tired from the flights."

"Did you get into any trouble down there?"

"Not really. You know me."

"That's just it. I do know you. Or I did."

Stranahan shut his eyes. When he spoke, his voice could barely be heard above the engine. "Whose fault is that, Martha? Do you have any idea how many nights I walked Choti up the road last fall, just so I could see if your light was on?"

"You know I can't talk about that."

"Then let's not talk about it."

Martha downshifted. "Quit staring at me," she said.

"I'm sorry."

"Sorry for staring?"

"Sorry for bringing it up."

"Just don't start being someone I don't know, okay? That fight you had with Buster Garrett, February, right? I heard about that. The man I know doesn't go into a bar picking fights."

"He said the next time he saw me he was going to flush my head in the toilet."

"That was two years ago, Sean. I'm the one who told you he'd said that, remember?"

"Two days, two years, it was out there. It needed to be addressed. I addressed it."

"The way I heard it, he didn't even remember who you were."

"I reminded him. He swung on me, I put him down. Long story short, as Sam would say."

"You could have wound up in jail."

"The Roadkill Saloon's in Park County. It wouldn't have been your jail."

"That isn't the point." Her exhalation made a bubbling sound. "You have a way with people, they're drawn to you. It isn't because you're all that goddamned charming, either. It's because they sense you're genuine. No, don't give me that roll of your eyes. I care about you. I don't want to see you lose what makes you you."

"Is that why you're trying to throw a bone my way, to bring me out of my funk?"

"No. Because I'm a mother and it could have been my child in that chimney. Because Cindy was special. But that's only part of it. This one gets to you. You don't walk away from it the same person. We'll be there in a few minutes. You'll understand what I'm trying to say."

She took her right hand off the steering wheel and again pressed her first two fingers against Stranahan's arm. "We okay?"

"Sure. We're okay, Martha." He moved his arm away.

CHAPTER SIX

Sleeping with the Devil

As a boy, Sean Stranahan had befriended a trapper in the Berkshire Mountains who bequeathed him the uncured hide of a red fox. His mother wouldn't let him bring it into the house, so Sean hung it in a tree until the taxidermy kit his father mail-ordered arrived. The result, his father told him, looked like the Tasmanian devil and smelled to high heaven. The odor inside the cabin recalled the memory. Ettinger left the door standing open and showed Sean the fireplace where the body had fallen onto Harold's lap.

"She looked like a Raggedy Ann with her eye buttons missing." Martha shook her head. "In all my days . . ."

Stranahan nodded. He could feel it, all right, what she'd talked about earlier. There was death in the room, in this cabin in the woods. A different kind of darkness.

"I didn't tell you before," she was saying, "but Cinderella was wearing a Santa hat. When your buddy Gallagher jabbed the poker up the chimney, the hat fell down into the fireplace." She made a face. "I guess it makes more sense if she had it in a pants pocket. Wilkerson found some strands of Cinderella's hair on it; it matches hairs she found on the elkskin jacket I told you about. But there were hairs on the hat that weren't hers, too."

"Oh?"

"Darker."

"Does that mean anything to you?"

"Just that someone else had worn the hat."

Sean nodded. "I really can't see Max being mixed up in this," he said. "He comes across as a rogue, but that's an act."

"Wrong man, wrong place, wrong time, huh? Yeah, I can't see him for it, either. Still, he's covering up. Maybe you can ask him about it. If I call on him he'll just antebellum up with the charm and turn his head so I'm looking at the pretty side of his face."

"Is that even a word?"

"You know what I mean. I told him not to leave the valley."

"I'll pay him a visit. What are we looking for, Martha?"

"I wish I knew." They moved back into the main room and Martha began pulling drawers out of the built-in cupboards and setting them onto the floor. "Nobody ever detail searched this place," she said, squatting down and shining a flashlight into the dark recesses. "Gigi bagged a lot of fiber evidence—that's another thing . . ."

"What?"

"She found fibers from the girl's shirt both above and below where she was found. It makes you think she broke into the cabin by shimmying down the chimney, then got stuck trying to climb back up."

"But once she was inside, couldn't she get out by opening the door?"

"No, the lock's on the outside. You saw it."

"How about climbing out a window?"

"I suppose she could have. If I had all the answers we wouldn't be here. You can stand around with your thumbs in your pockets or help me look."

"Anyone check the root cellar?"

Ettinger shook her head. "You want the honor?"

"Not really. Last time I climbed down into one of these things the situation went south, if you recall." He was remembering a cabin in the Cabinet Mountains, where he'd been shot at while cowering in the cellar.

Ettinger's grunt was unsympathetic. She handed Stranahan her flashlight. "I'll notify next of kin."

The table was positioned over the cellar entrance and Sean had to pull it aside to lift the iron rung recessed into the door. He pulled the door up and over, the hinges groaning. The cellar was little more than a crawl space, about the size of two stacked coffins. The earth had a smell like leaf rot, but compared to the odor above the floorboards, it wasn't unpleasant. Sean noted scattered pieces of two-by-four, not much else except a chipped shovel with half a handle. That wasn't surprising, given that the cellar had doubtlessly been ransacked by every teenager who skied in with a rental party. A trapdoor exerts a magnetic pull akin to the attic door in a horror movie. The skin crawls when you open it, but you open it.

Stranahan smiled at the way his mind tended to wander, and then his brow furrowed. He was looking at an anthill of dirt a half tone lighter than the rest of the floor. He shone his light on it, then raised the light up the nearest wall. At about waist height, there was a discoloration in the packed earth. The soil here was loose and he dug with his fingers. Only a few inches behind the wall his fingernails scraped against metal. He picked up the shovel. In less than a minute he had unearthed a rectangular metal box the size of a brick. He thumbed the soil away from the lid. It was a shortbread cookie tin with the image of a Swiss miss on the lid, wearing a scoop-neck frock that strained to contain her charms. She was holding a plate of cookies. He carried the tin up the steps and replaced the trapdoor.

"Buried treasure," he announced, placing the tin on the table.

Martha grunted. "Gimme. No, don't touch it again. Let me put on my rubbers." She donned a pair of latex gloves to examine the box. "This reminds me of the fruitcake tin my mother would bring out every Christmas. We'd put sugar cookies in it." She pried the lid off with her fingernails. Inside was an unopened pack of playing cards with pictures of old fishing lures on the backs. She extracted a paperback book with a blonde on the cover. *A Purple Place for Dying,* by John D. MacDonald. She fished out the last item in the box, a miniature troll doll with green hair.

She bit her lip. "I think this is a geocache. I've never seen one before, but I think that's what this is. Do you know how they work?"

Stranahan nodded. "Last fall I found one in an abandoned boxcar up on the Big Hole. You sign up online to access a databank that lists a bunch of coordinates. Then you pick one in the area where you're headed and find your way with a GPS. There's an online logbook you sign when you get back home."

"Uh-huh. And these are what, gifts?"

"The etiquette is, if you take something, you leave something else in its place."

Ettinger fingered the troll doll. "There's something in it," she said. She shook it. "Hear that?"

"Pop its head off," Stranahan said.

The ticking sound had been made by a wafer of black plastic the size of a postage stamp. It was a four-gigabyte memory card for a digital camera, sealed in a plastic snap case.

"You wanted to know why I brought you along, Stranny? It's 'cause of stuff like this." Ettinger pointed an accusatory finger. "This is what I mean when I tell people you manage to step into shit even if there's only one horse in the pasture."

She got her laptop from the Cherokee. The card held one file, a high-definition video that opened with a wide-angle view of a narrow bed. The date of recording showed in white letters in the upper left corner—February 14. There was a woman's indistinct voice. Ettinger tapped the volume key.

"Go sit down," the woman was saying. A man appeared, shirtless, and sat down on the edge of the bed, which squeaked under his weight. His face was obscured by a Venetian carnival mask, a devil face with red-and-black ram's horns. He was thin and looked tall, with a slight potbelly and chest hair distinguished by a whitish skunk stripe along the sternum. The hair on his head was combed straight back.

The video shook as the woman pulled the camera backwards. The frame settled. Now most of the bed was in view, as well as the chinked walls behind it.

"Stop it there," Stranahan said.

Ettinger gave him a quizzical look.

"See that knot in the log? It's shaped like a heart."

"I know what you're getting at," Martha said. She paused the video.

They got up from the table and went into the bunkroom. There was a knot in the cabin's north wall identical to the one in the video. The bedframe in the video must have been one of the rusty steel frames stacked against the west wall. Stranahan's eyes ran up to the mattresses, which were suspended in loops of rope from J-hooks screwed into the ceiling beam, to keep mice out of the ticking.

"What are we looking at, Martha?"

The question was rhetorical and they sat back down and Martha resumed the video. In a few moments, the man was joined by a un-masked woman whose slightly bulging eyes made the rest of her face look narrow. A horse's tail of dark curly hair cascaded to her waist. She reached out of the frame to find what looked like a joint and took a hit, then placed the joint into the slit in the mouth of the mask. The man exhaled, a cloud of smoke rising from the sides of the mask, as if the devil was breathing fire. In a matter-of-fact manner, the woman removed her clothes, showing tufts of hair under her arms as she pulled up her gauzy top, and fished the man's penis out of his shorts. She performed oral sex in a lazy manner, like a cat washing itself, and lifted her eyes to look into the camera. "Welcome to the Mile and a Half High Club," she said.

They made love, or rather had sex, in half a dozen positions. At first the woman would glance over at the camera and seemed to be putting on an act. Then for a while there was just the sound of the springs squeaking and the woman's moaning. She moaned for a long time, dragging her hair back and forth across the man's chest. When the man clasped the woman's buttocks, his right shoulder revealed an ink-blue tattoo the size of a silver dollar. Some kind of face, Strana-han thought, with words in a scroll banner. The resolution was too poor to reveal details. Finally the woman collapsed on top of him. The microphone picked up the sound of their breathing. The woman sat up and reached to turn off the camera. Rings glinted from all her fingers. "Put that in your pipe and smoke it," she said. And then to the man: "Talk about sleeping with the devil. Wow, huh?" The screen went blank.

Ettinger's face was crimson.

"I think I need a cigarette," Stranahan said.

"Shut up."

"Martha, come on, I mean you got to be able to see the humorous—"

"I said shut up." She ejected the card and checked to make sure she'd properly copied the file onto the hard drive. She fast-forwarded through the video to the twelve-minute mark, when the couple shifted positions for the last time, the woman climbing on top, then leaning over to reach out of the frame, toward the floor. "Happy Valentine's Day," the woman said, pulling a Santa hat over her head and tucking her hair behind her ears.

CHAPTER SEVEN

A Patient Wolf

By the time Ettinger reunited Stranahan with his dog and dropped them at the tipi, the evening had all but died. He checked the fluid levels in his '76 Land Cruiser, made a note to change the oil, and settled behind the wheel as the engine thundered out of a month-long slumber. He motored into town to check the mail that had been held for him at the Bridger Mountain Cultural Center, mulling over Martha's advice to get in touch with Max Gallagher. The truth was, buying a tank of gas to drive up the Madison Valley didn't appeal to him. Still, it was the logical step and he thought about it for the twenty minutes it took to drive into town and climb the stairs to his art studio. Gallagher, standing outside the studio door, saved him the decision.

"Blue Ribbon Watercolors. Private Investigations." Gallagher read aloud the lettering etched into the frosted glass. "All you need is somebody to scratch in a pistol with smoke curling out the barrel."

Stranahan ushered him inside. "You need a bath, Max," he said.

"I haven't exactly been sleeping. Or eating. Or washing up."

Stranahan waited while Gallagher's bloodshot eyes crawled around the paintings on the walls. When they stopped and narrowed, Stranahan knew that he'd noticed the watercolor of the Madison River Liars and Fly Tiers Club. It was evening in the painting, the co-owners gearing up on the porch as a swarm of caddis flies mobbed the light over the door. Gallagher was flanked by Robin Hurt Cowdry, who was stringing his fly rod, and by Kenneth Winston, whose long ebony fingers were tying on a fly. Patrick Willoughby, the club president, sat on the bench pulling up his waders, his round glasses giving him the look of a professorial owl. The initials P.S. were carved into the door, as homage to Polly Sorenson, the club's founder who had died on the bank of one of his beloved Catskill streams a couple years before.

"Don't tell anybody yet," Stranahan said. "It's a gift to the club for voting me an honorary member."

"Maybe if I had your talent I wouldn't have to pay my dues, either," Gallagher said. "I've been a little strapped lately."

"So the sheriff informed me."

Gallagher nodded. "Does she really think I had anything to do with that girl dying in the chimney? I've done a lot of things I'm not proud of, but the only person I ever hurt was myself."

"Would your exes agree to that assessment?"

"Well, those two witches aside." He grinned, the canine leer Stranahan remembered from the day he'd introduced Martinique to the club members, some two summers ago. Gallagher had bent to kiss her hand, making a *titching* sound, as if he wanted to devour her arm with a side of fava beans. Martinique had told Sean it made her think of the quote by Lana Turner—"A gentleman is simply a patient wolf."

Martinique. That sweet, unaccountably shy woman with a soft spot for cats had become the love of his life, long before he'd ever worked a jigsaw puzzle with Martha Ettinger. No one could have told him that the relationship would falter after Martinique had been accepted into the veterinary medicine program at Oregon State in Corvallis, that she would gradually pull away, his phone calls going straight to message.

"I seem to have caught you at a bad time."

Sean swam out of his reverie. "No, I've just got jet lag. Why are you here, Max?"

"There may have been something I didn't think to tell the sheriff. I'd like to ask your advice."

"In a professional capacity, or as a friend?"

"I can't afford to pay you."

Sean reached for the lower right-hand drawer of his desk, brought out the fifth of The Famous Grouse, and poured shots into two cups. He brought out the nose with a few drops of tap water. "It isn't branch water from your creek," he said, "but I doubt you'll object."

Gallagher didn't.

Stranahan said, "I heard you tried to go back to the cabin in the middle of the night. Why don't we start with what you were looking for. It certainly wasn't your computer."

"Oh, that. I thought I'd left some blow in the drawer of the table. But it was in my duffel, stuffed in a sock. I'd forgotten." He dismissed the matter with a flick of his hand. "You could say I was understandably confused."

"So, false alarm."

He nodded. "Scared the shit out of me at the time, though."

Stranahan smiled unsympathetically.

"It's just a damned coincidence, the girl dying like that."

"How's that?"

"Do you have time for a story about how bad a man can fuck himself?"

"It's what pays the rent."

"Good line. Don't sue me if I steal it."

"I won't."

"Okay. You know I used to be a reporter? Well, it's been back a few years, but I wrote a story about a professor at UC Santa Cruz who tried to break into her former lover's house. He had a restraining order against her and she wanted to confront him about why he'd left. So guess what she did?"

"She crawled down his chimney."

"How did you know that?"

"Why else would you be telling me?"

"Yeah, okay. Well, it gets better, I mean worse. The boyfriend was part of a farming co-op and had signed up to harvest artichokes in Castroville, see what it's like to fill immigrant shoes. When he returned home two days later, the ex was dripping body fluids into the fireplace. They had to jackhammer a hole in the chimney to get her out."

"Did she live?"

"She not only lived. She married him."

"True love," Stranahan suggested.

"True story. So you see my predicament? I had knowledge of a particularly unusual circumstance, and now the same scenario is repeated. It stinks of coincidence, or I guess the opposite."

"Every newspaper in the state must have carried that story."

"Well, yes, but that isn't the end of it. My last relationship was a literature professor at San Jose State. Barbara Louganis. The night she broke up with me—mind you I'd told her that story—I said she was going to change her mind and come back to me. She said, 'Like hell I will,' and then she started throwing books. My books. I have all the editions in this wall case and she was picking them out and throwing them at me one after another. I sort of tackled her to get her to stop and she called the police. We were standing at crossed swords when they arrived.

"And"—he laughed mirthlessly—"this you gotta love. I told her I wouldn't take her back even if she wrapped herself in cellophane and came down the chimney with a red ribbon around her neck. I told her that *in front of officers of the law*. When I saw the Santa hat and climbed up on the roof, guess what was crawling around the back of my mind? I mean, Barbara's certifiable. For all I know she followed me here and that was her in the chimney."

Gallagher had elbowed forward on the desk as he talked, his whiskey breath heavy in Stranahan's nostrils. "Now is that fucking yourself, or is that fucking yourself?" He nodded, looking straight into Sean's eyes. Then he sat back in his chair.

Sean shook his head. "The body in the chimney's a teenage girl who went missing last fall. How old is Barbara Louganis?"

"Barbara's thirty-five, but she looks younger. That thing I was looking at in the chimney had a round face. Barbara has a round face. I don't know how the hell she could have followed me out here, I didn't know I was coming myself until I did. But it scares the hell out of me."

"The CSI says the person in the chimney was dead two or three weeks, so that scenario is impossible."

Gallagher shook his head. "They could say I was here earlier and came back just to report the body, to remove myself from the suspect pool. I work alone, I live alone. It's not like I have a fucking alibi for every night in April. There'd be gaps in credit card records, phone—"

Stranahan held up a hand. "I can think of about ten reasons it can't be your girlfriend, starting with how she could get here. But I'll tell you what I'll do. If this doesn't turn out to be the person we think it is, I'll make some calls." He tore a Post-it note, scribbled a few lines, and pushed it over. "These are directions to Law and Justice. The sheriff's at the morgue, so ask to see Warren Jarrett. Tell him what you told me. He'll make you squirm, but it's better to do this now rather than wait and have it come out. Besides, if you don't, I will."

"I talked to you in confidence, Sean. Isn't that what private investigator means, your communication is private?"

Stranahan shook his head. "You ought to know better. In criminal matters, I turn over any pertinent information I get to the authorities. I'm just on someone else's payroll."

"Is this a criminal matter?"

"Not yet. Think of it this way. Even if it was this woman, as long as she died of exposure, she's just a crazy person lusting after her former lover. It would be one hell of a story and you'd get burned as a contributing cause, but my guess is it would sell books."

"Any publicity is good publicity?" Gallagher cocked his head. "I suppose you're right about that."

"Get out of here."

Sean felt his cell phone vibrating against his thigh. He checked the number. It was none that he knew, but the 578 prefix included the Shields River Valley.

"Hello, this is Sean Stranahan. Could you hold a second?"

He took the phone from his ear and shooed Gallagher out the door. "I'll call Warren and tell him you're coming."

"Why do I think I'm off to the gallows?" Gallagher said. He smiled, the commas fissuring his stubbled cheeks. He shut the door. Stranahan waited until his footsteps faded on the travertine floor tiles.

"Mr. Stranahan, are you there?" It was a woman's voice, a nervous one.

"Yes, I'm back."

"This is Etta Huntington. I've just had a call from Dr. Hanson at the coroner's office. That was my daughter who died that horrible way." The voice broke up and Stranahan could hear her ragged breaths.

"Mrs. Huntington—"

"It's Ms. Huntington."

"Ms. Huntington, I'm very sorry for your loss. It's a terrible tragedy."

"Yes, I suppose those are the words people say at a time like this. But they are little consolation, even though I have been preparing for this day for almost five months, or trying to. I felt her spirit for so long and so I thought she was alive, and now I know she really was, all that time she was alive and I was right to hope . . ."

Stranahan could hear her labored breathing.

"Could you drive down to the ranch? I would like to see you before dark, so you get a sense of the place."

"Did Sheriff Ettinger give you my number?"

"She said you're a man who can get to the bottom of a dark river. I intend to hire you to find out how my daughter ended up in a . . . in that place." There was a silence, a sound Stranahan took as a swallow and a dull rap like a lowball glass being set down on a tabletop. *Well, I might be drinking too under the circumstances,* he thought.

"You understand that this is an active investigation. You'd be paying me to do a job that people with more resources are doing as we speak. It might be wiser to wait—"

"I have already waited once for authorities to fail Cinderella before taking matters into my own hands. I won't make that mistake again."

Stranahan told her he could be on the road in an hour. "I might be intruding on your dinner. I wouldn't want to disturb you."

"Mr. Stranahan, you must not have children. I have not eaten. I don't know when I will ever eat again. I have no appetite for food. Surely you understand that."

Again he heard the swallowing sound and the click of the imagined glass.

"Ms. Huntington?"

There was no answer. She had hung up.

CHAPTER EIGHT

Acts of Kindness

How are the boys?" The county medical examiner's customary greeting came out as one word, "Howrtheboys?"

"David will be here for four weeks starting Memorial Day." Martha Ettinger paused a beat. "I can't wait." She lifted her eyebrows and let them fall.

"Are you being sarcastic, or do I detect a note of apprehension?"

"I'm scared to death. Ever since he went to college I'm down to seeing him three weeks a year, tops. He chose his dad after the divorce, you know that, everybody knows that and it makes people look at me funny, like I must be a cold fish. I can live with looks. What you don't know is David's been having a lot harder time growing up than Derek. I guess because Derek's older and he just came out of the chute sure of himself and rolling with the punches. But David's sensitive. He just hides it well."

"Like you hide it?"

Martha grunted. She shifted her eyes to the sheet covering the body on the morgue's examination table. "You said you confirmed the ID. Teeth or bone?"

"I got the X-rays from the compound fracture of Cinderella Huntington's forearm and compared it with the ulna of the body."

"Cause?"

"That's harder to determine. No brain or spinal injury, no sign of aneurism, and no arterial failure or scarring of the heart muscle or lining. Frankly I would be surprised if there was coronary system damage with a person this young. Toxicology was negative. Her body, under her clothing, was filthy, her palms and the pads of her fingers are cracked and callused to a very unusual degree for anyone but a homeless person. Third degree frostbite on four fingertips of the right hand. And she'd lost three toenails. It's all consistent with a life of exposure, hiking around on rough ground. But that's immaterial with regard to health. The only signs of trauma, beside the dislocation of her hip, which I understand was a result of the extraction, are two pairs of nodules on the vocal cords and an injury to her right foot. The nodules are sometimes called screamer's nodules. No doubt the poor girl hollered her head off."

"Could she have been moved postmortem?"

"Stuffed down the chimney?" Hanson shook his head. "Livor mortis is as you'd expect in the dependent portion of the body, in her case the feet and right hip. There's no evidence that the body was shifted or that she died anywhere but the chimney."

"So we're going with exposure?"

Hanson nodded. "Hypothermia. The time of death is mid-April, give or take a week. During that period average nighttime lows were right at the freezing mark. They dipped as low as the upper teens. This is at the nearest weather collecting station with similar elevation. So we're guessing a corresponding temperature curve, but the bottom line is it was cold. All she had on were jeans and a polyester pullover and maybe that Santa hat. Even with the highest temperatures of the period, we're looking at death within twenty-four hours. She may have survived a day but probably not a night. I made the call to the family an hour ago. Her mother had heard about the crows, so I took the liberty of assuring her that in all probability her daughter had died before that happened. I hope I didn't overstep my authority."

"No, that's fine. You said something about her foot."

Hanson led Ettinger to the table. The antiseptic odor was very strong, but not strong enough. He pulled back the sheet covering the victim's feet.

"Note the pooling of blood during her time of suspension." He lifted the curled toes and pointed with a steel probe to a circular puncture wound under the right arch. A starburst of angry red lines radiated from the wound. "The puncture extends to the distal area. It stops just under the skin, you can see the contusion. The infection is in an early stage. That suggests the wound occurred in the same time frame as her death."

"What made it?"

"A corroded iron nail. I can say that with certainty because the last centimeter broke off inside her foot. I extracted it and carried it to the forensics lab, handed it to Wilkerson personally. Isn't it a relief to finally have a facility of our own? It got so tiresome sending everything to the state lab in Missoula, flagging for priority and waiting in the queue. I heard Gigi helped make that happen."

"She's a wonder."

"Is that sarcasm I detect?" The furry caterpillars that were the medical examiner's eyebrows flexed half an inch.

Martha ignored the comment. "There's been talk about this girl having a relationship with the young man who disappeared at the same time. Is it possible to determine if she was a virgin?"

Hanson shook his head. "The hymen is far from a perfect indicator of virginity, if that is what you're getting at. But in this case the state of intactness is irrelevant. What you may have mistaken for postmortem bloating—I initially did—was the swelling of a second-trimester pregnancy. The fetus was 13.3 centimeters long. It's hard to close the window on the time of conception because the fetus has lost weight since the mother died and mortality presents other complicating factors."

Martha felt her gut knot. "How far along?"

"Five months, that's approximate."

Martha thought back to her own pregnancies. At five months, could she feel the baby kick? Wasn't that about the time it had started?

"So it had hair, teeth?"

"She. It was a girl. The fetus can make faces at that age, even what looks like a smile."

Martha sought the pulse in her throat, feeling for it with the latex sheath on her forefinger. It took effort to control her voice. "So that means she got pregnant at the time of her disappearance."

"Just before or after. If before, the obvious question is did she know. Did she perform a pregnancy test and that's why she decided to run away? Perhaps she felt like she couldn't go to her parents. I know I don't need to tell you this."

Martha had stared off toward a shuttered window.

"Martha?"

"I heard you, Bob. I suppose I shouldn't be surprised. Did you inform Loretta Huntington?"

"No. I called to provide cause of death only."

"This is going to strengthen her belief that it's the young man who worked at the ranch. I'll have to contact his family for a DNA sample to confirm paternity. What's best, a sibling?"

"Or the parents. But she was age of consent at the time of conception. According to the form I was provided, she turned sixteen the previous June. If no crime has been committed, I wouldn't think there would be a legal obligation to comply with your request."

Martha pressed her lips together. "They'll want to know. I would if it was my son."

"Yes, you're probably right. We've seen this kind of story before, haven't we? The sexual urge is so strong. I just wish we were better at convincing teenage boys to put a wrapper on it."

Martha nodded. She noticed that Hanson was tapping the floor, though the paper booties he wore over his sandals smothered the sound.

"How do I put this?" He seemed uneasy. "No, I won't go there."

"Go where, Bob?"

Hanson turned his eyes from Ettinger to pull the sheet back over the foot. He spoke with his back to her. "It's none of my business, Martha, but what happened with you and Sean?"

"You're right. It isn't any of your business. But I'd appreciate it if you looked at me when you ask about my personal life."

Hanson looked at her, peering over the top of his glasses.

Martha pressed her lips together. "Are you guessing or is it common knowledge around the department?"

"It's all over town, just as everyone knew about you and Harold breaking up a couple years ago."

"If you know, why are you asking?"

"Because I care about you. Because . . . oh, I'm just going to say something I'll regret . . ."

Martha saw a slight tremor of the salt-and-pepper mustache.

"It's me. What's this about, Bob?"

He sighed and folded his glasses into the pocket of his lab coat. He motioned with a latex finger for them to walk away from the table. "Do you remember the bucket list I made after my coronary last year?"

"You told me. I was moved. We were all worried about you."

"Do you remember me mentioning a night I'd like to relive up on Lake Superior?"

"You made love with a young woman."

"Vicki Pendergrass. Do you know the reason I thought about her?"

"Just tell me, Bob."

"Well, God knows I love Elizabeth, we'll have been together forty years in August, but people change. We've been living separate lives now for a long time. She has her book group, her knitting circle, all the volunteer work she does for the university's foreign students, and bless her for that, but that's not my world. I have to be outdoors. I have to feel air moving over my skin or I get grumpy and start feeling old."

"Are you thinking about separating?"

"No, no, we're comfortable, we take care of each other. And there are the kids—even though they're grown it would come as a shock. But, and this is hard to say, in terms of sexual energy we're not on the same page at all. To look at me I'm just an old walrus like everyone says, but I still have a libido, and facing my own mortality made me realize how precious life is, how precious having a full life is in the time I have left. My wife has put all matters of the flesh behind her, it's like her body's gone into hibernation or lost its nerve endings. The medication she's taking is a good part of it, but knowing why doesn't help. We've moved into separate bedrooms, it's been more than a year. Now when she lets me in the door it's an act of kindness, there's really nothing there but the act and it doesn't even bring us closer, it just makes us aware of the distance we lack the courage to bring up." He shook his head. "Listen to me go on."

"You're really broken up about this, aren't you?"

"I just thought . . . oh hell, you're going to slap me or quit talking to me, and that's the last thing I want, and I'm too old for you." He smiled while shaking his head.

"Are you propositioning me?"

He couldn't meet her eyes. "I've always been attracted to you, Martha. In every way."

"But we're friends."

"Are we? I can count the times we've seen each other on social occasions on one hand. All we've ever really shared is a body on an examining table. But I've always felt a connection."

"I don't know what to say." Martha shifted her weight from one foot to the other.

"Say you'll think about it. I just want to touch somebody who wants to touch me back. To feel alive that way, even if it's only one time. That's what a bucket list is, whether it's climbing Pilot Peak or the last kiss, you want that shudder in the bloodstream before the hands reach midnight."

"I don't do things lightly." Martha heard herself saying the words she'd uttered to Stranahan before she finally relented and unbuckled her gun belt—how long ago had it been, ten months?

"Look where that's got you," Hanson said. "I sense you're as alone as I am."

"I . . . I'm just not built for casual sex."

"Nor am I."

"Bob, this isn't the time—"

"Of course not. Please forgive me. It's just it's something I've been thinking about."

"Let's just—"

"Martha, you don't have to say a word. No, really. I'm actually proud of myself for getting it off my chest. Holding things in may have contributed to my heart attack last year." He shook his head as if to clear it. "So with regard to Cinderella Huntington, I'll have the full report to you tomorrow morning."

Martha pressed her lips tightly together. "I want to see her."

Hanson nodded and started walking back toward the examining table.

"No, the fetus."

"There's nothing to—"

"I have to see it."

The stainless steel tray on the counter was a cold bed for the question-mark curl of Cinderella's unborn child. For two weeks it had lain in decomposing amniotic fluid and yet its color remained and the expression of the face was calm under the fair, nearly invisible eyebrows. She could see the tiny hands, even the fingernails. Martha's lips moved in unspoken words.

"Did I ever tell you you're a scary woman?"

"Yeah, Bob. Everybody has." She nodded. "Okay. Now the mother."

At first Martha avoided the face. Her eyes traveled from the blackened feet to the flaccid belly, the small freckled breasts to either side of the zipper incision, the thin but muscular arms and surprisingly large hands with broken fingernails, where Huntington must have clawed at the walls of the chimney. She looked at the hair, lank and dirty. Finally she looked at the eye sockets. She looked at them, into them, for a long time. She wanted to believe the story of the crow, but she also remembered the opposite coin of the folklore, that sometimes something so bad had happened that the gods could not restore the soul, and the crow would then fly back to earth as an avenging angel. *In that case,* Martha thought, *I'll be the goddamned crow.*

"That's long enough." Doc Hanson put a hand on her shoulder and pulled her aside. He reverently pulled the sheet back over the body.

He turned to Martha with his mustache quivering and they were where they were before.

"Come here, Bob. Come on, we can be adults about this."

He didn't move, and Martha took a step and hugged him to her. *Why can't someone give him what he needs?* she thought. She couldn't, though, and when she turned to leave she heard the two-step intake of his breath.

"I'll see you around," she said. The words meant nothing and she instantly regretted them, but there they were, reinforcing the gulf that had spread across the marble floor.

"Sure, Martha," he said. "Around."

CHAPTER NINE

The Woman Who Kicked Out the Stars

At first glance the arm looked real. The skin tone was too light for a perfect match with the tanned left arm, but the raised veins were a realistic touch and the casually bent wrist showing the back of the hand, the fingers in relaxed contraction, would have passed muster in a dark room. They nearly did in the gloom of the glassed-in sunroom of the ranch house at the Bar-4.

"After the accident," Loretta Huntington said, as she handed Stranahan a squat glass and settled herself in a wicker chair, "I instinctively sat on the right side of people, so that my left arm, my natural arm, was closest to them. You want to hide your injury, it's a self-defense response. But you learn very quickly that you need the good hand to do things, pick up your drink"—she sipped from the drink that had been sitting on the coffee table making a wet ring on the wood, one of many—"anyway, with one thing or another your hand keeps bumping into them. So I've had to become comfortable with people sitting to my right, with this useless appendage in full sight between us."

"I'm on your left," Stranahan said.

"So you are. Are you going to be one of those people who are always correcting what others say? I hate those people." She drank. "Anyway"—her hand waved the glass—"I have grown to despise it. I only answered the door this way so your first impression wasn't a shock. As we will be working closely together, I'll remove it if you don't mind."

The artificial forearm fitted over the stump of arm just below the elbow with a sort of compression sock. She took it off and scratched at the puckered skin on the stump with the fingers of her left hand.

"It has mechanical knuckles so you can position the fingers." She demonstrated, holding the arm close to Sean and folding all but the middle finger down. She placed the arm on the sill of a casement window that looked down the Shields River Valley, the outstretched digit jutting from the skyline into purpling, gold-limned clouds.

"This is all I have to say to God," she said, dropping back into the chair. "Are you a religious man, Mr. Stranahan?"

"I am on a trout stream."

"That's a cop-out. I was raised a Catholic, but my belief system is pagan. I like to think it's the influence of the Cherokee blood on my mother's side. Here's to you, Mom, wherever you are." She picked up the drink and swallowed. Stranahan sipped from his. It was scotch on the rocks. She was one of those people who when they offer a drink don't offer a choice because they only drink scotch.

"If you're wondering what number I'm on, it's four. It seems the appropriate dosage. Did you know that you are a good-looking man? No? Well, you are. You have kissable lips. I ought to know about that, before the accident I made a lot of money kissing men. It could be my epitaph. 'The Good, the Bad, and the Ugly—She Kissed Them All.' And you shave. That's a plus. Kissing scenes, even if you like the guy and you decide to just go for it, get old by about the fifth take. You spend all morning kissing for eight seconds onscreen. Your lips get chapped and they have to keep stopping the shoot to apply makeup to cover the stubble burn. It hurts when you smile for a week after. My husband, that is my first husband, Scott, would want to have sex and I'd lay down the rules like a prostitute. 'Honey, you can have me any way you want, but if you want to kiss me, we're going to have dinner at Chico.' I don't know why I'm telling you this."

"Because you're drunk, Ms. Huntington."

She drew her head back and for just a moment a smile played at her lips. Loretta Huntington, even with her expression dulled by alcohol, was one of the most striking women Stranahan had ever seen.

Her hair was a rich dark chestnut, what horse people called liver chestnut, long and falling over her shoulders. Her eyebrows, a shade darker, were dead straight over almond-shaped eyes. High cheekbones, a bold, slightly crooked nose. You would not call her beautiful in any conventional meaning of the word. Rather, she was a predatory bird with the bird's aloof posture, her head not turning so much as jerking from one position to another, now to Stranahan, now to dismiss him and look toward the silver winding of the river. All her movements were those of the hunter. The pools of her irises were steadily hunting, green and as sharp as a cat's eyes, but impenetrable— the windless surface of a lake. They reminded him of something else, too. What was it?

"I am indeed," she said. "How refreshing to entertain a straight-talking man."

"Ms. Huntington—"

"Etta."

"Etta, I came here because you asked me to. You seemed to be very anxious that I come tonight. I drove fifty miles and so far you haven't mentioned your daughter's name."

"Cinderella turned into a pumpkin, don't you know? All her horses changed back into mice."

Stranahan stood up. "I'll come back at a better time. Thanks for the scotch."

The hand that stopped him, the blood and muscle hand, closed over his forearm like a vise. "Don't . . . you . . . dare." Her voice spit venom.

He looked down at her, feeling slightly absurd. He was acutely aware of the power in her grip, the fact that she had once made a living with a lariat in her hands.

"Oh, sit down," she said. "What are you going to do, walk away from my money?"

"I came here for your daughter."

"Yeah, right," she said, under her breath. "You who knew her so well." For a long moment her eyes focused on his, then the pools of still water began to waver. Her chest heaved and she raised the stump of her arm to wipe angrily at the tears tracking down her right cheekbone. Stranahan saw the gesture as intimate, the revealing of her arm more so than the tears. When she released him from her grip, Stranahan tentatively touched her left shoulder, not knowing if she was seeking his comfort. She took his hand in hers and rubbed her thumb into the tissues of his palm. The pad of her thumb was rough.

She seemed to sense his reaction. "They called me Hundred Grit Huntington because my skin was so rough. But isn't it funny, I keep people to the left of me and I only cry with my right eye, so nobody can see."

"What should I call you?"

"Etta."

"Etta, what can you tell me that might help my investigation? Sheriff Ettinger mentioned that you suspected Cinderella of running away with Landon Anker, the young man your husband hired."

"I would prefer you not to refer to Jasper as my husband. When he is in town we share a roof, but we do not sit together at a dinner table. I have been trying to forgive him for hiring that boy, I could have told him he would take advantage, but forgiveness is not in my nature."

She gripped Stranahan's hand harder still. "Here's all you need to know about Jasper Fey. When the sheriff asked me to identify the belt buckle on a body found in a chimney, mind you, in a fucking chimney, he was the first call I made. He is her stepfather, after all. I reached him on the set. He said it was only a matter of time before the body surfaced and I should view it as a relief. But she had been alive all winter, didn't he want to know what had happened to her? You know what he did? He *thought* about it. Then, this is what he said, the exact words. 'That's all behind us now, dust in the wind.' What the fuck is that supposed to mean? I told him I wanted to hold a memorial service, but he saw any more grieving as redundant, a sign of weakness. What a silver-tongued, self-aggrandizing bastard he's become. 'Mama, don't let your babies grow up to be cowboys.' I should have taken that one to heart. I only married two of them. The service is tomorrow. My sister's coming all the way from Sweden. Guess who *won't* be there?"

She reached for her drink, frowning at the empty glass. She caught Stranahan's eyes and lifted her head to gesture toward the door through which they had entered the sunroom. "The bottl'ze in the kishen, I mean kitchen." It was the first time he'd heard her slur her words.

"I'll make us some coffee." He held up a hand. "I know, how dare I? But either we drink coffee and discuss your daughter or this time I really will leave. Cream, sugar?"

She glared at him, then the opaque pools lost focus. "Black. You'll find it on the counter. Knock yourself out."

He left her sitting in minor defeat, the hawk with her primary feathers ruffled. He found the coffee and a French press. While he waited for water to boil, he heard the door open and she walked past him, holding her body carefully erect. He could hear water running in the pipes. A minute later, her voice: "Bring the coffee into the saddle room."

The request had come from a hall that led into a bunkhouse. Like the rest of the house, as much as he'd seen of it, the room was straight out of *Western Living*, the walls and peaked ceiling constructed of blond logs joined by cream chinking. The floorboards were rough wood twelve-by-twos laid on a diagonal, the walls hung with copper wall sconces that illuminated an ornate pool table with feet carved like cat's paws. A stained glass lighting fixture over the pool table reflected on a display case on one wall. The case was stacked five shelves deep with rodeo trophies and belt buckles. Cowboy hats hung on the squared posts of the bunk beds, ropes from wall pegs. An open steamer chest was stacked with expensive-looking wool blankets.

"I'm in here."

Stranahan walked past the pool table, which was racked for nine-ball. He absently rolled the cue toward a corner pocket. "You have tight pockets," he said, entering the saddle room.

She was hoisting a cardboard filing box onto a corner table. "I beg your pardon?"

"Nothing. I was talking about the pool table."

"That's a game I haven't touched since the accident. This is my lair."

Etta Huntington's saddle room was decidedly a work space, with track lighting and drop cloths covering the floor. An intricately tooled saddle rode the back of a sawhorse. Another saddle, half finished, rested on a bench dominated by a massive, bolted-in vise. The bench was strewn with odd-looking punches and awls. There were spools of rawhide thread and silver lace, racks draped with sheepskins, the pungent scent of chrome-tanned leather.

"A hand-tooled Huntington roping saddle," Etta was saying, "like that one in progress, double rigged, is worth eight thousand dollars. *If* I ever finish it." Her back was to Stranahan, her broad shoulders tapering to a wasp waist. She was looking out a picture window, the intermittent thread of the river faded to pewter. "I used to love last light," she said. She spoke without turning her head. "The doctors assure me I'm a good candidate for one of those bionic arms you control by telepathic impulse. So I could do leatherwork again. Or flip steaks on the grill or pick up runaway lobsters. Strangle someone. You know, stuff normal people do." She waved her good arm dismissively. "Jasper wanted to hire somebody to carry on the business because it was lucrative, but I have my integrity. I won't be a 'designed by'—if I put my name on a saddle, I'll damned well make it."

She took the cup of coffee from Stranahan's hand. "That's too hot," she said, blowing the steam off. As she stood close to him, her green eyes made a frank assessment. She was wearing a pearl snap shirt with piping in the outline of stallions facing each other, one rearing from each swell of breast. Her mouth parted and she breathed in, then slowly, audibly let the breath out. She was only a couple inches shorter than Stranahan and her animal vitality was palpable.

"My mother used to say she could read my heart rate just by

watching my veins jump. It makes some people uncomfortable, standing this close to me. Do I disturb you, Sean?"

Stranahan wasn't going to play the game. He lifted his chin to indicate the table. "What's in the box?"

"That's Cindy. School projects, letters, photos. It's what's left of her. Besides the rodeo trophies. You'd need a U-Haul to fit them in. I put it together for Harold with the girl's last name, the Indian detective. He returned it a few months ago."

"Little Feather."

She sipped at the coffee. "Now there's . . . well, he's a man, that's all." She stared at the ceiling. "That same spider's been there all spring." She shook her head. "I had most of the papers copied to turn over to Bullock and Bullock, the detective firm. That was a waste of money. I still have a stack of their reports somewhere, every nickel accounted for. If all I wanted was paperwork I could have hired a secretary. Anyway, you can go through the box. There's a disk I put together of Cindy riding, different rodeos. Nothing seems to have the slightest bearing on why she disappeared. But you're the one gets to the bottom of the dark river. Just come back to me with something I don't know."

"Nothing I do will bring her back."

"I'm acutely aware of that."

"There's also the possibility that I'll discover something that points a finger. You can develop an obsession about bringing someone to justice with no realistic chance of it happening. They go on living while your life dies inside you. It's like a cancer. I've seen it before."

"And how is that worse than what I have now, the not knowing? Sometimes I wish the detective had been right, that she'd died when she went missing."

"Is that what Harold said?"

She shook her head. She struck Stranahan as being sober now; it was a remarkable transformation. "No, Mr. Bullock the elder. He said only hippies and the homeless disappear, that when someone is missing who has people who are looking out for their welfare, who care about them, they pick up an electronic trail or find receipts or someone talks, that if they don't surface in a few days it means they're dead." Her voice was matter-of-fact, but her eyes were wavering. "He thought . . . when they got the flat, somebody picked them up and killed them. Like a serial killer. But he was wrong. She didn't die, she was alive up until last month. I have to know what happened."

"Did Cinderella use drugs?"

"No, never. The only time I ever saw her with a drink was at Christmas, a glass of spiked eggnog. If somebody offered her a beer, she'd wrinkle up her nose."

"Tell me about Landon Anker."

"What's to tell? Jasper hired him last summer to take care of the horses when I was back in West Virginia, trying to find my mother. I'm a hills and hollows girl. My mother said I'd sleepwalk and she'd find me curled up by the woodstove, that she should have named me Cinderella. That's how I picked the name for my daughter."

"Did you find her?"

"Mother? No, but that's a story you don't need to hear. Anyway, you asked about Landon. He was a couple years older. They went to the same school." She shrugged. "He was soft-spoken, had good country manners. I know she had . . . certain feelings for him. I just wish she'd talked to me about it. We used to be so close."

"How do you know she had feelings?"

"Cindy kept a diary. I came across it one day, I think it was the first day of school. That's not true, I was looking for it. Since the accident she'd become distant. I felt guilty, but I wanted to know what she was thinking. There was an entry in it about how handsome he was and how he didn't notice her. She wrote about how she wanted to twirl his hair in her fingers, how she'd . . . satisfy herself when she thought about him. I wasn't shocked. I was her age once and dreamed about boys. But nothing in the diary gave the impression they had a physical relationship. It's just within the past couple weeks I heard he might have been gay. If he was, maybe that would explain it. But I never voiced my disapproval of him, certainly not within my daughter's hearing. I can't begin to understand why she should feel the need to run away."

"Did you turn the diary over to Harold?"

"No, where I'd found it in her room, it wasn't there. We looked hard for it. I think she took it with her, wherever she was going."

"Etta, I talked to Sheriff Ettinger on the phone before driving down here. She attended your daughter's autopsy. There's no easing into this. Cinderella was pregnant."

For a moment her face didn't change. "Why," she started to say. A slight tremor blurred her lower jaw. "Why wasn't I told this?" Her eyes had a wave in their focus. "For God's sake—"

"I *am* telling you. Sheriff Ettinger didn't call because she thought it would be better if someone told you in person."

A cloud had come over her face. When she spoke again, her voice had lost its frantic quality. It was if she was half talking to herself.

"I never suspected."

Her eyes settled back on Stranahan. "I never suspected," she said again.

"The medical examiner says five months. It could be why they ran away, that she'd found out. How would your husband"—Stranahan remembered he wasn't to use the word—"how would Jasper Fey have reacted if he'd known?"

"He . . ." She bit her lower lip. "I don't know really. I . . . I'm not sure how *I* would have reacted." She blinked and looked far off, seeming to seek exactly the right words. "I would have been disappointed, but I would never disown her. I would have been there for her, for them as a couple if he stayed in the picture. Jasper, I would have said he'd kill the kid, but he seems to be trying to forget all about his stepdaughter. He did love her, though, he never had children with his first wife; you couldn't have found a more doting father. Despite what I've said, we actually were a family once, before the accident changed things."

It was the fourth or fifth time she'd brought up the accident, speaking as if it was common knowledge. Stranahan, though, hadn't known anything about it until a couple hours ago, when he used the computer in his art studio to scan websites, trying to get a feel for Huntington before making her acquaintance. He'd found a newspaper account in the *Bridger Mountain Star*. The accident had occurred a year ago March when Huntington was pulling a horse trailer, driving her daughter to compete in a rodeo in Sheridan, Wyoming, and had swerved to avoid hitting a deer. The truck had caromed off the road into a stack of culvert pipe, one of which slammed through the windshield and severed her right arm below the elbow. Though the pipe had an eighteen inch diameter, it had miraculously missed Cinderella, who was sitting in the passenger seat. The story was newsworthy not only because Etta had gained a measure of notoriety as the face of Chevy Absaroka, and it was a half-ton Absaroka that she'd crashed, but because less than twenty-four hours later she had ripped out her IV and walked out of the hospital to watch her daughter win the junior division in barrel racing. Fans had seen the blood seeping through the heavy sterile wraps on her arm, as well as the head bandages on her daughter, who had suffered cuts and contusions in the crash, and whose hat had blown off as she laid her head on her horse's neck while rounding the first barrel. A video posted on YouTube received more than thirty thousand hits.

"This accident," Stranahan prompted.

"Yes. It seems like everyone knows about that particular incident. And the commercial. People who don't know you form . . . opinions." She drew the last word out, her voice turning bitter.

"How did it change things, Etta?"

"I don't know where to begin. I'd been stamped as the brazen cowgirl. 'Hellcat in a cowgirl hat' is what a director called me once. 'Puma on a painted horse.' I was called a lot of things relating to cats. But it's hard to live up to the image when you lose your arm. It puts a damper on the male fantasy. For Cindy, it was . . . more a personality change. She was wearing a seat belt, but her head whiplashed against the pipe. The damage to her brain wasn't determined for several months. But I could see she was different. Cindy never took decisions lightly—the decision to buy a filly, or whether to go to the school in Clyde Park or be homeschooled—she'd agonize. She was always at odds with herself, head versus heart. The accident resulted in an injury to the cerebral cortex. It removed a filtering process and made her more likely to act on impulse than consider consequences. One thing that upset me about Jasper's decision to hire Landon was that he knew how vulnerable Cindy would be to act on her . . . urges. He should have known that bringing him in here would be giving her a green card to explore her sexuality."

"Wouldn't an injury like hers make it more dangerous to ride?"

She looked querulously at Stranahan, held the look, then slowly nodded. "You're absolutely right. In rodeo, you're always riding on edge. People think only the guys take risks, but I would tell them to climb on the back of a blooded quarter horse and do a one-eighty at full gallop and try not to fly off the pommel. Cindy threw all caution to the wind to win that buckle in Laramie."

"Was she still riding when she went missing?"

"Not competitively. I'd made her stop. It was for her own safety." She paused. "It was . . . hard for her to take. Another effect of the injury was that she didn't fully understand what had happened to her, why I had to take her off her horse. We were already getting recruitment letters from rodeo schools—Cal Poly, Montana State, New Mexico State. She would be offered a full-ride scholarship, she was that good. I was taking her dream away from her."

"Maybe that's why she didn't come to you about Landon. She was afraid you'd take him away, too."

"It would break my heart that she didn't know me better. But I have wondered about it. You're a perceptive man. Do you have a contract, something for me to sign? Now that you'll deign to work for me."

He watched the corners of her lips shrug, a smile that made her look ten years younger. Stranahan kept a portable fly-tying kit in the Land Cruiser, and he excused himself to retrieve his "emergency" contract, which was folded under a rooster hackle used to tie dry flies. She signed on the line.

"In case you're wondering, I've always been ambidextrous. Its helped with the adjustment. But the signature's the hardest."

"I'll need to talk to you again, everyone who works here for that matter. And I'd like to see your daughter's room."

She nodded. "The memorial service is at noon. It's at the Episcopal church in Pony. It's a bit of a drive, but that's where we lived before I bought this place. Do you know Pony?"

Stranahan nodded as she handed him back the pen.

"We're having a potluck. I can introduce you to people who were part of her life."

Stranahan said he'd be there and offered his hand. She wrapped it in her strong rough fingers and then reached to touch his face. She spread her fingers along his jaw and drew them back until only her fingertips touched the point of his chin, leaving lines of heat. She placed her forefinger against her lips and pressed. Then she pressed the finger against his lips, before placing her hand on her heart. "That's the way I would say good night to Cindy," she said. "She called it the Crazy Mountain kiss. It was our secret."

"I'll find out what happened to her, Etta."

"That's good to hear. It's the first time anyone has said that to me."

She fingered a cream-colored doeskin dress that hung from a peg in the wall. "My heritage is Cherokee, but this is a traditional Lakota design; you can tell by the ragged hem. I haven't finished the bead-work on the yoke and there's still the elk teeth to sew on. It was to have been Cindy's wedding dress, if she ever married. Now I suppose I'll be buried in it."

"You're still a young woman, Etta."

"Am I?" She walked to the sawhorse and swung a leg over the saddle. "God I'm tired."

She draped a sheepskin over the two-by-fours that crossed in front of the pommel, then leaned forward so that her cheek lay against the makeshift pillow, the neck of an invisible horse. To Stranahan the position looked awkward, one of those impossible positions cats contort themselves into. It struck him that this wasn't the first time she'd done it, and that had he not merited a measure of her trust she wouldn't have let him see her in the position. She closed her eyes and, without lifting her head, drew a lazy circle in his direction with the stump of her right arm. He had forgotten all about the arm.

"Good night," she said.

———

It was past midnight when Stranahan let himself into his studio. He booted the computer and found the video. The volume key had stopped working, so there would be no soundtrack to the commercial.

She was leaning against the rail of a lunging pen. Noticeably younger, her cheekbones sharp as ax blades. Red cowboy boots well worn, morning sun glinting off a spur. She brushed the hair back from her eyes and centered a black Stetson as she strode into the pen, holding the lariat at her side. The horse reared when she roped him, she brought her cheek to his to settle him down. Whispered to him, the camera having a love affair with her lips. She loaded the horse into a trailer and climbed into the truck. Mountains passed by, snow on the escarpment. Then she was in sagebrush country on a road like an arrow, a line of dust in her wake, her hand on the wheel ropy with veins.

At the rodeo, she paired up with a man for the team roping, gave a grim-faced nod to the gatekeeper for the break. She headed, he heeled, the steer stretched out as the flag went up. A glance at the clock, her eyes fierce. Six point two seconds.

She trailered her horse, parked the Chevy under a hangnail moon. Middle of nowhere, didn't turn her head as he drove up in a battered pickup. The kiss was deep, somehow the hats stayed on. They looked toward his truck, then hers with the longer bed. No comparison. The camera pulled back, the Chevy was center frame. You couldn't see them over the sidewalls, but the implication was clear. The sky black with white pepper until now, a single red cowboy boot kicked high against the stars. Then the other.

Stranahan read the banner as the frame froze:

ABSAROKA, FOR THE WOMAN WHO KICKS OUT THE STARS.

PART TWO

THE MILE AND A HALF HIGH CLUB

CHAPTER TEN

Love in Thin Air

In the tipi, Stranahan sat behind the center fire looking toward the flap, Martha Ettinger sitting cross-legged to his right. If his guest had been a man, Stranahan would have indicated the space to his left. It was the Blackfeet custom Harold Little Feather had impressed upon him when he'd lent Stranahan the tipi. Martha brought the coffee cup to her lips, pursing them out tentatively. She made a face.

"Don't you know better than to serve a hot drink in an enamel cup? You might as well kiss a branding iron."

Stranahan smiled. It was the first time she had visited since their breakup and already she was being critical. Vintage Martha.

"All I have for breakfast is tuna jerky Sam made in Florida."

"I'll pass. How is Sam?"

"He's in Sam heaven. The fishing clients down there expect the guide to berate them for their incompetence. His only regret is it's against the law to put a shock collar on them."

"Sam," Ettinger said. "You're waiting for me to smile when I think about him."

"You never did like Sam."

"I don't have as much tolerance for bullshit as you do."

"Did you see Wilkerson after the autopsy? Now that I'm officially on the clock for Etta Huntington, I'm interested to hear what she's found out."

"Not much we don't know. She confirmed that the fibers collected above and below her position were in fact from her clothing. So she went down, but she went up, too, and we don't have an acceptable explanation for that. Her body hair had grown out and it didn't look like she'd washed in weeks. Gigi found abnormally large red blood cells that suggest a folic acid deficiency. She wasn't eating enough vegetables. It all points to her living very rough. Not much else except the nail broken off in her foot is made of iron. It's called a type B cut nail. They started being replaced by steel nails about the turn of the century, but of course there must be millions rusting in coffee cans and wherever."

"Where do you think she stepped on it?"

"The only place we know she's been is the forest cabin, so I suggest that's where you'd start. But that's not why I stopped by."

"Why did you?"

"I'll get to it, but tell me, what did you make of Loretta Huntington?"

Stranahan pressed his lips together. "She was drunk. Mad at the world. I got some coffee in her you could stand a snake in and she became a human being, but that only went so far. There's a wild animal quality about her."

Martha nodded. "Walt YouTubed her to see the truck commercial and said that she was, and I quote the man, 'a Johnson straightener of the first order.'"

"That's one way of putting it. She has an excess of vitality, like she breathes a purer form of air. She places a lot of blame on her second husband, who's in Roundup shooting a series TV show about a modern-day sheriff. The actor had never been on a horse. Jasper Fey is his coach."

Martha grunted. "Seems like for every real cowboy, you have someone sitting saddle who plays the part on camera. 'All hat, no cattle.' It ought to be the new state motto."

"From what I heard, Jasper's the real deal. Etta told me he was a pickup man, one of the horsemen who rescues the bronc and bareback riders from bucking horses. Before that he was a bullfighter, the guy with the baggy britches who distracts the bull so it doesn't kill the cowboy it's tossed in the air. He was a champion bronc rider before he was twenty. A walking catalog of broken bones."

"How did the pregnancy news go over?"

"About as you'd expect. She got mad at the messenger. But I don't think Cinderella being pregnant came as that much of a surprise. She stills thinks it was Anker, the hired hand. By the way, why didn't you tell me she had only one arm?"

"I didn't want you to have preconceived notions. Did she talk about any of her daughter's relationships besides the one with the boy?"

"Well, the mother-daughter bond was strained. They had a falling-out after the accident." Stranahan related the story of Cinderella's brain injury and its effect on her behavior.

Ettinger took a swallow from her cup. It was just cool enough.

"I did not know that. And I don't remember Harold mentioning it last fall."

"I don't think it's something the family wants to advertise."

Ettinger nodded thoughtfully and they sat in easy silence, watching the smoke curl up toward the tipi's top flap.

"I better get my butt to work. What's on your schedule today?"

"The memorial service is at one. I was thinking about looking up Anker's parents for their side of the story. The news that Cindy was alive all winter must be hard on them. You've been trying to come to terms with the likelihood your son is dead, and now you have to think if she was alive, maybe he was, too. Or still is."

"Won't they be at the memorial?"

"I'll find out."

"So that leaves you the morning. I have a suggestion. Remember the date on that sex tape?"

"February fourteenth, wasn't it?"

Martha nodded. "I called the Forest Service and got a scan of the reservation. Ariana Dimitri." She fished a piece of notepaper from her shirt pocket. "You might want to find out how she came to be wearing a Santa hat two months before it dropped out of a chimney."

"It will be interesting to see if I recognize her in clothes."

"Somebody has to point you in the right direction. Say, 'Thank you, Martha.'" She uncrossed her legs and got stiffly to her feet. "Now I'm going to smell like woodsmoke all day."

"Thank you, Martha," Stranahan said.

Ettinger squared her hat. "All part of the service."

The address led Stranahan to a one-story clapboard house on the north side of Bozeman. Stranahan generally avoided the Bo-Zone, as the sprawling community was called, preferring the quieter backwaters of Bridger and Ennis, but had to admit parts of the town were attractive. This wasn't one of them, the houses run-down and this one needing a roof and a coat of paint it would probably never get. Stranahan would place a bet that it would be torn down to make way for a Craftsman cottage for a California couple before the decade was out, protection provided by ADT Security. As it was, the patch of dandilion lawn was protected by a cocker doodle leashed to the rail of the porch. Or not protected. The cocker doodle raised his head to be patted when Stranahan approached. The girl who answered his knock had twin braids and was a younger image of the woman Stranahan had seen in the video, with thin facial features and a bulging forehead. All of ten. No, her mother wasn't in. Was her father around? Her father lived in Boise. "They're D-I-V-O-R-C-E." Was there anyone else at home. "I'm supposed to say there is because you're a stranger." Where is your mother? "She works at the library."

Of course she's a librarian, Stranahan thought.

He thanked the little speller and found his way to the library. The woman manning the checkout desk was wearing a name tag on a scoop top that played peekaboo with a lacy camisole. The tag read ARI. Her glasses were big for her eyes, magnifying dark brown irises.

"I'm Sean Stranahan," he said, and offered his hand.

She took it unhesitatingly, her rings pressing into his fingers. He had that effect on people, disarming them with his touch before they could erect a subconscious skin of posture to keep their distance. It had the desired effect now, for she brightened and smiled up at him from her chair, a little magenta lipstick smeared on her front teeth. Her face was its own constellation, with silver glitter twinkling from blushed cheeks and half moons of midnight blue eye shadow. Her earrings were bolts of pewter lightning. Her bracelets clicked. It was the gypsy look, but not unattractive.

"Can I make you a card? You look like a reader of . . . let me guess"—her voice fell to a delicious whisper—"espionage. John Le Carré, Alan Furst. I love Alan Furst. He puts you right there in prewar Europe." She worked a finger into her curls—her nails matched the color of her lips—and raised her eyebrows.

Stranahan told her he'd got into the habit of listening to books on tape. Like a lot of immigrant Montanans, he'd found audiobooks to be something of a necessity in a country where driving distances were so enormous.

"We have quite a few of those," she said. "CD, cassette, Playaway. If you're into police procedurals, I recommend the Harry Bosch novels by Michael Connelly. Len Cariou is the reader, what a voice. And anything that Simon Vance or Rick Holmes narrates. It's the reader makes the book."

"Thanks. I'll look into them, but that's not why I came here, Ariana."

"You know my name," she said. She was smiling but her eyes had narrowed.

"Is there a place we can talk privately?" He awarded her his best smile while inwardly wincing. He was getting to be as bad as Max Gallagher, offering the better half of his face.

"Are you flirting with me?" she said. "I'm not that kind of librarian." *Yes you are,* thought Stranahan.

She pulled a shawl over her bare shoulders and he followed her outside, past a homeless man curled around an open guitar case on a manicured lawn. The guitar was minus three strings. She paused to rummage in her purse and dropped a five-dollar bill into the case. "That's for food, Henry," she said in a loud voice.

The man stirred and opened his eyes. "God bless you," he said.

They walked toward a picnic table bolted to a concrete slab.

"Jackie wants us to run him off, but I don't have the heart. He's like a bird, all the homeless are this far north. In November they fly away and you never know if you'll see them again."

Stranahan saw that the library grounds bordered a big park. He produced his card, the one with the eye under the logo—*Blue Ribbon Investigations.*

She fidgeted with the shawl. "Are you a private detective? I've never met a private detective."

"Then you're in luck."

She smiled again, but her expression had become guarded. "Is this about Jeremy Cusack? He has an overactive imagination, that boy."

"No." Sean saw the relief in her eyes. "It's about the night you rented a Forest Service cabin in the Crazy Mountains."

"Oh." She was still worried, but it seemed a milder apprehension. Stranahan had a feeling that her problem with Jeremy Cusack—or maybe it was his parents who had the problem with her—was more serious in nature. He was sure that the boy, underage or not, considered himself lucky.

"Ari, I know about the video you made in the cabin. Now, you're not in any trouble, it's consenting adults and there's no law against what you did. But I'm working with the Hyalite sheriff's department on an open investigation and I need to know a few things about that night. I can put you in touch with Sheriff Ettinger if you want to verify my credentials."

She was looking down at her shoes. "No, I have nothing to hide." A small laugh, then a shake of her head as she looked up. Her cheeks were blushing under the blush. "Nothing to hide, I guess that's a Freudian slip."

"You were wearing a hat, a Santa hat. Where did you get it?"

"It wasn't mine. I found it in the box, the geocache. You . . . know about that, too, right? I guess you'd have to."

"I know about the box in the cellar."

She nodded. "When you take something you're supposed to put

something of equal value back. My uncle gave me some playing cards with fishing lures on them, so I took the hat and left the pack."

"What did you do with the hat?"

"I was going to take it home, like a souvenir. But then I didn't because, in the end, the next day, I wasn't so wild about the guy. He wasn't as advertised and it's not written or anything, but wearing a mask seems like a cop-out. I tried to get into the spirit, but the devil face freaked me out." She spoke quickly, nervously. "And there were other things, not so good at all. No, he was a creep. So I just hung the hat on a nail and left it. Am I in trouble?"

"Not if you're telling the truth."

She was shaking her head from side to side, her hair falling in loose curls that alternately hid one or the other side of her face. "Dumb, dumb, dumb," she muttered to herself. "You make one little sex tape, next thing you know the world's seeing it."

"Just two people," Stranahan said. "And it's probably all that ever will."

"You're not, like, passing it around the office?"

"No. You mentioned the guy you were with. What's his name?"

"Well, we all choose our club names. I'm Book Girl and his was . . . I can't remember. It was a girl's name. Shirley, that was it. But I said that was silly, so he said call him Gus. I don't think it's his real name."

"You didn't know him?"

"No, the way it works is Amoretta matches me up with someone from her list. After we make the video, we put the card into the troll doll for the next couple."

"Does Amoretta rent the cabin?"

She nodded. "That's what the dues are for. We each put in a hundred dollars a year and the cabin costs fifty, so divide it by two 'cause it takes two to tango, that's twenty-five. So the dues cover four assignations a year. That's what Amoretta calls them, assignations."

"Who is Amoretta?"

"She's the one who does the matching up. It's called the Mile and a Half High Club because the assignations are in the mountains."

"So you're a swingers' club."

"Kind of, but there's no group sex or anything." Her smile flickered back. When she spoke next, her voice was singsong and dreamy. "Not that there's anything wrong with that." She touched her tongue to her upper lip.

"Are these assignations arranged through email?"

"No, the Internet's too public. Amoretta puts an ad in the classi-fieds at the *Star*, first of the month. It will have the date and the coor-dinates of the geocache and the combination to the cabin door. All the numbers are in reverse, like a code. So every month I look for an ad that says 'Love in Thin Air,' and if Book Girl's one of the two names in it, then I have an assignation."

"But it's your name on the register with the Forest Service, not Amoretta's."

"Well, she does the renting but puts the rental party and contract and all that kind of stuff in the name of one of the participating members."

"How long has the club been going?"

"About two years, but I only joined up last fall. You have to be recommended by somebody who's a member."

"Are the assignations always in the same cabin?"

"They weren't at first, but they are now. I think Amoretta has a connection that makes it available."

"Have you met this person?"

"I might have. But I didn't, like, *meet her* meet her. I was told that she'd seen me at a party and was going to give me a call. Amoretta interviews all of us before we're invited to join. You don't want any weirdos."

"So you don't know her real identity?"

"No. The whole point is the anonymity."

"Why do you think she chose you?"

"Well, it was a certain kind of party. She must have liked what she saw. Is this going to take much longer? Because if it is, I have to get somebody to cover for me."

"Let me make certain I have this straight. You make a video and put the chip into the doll and hide the doll in the geocache for the next couple to find. And then they make a video and put it into the doll and so on?"

"Pay it forward. Now you get the picture."

"How does Amoretta know you'll find the box? It was in the wall of the cellar."

"Well, the coordinates are for the cache, not the cabin. That gets you within a few feet. And she puts a clue in the ad. Our clue was 'Trapdoor.'"

"Was there a memory card in the doll when you got there?"

"*Mmm—hmm*. A busty blonde who looked sort of dyke-ish. And a little bitty thing. Oh, but she was the contortionist."

"Lesbians."

"Or bi. I'm bi. Why limit yourself, is what I say."

"Do you have that card?"

She hesitated. "Maybe."

"Look, Ari, this could be important." Sean wasn't sure how it could be important, but you could never collect too much information.

"It's at home. I could mail it to you."

"No, I'm going to need it now."

"All right. I rode my bike here, so you'll have to drive."

Stranahan climbed into the Land Cruiser. He turned the key when he saw her reemerge from the library. "I got somebody to cover until lunch." She flounced into the passenger seat, turning herself sideways to face him. She'd brought a scent of perfume with her and had reapplied her lipstick. "I like an engine with a good rumble," she said. Deliberately, she hooked her left leg over the stick shift. Whatever misgivings she had harbored were all gone now.

"Ari."

A pause, her eyebrows going up. Innocently: "Yes?"

"Your leg."

"This leg?" She moved her leg an inch.

Stranahan lifted the leg and put it where it belonged.

"You're no fun."

"I'll tell you something that isn't fun. Letting a stranger hook you up in the middle of nowhere with a stranger. You could get killed over a cheap thrill like that."

But she wasn't listening. Stranahan heard her humming, her eyes teasing him, her smile wicked.

When he pulled up in front of the house, she said, "I'll just get it," and ran to the door the way a girl would run, legs flying as she jumped over the dog, and then a minute later ran out again, taking the dog in stride. She leaned inside the open driver's side window, breathing hard. "Feel my heart," she said, and brought Stranahan's hand to her chest as she folded his fingers over the camera card. Her heart beat hard, her breath was warm. Her hand was very warm, with rings on every finger. Stranahan recalled her words at the end of the video, when she'd reached out that hand to turn the camera off: *"Put that in your pipe and smoke it."*

"Ari?"

"Yes?"

"My hand."

She didn't release it. Instead, she reached her free hand to take a pen from the cracked dashboard and inked numbers onto the back of Stranahan's hand. "Will you come and see me sometime? Or maybe you don't like natural women. Do you like natural women?"

"I even like the unnatural ones."

"I'm off Sundays and Mondays."

"Sure," Stranahan said. "Maybe I'll come by and we can rent a book on tape or something."

She rubbed her thumb into the palm of his hand. The skin was smooth, in contrast to the sandpaper grip of Etta Huntington. "A book could be nice. But I vote for 'or something.'"

She brought the tips of her first two fingers to her lips, then touched Stranahan's. She straightened up and walked to join her daughter, who had appeared on the front step. The dog hadn't moved an inch since Sean's earlier visit, even after being hurdled twice.

"Wave goodbye to the detective man," she said to the girl.

"Don't you need a ride back to work?" Stranahan called out.

"No, I'll walk."

The girl waved goodbye and then they both were waving as he drove away, and were still waving when he glanced at the rearview mirror, as if they were a family and he was catching a train for work.

CHAPTER ELEVEN

True Love

As far as Sean Stranahan was concerned, Pony, Montana's motto—"The Last Best Town in the Last Best Place"—wasn't a stretch, not if you liked a one-street, know-your-neighbors town. A gold rush settlement of five thousand dreamers in the 1860s, complete with a blacksmith's shop and two Chinese laundries, it was down to less than a hundred souls, no longer even a whorehouse to its name, but the one essential business was open 365 days a year. Stranahan took a stool in the Pony Bar under a graveyard of cracked cowboy hats hanging from nails and put his boots on the brass rail.

A bartender wearing sleeve garters cut the foam off a Guinness and set it on the bar as Stranahan caught snatches of conversation:

> "When the boy and I climbed Hollow Top last summer I told him that's where I proposed to his mother. I was thinking it was a tender moment. He said the mosquitoes up here are big enough to rape a chicken. Where do you suppose he heard a thing like that at?"

> "I'm telling you there must have been a dozen dogs fighting. I jumped up onto the bar and yelled, 'Okay, anything with a tail, out of here!' And Rose Marie, you got to love her, I get the last one out the door and she says, 'Does that mean me, too?'"

"Now he wants twenty percent of the calves in addition to twenty-a-head grazing rights. I said why not take my third cutting and have a poke at my wife while you're at it?"

Stranahan's focus wavered as he finished his beer. He had decompressed from the drive and now he was just tired. He raised a finger to the bartender. "Coffee."

The coffee came and he blew on it as he heard a man behind him talking in a loud voice. "I told that one-armed bitch the dog was coming through my fence and I was going to shoot him, and then she gets her panties in a bunch when I foller through. She said the dog wasn't getting into livestock and I said it's the principle, can't you understand that? This isn't Indi-fucking-ana. Out here people have a respect for property rights. She wrapped the dog in a Navajo blanket must be worth a grand. Took him without a goddamned word. But if those eyes could kill I'd be bullshitting from the grave. I do feel sorry for her girl. That was a hell of a thing."

Stranahan swiveled the stool around to see who was talking about Etta Huntington as a fist flashed by his face. He heard a hollow thump like a bat striking a watermelon and the man who'd been speaking hit the floor hard, his legs twitching, his eyes rolled right back into his head. Everything locked into freeze frame, bottles stopped midway to lips, the bartender's face agape, the jukebox loud in the silence. Then the man was on his knees and trying to stand and the one who'd hit him cocked his fist to swing and Stranahan, without thinking, tossed his coffee into the man's face, then flung himself off the stool and tackled him at his ankles, immediately registering that he might have taken on more adrenaline-stoked muscle than he could handle. But the balance shifted when the bartender vaulted the bar and got the man in a headlock, his blousy shirt stretched tight across his thick right arm. Stranahan heard a muffled, "Okay, okay," and they manhandled him to his feet and half dragged him outside, the bartender's face red as a beet and the cords in his neck standing with the strain.

"I'm going to smack shit out of you next, boy-oh," the man said to Stranahan when they released him. Sean was surprised to see he was looking down at the top of the man's head and that the hair—the man's cowboy hat had come off in the melee—was as silver as last night's moon.

"No, you're not going to do anything of the kind, Jasper." The bartender had stepped between them. "They're inside thinking about calling the cops right now, if they haven't already. If you'd hit that fellow a second time you'd be cooling those snakeskins in jail tonight. This young man saved the county the expense. What the hell were you trying to do, upstage your own daughter's memorial?"

"He insulted my wife, my own goddamned neighbor." The man had a way-down-in-the-well voice, but with melody in it, despite the vitriol of the words. "A silver-tongued bastard," Etta had called him. Now that bastard was looking around the bartender's barrel chest toward Stranahan. He may have been short, but Sean saw that the body was tight with muscle that strained the seams of his snap-up shirt.

"You burned about half my goddamned face off, mister," the man said.

"So you're Jasper Fey. Your wife told me you'd be skipping this occasion."

"My wife?" He said it a second time, his voice rising. "What's my wife have to do with you throwing coffee in my face? Shit. Everything's a blur, I can't hardly see. If I—"

"It's just the surface of the cornea that's burned. You stay out of bright lights and you'll be fine tomorrow."

"What are you, an ophthalmologist?"

"I'm a private detective. But I've been snow-blind and it's the same burn. Your wife hired me to find out about Cinderella. You mind your manners, I'll take you to the service. You're in no condition to drive and it's going to start in ten minutes."

"You sure you got this under control?" the bartender said.

Stranahan nodded.

"Then I got to go back in there and pick up the goddamned pieces. This isn't a fighting bar; there's families, for Chrise sakes. I'm not back in five minutes means nobody's pressing charges—yet. Either or, don't you never come through the door again, Jasper. Not never." He straightened his bolo tie and shot his cuffs.

"It's not like you own the place, Sidwell," Jasper Fey said. But he said it under his breath after the bartender had gone.

———

In the cut stone Episcopal church with its towering steeple and stained glass windows, Loretta Huntington sat in the front left pew, beside her an equally tall but considerably blonder version of herself, undoubtedly the sister from Sweden she'd mentioned. When Jasper Fey made his appearance, standing in the aisle with his hat in hand and his silver head catching the prism light, the two women edged down the pew to make room for him. He sat; the crown of his head came up a little past his wife's ears. From where Stranahan was standing against the back wall, he saw Etta glance at her husband's burned face and abruptly turn her head away. Sean took in the gathering, bowlegged men with middle-age spread and two-tone foreheads, women who had meat on their bones. Ranch people—knuckled hands folded on top of each other, skin that had spots. Among them were a smattering of suits, or rather what passed for them—crisp shirts, silk accent scarves, jeans with decorative stitching, the main difference being the faces weren't so leathered, having seen the seasons change from behind the picture window. Toward the back on both sides of the aisle were at least a dozen teenagers, Cinderella's schoolmates, Sean surmised.

What he learned about her from the Reverend George Crookshaw he could sum up in a sentence—"She had too much life to be called to heaven so young, but who are we to question the ways of the Lord?"

Etta was the first speaker from the family; she took the steps holding herself carefully erect. She'd braided her hair and was dressed in western mourning attire—a black pearl snap shirt, black skirt, and black boots with embroidered pink roses. Her right arm looked natural from a distance, but the plastic clacked off the wood of the lectern as she leaned forward. In the silence that stretched she seemed shaky—for a moment Stranahan wondered if she'd been drinking—but she steadied as she found her voice.

"As some of you know, my spiritual belief system is more aboriginal than the prevailing Christian doctrines you subscribe to. My daughter also adopted my beliefs, and as we do not disparage your faith I would hope that you respect our belief that the sun, dawn light, is our father god, as it is for Native Americans of many tribes, and that the moon, night light, is the sun's wife. What some of you may not know is that Cinderella was my third child. My first son died shortly after childbirth, and my second, a girl, died in a miscarriage. In Native belief, the only surviving child of the union between the sun and the moon was called A-pi-su-ahts, the morning star. Cinderella was my morning star. Since the day she disappeared I have risen in the night and gone outside the house and stared at those rising stars, trying to find that one that is the vessel containing her light. I could not move forward with a new day until I knew that one of those stars was her, because, as I've come to understand, the heart never buries the dead. They remain alive in here." She placed her hand over her breast. "So when I learned that a crow had pecked out her eyes I did not react with horror. Rather I rejoiced, knowing that it had taken her eyes to heaven so that she might be whole again, that today she is there among those stars with her soul restored, and someday I might follow her and we will be reunited.

"I would like to tell you about Cindy . . ."

Stranahan listened as Etta talked about the girl with the unbridled ambitions and love of horses, hoping to hear something he didn't know before his mind inevitably strayed. Ever since he was a child going stir crazy while the reverend droned, Stranahan had adopted a habit in church of examining the faces in the congregation and attaching stories to them that were spun entirely from whole cloth. This habit had not gone over well with his mother, who'd once taken his bicycle away when Sean convinced Karen, his younger sister, that old Mr. McManus had brained his wife with a shovel.

Now, his attention flagging, he turned his eyes to a man sitting down the pew whose crew cut was gray and whose hands, clasped together on top of his Bible, bulged with muscles as they kneaded each other, writhing in isometric turmoil. The man, who wore a frayed Carhartt jack shirt, had made the floor creak when he'd walked by Stranahan earlier, and, with piglike eyes, broad nostrils, and hair sprouting from his collar and curling out of his ears, brought to mind a semi-domesticated boar. Stranahan watched his head bend forward so that his heavy jowls sagged over his Bible. The man's eyes closed, and Stranahan was beginning to build a story of a sinner overcome with remorse who prayed for God's forgiveness, when he heard the church door open. He turned his head to see a couple enter, the man Depression-era thin in defeated overalls, battered felt fedora, and shirt buttoned to the collar, an embarrassed expression on his face. Sean's eyes settled on the woman, who stepped past the man as he held the door and stared incuriously back at the gawkers, for now all the eyes of the church were on her. She looked to the left, then to the right, then to the stage at the back of the church. Etta Huntington had surrendered the microphone to a young woman who was fingerpicking a guitar, singing a song said to have been a favorite of Cinderella's but that Stranahan had never heard before, and held the last note. The strings rang into silence and it was the bar again, everyone holding a collective breath.

"Well don't mind me for livin'," the woman said.

The pastor rose to offer his professional smile. "Donna, Clyde, you're welcome to—"

"You're right I'm welcome. Grieving for this young woman is as much my right as anyone's. But who sitting here is grieving for my son? My son"—her jaw began to tremble—"my son who is, who is"— Stranahan could hear indrawn breath as she tried to calm herself—"the sweetest boy . . ." She had become unsteady and the man took her arm in support. "Landon never did a wrong thing. I know what people been saying, but he would not hurt Cindy, he thought the world of that girl, and you should be, well you should be ashamed, who think he could possibly, who don't understand the way he is . . ."

"Come on, Donna. You said your piece." It was the first the man had spoken, and she leaned into him and then went down to her knees, hugging his waist like the trunk of a tree. "Come on now, Donna."

Stranahan rose and helped the man get her to her feet.

"Thank you," he said. "I can take this from here."

"I'll hold the door." Stranahan stepped out with the couple and steered them to one of the picnic tables set end to end for the potluck. The woman had composed herself, and after sitting down she wiped at the tears that streaked her face. She wore no makeup and her face was as plain as her front-button prairie dress that belonged to another era. Her eyes searched Stranahan's face and then turned to her husband. "Oh, I shouldn't have done that, you shouldn't have let me done that."

The man patted her back. His colorless lips played with a smile as he turned to look at Stranahan. "As if I had a choice," he said. He coughed. It was a smoker's cough; Stranahan could see the outline of the cigarette pack in his shirt pocket. "I'd like to thank you for helping us back there," he said. "There was no one else got out of their seats, it was like they'd all sat down in a puddle of glue. I guess a person isn't worth saying a prayer over but that she's pretty or their folks have the money. At least they know what happened to Cindy. But our boy, it's like the world went flat and he stepped off the edge."

"I'm Sean," Stranahan said. "I know this is a difficult time for you, but I came here today because I'm trying to find out what led to Cindy's death. If I can find out how she disappeared, there's a good chance I'll find out about your son, too."

"What exactly is it you're trying to say?"

Stranahan told them and watched the man's face harden.

"So that's why you got the door?"

"No, that's the way I was brought up. But yes, I would have wanted to talk to you at some point. For what it's worth, Etta Huntington found Landon to be a nice young man."

"Just not good enough for her daughter."

"No, she worried that her daughter was too young to get too serious." That Cinderella had become pregnant was not public knowledge and Stranahan refrained from mentioning it.

The woman, Donna, didn't seem to listen. For some time she had been staring off to the west, where the cone of Hollowtop Mountain carried striations of snow under a gray sky.

"Tell him," she said presently. She turned to her husband and raised her chin. "He's gonna find out. Just tell him."

The man shook his head. "We can't have something like that getting around."

"It is around, Clyde. Ask any one of those kids in there. Mr. Stranahan, I don't know if you're being disingenuous or you're as nice as you seem . . ." Her voice trailed off.

Stranahan let the silence settle like a cloud about them. An organ started playing in the church and it would be only minutes now, he thought, before the mourners would be trickling out the door.

"I guess it really doesn't matter what you are," she said, her voice almost a whisper. "It's not going to change anything. Landon loved that girl, but not in the way that you think. He was gay. He told us last year. Oh, I'm not saying I didn't have my suspicions."

"Did Etta Huntington know that?"

"If you're asking did I tell her, I didn't. Not because I was ashamed, just because it was none of her business."

"Cinderella had a crush on your son. Did Landon speak of it?"

Clyde Anker was working the muscles in his face. "I think we talked enough. I don't aim to be standing here when they come out for that potluck."

"Then I'm going to ask you to go wait in the truck," his wife said without looking over at him. "I'll be there directly."

He started to say something, then walked away without a word.

"I'd apologize for my husband's behavior, but I'm about all apologized out. Landon never said anything about Cindy pining for him, but it doesn't surprise me. I'm going to give you the phone number to the house. Anything you want to know, you call that number. I'd hire you myself if I had Etta's money."

She said goodbye and Stranahan found himself in the awkward position of interrogator at a memorial. He made a number of acquaintances, telling people to call if they thought they could be of help. Many had already said what they had to say at the time of the disappearance, and others had been interviewed by Harold Little Feather within the last few days. Stranahan was going through motions.

At one point he found himself in conversation with a high school girl named Celeste, who claimed to have been Landon Anker's closest friend and whose left upper arm was tattooed with the words *Made in Montana* in a dripping heart and her right with *Laid in North Dakota* inside a cracked egg. She explained that she'd been conceived in Billings and born in Bismarck, adding that it had been a "fucked-up" time in her life. "Not being born—I mean, when I got the tats," she clarified. He asked her about Landon, when she'd found out he was gay.

"When I put his hand on my ass at the Sweet Pea Festival. Most guys, you do that when you're rubbing belly buttons, they've got timber hard enough to chainsaw. I told him that's okay, we could just be friends. We were up all night talking; he told me I was the first person he ever came out to."

Stranahan asked if she was jealous of Cinderella. She said no, not jealous. Well, maybe. The girl had stripped for him, after all.

"Yeah, starkers," she said. She told Stranahan that one of the nights he was lying in wait for the horsehair thief, Cindy had come into the stables wearing a bathrobe with nothing underneath. She'd taken it off and spread it out on some straw. She started kissing him, and when he said he didn't think of her that way, she started to cry. He'd spent an hour trying to talk her down and worrying that the horse trainer or somebody else might walk in on them.

"So yeah, I was pissed. She put him in that position."

Stranahan excused himself when he saw Etta Huntington standing alone. She gestured with a glass of white wine as he walked up.

"I thought it went well," she said with understated sarcasm. "Only one person made a scene and I didn't drop my arm on the floor."

"Did your husband tell you he cold-cocked a man in the bar?"

She made a dismissive snort. "Try to find someone he hasn't by now." She pointed her chin back toward the door of the church. "He said he was going to the bathroom to soak his handkerchief in cold water because his face is burning. I'd hope he was arrested if it wasn't for drawing attention from Cindy."

"He said he was protecting your honor."

"Yeah, that's a good one."

"Somebody else told me about Anker sleeping in your stable to catch a horsehair thief. Wouldn't it be hard to drive in without someone noticing?"

"Not really, not after dark. You've seen the stables; they're a couple hundred yards below the house. But what's hard to believe is how he cut off so much hair without the horses raising a ruckus. When a horse squeals with his mouth shut, the sound carries. That's why Harold thought it was an inside job."

"But no one was ever suspected?"

"No. Our manager and trainer have been with us for ages. It would have to have been someone who used to work at the ranch."

"Could you get me a list?"

"Earl Hightower could." She looked nervously past Stranahan. "Jasper's coming."

"Does that mean it's time for me to leave?"

"If you don't mind. I didn't expect to see him here at all, but now that he is, I have to at least try to keep a civil face. He'll be back on the set in a few days; we can talk all you want then."

"I'd like to ask him about Cinderella."

"Good luck with that. He's not so wild about my hiring you, as you might guess. But it's my money and she was my daughter."

"Try to convince him."

Sean could see the nervous jumping of her eyes. "Just go. I'll call you."

When Stranahan got to his rig, he found the girl who claimed to be Landon's friend sitting on the grass, smoking a cigarette. When she looked up, Sean saw that her eyes were shiny. "I didn't want you to leave thinking I was mad at Cindy or something," she said. "She was a nice girl. It's just that I was in love with him for who he was, not for somebody I wanted him to be. I mean, I'd have married him as is and just bought batteries for my vibrator. I'd have given up other guys."

Stranahan thumbed a card out of his wallet and she caught it as it fluttered down.

"Call me if you think of anything that could help," he said, and left her sitting on the grass, contemplating the sacrifices of love.

CHAPTER TWELVE

Bumps in the Night

You dating somebody with a Bozeman prefix now?" Martha Ettinger turned Sean's wrist over to examine the numbers on the back of his hand.

"Our lady of the cabin did that."

"Uh-huh." She leaned back in her office chair and laced her fingers behind her head.

"What did you expect, that she'd be a wallflower?"

"She isn't a Ginny Gin Jenny, is she?" Ginny Gin Jenny, a.k.a. Virginia Jenkins, a.k.a. the Elk Camp Madam, held the record for arrests for soliciting in Hyalite County, but had never done time because her clientele, whom she serviced in wall tents and camper trucks during hunting season, was rumored to include the current mayor, as well as officers in the police and fire departments. No one in the DA's office seemed eager to follow up on her arrests.

"No, she's strictly an amateur enthusiast," Sean said. He conveyed the gist of his interview with Ariana Dimitri.

Martha rolled her eyes. "She might as well hang a target around her neck with a bull's-eye."

"I told her. But she looks at it as an extreme sport, like parasailing off mountains. Anything for the thrill."

"Humpff. So how does this tie in with Cinderella Huntington?"

"Maybe it doesn't. According to Ari—"

"So it's Ari?"

"—Ariana. According to *her*, the Santa hat was in the geocache when she arrived at the cabin. She left it hanging on the wall. You could call the parties that came after, see if they remember seeing it."

"I can do that. How did the memorial go? "

"I made the acquaintance of Jasper Fey."

He related the circumstances of their meeting as Ettinger harrumphed. She placed her palms flat on her desk.

"While you were eating deviled eggs and throwing your coffee, Harold dropped this on the desk." She tapped a forefinger on a file folder. "Fifty-two interviews, headwaters of the Shields right on down to the Yellowstone." She flipped her fingers in a dismissive gesture. "'We have some interesting individuals residing in our county.' That was the whole of Harold's summation. Nothing remotely relatable. You know, I misjudged the fallout on this. I thought there'd be a flurry of interest and then it would go away and we'd be left with Loretta Huntington's grief, which would be tough enough to deal with. But I guess girls don't die in chimneys every day. If I put my phone in my pocket on vibrate, I could have orgasms all day long just from journalist calls. What? Why are you laughing?"

Stranahan shook his head. "This is what I miss about you. The only other person who makes me laugh like this is Sam."

"Glad to be of service. So why are you here? Don't you have any other sexy librarians waiting to put their number on your hand?"

"I thought I'd take a peek at the cabin's guestbook. It's in evidence, right?"

Ettinger nodded. "I leafed through it."

"Did anything stand out?"

"I didn't put on my deerstalker cap, but no. I'll have somebody walk it up. You can examine it in my presence. All I'm doing for the next couple hours is filling out evaluation forms. Be happy yours isn't on the list."

When the book came up, Ettinger signed for it and provided Stranahan with a legal pad and a pair of latex gloves. She shrugged. "Safe than sorry," she said.

The first entry was dated three winters in the wind and Stranahan turned pages until he found the December 1 entry of the prior calendar year, when the rental season opened. Like most of the cabins, it opened just as elk and deer season closed. The Forest Service didn't want to chance liability suits with hunters carrying firearms into the cabins. There were the expected smiley faces and a smattering of childish artwork. One entry brought a smile to Sean's lips, a pencil sketch of dancing mice to accompany complaints about said mice, with a note to stock more Victor traps. A curl of something that looked like a dried-up mouse tail was taped to the sketch.

An hour passed. Stranahan looked up to see Martha shaking her head.

"I just terminated someone's employment."

"Was it an easy decision?"

"No." She rubbed her knuckles into her eyes and blew out a breath.

"Well?"

"A couple things."

Martha walked around her desk to peer over Stranahan's shoulder. He tapped his pencil eraser on an entry marked December 3:

> *About midnight Chester went bonkers and woke us up. He was growling like I'd never heard before, I mean like a wolf. Hal went outside, the idiot, and said he smelled something really rank and in the morning there were big tracks in the snow where the kids went sledding. Like somebody wearing snowshoes, but it was powder so I can't say. Al thought a bear, but aren't the bears supposed to be hibernating by now, I mean global warming hasn't made that much of an impact yet, has it? Other than that it was the peace and quiet we needed. Just a million stars and perfect snow. We skinned up to the pass and just floated back to the cabin. <u>Whooooosh.</u>*

"I read a story about how some of the grizzlies don't even go into hibernation," Sean said. "They just scavenge food and steal from wolf kills."

Martha shook her head. "I don't see what this has to do with anything."

Stranahan turned to the next page he'd bookmarked. It was another entry about a dog getting his back hair up after dark.

Martha shrugged. "It's Montana. Things go bump in the night."

Stranahan turned to the entry for January 12. The words were neatly printed and small, the hand masculine.

> *The previous occupants did _not_ clean up after. The pots were _disgusting_. I had to melt a ton of snow to get enough water to clean them. Shame on you. Other than that beautiful as ever, every pleasure life has to offer, indoor and out. Even a ghost.*
> *And _no_ xxxxxx-ing men!*

"This was written by the couple in the video Ari gave me," Sean said. "The one that was in the geocache when she skied in. They're lesbians, hence 'no fucking men.'"

"Men are equal-opportunity assholes. They don't just piss off gay women. But how can you be sure it's their entry?"

"It's the date on the recording."

"Have you seen it?"

He nodded.

"Is there any reason I need to look at it?" Her voice said she'd rather not.

"No. They did what two women do, I guess. I'm not an expert."

"You're thinking because it mentions a ghost that it means something?"

"It's the third entry that mentions something big and scary in the nighttime."

"People have imaginations."

Stranahan wasn't going to win the point and leafed to the last page bookmarked. It was an early January entry from two years before, exactly halfway through the journal.

Perfect weather (smiley face). Perfect people (smiley face). The dog threw up on my sleeping bag (frowny face). I had an epiphany. God is the mountain. The mountain is God. Perfect! Perfect! Perfect! (three smiley faces)

"See it? It's scrawled over the other writing, but the pen was almost out of ink. It says—"

"I see it. 'THE CLOWNS ARE HERE.'"

"It could be a cry for help. Whoever wrote it felt panicked, grabbed the closest pen, and wrote over the top of the entry."

"Why not tear out a blank page and leave it where it could be spotted?"

"The same reason *she* didn't change pens. There wasn't time. And the page is smeared by soot, or what looks like it."

"I'll bite. Assume it's Cinderella Huntington."

Stranahan nodded. "She's dirty from climbing down the chimney, she sees something that scares the hell out of her, she looks frantically around for a place to leave a message and finds the logbook on the table. Now watch." Stranahan shut the journal. Then carelessly flipped it open. It opened to the same page. "It's where the seam is, you can see the binding cord. If you found the book closed and flipped it open, it's going to open to this page. I'll bet if you go back to the cabin, you'll find a pen on the table where the guestbook was and it will be almost out of purple ink. Maybe you could lift her prints off it."

"Doubtful. Only if she was the last to handle it. So, she tries to hide by climbing into the chimney?"

"The fibers tell us she went down the chimney, but they also suggest she climbed up. In her panic she tries to climb too fast, brings her leg up past her hip, and gets stuck. She dies."

Martha made a face. *I don't agree. I don't disagree.* "Where's the camera card the librarian gave you?"

"It's in the glove compartment. I'll get it. While I'm gone, could you call the Forest Service and get the name and address on the reservation? I'd like to hear about this 'ghost.'"

"I'll remind you I'm the sheriff," Martha said.

"And coffee for the road."

"Maybe I just thought I was the sheriff," she said under her breath.

———

The sign at the turnoff read WILLOW CREEK POTTERY—EILEEN BARNES, MASTER POTTER AND GLASSBLOWER. Stranahan clattered across a one-lane bridge over the East Fork of the Gallatin River, swollen with mid-elevation snowmelt, then had to slow for several peahens to cross the road. The lone cock turned its butt to the Land Cruiser, flaring his tail like a psychedelic turkey. Stranahan idled up to a clapboard house with peeling white paint. A Datsun pickup caked with mayfly carcasses sat in the drive.

No answer at his knock, he went around back to check the outbuildings. A broken-backed barn with a bird coop constructed of sagging chicken wire had a red arrow painted on its side, and Stranahan, following in the direction it pointed, saw a prefab shed, billowing white smoke. Three domestic geese announced his arrival by honking like train whistles.

"Wait outside." The voice came from the shed.

Stranahan pushed at the muscular neck of the largest goose, whose bulbous orange bill was poised to snap at his crotch. The goose bit at his hand.

"They're like horses, you've got to show them who's boss." The woman who emerged from the shed had a welcoming voice that belied the stern countenance of her face. "Are you here for the majolica fish? Hal said his brother was picking it up." Stranahan said he wasn't and she seemed to ponder his answer. Her hair was short and layered, with pink stripes. She was the butch-looking straw blonde he'd seen in the video.

"I guess I should have known. You get to know a little about genetic phenotypes after raising exotics half your life. No, you're not Hal's brother at all."

Stranahan introduced himself. The handshake and the smile

didn't have the effect they'd had on Ariana; the hazel eyes were guarded as he explained his reason for coming. The potter's arms crossed defensively, thick hands cupping her elbows. Stranahan expected her to tell him to get off her property any second. But she listened, a look of chagrin crossing her face as he wound down.

"This is about the girl who died in the chimney," she said. "The coincidence struck me as soon as I heard it on the radio. I'm embarrassed you saw that video. It makes me feel like I'm standing here naked. How did you get the card?"

Stranahan didn't say, and after a short silence she spoke for him. "It was Book Girl, wasn't it? Either her or the guy she met. They were up next in the classifieds. I ought to be peeved, but I guess I can't blame someone for cooperating. I understand you have to explore all avenues."

"We think Cinderella Huntington could have become scared by something and tried to crawl up the chimney. Several renters wrote about their dogs barking and finding big tracks in the snow. Your entry mentioned a ghost. I'm following up."

The woman nodded. "Maria was the author of that little diatribe. I'll bet you thought it was me, me being the stereotype. You're probably a little confused, her acting as the dominant."

"I don't know much about gay women."

"Dominant-submissive doesn't have anything to do with sexual orientation." She hesitated. "Imagine what it was like growing up in this valley in the seventies, your father's life perspective gained from the seat of a tractor. Here he is, a single-parent farmer with a daughter who bats cleanup on the Little League team."

"It must have been hard on him."

"Not as hard as it was on me. I played with boys but I wanted to be with girls. It made me feel ashamed. Montana was different then. Everybody chewed tobacco, the times passing them right by while they put up their boots and tipped their hats and talked about weather and wheat stem sawfly. Boys looked at me like I was misshapen and said horrible things, these being the same boys who wouldn't turn down a shorn ewe. Now it's different, we're a purple state now, all so enlightened." The last sentence came out bitter.

"Now who's doing the stereotyping."

"I am. But not without reason. You said your name was Stranahan. Aren't you the guy who found the man with the trout fly in his lip a few years ago? That guy who got stuck with a knife?"

"I actually didn't find him, I just got the knife." He unbuttoned his shirt and pulled it over his left shoulder, where the scar showed white against his skin.

"And you're still asking for trouble."

"It seems to find me."

She nodded. "I might have something for you."

She led him to the house and told him to wait on the stoop. Inside, Stranahan heard xylophone tones as a computer booted up. A few minutes passed and she called him in. A video was paused on a laptop on the kitchen table. The screen showed a corner of a cabin porch with a pine pillar and, beyond, the snowy darkness.

"That card you have is the video we made the first night. It maxed out and Maria put in a new card to record the next night; it was her camera. After our . . . intimacies, we heard something. It was cold, but the fire drew better with the window open. Otherwise I don't think we would have noticed."

"What was it you heard?"

"Like a clattering sound. Maria was shutting down the camera and ran right out the door. She's one of those people who'd walk up to a lion and it would be the lion that backed down. So this is her shooting what she saw. It's shaky because she had her shotgun in her hand." She pressed the play button.

A shadow, imprinted against the darker forest background, appeared at the center of the screen and seemed to jerk a few steps, as if dragging a leg, then disappeared. The eye of the camera panned up and down. Then a voice—"There's the bastard"—and the camera zoomed to a horizon line at a break in the forest. There was the sound of a shot as the frame jerked wildly. Moments later the camera steadied to show a circular shape imprinted under the silver orb of a moon a day off the full, the image looking like two-thirds of a two-tone snowman. The opacity blotted out the early stars, then the stars were back and the pelt of snow in the foreground shimmered with an eerie lambency.

"You fucking better be gone!" The voice on the video was scared and full of vitriol at the same time. "Would you believe the nerve, the fucking Tom. Yeah, that's right, I'll shoot you again if you come back." The camera panned to the porch, littered with quarter rounds that had fallen from a woodpile, then switched off.

"I only heard one shot," Stranahan said.

"The other one was as soon as she went out the door, before she switched the camera on. I think it bumped into the wood, that's what we heard."

"Do you think she hit anything?"

"No. She shot the first barrel straight up through the roof and she was shooting with the camera in her hand the second time. I think she just pointed in the vague direction. There wasn't any blood in the snow, anyway."

"It or he?"

She shrugged. "We ran this a hundred times and you just can't tell. The tracks were just troughs in the snow."

"Back it up."

He had her freeze the frame when the orb appeared above the horizon. "It's either a human or a bear standing on his hind legs with his face forward, so you can't see the nose."

"Wouldn't bears be in hibernation?"

"Most of them," Stranahan said. "A few are known to stay out all winter, more often now because they can get by scavenging wolf kills. Could you burn this onto a DVD? We have analysts who can do amazing things with video."

She pulled out a thumb drive from the back of the computer. "I was copying it onto here while you watched. What you're getting is the intruder part, not the other." She handed him the thumb drive.

"That's all we're interested in. You saw it, right?"

She nodded. "I was standing at the door."

"Did you take it for a man and later think it could have been a bear, or the other way around?"

"A man. It scared the hell out of me. Maria, too, though she'd never admit it. Her whole body was trembling."

"You talk about her as if you're a couple. My understanding was the club matched up one-night stands."

"One-night stands don't have to stay that way."

"So you're still with her?"

"Four months. She'll be here in about half an hour." She seemed to anticipate Stranahan's next question. "No, it would not be a good thing if you stayed. She'd be suspicious and you wouldn't get a single thing out of her you haven't already learned. I've betrayed her trust by talking to you at all. I only did it because of the girl. I lost my own daughter. I know how important it is for a family to have closure."

"So you were married, Eileen?"

"I was many things before I came out." She regarded Stranahan with a sober expression. "Let me tell you something about the dominant-submissive relationship. The people involved have to be completely open. When you are the submissive, you have to have absolute trust that your dominant will stay within specified bounds, and when you are the dominant, you have to inspire that trust with your actions. People think we're role-playing, but that's a misconception, because you are not playing a part. What you *are* doing is awakening a part of you, a part that you may not even have known you possessed. The intimacy you share, not trust now but honesty, is absolute. It's something most conventional relationships fall far short of."

She paused. "When you came here, the way you approached me, it's clear you rely on your charisma to get people to open up to you. Correct me if I'm wrong. Now, I'm not going to tell you there's anything wrong with that, it's just a tool and you'd be a fool not to use it, but I also sensed a detachment or disillusionment. Not boredom, but a sort of recklessness, a hell-with-the-consequences, that I don't see as being you."

"You've known me a half hour."

She shook her head. "What's time? You can look into another person's eyes, someone you've only met, and read a story there that the person has never shared with anyone else. Has that never happened to you?"

"I knew a woman named Vareda Beaudreux," Stranahan said. "It was that way with us."

"All I'm saying is that when people affect a manner or play the part of someone they aren't, they risk becoming the fiction they've created. Take it from someone who knows. I played a part for more than thirty years. It isn't worth it. Whatever you're going through, just face it by being yourself."

"What if every person you let yourself get close to sees something that makes them turn away? Isn't that telling you something needs to change?"

"Is that all it is? Why no, young man. That's just called unlucky in love. You have to have the courage to keep stepping up to the plate."

At the door they shook hands rather formally. It had been a thought-provoking forty minutes and Stranahan said so. "Maybe when this is over we could have a cup of coffee," he said.

"I'd like that. Maria tolerates my male friends, but just barely. And she's always packing. I tell men my friendship comes with the advice to buy a flak jacket. But then as you say, trouble seems to find you, so it would be nothing new. You stay right here, I want to give you something." She returned to hand him a glazed coffee cup with a line of elk around the center. Sean knew nothing about pottery but liked the angular lines of the elk.

"It looks like cave art," he said.

"It's based on pictographs I saw up on the Smith River. An archaeologist I was with said it was probably a place where Indian boys went on vision quests."

She shook hands with him. "I hope you find out what happened to that girl."

A flock of spotted guinea fowl escorted Stranahan to his Land Cruiser and he was a mile down Schoolhouse Road when he realized he hadn't asked Barnes if she had put the Santa hat inside the geocache. A rusted Suburban was approaching from the other direction and he slowed and raised a forefinger in salute. All he could see of the driver as the Suburban sped past, a sting of gravel clattering off the Land Cruiser, was a flash of dark hair under a hat tilted to the bridge of the nose.

"Good morning to you, too, Maria," Stranahan said under his breath, and reached for the knob of the radio.

CHAPTER THIRTEEN

Rolling Thunder

So whatcha thinkin', somebody was burning boards with nails sticking out of them?"

Katie Sparrow, standing before the fireplace at the Forest Service cabin, blew at her bangs as she worked a hand under her undershirt. Sean didn't need to see the chain to know that she was fingering a locket that carried a photograph of her fiancé, who had died in an avalanche ten years earlier. It was watching the search dogs work to find his body that persuaded her to become a handler.

"It makes sense," Stranahan said. "When she climbed down the chimney, she wouldn't be able to see where she set her feet when she got to the bottom."

"But why would anybody burn boards when there's enough firewood stacked in this place to heat the Old Faithful Inn?" Katie shook her head. "Let me put my thinking cap on." She took the bill of her ball cap between her right thumb and forefinger and swiveled it from the back to the front.

Stranahan raised an eyebrow.

"Haven't you ever seen someone do that before? It's like the Montana dress code. You wear your cap backwards on your way to work, then when you step out of the truck you turn it around so you're presentable."

"Just switch that machine on and prove me wrong."

When Stranahan had left the memorial service the afternoon before, he'd called Katie at her home outside West Yellowstone—her day job was as a park ranger—and invited her to breakfast at Josie's in

Bridger. Katie was the only person Stranahan knew who owned a metal detector, and he thought if he could find the source for the nail that Cinderella Huntington had lodged in her foot, it might shed light on the circumstances of her death. Besides, Katie brought a level head to a search, not to mention a Class III tracking-trailing dog in Lothar, her German shepherd. It was worth parting with a little of Loretta Huntington's money to have her along.

"I'd do it for a French kiss," she'd told him over the phone. Their flirtation was the basis of their relationship.

Now she was peering at the fireplace skeptically. "Looks like the techs swept it," she said.

"Wilkerson bagged the ashes, but I was thinking if there were old rusty nails, one could have fallen into the cracks of the concrete."

"Okay." She tapped at the keypad of the detector and swept the coil over the fireplace. "I got it set to all metals, so if this doesn't beep it isn't there."

No more than a few seconds passed before Stranahan cocked his ear. "There's something, huh?"

Katie plugged a headphone set into the detector and fiddled with the keypad to isolate the source. She nodded and took off the head-phones.

"There's something down there all right, but it's steel. You said the nail was iron."

"That's what Ettinger told me. Let's get it out."

Katie removed a heavy magnet from her pack. After a bit of ma-neuvering, she withdrew the lid of a can from a crack at the base of the fireplace.

"Folks throw what-all into the fire so they don't have to pack out the trash." Katie, whose face reminded Stranahan of an inquisitive wren, looked pensive, then she nodded. "Let's try outside. I got an idea."

The cabin was built on the west-facing slope of the range and still held troughs of snow along the northern and eastern walls, where accumulations from winter storms had slid off the roof. The snow was too rotted to hold her weight, so Katie took the broom from the cabin and used its long handle to etch lines on the snow into a grid pattern.

"You got to be methodical with these things," she explained. "Go keep Lothar company and I'll call if I get a hit."

Stranahan had no more than sat down on a chopping block and worked his fingers into the dense hair on the shepherd's neck when he heard Katie's whistle.

"Hey, I think I got something," she called out. "Get the shovel from the cabin."

When Sean got to her side, he saw where she'd used the broom handle to open a trough in the snow. "Whatcha think?" Katie said. "She wouldn't be going anywhere quick after driving that into her foot."

Sean cleared the snow from a line of nails protruding about three inches from a piece of wood. A few minutes of digging uncovered a rectangle of warped boards nailed together with crosspieces. The rectangle was roughly three feet by four feet and had corroded nails pounded through it; it was as heavily quilled as a porcupine.

"It's a bear window," Katie said. "Back in the day, they used to nail these things over the windows so mister grizzly bear would think twice before inviting himself to dinner. Same with the doors. This is what I thought we might find, but I didn't get my hopes up 'cause folks take them for souvenirs. You think the techs could get blood off the boards for a match?"

"Maybe." Stranahan fingered his chin, a subconscious habit he'd picked up from Ettinger. "But it's not like I have a free pass to the lab."

"Call Martha. She could make it happen. She's got the hots for you."

"Who says that?"

"Everybody. The both of you living up in that canyon, Martha knocking on the door of your tipi asking you got any sugar, when what she really needs is salt. That woman's desperate for love. Or at least some buck-nekkid howling at the moon."

"Let's concentrate on Cinderella," Sean said.

"Hey, I'm sorry I brought it up. You know how people talk."

"I do."

"Even if this is what she stepped on, it still doesn't tell you what she was doing here."

"No, it doesn't."

Katie shrugged. "Maybe she was scared of that Bigfoot creature. She was running and that's when she stepped on the nail. She climbs up the ladder and down the chimney to get away."

They had moved to the porch and were sitting at either end of a bench with Lothar between them, his head on Katie's lap. Sean looked up. Eileen Barnes had mentioned a shot going through the roof. He noticed a ragged hole and climbed onto the splitting block. Digging with his knife, he freed a shotgun pellet that was stuck in the wood, put it in his pocket. He told Katie the story of the maybe man, maybe bear that the lovers had seen.

Katie frowned. "Maybe her being in the chimney has something to do with the sex club. Maybe it isn't a coincidence that she dies only a few feet from the bed where these people were doing the nasty."

"No, I can't see Cinderella Huntington involved in something like that."

"Can't or don't want to?"

"Either. Doc told Martha she was covered in filth, not from being in the chimney but from living rough, like a homeless person. Except for the jacket, she was wearing the same clothes she'd had on when she disappeared. Or that's the assumption. Anyway, it's not exactly being dressed for sex."

They sat and mulled it over, ball cap bills forward.

Katie said, "Did I ever tell you I tried to patent a sex move?"

"I think I would have remembered that."

"Yeah. You know how girls are when they get together."

"Not really."

"Well, they're no different than guys, trust me. Back after Colin died I went through a phase when I got a little wild, and I was with some friends and we were talking the way girls talk, and I said this guy told me I had a sex move that ought to be against the law. I think he meant this twisty thing I did to get him off. He said I ought to patent it. This guy, he was funny. After we'd have sex, he'd break out these candy cigarettes and we'd lie there acting like we were smoking and talking, like, philosophically. I wonder whatever happened to him?" She was quiet a moment. "Anyway, I told the girls, and one of them, Heather, she said her brother-in-law was a patent lawyer and she flips open her phone, it's two in the morning but he picks up and she tells him. He says to put me on, wants me to describe it for him. Wants details. Pretty soon he's asking what I'm wearing. I say use your imagination. We got him on speaker and the girls are just rolling, they're laughing so hard. He wants to ask me out, yeah." Katie had started laughing.

"So what did you say?"

"I told him he only wanted me for my move and hung up. He never did say if it was patentable."

"As opposed to someone like me," Stranahan said, "who only wants you for your dog biscuits."

"No, you want me for my move, too, you're just not ready for it. But I'll share a biscuit with you. I baked them last night."

Katie reached into her chest pocket and cracked a biscuit shaped like a heart into thirds, handed a piece to Sean, and gave another to Lothar. Among the search-and-rescue hasty team she was known as Dog Breath because she snacked on dog biscuits while Lothar worked the trail. Sean had helped her bake a batch at her place in West Yellowstone once, knowing it might lead to something, and it almost had, then didn't.

"Not bad," he said, and he was chewing when a shot echoed off the ridge behind the cabin.

They looked at each other. Katie swallowed. "Spring bear hunter," she said, taking a swig of water from a bottle. "Somebody just got himself a rug."

"If it's a bear hunter, wouldn't we have seen his rig? This is the only public access."

Katie shook her head. "No, you can drive roundabout and get into this country from the north, up Sunlight Creek. But hey"—she shrugged her slight shoulders—"it's Montana. Gunshot's part of the soundtrack. Back when I worked in the Forest Service I could tell you the caliber, the difference, say, between a .270 that sounds like the crack of whip echoing away and the boom of a .35 Whelan that's more like rolling thunder."

"What did we just hear?"

"A deep boom. A rifle that shoots a heavy bullet at a low muzzle velocity. Like a .45-70 or .444 Marlin."

"You can say that with certainty?"

"Nah, it's a guess. But that doesn't mean anything. People hunt bears with a bunch of different guns."

"What else is in season?"

"Just turkeys. And cheatin' boyfriends. They're always fair game."

CHAPTER FOURTEEN

The Man with the Lobster Hand

How do you like your coffee?" Jasper Fey's voice came from the kitchen. Stranahan was standing in the ranch living room dominated by a spectacular piece of landscape art, an immensity of sky over a flat-topped butte.

"Is that an original Charlie Russell?" he said.

"That it is. I raised my paddle one time too many at an auction at the Sappington Ranch 'bout five years ago, when the getting was good. Nobody painted sunsets the way old Charlie did, except maybe God. How do want your coffee?"

"Black," Stranahan said.

"Good, 'cause that's what you're getting." He heard Fey whistling as he walked into the room and handed Sean a cup with his left hand. His right hand and wrist sported a cast. "Etta's lactose-intolerant, and I'm, well, I'm off on shoots so much, milk would sour waiting for me."

Stranahan needn't have worried about his reception. At the door a few minutes before, Fey had looked incuriously at him for only a moment before smiling broadly and ushering him in, saying, "Welcome to my dacha." He was wearing the rolled-brim silver Stetson he'd worn to the memorial and a knotted gray silk scarf with a pattern of scrolls. As a man whose preparation for the day consisted of splashing water and running his fingers through his hair, Stranahan got the impression that Jasper Fey's appearance was as meticulously planned as a politician's. He said that Etta was off on a horse ride, but he'd be happy to help Stranahan's investigation in any way that he could.

"Jam a knuckle?" Stranahan said.

Fey held up two fingers. "They throb like the dickens. You ever have one?"

"A few. I used to box."

Fey's eyebrows said *I'm impressed.* "I guess it was wise of me not to throw down on you after you hit me with that coffee."

"I'm sorry about that. It was just instinct. I didn't know who you were. I didn't know who the man was you hit."

"That would be the Leroy Hunt what people call Pickle. He cowboyed up and didn't press charges, so I'm indebted. Maybe it's God's warning that I ought to get my skinny butt back to Roundup. I was just packing up."

Fey indicated a sofa patterned with bison and they sat down.

"Tell me what it is you do besides teach people how to ride," Sean said.

"Oh, everything. Anything to do with the West."

Stranahan had pegged Fey for a man whose first subject was himself and noticed his eyes brighten.

"A lot of the actors are from New York, L.A., the lead's from Melbourne, Australia. He's actually the easiest to work with, just a natural actor and a hell of a nice guy. Most Aussies are. But a lot of the talent that comes onto the set, they don't know the first thing about country life. They don't know how to put a hat on, they don't know how to take it off. They don't know that if you're knocking on someone's door to give them the bad news about their son, that you place the hat over your heart before you step inside." Fey removed his Stetson, spread his fingers across the crown, and placed it over his chest. "Or that when you kneel down to ask a girl to dance, you take off your hat and put it on the knee that's raised." He slipped from the sofa and demonstrated. "Ma'am, may I have the honor?"

Fey stood and repositioned his hat. "Or just bearing, how to hold your body in different situations. Women need to push their hips more forward to play a western part, which is something they don't teach in acting class. Some of the mistakes are right in the script, so the first thing I do is go over the day's pages. Horses, of course, any-thing to do with livestock I'm the guy."

"Fight scenes?"

"No, we got a choreographer for that, an old stuntman. He's good at staging the action, but it's still too much Hollywood. No one gets anything worse than a black eye, when in a real fight, you break bones and lose teeth. Or at least you jam your knuckles like I did. I thought I had my drinking under control until Etta called about Cindy. I fell off the wagon. I'm ashamed of my behavior yesterday and I hope you'll accept my apology. I want you to have something. It's in the other room."

Fey came back holding a DVD case. "This is season one. Three disks. It won't be released till July, so this is hot off the press. I haven't even cracked the cellophane."

Sean started to object.

"I insist. I'll get another and probably won't watch it anyway. All the stuff you went to so much trouble to get right either gets cut out or screwed with. It's depressing. Make a man wonder why they hired him in the first place."

Stranahan thanked him and asked Fey if he did the gun scenes.

Fey nodded. "They're my guns. I have a collection I rent out for a lot of productions, not just ones I work on. I like to get the details exactly right. I worked on a biopic of Bad Man Soapy Smith a couple years back. Now he used a Model 1892 Winchester in .44-40 in the Frank Reid gunfight on the Skagway docks. Had it wrested out of his hands and was killed by his own gun. They were going to shoot the scene using an 1866 'cause it's got the brass action. I said that's like putting a push-up bra on a flapper. It's just wrong. Threatened to quit. I told myself that's a stupid move, Jasper, you're going to get your ass fired. But they ended up rearranging the schedule until I could get my hands on the right rifle." He paused, and Sean saw Fey's face flush. He used the wrap on his cast to wipe at the corners of his eyes. "Here I'm talking guns and my Cinderella's ashes are in an urn."

Despite his reservations, Sean felt himself warming to Fey. He was not at all what Etta had led him to expect, but then most people were surprises. He decided to get down to the business that had brought him here.

"Jasper, did your wife tell you that Cindy was pregnant when she disappeared last November?"

Fey nodded. "She blames Landon. Between you, me, and old Charlie here, that boy's as queer as a Lauderdale decorator. And in my business you learn gay from good-looking. It's part of why I took him on. I needed a hand and figured he'd be the one boy who *wouldn't* be trying to clip the rose off the vine. But I don't know. Maybe he thought if he slept with her, he'd find out he wasn't really gay, that it was a software malfunction but the hard drive was okay. Kids experiment. Will they do a DNA test on the fetus?"

"That's in the works. You knew her friends. Who else would be a candidate?"

He shook his head. "When it comes to your own daughter, you're the last to know. Any parent will tell you that."

"How old was Cinderella when you married Etta?"

"She was twelve, but I'd already been in the picture a couple years. But that's not what you're asking, is it? You're asking if our relationship was that of a father and his daughter. It was. Oh, we circled each other at the beginning. She was afraid I'd steal the affections of her mother, and she'd already lost one parent. But then I think she realized that I wanted to add to her life, not subtract from it. Cindy's birth father died when she was five. My understanding is that's about the youngest age that children form lasting memories. She'd cry sometimes because she couldn't remember his face. I grew up in a one-parent household myself. I understood. One of the first things I did after the honeymoon was make her a scrapbook with old photos and newspaper clippings about her father. He was a hard-luck horseman, all-around rodeo bum, just like I was. I'll admit I was trying to win her over, but it came from the heart."

"Etta told me you didn't approve of the memorial."

"My feeling was we'd dwelled on our loss long enough. To me Cindy's been gone quite a long time."

"Didn't it seem reasonable to spend an afternoon remembering her life?"

"What they were remembering in that church . . ." He let the thought die and for a few moments his eyes drifted around the room. "I'll get us some more coffee," he said abruptly. Stranahan heard whistling from the kitchen. When Fey returned, the smile was back on his face, but his voice was sober.

"I'll be perfectly frank with you. The young woman we're talking about died in a traffic accident on March 26 last spring, or might as well have. My wife lost an arm in that accident. What Cindy lost was not so visible, but she was a changed person. She'd had it all—the looks, athletic ability, a personality that could coax a smile out of a stone. And top of her class. All that changed. The way the doctor put it to me, that cerebral cortex acts like a lid, a restraint on acting upon your urges. It's like snakes in a bottle. You take off the lid, they slither out and they're everywhere. After the accident, you couldn't trust Cindy on a horse not to kill herself. You couldn't trust her to show simple modesty about bodily functions. Any itch, she scratched it. It made visitors uncomfortable; hell, it made me uncomfortable. Could she have taken care of herself well enough to lead a productive and independent life? The doctors said she could. Her age was in her favor. Young people recover from brain injuries better than adults. But would she ever reach the potential she had before the accident? No, that wasn't going to happen. They talk about the new normal, how you change your expectations and set your sights accordingly. It's easy to say. But it broke my heart. It was worse for Etta, because she was the one in the driver's seat. She took all the blame. I told her she needs help from a therapist. But she won't get it. You don't win the women's all-around five times asking for people's help."

"She was drunk when I came here the other night," Stranahan said. "Does that happen often?"

"If you'd asked me that before the accident, I'd say that isn't the woman I know. She drank socially. We were a drinking couple. But we were never behind-your-back drinkers and it never got out of hand. Now I'm afraid she drinks more than she should, but it's the insomnia that makes me worry the most. What she said in that church was dead true. Every night, small hours, she's up. I feel the cold sweep into the house and know she's standing with the door open. Back in February it fell to twenty-six below at the airport. God knows how cold it got up here. And four in the morning she's outside looking at the stars, just shaking like an aspen leaf. Now it's the horse rides. Every morning she saddles up and I don't see her until noon earliest. She won't let me go with her. There's no cell service up there, she rides up with no saying goodbye, she comes back with no explanation. I'm watching my wife fall apart day by day, piece by piece, and there's nothing I can do about it."

You could be here more, Stranahan thought, but as Fey had opened up, he thought better than to interrupt.

"Etta has dismissed me from her life. I speak to her when she walks into the living room, into the kitchen. She looks straight ahead. We could have been a comfort to each other. Instead, she's created a gulf. To tell you the truth I don't think we're going to make it. We've lost our daughter and now we're losing each other."

"You could take some time from the series."

"No, you're wrong there. Work keeps me sane and all Etta's money has been swallowed by medical bills. We couldn't afford full-coverage insurance. The premiums are too high for people who make their living on the back of a horse. We turn a breeding dollar and she gives riding lessons, but she doesn't have anything coming in now from the outside. The income from my television work is the only thing that keeps the horses in the stable. If I quit, we'd have to sell the place."

"Maybe that wouldn't be a bad idea."

Fey nodded. "Get away from the memories. Move someplace she has to see people, engage in conversation, not be so isolated. Don't think I haven't thought about it."

"Do you have a problem with me doing the job Etta's paid me to?"

"You mean do I take issue with you airing our dirty laundry to anyone you please? Hell yes I do, and I made that clear to Etta."

"Then why did you let me in when I knocked?"

"Because I had all last night to think about it. This isn't about me. And it isn't really about Cindy, because Cindy's past caring. It's about Etta, and nobody says no to Etta, not me, not anyone. She's going to keep riding off into the mountains and staring at stars until she knows what happened. The way I see it is you're the only one standing between someone I love and the woman's descent into madness. You've seen her yourself; she can't turn the corner on this thing. Do you know how the Crazy Mountains got their name?"

"I know the legend."

"Which legend? There's a couple."

"I know the story of the settler woman."

Fey nodded. "She became a wanderer whose spirit haunted the mountains. A woman who'd lost her children, now who does that bring to mind? What's clear to me is that if somebody doesn't find out what happened to our daughter, Etta's going to ride out one day and she won't come back. It will be her spirit that haunts the mountains then."

"Do you think she'd commit suicide?"

"I was speaking metaphorically. This morning, when I got a cup of coffee and some eggs under my belt, I went up to Cindy's room. I do that sometimes because . . . well, just because. I stand there for a minute or two. Anyway, I found myself looking at this Wonder Horse Cindy rocked till she wore the paint off it. It got me thinking about how much time she spent in the stables, so I went out there, nothing particular in mind, but by God I found something. I left it where it was because Etta will want to see for herself. Now that you're here, I don't see a reason to wait."

Sean followed Fey's compact shoulders into a mudroom, where he buckled a tool belt over his jeans. "No, you stay here, Poupette," he said as a diminutive terrier-like dog appeared, licking at his boot.

"Etta calls Poupette my ten-gallon-hat dog account of her being small and she likes to sleep in the crown of my Stetson. But she's a sweetie, yes she is." He moved the dog with his toe, a gentle nudge, and they stepped out and he shut the door.

Jasper Fey had a bowlegged walk with a limp that hadn't registered with Stranahan at the church service. "I slow people down," he said as Sean matched his stride. "Would you believe I've broken thirty-three bones? This hand I punched Pickle with, it was broken five times before I turned thirty. You look at it compared to the left and it's half again larger. That's not just because it built up more muscle. How it happens is, you wrap your hand in the bull rope and get tossed, you got three-quarter ton of grade A flopping and your hand stuck on his back. Something's got to give and it isn't the rope and it sure as hell isn't the bull. My hand, it's been yanked, broke, stretched, everything but dropped in the boil and buttered. That was my nickname when I rode—Lobster Fey. I've had my collarbones snapped like wishbones, upper radius stress fractures both arms, I mean corkscrewed, the long tendon of the biceps torn from my right shoulder, compressed neck vertebrae, smashed pelvis, cracked tailbone, surgeries both knees. The reason I limp is a bull sired by Whitewater came out of the chute dipping like his pa, then he spun on a dime with change left over." Fey inscribed a circle with his arm. "When I stopped sailing, he stepped on my foot and broke all the metatarsals. It was no more use than a flipper for damn near a year."

The Quonset-style stables had a metal corrugated roof that they entered at one end into a center aisle separating rows of stalls. It was dark, damp, and chill. Horses nickered as they walked past them. At the far end of the corridor, Stranahan could hear echoey voices. Two figures came together in the light pouring in from the east-facing doors and separated, one walking into blinding whiteness, one approaching. A tall, gaunt man with slack skin on his throat and grizzled cheeks stooped into focus, wearing overalls and a pinstripe railroader's cap. He was carrying a blue lead rope.

Fey made the introductions and the man crooked baseball-glove fingers around Stranahan's palm. Despite the overall appearance of a Depression-era farmer, he was younger than Stranahan had first thought, midforties maybe, with a handsomely angular, well-worn face that reminded Sean of the Band's Levon Helm, who had been his father's favorite musician.

"Charlie Watt, singular, not the drummer," he said, his smile revealing nicotine-stained teeth. "Etta told me I was to tolerate your questions. I'll do you better. You come look me up, I can talk about that sweet Cindy all day long." He put a hand on Jasper Fey's shoulder. "How are you holding up, J.P.?" he asked.

"I'm okay, Charlie. I was just going to show Mr. Stranahan Snapdragon's stall."

"I'll take him the paddock while you do."

Watt led the way to a stall housing a chestnut quarter horse mare with a star blaze. He pulled a carrot out of the bib pocket of the overalls and fed it to the horse, then buckled the lead to the horse's halter and led her away, chasing his own long shadow. Stranahan saw that the animal had a bobbed tail.

"The horsehair thief?" he said.

Fey nodded. "And not a clue to the culprit. You saw our trainer Charlie there, salt of the earth. We used to be bullfighters together, saving cowboys' asses after they got tossed. Charlie said we controlled hell inside the arena and raised it on the outside. Why, the man saved my life once by stepping in front of a bull that hooked me before I could duck into the barrel. Took a horn in the gut. Retired to a job with Burlington Northern. Brakeman. I hired him away to work the horses, man's a sure enough whisperer. Now Earl Hightower, the ranch manager you saw down the way, he's an AA sponsor done a lot of good for a lot of people. He'd lay right down on the tracks for me."

"I'd still like to meet him."

"Sure, sure. We had a colt die of the colic and Earl's got to hitch up the Mantis to bury it, but anytime, anytime at all. I was just saying that these are old friends and they're above suspicion. I suppose one of the hands we had in years past might have done it."

"What's the Mantis?"

"That's what we call the tractor when you attach the backhoe. Looks like a praying mantis. We got a place for the deadstock up on the northeast corner."

"Would Charlie have been Landon's boss, or Earl?"

"That's splitting a hair. They both gave him his chores, but I doubt either will hear a word against him. I understand why the boy's mother said what she said at the church, but she was wrong to think we thought poorly of her son, and I'm saying that knowing he could have been the one who got her pregnant. It's just that when two young people disappear on the same day and you're settin' in a pew on one side of the aisle, you can't help blaming the person whose people are settin' on the other side."

"Etta said Anker spent a few nights out here. Where did he sleep?"

"In one of the empty stalls. I never asked what one. Our horses are pastured most of the year, so there are a lot of unoccupied stalls. It's only when cold weather sets in we bring them inside. Snapdragon was stalled more than most just because Cindy liked to sit up with her."

"Could Landon Anker have slept in this stall?"

"Not if it was occupied. Somebody could cut loose on a coyote with the .220 Swift and Dragonfly would have four shod feet in the air. You could get your brains kicked out." He pressed his lips together and slowly nodded. "Only Cindy, she did sleep here some. I cautioned against it and Etta backed me up, between the two of us we've only known about a dozen paraplegics. But Cindy made her own rules; she was Etta's daughter that way, but with considerably less horse sense. She'd sit here doing homework almost every school night." He pointed to a folding chair tilted against the stall wall. "I hooked up a light for her." He flicked a switch in the corridor to illuminate a fluorescent tube nailed to one wall of the stall. "A bulb would have been cheaper, but you got to consider the fire hazard."

"And this is where you say you found something?"

He nodded. "You'll notice the only thing separating one stall from the next is a wall that's one plank thickness. But this one's got two walls side by side with about ten inches of space in between. I insisted on the design because you sometimes stable a horse that doesn't make a good neighbor. When that happens, you isolate him in this stall. It helps that the stall is smaller so he can't turn around so easy, and that cuts down on the bucking. Everybody sleeps better."

"Is Dragonfly unneighborly?"

"Christ no, Dragonfly has the same personality Cindy did. Never met a stranger. But the horse before Dragonfly was a surly cuss." Fey fingered a screwdriver from his tool belt. He backed out a screw from a plank of pine. The plank swung down from the pivot point of the loosened screw, revealing the space between the double walls. Fey shone a flashlight into the dark recess. Glinting from the light were the heads of three nails that protruded from the inside wall of the neighboring stall. A length of red string looped to each nail head trailed down into the darkness. Fey pulled up the strings one by one. The first was knotted to the handle of a plastic grocery bag holding two paperback books: *A Girl's Guide to Sweet Sixteen: Why It's Okay to Pleasure Your Body and Save Yourself for Love,* and a Harlequin suspense novel by B. J. Daniels, a woman on the cover held by a man who had forgotten to button his shirt. The second string was tied to a powder horn like those used in the era of muzzle-loading rifles.

Fey handed Stranahan the horn, which had been rubbed to a high polish. The horn had a graceful curve and was stoppered with a wood plug. Sean shook it. Raised his eyebrows.

"Be my guest," Fey said.

Sean pulled the wood plug and trickled black powder into his palm. It was the texture of coarse sugar and smelled like rotten eggs.

"Does anyone on the ranch shoot a muzzle-loader?" Sean said.

"Not to my knowledge. Where do you think Cindy would get something like this?"

"I should be asking you that question."

"I haven't the faintest idea."

"What's on the third string?"

"Nothing. This is all there was."

"What made you know where to look?"

"I didn't. It just occurred to me that nobody had looked in the space between the walls."

Stranahan held the horn up to the light. It was carved in bas-relief, a mountain front of sharp-sided peaks against a recessed sky and the raised images of several birds, including a bald eagle. Inlays of what looked like bone represented mantles of snow on the peaks and the head and tail of the eagle. Sean ran the pad of a finger over letters detailed into the horn with brass tacks.

"The initials B.P.B. mean anything to you?"

"Doesn't ring a bell," Fey said. "But I watch *Antiques Roadshow*. Some of these horns, if you can connect them to pioneers, are worth a lot of money."

Sean nodded. "I have a friend who makes muzzle-loading rifles. I don't know if he makes horns, too." He was thinking of Sam Meslik. During the winter months, Sam crafted stocks for muzzle-loading rifles from blanks of curly maple, mostly for hunters from states that had special black powder hunting seasons. He called the business "Uncle Sam's Smoke Poles."

"Show it to your friend and see what he thinks."

"He's in Florida, but I'll give him a call. You don't mind if I borrow it?"

"I trust you to return it."

Stranahan heard a horse nicker.

"That'll be Etta," Fey said. "I can pick Amberjack's clop out of a dozen horses."

Stranahan heard the horse's footfalls echoing hollowly in the metal building. Jasper Fey led Stranahan to the tack room, where Etta Huntington was removing the cinch strap.

"Here, let me help with that saddle," Fey said.

"I'm not a cripple." She hoisted the saddle with her good arm and trapped it against her chest, using her stump to steady the weight. It took her three tries to hang it over the timber sawhorse that ran the length of the room.

"I see he didn't shoot you," she said before turning around.

"Your husband's found something of Cindy's," Stranahan said.

"Oh, what?" She walked over, exuding a smell of tannin mixed with sweat and horseflesh. She examined the powder horn while Jasper Fey explained the circumstances of the discovery. She said, "It came to you, huh, just like that?" She didn't look at him.

"Do you recognize it?"

"I would have said by now if I did. I'd like you to show me where it was, please."

They showed her. "Give me your hammer," she said. Fey handed her the hammer hanging from his tool belt and she started prying up boards with the claw. Fey gave Stranahan a *you see what I have to deal with?* shrug.

"I could care less what you think of me," Etta said. She grunted with each pull of the claw. "I don't care what anyone thinks." She dropped the hammer and stuck her head in the hole she'd made in the wall. She snapped the fingers of her left hand and Fey handed her his flashlight without waiting to be asked. When she tried to sit back, her braid got stuck on splinters of wood.

Stranahan moved to help her and Fey held up a hand. He mouthed the word, "No."

Etta extracted herself and sat heavily on the floor of the stall.

"Was there anything else down there, Etta?"

"Quit asking me questions you know the answers to . . . Dammit, why couldn't she have told me? A romance novel? A fucking romance novel. My own daughter was afraid to let me know she was reading a *book*." She wiped at her tears. "I don't believe in God," she said to herself. "How can I? All he's done is take my husband, take my Cindy, take my boy, take my unborn daughter." Her voice had risen half an octave. She was speaking as if they weren't in the stall with her. "The sun is my father, the moon is my mother. My daughter lives in the stars." She buried her head in her hands. "The sun is my father, the moon is my mother. My daughter lives in the stars." Slowly she lifted her head. Her eyes swept the stall, at first with dreamy languor, then frantically, her head snapping side to side as her eyes rolled in the sockets.

"Look at me," Stranahan said.

The eyes stopped on him. "If there is a god, why doesn't he kill me, too?" she said. "Wouldn't that be the mercy of a gracious being, to unite me with the only people who ever loved me?"

"I loved you, Etta." Jasper Fey's voice was tender. "I love you."

"You loved the woman who kicked out the stars." The panic had gone and she'd settled back to earth again, but a very cold hard earth.

"That isn't fair. I loved every part of you. I loved your spirit."

"You rode me like one of your horses." She looked at Stranahan. "He wore his fucking spurs to bed."

"You wanted me, Etta. We wanted each other."

"You just climbed on board and had at it. That isn't love."

"It turned into love."

"Don't flatter yourself. All I ever wanted to do was disappear. You just provided the oblivion. You can't love, Jasper Fey. You don't know what love is. You just lust."

Fey had sat down beside her. He stroked the empty sleeve of her jacket.

"Don't do that." She turned her face away from him.

He put his arm around her and Stranahan saw her body stiffen. Then abruptly, she turned and buried her head against his shoulder.

Stranahan heard her sobbing as he walked away, past the tack room and the steady eye of Amberjack, out of the poison and into the sunlight.

CHAPTER FIFTEEN

Watch Your Topknot

In early May, the water is low but rising, clear but coloring, the trout thin but beginning to butter up. This is when a river makes its promise to a fisherman, before it breaks its vow a week or two later, when the snow on the peaks melts, the sound of the current rises to a roar, and you have to find somewhere else to cast a fly.

Sean whistled to himself as he stepped into a ledge rock reach of the Yellowstone River east of Livingston. The caddis hatch he was hoping for didn't materialize, so he tied on a streamer fly called the Madonna, which had twin strips of rabbit in a rust color to emulate the claws of a crawfish. He gave it a chance, gave up on it, and went to his ace in the hole, a marabou of his own design that Sam had appropriated and marketed out of his shop as "Sam's Skinny Minnow." This one was black over olive, and the trout that came to his hand after walloping the surface was just over eighteen inches long and thick with muscle. He slipped the hook and watched the fish glimmer back into the depths.

One more cast would be one too many. Stranahan hooked the fly in the keeper ring and found a comfortable log on the bank. He'd driven to the river to clear his head after the scene in the stables and fished the cell phone from a sealed plastic bag in his vest. Idly, he watched a kingfisher beat a small silver fish against a river rock, then swallow it headfirst. The call went through.

"Kemo-fucking-sabe. I was just thinking how much I missed you."

"That so, Sam?"

"Hell, no. My client just boated a permit on a crab fly. I'm tied off at Boca Grande waiting for the incoming while he's wading around congratulating himself. I sure as hell better get a Benjamin for a tip. I was going to call you about something, what was it? Oh, I met somebody. That waitress at Louie's Backyard, the one with the Jennifer Lopez glutes, says I look like Satan."

"You're ruining the reputation of a waitress now?"

"And she's a fucking Zumba instructor."

"I don't know what that is."

"It's Latin dance, rumba, samba, that kind of shit. Carolina's from Brazil."

"She can move, huh?"

"Oh, my goodness gracious."

"All right, Sam, I'll leave you to your dance card. But tell me something. I'm working the chimney case and there's an artifact that's surfaced, a powder horn with a lot of carving. Who would know about that?"

"If it's an antique? Brad Amundson, he's an adjunct prof at MSU. Brad's a Lewis and Clark scholar, one of those people who are always digging around up on the Missouri. Drop in to the Mint at happy hour. He's the one looks like Custer."

"Thanks, Sam."

"Watch your topknot."

Stranahan smiled. It was a line from *Jeremiah Johnson,* Bear Claw Chris Lapp warning the famous mountain man to watch out for Indians. Sam quoted from it almost daily.

Sean picked up the thread. "Yep, watch your'n," he said.

————

Stranahan drove to the university, where he was kicked around from office to office in predictable fashion—bureaucracy at Montana State being no different than at any other academic institution—finally learning that Amundson taught a morning class and was gone for the day. No, they wouldn't give him a phone number. Stranahan could have played the Ettinger card but didn't; he'd catch the professor at the bar later. With a couple hours to kill, he drove to the tipi and took Choti on a walk up the road, and was surprised to see the department Cherokee parked in Ettinger's drive. His feet took him to the door.

"Martha, you look—"

"I'm blaming you," she said, ushering him in, her voice scolding but not cross. She pulled up the tail of her flannel shirt and rubbed at the black filth streaking her face. "I was putting in the new faucet when I heard Goldie barking. I got distracted."

"Tell you what. You go take a shower and I'll replace your faucet."

"Are you a plumber now? Toolman Stranahan? Let's see. Artist, fishing guide, detective, tracker, boxer, bricklayer, candlestick maker."

"I'm my father's son. I got a Craftsman socket set for my tenth birthday."

"What are you doing here?"

"Can't I just drop in on an old friend?"

Martha grunted. "Make yourself useful. Everything you need's in that box."

When she came back in freshly laundered Carhartts and work shirt, Stranahan poured water from the new tap and set a kettle on the stove.

"Montana's the only state I've ever lived in," he said, pouring the tea, "where the only difference between your work clothes and your dress clothes is date of purchase. Do you know a prof named Brad Amundson?"

"Buckskin Brad. Sure."

He told her about the powder horn and the drama that had unfolded in the Bar-4 stables.

Ettinger nodded, speaking as if to herself. "'Happy families are all alike; every unhappy family is unhappy in its own way.'"

"What's that mean?"

"It's the first line of *Anna Karenina*. Tolstoy."

"I've heard of him."

"I hope so. What he's saying is that for a marriage to be happy, it has to avoid a deficiency in any aspect. Just one deficiency dooms it to failure."

"Sounds like an impossible standard."

"It's called the Anna Karenina principle. It's why I've been divorced twice. It's why you couldn't maintain a relationship with Martinique. It's why Harold and I didn't work out, and it's why the two of us are fixing faucets and not working a puzzle."

"If you apply that logic to Etta Huntington and Jasper Fey, they don't stand a chance. So where do I go from here?"

"You're doing fine. In my experience, all roads lead back to the family. Find the deficiencies, you'll find the answers to your questions."

"Do you want to go to the Mint? Happy hour ought to be starting."

"Nah, bars where women nail their bras to the ceiling aren't my thing."

———

The Mint was west of Bridger, out by the railroad tracks along the lower Gallatin River. It was only a few hundred yards from the limestone bluffs where Lewis and Clark camped at Three Forks, pondering a route to the Pacific. The man sitting on the barstool in period attire looked to be contemplating his own way west in the reflection of an empty beer glass. Stranahan took a neighboring stool, noting the bras nailed to the low ceiling. Holding the position of honor over the bartender's station was a pink underwire with cups that looked big enough to coddle marmots.

"Last Cast Pale Ale," he said to the bartender. "And another for my friend here, whatever's his pleasure."

The man who turned toward him wore a buckskin jacket with fringe, had an impeccably coiffed goatee, and wore his long golden hair in a braid. Despite a baby beer gut pressing against his shirt, he was as handsome a human being as Stranahan had ever seen, with a profile that belonged on a shiny coin. "One always depends on the kindness of strangers," the man said, and rolled his right hand on a loose wrist in the pantomime of a bow.

Sean extended his hand and the man took it and the beers came and they knocked them back. Brad Amundson set his glass down and licked the foam off his mustache. "Now that we're drinking friends, I'll tell you a story. That bra"—he indicated the pink one—"is a 40 double D, and the woman who wore it wasn't just any woman with a mature set of hushpuppies. Her name is Dora Evans and she was hiking with her husband in Glacier Park when they startled mama grizzly. This is back before everybody carried bear spray and the going wisdom was you lie down and play dead. It's one of those things sounds good before you try it. Well, the bear got her husband on the ground and playing dead wasn't doing the trick, so she whipped off her bra, filled the cups with rocks, and smacked that bear in the head, whirling it like a bolo. Bear ran off. It made all the papers—'Woman Fends Off Grizzly Attack with Bra.' The next time she came in here—they live just up the road in Logan—I said, "Dora, darling, may I have the honor?' She took it off and I nailed it to the ceiling with the butt of a Colt revolver." The man finished his beer and cocked a finger at the bartender for another round. "Do you know what the moral of the story is?"

"Wear a bra?"

"No, it's if you got them, God put them there for a reason. Dora was going to get chest reduction surgery because lugging all that weight around was giving her back pain."

"Did she end up getting the surgery?"

"Sit here another hour she'll put your hand down her shirt and make you guess. You want to know the second lesson of the story?"

"That's why I'm here."

"Don't use an antique firearm as a hammer. It reduces the value."

Amundson drained his glass and raised a finger for another round. "Are you drinking here per chance or did you have a question for me? Either way is fine, I just like to know who I'm telling my stories to."

"Sam Meslik told me you were the man to see about Lewis and Clark–era artifacts."

"There's a fellow knows how to warm a barstool. How may I be of service?"

Stranahan took the powder horn from his knapsack and unfolded the handkerchief he'd wrapped around it.

Amundson brought up a monocle he wore on a silver chain and screwed it into his right eye. He nodded, looking at the horn. "It's bison, that puts it post-1830. Prior to that, most horns were cattle; people brought their horns with them when they came west. After settlers were here in better numbers, you start seeing buffalo horns taking over, because pre–*Lonesome Dove* there were a hell of a lot more buffalo than cattle. So Lewis and Clark I don't think. More likely it's later mountain man era, American-Indian war era, roughly 1840 to 1890. Or that's what who made it wants you to think." He nodded to the bartender. "We're just going to be outside, Lou."

Amundson studied the horn in the better light of the parking lot, resting it on the hood of Sean's Land Cruiser. "Interesting," Sean heard him say a couple of times.

"Is it authentic?"

Amundson removed his monocle. "The base plug is convex, round rather than oval, and secured by wood pegs, not tacks. Iron staple for securing the cord. And here, at the bulb end, just a simple hardwood plug with a carved ring to hold the end of the suspension cord. All true to the period. Beautiful patina, some mouse gnawing, hairline cracks, what we call good attic condition. The horn is original. If it was left the way it was found, I would appraise it at two hundred to three hundred dollars."

"But the engraving—"

"—is not original to the horn. Nicely done, none of that folksy, whimsical design you see on eastern horns. The bone inlays representing the snow are very well fitted and something I've never seen before. The head and tail of the eagle, also. But the etching is raised slightly, the scrimshaw. Feel it." He took Stranahan's finger and ran it across the grain of the mountains. "After a hundred and sixty years or so, that would be worn perfectly smooth and you'd start losing detail, but this is crisp. The birds are quite interesting. Most horns from this era are plain, but if there's engraving of any sort, it tends toward hunting motif. Yet here we have several species of birds— eagle, raven, even a songbird. My guess is that the horn was bought plain, or found that way, and someone altered it within the last thirty or forty years, probably whoever added these initials. I'd speculate that the artwork is highly personal, that the mountains represent an actual mountain range that is part of this person's life and that the birds tell a story. I hate to see history defaced like this, but would almost make an exception for this horn. I'd like to meet its maker."

"So would I," Stranahan said.

"May I ask what your interest is in the horn?"

"It came into someone's possession and I was hired partly to find out how that happened. I'm a private investigator." He handed Amundson one of his cards.

"You could have said so earlier."

"And missed the story of the bra?"

"Hell, I would have told you anyway. Come on back inside. It's your turn to buy. I'm a licensed appraiser and you just took up my valuable time."

"All right, but only one more." Stranahan looked west toward the bluff where Lewis and Clark had camped. "Have you been up there?"

"Many times."

"What do you look for—musket balls, canteens?"

"I should be so lucky. No, mostly what I do is triangulate possible campsites using the best data available, which is the journals and other personal accounts, and then search for evidence of a latrine. The corps carried a laxative in which the active agent was mercury. Mercury does not dissolve from the soil."

"Here I thought your work was glamorous."

"That's Dora driving in. She'll nudge you with her fenders, just remember to come up for air and you'll be okay."

CHAPTER SIXTEEN

The Crazy Mountain Horsetail Detective

As an old-fashioned man living in a state of anachronisms, the yawning gaps between cell towers paramount among them, Sean Stranahan embraced communications technology with reluctant arms. Though it was mighty convenient to receive calls from the road, most of the time the phone was just draining the battery, searching for service. As usual he had forgotten the charger and was about out of juice when he saw that he had two text messages.

The first was from a number he didn't recognize and had five question marks in as many sentences.

> This is Celeste? Landon's friend? At the memorial? You said to call if I found anything that might help? Can you call me?

"Kids these days," Sean said to Choti, who was riding shotgun and opened her blue eye and then shut it when a dog biscuit failed to materialize.

He scrolled to the second text.

> Please join me for dinner tonight at Chico Hot Springs. 7. Best behavior. Etta.

The phone died halfway through Sean's muttered "Hmm." He grabbed the pen that the librarian from the Mile and a Half High

Club had used to scrawl on his hand, found a gas pump receipt, and jotted the number as best as he could recall it. At the Town Pump in Three Forks he dropped coins into a pay phone. Wrong number. Tried again, switching the last two digits, and got a professionally pleasant voice saying, "Three Rivers Realty." Down to his last two quarters, he tried reversing the first two of the last four numbers.

"Hello?"

"Celeste?"

"This is me."

———

The address was two blocks off Main Street in Ennis, a rental with a plastic tricycle and a swing set minus swings in the front yard. Celeste lived on the upper story, each narrow step a creak from a horror movie. She seemed nervous to the point of hyperventilation, rattling in run-on sentences about a bear in the yard the night before and how driving back from the dude ranch where she waitressed she was afraid to walk from the car to the door and the couple downstairs were fighting all the time while the baby cried and how it was driving her crazy, that and the washing machine going night and day because they were using cloth diapers and she was paying half the utilities which wasn't fair, and it was a month before the lease was up and she wanted to move but couldn't afford the deposit. Stranahan tried to calm her down by having her busy herself making espresso. He'd seen the machine on the counter; it was a studio, the kitchen and living area in the same room. She said that she'd got the expresso maker as a gift from the owner of the drugstore when they upgraded and wished she hadn't because he was divorced and now he was coming on to her and he was like, forty, no offense.

"None taken," Sean said. "I got three years to go."

"Sorry about the mess," she said. She was wearing a Woody Wood-pecker T-shirt and distressed jeans with horizontal slashes at the knees. She was actually an attractive girl, Sean realized, and as she sat beside him and took her first sip of espresso, a changed one. She seemed to lose her breathless quality and for a moment they sat in an unexpected silence.

"Quaalude in a cup," she said quietly. "The doctor thinks I'm ADHD. When coffee slows you down, that's like a red flag. But he wants to try relaxation techniques before dosing me with Ritalin." She took another sip. "I've got something to show you. It's probably nothing, but you said call, so I did." She walked to a television set opposite the couch and inserted a DVD. "These are documentaries Cindy made for class. We all did them, either on phones or renting out video recorders at the library. She made one about Landon last year, when he was working at her parents' ranch. She gave me a copy because she knew him and me hung out. I don't know how it can help you but I'd feel really bad, well, you know, he's still missing and he could be alive and—"

"You did the right thing, Celeste. Let's watch it." Sean had a mild sense of anticipation. Knock on enough doors and the first cog on the wheel clicks over. It was like fishing for steelhead; the first five hundred casts were just finding the rhythm, but the five hundred and first . . .

The title was in white block letters on a black screen—THE CRAZY MOUNTAIN HORSETAIL DETECTIVE. At the bottom of the screen was "Produced and Directed by Cinderella Huntington." The video opened with horses in a hayfield shot through with golden light. Stranahan heard a young woman in voice-over. "In this peaceful valley, nobody would dream of locking their doors. Nothing ever happens here except the bear getting into the bee houses or mister wolf passing through, taking a bite out of missus sheep. That is, nothing ever happened until this summer." Stranahan realized he was listening to Cinderella for the first time. It was a lilting voice with a melodramatic flair, and it went on to say how on the night of October 7—now the title theme of *Jaws* was playing—someone had sneaked into the stables and cut the tails off eleven horses, even Goldilocks, the prize palomino whose tail was so long it swept the ground. "Something had to be done," Cinderella said, "so we employed the services of the fearless Landon Anker. Say hello to the camera, mister horsetail detective."

The camera lens that had been swooping over the ranch entered the long corridor of the stables. It focused on a young man sitting in a horse stall, grinning sheepishly and scratching at strands of straw in his tousled blond hair.

"Sleeping on the job, are we? We have a way of dealing with slackards where I come from."

The young man pointed to his sleeping bag. "Sleeping here *is* my job," he said. He was fighting a smile, trying to keep a straight face.

"And what precisely are you going to do when the dastardly criminal sweeps in with the night? Leap on Snapdragon and lasso him like a steer out of the chute, tie him up like a rodeo calf? 'And the flag comes up and it's, no, I can't believe it, two point three seconds. It's a world record for catching a horsetail thief.'" Stranahan could hear Cinderella laughing; it was a wonderful laugh, full of music. "Let me just set this camera on the tripod so I can punish our employee for sleeping on the job. What is the appropriate sentence? Forty lashes? No, I say. Forty kisses."

The camera steadied on Landon Anker as Cinderella leapt on top of him, the video jolting as she bowled the young man over and hugged him while he tried to struggle up, Cinderella making kissing noises as her lips sought holes in his defense. Wrestling and laughing, he managed to get back to a sitting position. His cheeks were flushed.

"That's enough punishment," he said. "I can't take any more."

"No, I say, four more kisses!" She gave him a dozen more.

"Seriously," the young man said, "if I hear or see anything, all I do is ring the house extension."

"But what is this I see? Is this old Charlie Watt's .30-30 with the seal of Montana on the stock?" She grabbed a lever-action rifle and held it to the eye of the camera. "The one that's supposed to be in the tack room in case hungry varmints come a-calling?"

"He said I could keep it here."

"No, say no more." She ran a finger across her lips and shook her head dramatically. "Your secret is safe with me."

"Does—"

"Shhh, I said say no more. Until the Crazy Mountain Horsetail Thief dares to strike again, this is Cinderella Huntington reporting from the stables of the Bar-4, where Landon Anker keeps his lonely vigil through the wee hours of the night, so that men and horses may sleep. I think you need one more lash with the lips, young man." She kissed his cheek as the video showed the range of mountains behind the ranch, then crooked block letters reading THE END.

A few seconds later an image came onto the screen of what looked like the same mountains. Celeste stopped the video. Her cheeks were shiny. "I've seen this a zillion times and even though it makes me jealous it always makes me cry. It's all I have left of him."

Stranahan felt a wave of emotion. Anker seemed a very sweet young man, not without charisma. But it was Cinderella who had captivated him. Up until this point, Sean had been searching for a key to unlock the history of a name. Now there was a face to go with the name, dark golden hair to frame the face, eyes before the crow took them, a voice not yet stilled. He recalled Ettinger's words. *You just wanted to bottle her and carry her around in your pocket.*

"Play it again," he said.

"Okay." Celeste reached for the remote. Again there was the brief image of mountains before she stopped the video to return it to the beginning.

"No, wait," Sean said. "What was that?"

"That's the next documentary. She made three. There's Landon and then there's one about a beekeeper and then there's the mountain man. They all open with a shot of the mountains."

"Play them all."

THE BEEKEEPER OF SHIELDS VALLEY featured a bandy-legged man with a droopy mustache and cold blue eyes. Jimmy John Aaberg was a toothpick-in-the-mouth raconteur, holding forth as he drove with his left hand while his right dexterously rolled a cigarette.

Cinderella's camera followed him as he collected bee houses from three ranches. At one point, Aaberg took a grainy photograph from the glove compartment and held it up for Cindy's camera. The photo showed Aaberg standing among smashed bee houses holding a rifle, his cowboy boot on top of a dead bear. "That was at your ma's ranch, little lady," he said. "I called him Snaggletooth because of that right upper canine. Did I want to shoot him? No, I get no pleasure taking an animal's life lest it's going to grace the dinner table. But yours was the fourth place he hit inside a month. That bear durn near put me out of bees."

The video ended with a freeze-frame of Jimmy John, smiling as bees walked over his face.

The screen of the TV flickered and the third documentary came onto the screen: BEAR PAW BILL—LAST OF THE MOUNTAIN MEN. The camera swept peaks streaked with autumn snow, then focused on a Rocky Mountain goat nosing along a trail through rock scree. It panned from the goat to the foot of the slide, where an emerald lake was skimmed with ice.

Cinderella's voice-over began.

"Way far up in the Crazy Mountains, where Crow warriors sent their sons on vision quests and Billy Goat Gruff is king of the cliffs, lives the last of the old-time mountain men." The camera dipped to reveal a man sitting cross-legged before a small campfire. An ax gleamed in the firelight and Stranahan noticed a small rucksack propped beside it. Like the Lewis and Clark scholar, this man was dressed in animal skins, but there the similarity ended. Brad Amundson's jacket was chrome-tanned to a rich shade of chestnut. This man's skins were worn to a hard dark shine, and instead of a monocle on a chain, he wore a rawhide necklace strung with wickedly curved birds' talons.

The voice-over resumed: "Like the fur traders of yore, Bear Paw Bill doesn't talk much. I only know him because, riding my horse Snapdragon one day, I came across his camp and he offered this young reporter a leg of a rabbit to eat—"

"It wasn't rabbit. It was a stick of deer jerky. Journalism is a search for the truth." The man's voice was gravel rattling at the base of the kettle. The camera zoomed in to reveal a broad, bearded face with pale eyes and wild hair tamed into braids, at the ends of which fluttered feathers of various hues. "And we did not meet in my camp. We met at your school where I spoke to your American history class."

"Haven't you heard of poetic license?" The girl's voice was indignant. "Now we're going to have to start over."

"As you wish. But you may find my life worthy of record even if we stick to facts."

"The search for prophecy in the realm of the gods?"

"I see you have listened to at least a little of what I have told you. Someday you will see that life can take many paths and that the important thing is not the path but the courage to take it, and then the courage to take the next path if you find the first was a false trail to happiness. When faced with the opportunity to take a new path, most are reluctant, so that they live their lives at crossroads, frozen as time marches past them."

The frame shook as Cindy perched the camera on a rock and walked into the frame. She sat down cross-legged alongside the man. With Cinderella for scale, Sean saw that the man was immense, not tall or fat so much as wide and thick. The back of the hand that moved a stick to stir the embers was black with hair and Stranahan felt a shivering, as if tiny fish were swimming in his veins. He had seen this man before, or someone who reminded him of the man, but couldn't place the circumstance. Now the man had sat back and put an arm around Cindy, drawing her toward his shoulder. She rested her head and closed her eyes, their faces veiled by the smoke of the fire.

"It's a far way up here. You are kind to visit this old seeker."

Cinderella opened her eyes, her look one of beseechment. "What do you think it was really like for the Indians who came on vision quests? You went on one, but never told me about it." She bent herself to him as a smaller tree fetches up against the trunk of an oak. She appeared to have forgotten that she was making a film.

"I cannot put myself in the place of those who came before me. But I understand the concept of the quest, the search for the spirit animal that lends its wisdom so that one makes the right choice at life's crossroads. When the Crow warrior Plenty Coups came to these mountains, he dreamed of a time when the buffalo were replaced by spotted cattle and saw four great winds advancing, destroying all the forests. When the winds had passed, only one tree stood on the mountain. It was the pine from which the chickadee sings. To Plenty Coups, the dream meant the Crow must make peace with the white invaders or perish in their inferno. The bird was a symbol of peace."

"What did you see on your quest, Bear Paw Bill?"

"I saw the chickadee, too. But on the third day a great golden eagle knocked a mountain goat off the cliffs and it died down there by the lake. I took its skin for a blanket, but knew then that my soul would never be at rest, for the eagle is a bird of war. Forevermore, there would be a struggle for my heart between the chickadee and the eagle, between the goodness and the evil."

"But I think you are a good man."

"I fight against the rising of the violence inside me. I struggle mightily, but I am not a good man. Once I did a great evil in the valley. So have I become as Moses on his journey to the Promised Land. I sit atop this mountain and see the plains and the rivers, but God will not let me live at peace where men rest their heads, and so I am banished to wilderness."

"Where did you learn to speak like that? I've never heard anyone talk like you before."

"I seldom speak to people, but I read my Bible every day. Its language has reshaped my tongue. The animals that I talk to do not mind. That goat once passed by so close I could have stroked his nose. They sense that I mean no harm, but only take a deer every few weeks for my sustenance. Tomorrow my throat will be sore from talking to you, I have talked so much."

"Will you let me shoot your muzzle-loader? You can hold the camera."

"If you insist. But it kicks like the swat of a bear. I dare not use a full charge of powder."

As Stranahan watched the next part of the video, his hand came up to worry the stubble on his cheeks. Bear Paw Bill's hands were thick with muscle as he measured out the charge of black powder, poured it down the long octagonal barrel, and tamped the ball down onto the charge with the ramrod. He handed the gun to Cinderella.

"It's heavy," she said.

Sean watched her raise the rifle. "Pause it there," he said to Celeste.

Celeste paused the video. Up to this point, the powder horn that Bear Paw Bill wore on a thong around his neck had been obscured either by the campfire smoke or his hands as he measured out the charge. For a moment the wind had changed, revealing the crescent of the horn, but the resolution was poor. Still, Sean was certain it was the horn that Jasper Fey had found in the stall. He could see the white of the mountains. He motioned Celeste to resume the video and heard the click as Cindy pulled the set trigger to reduce the tension on the sear, then the *ka-boom* of the rifle as she touched the front trigger. A jet of fire shot from the muzzle. Cindy's head jerked back, instantly enveloped in a rope of smoke.

"Wow," she said. "That was cool." She had lowered the muzzle to the ground, and when she turned to face the camera, her cheeks were wet.

"Whatever are you crying for, dear girl?"

She set the rifle on the ground and walked toward the camera with her arms outstretched.

"What is the matter? Was it the rifle?"

The man had set the camera down and the screen showed the ground cover, the autofocus sharpening on grouse whortleberry leaves turning from green to yellow.

"Oh, I don't know," Sean heard her say. "My mom, all she does is cry and sit up drinking in a coffee cup, but I know it's her whiskey, I put a piece of tape on the bottle so I know how much, and it's all because I'm different now, I'm . . . all strange in my head. And my step-dad doesn't look at me and then sometimes he gives me the strangest looks and they both had such high hopes that I'd be . . . and I know they're only together because of me"—she was sobbing now—"I've let everybody down, and Landon, he calls me his little sister and I want him so but I can't have him and maybe if I hadn't had the accident he'd have liked me. Oh God, I can't even rodeo. Nobody will say it but I know I'm dumb. I just want to run away but I don't have anywhere to go."

"There, there, girl, things aren't so bad." Although Sean couldn't see them, he envisioned Cinderella wrapped in the mountain man's immense arms.

"Oh, can I come up here and stay with you? You could show me how to do a vision quest and I could sit in the cave and maybe an animal would tell me what to do."

"Leave the valley for the sanctity of the mountain? Become a seeker like this old man? But the ways of the mountain—"

Abruptly, the screen went blank. Then the video flicked back on, the camera steadying on Bear Paw Bill standing beside a dwarf white-bark pine shaped by the wind, His shaggy head silhouetted against the sky. The screen went black. There were no closing credits.

Celeste ejected the disk. Stranahan saw that he had the espresso cup in his hand, and he drank the cool bitter liquid.

"How many people have seen this?"

"No one, just you."

"I thought it was a school project."

"We only had to present one. Cindy's was the beekeeper guy. She said Landon could get in trouble if she showed that one, and the mountain man, people might come looking for him because he'd never told her what he did that made him go up there. She said she promised him she wouldn't show it to anyone."

"Including you?"

She nodded.

"Did you keep your promise?"

"Yes. When the title came on I turned it off. I'm not like popular or pretty, but I know people's secrets. They know I can keep a secret. That's why Landon came out to me. I want to be a counselor someday."

"I'm sure you will. I'm going to ask you to keep this a secret between us."

She nodded. "Do you think that's where she was, she ran away up into the mountains?"

"I don't know."

"He's not creepy or anything, though. Just sort of lonely and sad."

"I'm going to have to show it to the sheriff."

"Are you going to say where you got it?"

"Yes, but you aren't in any trouble."

"Can I burn it? It would just take a minute."

Though he could envision Martha Ettinger shaking her head—"He's not creepy or anything" wouldn't cut the mustard with her—Sean heard himself say sure, and while she was at it to burn a second copy for him. He knew that the video could be evidence, and if it got erased, the blame would fall squarely on him. But if it hadn't been for this girl who knew how to keep secrets, he would never have known there was a Bear Paw Bill, nor, for that matter, where to look for him. For when Cinderella shot the muzzle-loader, his mind heard in its echo the cracking boom of the rifle shot behind the forest cabin. A big bullet, going slow, Katie Sparrow had said. Someone getting himself a bearskin rug.

PART THREE

THE HUNT FOR BEAR PAW BILL

CHAPTER SEVENTEEN

The Shelby Southpaw and
the Red Death

Back at his studio, Stranahan spun the dial on his safe, three-zero-zero-six, the designation of the most popular rifle caliber in Montana and the first combination any thief with lukewarm IQ would try. He locked up the original DVD—the burned copy he'd left in the glove compartment of the Land Cruiser—and looked at the paintings on the walls. His gaze settled on a somber oil titled *Nocturne,* a man wading a twilight river, the cherry glow from his pipe as he pulled the flame of a match into the tobacco. The hands cupping the pipe bowl were his father's, but he wasn't thinking of his father. Rather, he was back on the ridge in Cinderella's video, Bear Paw Bill standing with his massive hands folded over the muzzle of his rifle. *Hands forested with hair.* Stranahan's fingers drummed the top of his fly-tying desk. He sat down, found a pack of #14 Partridge dry fly hooks, and spun elk hair and hackle, turning out tent-wing caddis imitations while deliberately turning his mind back to the river.

He heard Choti whimper. "It'll come to me only if I don't think about it, girl."

He was applying the whip finishing to the head of the third fly when it did.

————

Northern Hyalite County, worn-down mountains called the Bangtails, was a bluebird heaven in May, the cerulean males fighting over kingdoms of grass while the drab females preserved their modesty. A snowshoe hare the splotchy white of the mountains crossed the gravel road the preacher had told him to take. The double-wide was up a muddy two-track in a greening stand of aspens.

"What do you want?" The woman who came to the door cast a glance past Stranahan toward the Land Cruiser. "Well, he's around back in the shop," she said. Her eyes were small and distrustful in folds of fat. "But I'd leave that dog in the rig. Myron doesn't cater to strange animals mixing with the livestock."

As Stranahan walked around the back of the trailer, the only live-stock in sight a goat that nipped at his jacket cuff when he extended a hand, he became aware of a droning noise that rose in pitch, then ceased abruptly.

"Mr. McKutchen?"

Inside the open door of the shed, the man whose weight had made the floors creak at Cinderella Huntington's memorial service, whose appearance had reminded Stranahan of a domesticated boar, re-moved his work goggles. He ran a mittlike right hand across the stray hairs that clung to the barren landscape above his forehead.

"This number two board has more knots than plywood," he said.

"You need a table saw for that kind of work," Sean said.

"I've got a pack rat that chewed through the cord. You'd think he would have been satisfied gnawing the insulation off the spark plug wires in the tractor, but he's of a mind to put me out of business one piece of machinery at a time. If you're here for that cord of the sea-soned, just pull around back and I'll help you load."

"Actually, I'm here to ask after your brother."

The man's eyes changed.

"I'm trying to find out what happened to Cinderella Huntington. Your brother was a friend of hers. She calls him Bear Paw Bill."

Myron McKutchen replaced his goggles and picked up a jigsaw. He'd penciled a line on the board and bent to the saw, blowing the sawdust from the cut so that he could stay on the line. Stranahan stepped forward and held the edge of the board so that it wouldn't splinter as it fell. The blur of the blade passed within inches of his hand and finished cutting through the board. The man turned the saw off and set it down.

"How did you find me?"

"We sat in the same pew at the memorial service. I called Reverend Crookshaw. He gave me your name."

"That's not what I asked. How did you know Bill was my brother?"

"I saw a video Cinderella made with your brother. You two look alike, but I didn't put it together until I saw him fold his hands over the muzzle of his rifle. In the church, you folded your hands over your Bible." Stranahan shrugged. "You have a similar face and they were the same hands and you're too young to be his father."

The man looked at the backs of his hands, then turned them over so that the palms showed. "It was me they called Bear Paw first. Bear Paw Myron McKutchen, the Shelby Southpaw. I used to fight smokers on the reservation against these Indian bucks. One called himself the Red Death. He knocked two teeth out of my head before I got a right hand in and settled him down. It's the American way, isn't it, the disenfranchised beat the hell out of each other while the rich man collects the money?"

He looked off and Stranahan saw that his eyes were like blue watercolor, saturated around the pupils and then fading outward. "I thought it would be someone wearing a uniform," the man said. "Ever since they found that girl, I expected someone with a badge, but nobody came."

"How many people know Bill is your brother?"

McKutchen shook his head. "We moved here two years ago. A lot of people from up on the Hi-Line know our family; down here not so many. Bill moved here to be with us last spring, got a job building a barn in Ringling. He was a guest historian in the schools, traveling around and talking about life in the 1800s. He was taking medication to keep him on track. It was the most I saw of him in the last ten years and it was probably the best I saw of him in twenty."

"Is your brother mentally unstable?"

"He's on the more manageable end of some spectrum or other, not bipolar but like that. I looked it up on the Internet and it's just a catch-all term for a set of behaviors nobody understands. Bill says the meds dumb him down. In the past it's only been a matter of time before he dumped them into the river."

"Does he really live in the mountains?"

"For three or four months at a time. He was gone almost a year once. It's not entirely living off the land. He packs in a lot of dried peas and flour. And he's got the muzzle-loader he made here in the shop. He shoots a deer now and again, makes his own clothes."

"How long has he been gone this time?"

"He left Labor Day weekend." He counted on his fingers. "Just over eight months ago."

"Do you know how to find him?"

"He had me drop him off on the west side of the Crazies."

"Do you think he'd still be there?"

"There being where, exactly? It's a big mountain range. But I don't even know if he's alive. He's never spent a whole winter before."

"In the video, he talks about committing an act of evil."

"If you're not a policeman, who are you? Coming to my house, wanting to talk about Bill?"

Sean told him.

"I think you better explain to me about this video."

As he spoke, Sean watched the man lower his head and shake it. Then McKutchen removed his work goggles and looked up. His eyes held one of the saddest expressions Sean had ever seen.

"My brother," he began quietly, "equates not being able to prevent someone's death with killing a person. Bill was the promise of our family—class salutatorian, center on the basketball team, got a scholarship to play ball at MSU. It was a ticket out. But there was this girl who'd moved from the Rocky Boy Reservation who'd taken a fancy to him, trailed him around the halls like a puppy. You got to understand that on the reservations, basketball players are rock stars. Girls make no bones about wanting to have their babies. To hear Bill tell it, Lu-cinda lied to him about the pill and got pregnant to stop him from going to college. They had it out at a graduation party and he stuck to his guns, said she could come with him or not, but he was going. She stormed out, swearing on her mother's grave that she was going to kill herself and the baby, too. He said, 'Have it your way,' or something like that, depending on who was telling the story. I wasn't there.

"When I get a call, it's Bill saying someone came to the party talking about a crazy person out by the station who said she was going to lay down on the tracks and wait for the 6:47 from Malta. Well, I got alarmed, because that form of suicide isn't an unheard-of thing where you got liquored-up Indians passing out—that's not a politically correct thing to say, but there you have it. So Bill met me where this guy said he'd seen the girl, we were running because the train was due, and we heard the train passing and followed it out of town and there was what looked like a pile of clothes in the middle of the tracks. The wheels cut her right in half. The baby was still moving when the ambulance came. It was like a hairless puppy. Bill was holding it, trying to keep it warm. It didn't die for hours. I mean it was just awful." He looked at Stranahan. "How can you recover from something like that? It's been thirty years, but how do you get past it. I can understand why he feels like he's in exile."

"Did you know he was in touch with the Huntington girl?"

"No. But he'd talked about her. She'd made an impression on him when he went to her school. He said he hoped if his child had lived it would have grown up to be like her. That's why I went to the memorial."

"His baby was a girl?"

McKutchen nodded. "That's when he started going to the mountains. The first time, up there in the Little Belts, we thought he'd died. Then this man came out, full beard, dressed in some deerskins he'd made into clothes, quoting the Bible. You would never have known it was my brother."

"How would Cinderella have found Bill up there?"

"I didn't know she had. You're the one telling me."

"You had to have suspected when she went missing."

"I didn't, though. Not until last week when I read where they'd found her. That cabin, that's the trailhead where I dropped Bill off. If you're asking if he would have harmed her or taken advantage, I can't see it. Bill was a gentle man."

"A powder horn of your brother's was found among Cinderella's possessions. It had engraving on it, mountains and birds."

McKutchen was nodding. "We found that horn packed in a dynamite box after our uncle John passed. He had a lot of antiques and taped notes to them, the provenance and so forth. The note said his grandfather had found the horn up on the Musselshell. Bill cut the scrimshaw himself. I told him it would ruin the value, but then we weren't going to sell it, so I didn't stop him."

He looked away. "Have you gone to the sheriff?"

"I came to you first."

"They'll go after him." It was a statement.

"Cinderella talked about wanting to run away to the mountains to live with him."

McKutchen shook his head. "He isn't dangerous to anyone but himself."

"You need to tell that to the sheriff. Can you come in tomorrow morning, if I arrange it? You'd be helping your brother."

McKutchen bit his lips, his nod almost imperceptible. He was leaning forward as he had in the church, his heavy hands folded on the workbench.

"What are you making?" Sean said. They were just words, something to break the silence.

"A box to bury my dog. The coyotes got him last night." He shook his head. "I never let him out after sunset, but I was having an argument with the wife. What they do is send a female out to lure him from the house and then the pack kills him. We heard him yelp but it was too late to do anything but shoot into the air." He shrugged, made a helpless gesture. "You get to love a dog when you don't have kids."

Stranahan was sorry he'd asked. He said he'd call in the morning and left the Shelby Southpaw staring at the backs of his hands.

CHAPTER EIGHTEEN

The Second Thing She Did

Coming through the door, all Stranahan knew about Chico Lodge was what Sam had told him, that it had the prettiest waitresses in the Paradise Valley, but ever since the actor Jeff Bridges plucked one for his wife, they were all looking for love a little farther up the social ladder than a fishing guide could scale. "How about an artist who lives in a tipi?" Sean had asked. "Second base tops, my brother," the big man had said.

Etta Huntington smiled at the story, sipping her scotch in the bar at the back of the restaurant. She looked trim and western, wearing jeans and a white snap shirt under a rabbit-fur vest. "Oh, I wouldn't know about that," she said. "Some women might consider making love in a tipi to be the height of romance."

"Better than a truck under the stars?"

She leaned close to Sean on the red brocaded love seat, her hair falling forward and her scent light, slightly musky. Her voice fell to a whisper. "I'll let you in on a trade secret. I wasn't even in the bed of that truck. I couldn't kick the boots high enough."

"So how did they pull it off, some digital trick?"

"The AD on the shoot played club soccer. The woman who kicked out the stars had hairy legs and wore a man's size ten."

"You just ruined the fantasy of the adolescent male viewing public."

"Shhh. Don't tell anyone. Men might quit buying me drinks at the bar."

This was an Etta Huntington Stranahan had not seen before. He had seen her drunk and sarcastic. He had seen her stoic and bitter. And he had watched her cry. It was her vulnerability that touched him. But he had not seen this playful, flirting side of her, her eyes flashing in the lamplight of a dimly lit bar.

A waitress approached. "Ms. Huntington, your table is ready."

Stranahan was aware of the surreptitious glance from a man at a neighboring table as he pulled out Etta's chair.

"You must get used to people looking at you," he said.

She took the question seriously. "You mean men look at me. I'm told it's because I have a carnivorous face, all these sharp bones and prominent orbitals. 'Jaguar eyes,' the ad people called me. People think they've seen you before, so you must be somebody. That's a way of saying I'm not conventionally beautiful but men lick their lips anyway. Women are the opposite. They hate me on sight. Sometimes I feel like smiling back and then casually removing my arm, just to see the expressions."

"But not tonight."

"No, you don't have to worry. Best behavior, I promise. But let me tell you a story. Last summer after the accident, they'd already made the arm for me, the Chevy people asked me down to San Francisco. They wanted to make another ad, but they didn't want to show the arm. Could I ride a horse one-handed? I said, 'Get me a horse and I'll show you.' So they trailered in a horse and we're on Potrero Hill, where one of the execs lived, and we were going to drive to this park. I said, 'I'll show you right here,' and get on the horse, and my arm falls off and starts rolling down the street. It's really steep and it's just rolling like a bowling pin." Etta had started laughing. "These guys are running after it but they're too slow so I take off and pass it and bail off the horse. Full gallop. Like it was something I did every day, like heading a steer. By the time they got down to me I had the arm on. The exec, he's this skinny gay man who's got this way of considering things, rubbing his nose with these long fingers, they called him the Praying Hands, and he's praying and praying, and finally he nods and says, 'I guess you answered my question.'"

Stranahan started laughing with her. Etta's skin glowed, the diffuse candlelight softening the angles of her face. Even at their first meeting, when she had done her best to repel him, he had felt drawn by her honesty. She created an atmosphere of intimacy. There was Etta and you were with her, and the rest of the world bled away. He reached for her hand.

"Etta, there's something I need to show you later. It's a DVD, a documentary that Cinderella made."

"Yes, I know. J. J. Aaberg."

"There was—"

She put her fingers to his lips. "I saw it, but if there's something you have to say, please wait. Tomorrow, yes. But not tonight. By some miracle I have managed to escape from myself. Perhaps the reason is you. Perhaps it isn't. But you don't have to understand why to respect my decision."

"Does it have something to do with Jasper? The two of you looked—"

"It has nothing to do with Jasper Fey. Despite anything he might have told you, there is nothing between us. We haven't been in the same bed for more than a year, even before the accident. At the stables, I let him comfort me in a moment of weakness. That was all. He made his appearance. He spread his charm, his tender concern for the stepdaughter he has forgotten. He drove back to the set today. He's moved on." She squeezed Sean's hand and then touched her fingers to her heart. "He was never here. Not in here.

"Now"—she dismissed the topic by picking up the menu—"this is my treat. They make a bison Wellington in the most luscious puff pastry; it's only for two to share, they won't make it for one."

"Then it's the Wellington," Sean said.

"And a big red, a Zin if they have the Maryhill Reserve. But I'll only have one glass. As I said, 'best behavior.'"

———

The eye of the moon hung above the Crazy Mountains on the drive back to the ranch. They talked, or rather Sean talked as Etta drew him out, about his life on his grandfather's farm in the Berkshires, about his move west to the rivers his father had dreamed of fishing and hoped to take Sean to, until life got in the way, and then not having money got in the way, and finally his father's death got in the way. He told her he'd married his high school sweetheart, that at some point they had become unknown to each other and divorced, in the last years having to struggle to find topics to talk about. Etta laughed softly; it had been the same story with her first husband, whom she had loved dearly though it was a marriage steeped in silence before his untimely death. Now Jasper Fey, that was different. "I stopped talking. He kept yelling."

She asked Sean if he was in a relationship and he said he had been, with a veterinary student who lived in Oregon.

"Is it over?"

"I think it is. It's hard to have a relationship with someone who's eight hundred miles away and doesn't return your calls."

Etta looked ahead out the window. "Oh, I don't know. I still speak to someone who is as far from me as a star."

After that, for the last ten miles, as each became acutely aware of the breathing of the other, there was only the rumble of the Land Cruiser's straight six.

"You know what I like about you?" Etta said when Sean pulled up to the ranch house. "You're damaged goods like me. The difference is you think you've lost things so you act like you have nothing to lose. But your life is still ahead of you. Mine is behind me now. I might not last a lot longer."

"You're the woman who kicked out the stars."

"That's not me."

"Then who are you, Etta?"

"A woman who spent an evening with a very nice man who's going to kiss her good night." She leaned across the seat and kissed him, then pulled back, gently letting go of his lower lip to look at him in a questing way, the kiss the only point where their bodies had touched. The second time she kissed him, it managed not to be. She climbed out of the Land Cruiser and Stranahan watched her walk to the house and open the door. The house was dark. She disappeared inside. He waited for the door to close, part of him hoping it wouldn't.

Stranahan counted to ten. He recalled the video Cinderella had made, Bear Paw Bill talking about the crossroads. Stranahan felt he stood before one now. He walked to the open door and stepped inside. She was standing in the hall, her shoulders slumped a little. A sad smile. *This is me, all there is.* The first thing she did, after he shut the door, was come into his arms. "Don't worry," she said, "I won't bite you." She nuzzled her head under his chin and nipped his neck. "Well, maybe I will."

The second thing she did, as he followed her through the darkened house, was take off her arm and let it drop to the floor.

———

Hours later Stranahan awoke to feel the cold on the other side of the bed that meant she had gone. He found her in the sunroom with the moon in the window, curled into the wicker chair where she had sat when they first met.

"How long have you been here, Etta?" He dropped into the chair beside her.

"A while. I woke up about four." She sipped from a cup, then handed it to Sean and looked out the window.

"Which one is she?"

"It depends on the morning, what frame of mind I'm in. If I'm feeling melancholy, then a dim star, one fading out with the night. But it can be bright, it just depends."

"What one is it tonight?"

Wordlessly, she got to her feet, and Sean followed her onto the porch, where the universe reeled away in a pepper of stars. "Tonight it's that one in the east there, under Cassiopeia."

She zipped up the rabbit fur she'd worn to the restaurant and leaned back against Sean, reaching behind her to take his hands and cross them over her chest.

"This is where the man says, 'About last night,' and the woman feels her heart sink, knowing what he's going to say next."

"I didn't say anything."

"You don't have to. If you want me to let you off the hook, I can say you didn't have a choice and I'm releasing you now. I won't make a scene."

"But I did have a choice."

"Did you?"

"I don't make a habit of sleeping with married women. Even those who say they haven't been with their husbands in more than a year."

"Life is more complicated than marital status."

"No, I don't think it is."

"Aren't you young."

She extracted herself from his embrace and walked back into the house and switched on the light in the kitchen. She kept her back to him as she poured coffee. "If you aren't going to go," she said, "then tell me what it was you wanted to say last night, before I made you compromise your principles."

A bitter tone had crept into her voice and Stranahan was aware of her posture, how she had erected a wall against him and pulled into herself. Her face remained impassive as he spoke, and he told her everything, the Mile and a Half High Club, the ghostlike figure running on moonlit snow that the women had seen, and the mountain man, Bear Paw Bill.

"Where is this DVD?" she said. "I have a right to see it."

Stranahan got the copy from the Land Cruiser and they watched the documentaries on the flat-screen television in the den, the room slowly becoming pale with dawn. Etta began to cry silently halfway through the first video, the one with Cinderella and Landon Anker in the stables, but her eyes were dry by the end.

"Have you ever seen this man before?" Sean asked.

She shook her head. "I only knew Cindy was making one about J.J. I was worried she'd get stung by the bees. Do you think this mountain man, do you think he would . . ."

"We can't say for sure that he was even with her. But we'll certainly try to find him."

"Who will?"

"Anyone I can muster to help. The brother is seeing the sheriff this morning. I'll show Ettinger the video and see if she'll kick loose a couple of her men. It's a solid lead on a suspicious death. Plus, we have the shot I heard behind the cabin. So there's a starting point."

"I'll go with you."

"Etta—"

"Etta what? What do you expect me to do? Sit around and guess what star when I might be of actual use?"

———

Martha Ettinger ejected the DVD from her computer and leaned back in her office chair, staring past Stranahan to the Wanted posters on the corkboard. She rolled a dart between her right thumb and forefinger.

"So," she said, "this Bear Paw Bill, do we consider him kinda sorta armed, or sorta kinda armed? You see my predicament."

"Not really. But I saw his brother in the hall. You talked to him. What do you think? A muzzle-loading rifle is a far cry from an M-15."

"I think it was enough gun to kill grizzly bears in the day. Plus he has a history of antisocial behavior. So I'm going to come down on the side of discretion and consider him armed and dangerous. That rules out SAR volunteers because I can't send civilians up there." She scratched her chin with the point of the dart. "Here's what I will do. I'll call Katie because we might need her dog if we hit a track. I'll provide myself because I'm overdue for a horse ride and Walt can run the department. To hear him talk you'd think he's the sheriff, anyway—wait, Walt's off." She nodded. "That's actually better. We can pull him in, too. And I'll check Harold's schedule. Technically, he's in charge, and he's the one you want in the mountains, regardless. When do you want to go up?"

"This morning. They're forecasting snow above six thousand feet tonight. It hasn't snowed since Katie and I heard the shot. So we've got maybe eight hours before the white story—what's Harold call it?"

"The white book."

"Anyway, before it closes and the tracks get swallowed up."

"I understand the urgency." She nodded. "This could be coming together. I received a text from Wilkerson. She performed the test to compare the DNA of the fetus with DNA collected from a cheek swab of Anker's sister. Landon Anker wasn't the father. I was going to call Etta Huntington with the news."

"It would be better having it come from me."

"You two are close now." It was a statement. "Okay then, you."

She called her shot—"Ricardo Chicarelli, a.k.a. the Squid, third from the left"—the dart leapt from her hand and buried in the fugitive's right eye. She reached for the phone.

CHAPTER NINETEEN

A Taint of Sour Dog

By ten in the morning they were six, seven counting Lothar. At first, Ettinger had been adamant about refusing Loretta Huntington's request to join the search party. If she was injured the department could be sued. But she'd finally relented on a purely practical point. Huntington could have six mountain horses trailered to the junction of U.S. 89 and the Shields River Road inside an hour, together with the tack and saddlebags packed with lunches and thermoses of coffee, against the two hours or more it would take to round up and trailer their own mounts. All Ettinger's party needed to do was bring clothing to brunt the weather—it would drop into the lower twenties by nightfall—and the emergency gear all members of search and rescue had at the ready. The team was gathered at the crossroads around a topo map of the western front of the Crazy Mountains, spread out on the hood of Ettinger's Cherokee, when two trucks from the Bar-4 arrived, the trainer, Charles Watt, pulling a four-horse trailer, Earl Hightower, the ranch manager, pulling a two-horse. Stranahan had not met Hightower and he looked the part of a ranch manager—black Wranglers belted under a comfortably ample middle, Carhartt jacket frayed at the cuffs, rancher-style hat pushed high on his forehead. He'd heard Sean wanted to interview him and said anytime.

The headlights of Etta Huntington's longbed Absaroka bobbed onto the road. Perfunctory handshakes all around, left-handed for Huntington, the men purposely not looking at the empty sleeve of her jacket.

"Largest gathering of non-tattooed individuals this side of Two Dot," Walt said.

Harold Little Feather shrugged off his wool-lined jean jacket. He was wearing a flannel shirt with the arms cut off, elk tracks in blue ink circling his sculpted right biceps, weasel tracks his left.

"Our Native brother notwithstanding."

Earl Hightower spoke up. "Charlie, don't you have a bit of jailhouse art here or there?"

"I might. I might not."

"I got a heart on my boob," Katie said.

"Thank you for sharing that with us," Ettinger said. She rapped her knuckles on the hood. "Can we concentrate here?"

The truth was they were giddy. Manhunts brought up the heart rate. If your days were spent pushing a pencil, as too many of Ettinger's were, you lived for the open air and the track in the snow. It was one of the exhilarations of the job that attracted you to law enforcement in the first place, and that was experienced less often at every rung of the professional ladder.

"Here's what I'm thinking," Ettinger said. "We'll trailer four horses to the cabin where Sean and Katie heard the shot. Four of us will mount up and take this trail here"—she pointed at the map—"up and over the bald ridge. Where it drops into the South Fork we split up, two heading downstream, two heading up. The other two horses we trailer to the Sunlight Creek trailhead, ride up that trail, then take the loop trail back under Black Mountain." She waited for someone to object.

"The Sunlight road will be blown in." The team's eyes turned to Huntington, who spoke from under the brim of an old felt Stetson. "Even if you can bust through, it's a downhill grade that last half mile, and with snow on the way, we got to think about getting out." Her jacket was worn and her tin cloth pants had faded to the color of dirt. If you could ignore the sculpted planes of her face, she could have been any ranch woman of a certain type, long in the leg, broad in the shoulders, an inverted triangle in the saddle.

"What do you suggest?" Ettinger said.

"Take the other two horses up South Cottonwood, which is a better road, then ride them up to the divide that looks down onto the South Fork. That way you have riders strung out along two creeks and eight or nine miles of country. You'll never be more than an hour ride from each other if someone cuts track, and it's all good trail, so you can ride out at night if it comes down to that. There's water, tree belt shelter all along the route. That's where I'd camp if I had to survive a winter up there."

"She makes a good point, Marth." Walter Hess worked his Adam's apple.

Ettinger saw Harold nodding. In the mountains, he was her barometer.

"Okay then, we're agreed. How are your horses shod? I don't want to slide off a goddamn mountain."

"They got snowball pads and tungsten grit shoes. All except my horse. He's got aluminum front shoes and nothing on the back. Does that answer your question?"

Sean saw that she'd been offended. Etta Huntington knew more about shoeing horses than the rest of them put together.

Martha grunted. "Since you suggested Cottonwood, Etta, I'm going to have you pair up with Harold and go that route. The radios are synched, but in case anyone changes channel by accident, we're all on seventeen."

———

It took a little less than an hour to climb to the ridge, the horses straining against their chest straps. Ettinger rode ahead, pulling a string that included Stranahan, Hess, and Sparrow, with the shepherd trailing, his tail curved above the snow. On top they stopped to drink in the country, the forested ridges backdropped by jack-o'-lantern teeth. "Where did the shot come from?" Ettinger asked Stranahan.

"Not sure."

"If you had to say?"

"It was a dull echo, like from way off. I think if it was from here it would have been a sharper report. It wouldn't have had two walls to make the echo."

Ettinger's "Hmm" sounded skeptical. She touched the ribs of the horse and they switchbacked into the bottom where the South Fork of the Shields tinkled under glassy banks. The horses left it muddy, clopping through the ice and then climbing through spindly Engelmann spruce to the trail T-junction. So far the only tracks they had seen were snowshoe rabbit and a lone wolf.

"Remember what I said." Ettinger nodded toward Walt as they rested the horses. "You find a track, you radio it in before anyone follows." Hess pinched the brim of his hat and he and Katie Sparrow turned south, heading upstream.

Ettinger waited until they were swallowed by the forest. She shook her head. "This country can't get more than two, three hours of sunlight at the solstice. You'd have to be crazy to spend a winter here."

"You think we're wasting our time, don't you?"

"If McKutchen kidnapped Cindy and she escaped from him, you'd think he'd get as far away from the scene as he could. He'd expect us to come looking. He wouldn't know she had died in the cabin."

"You think that's what played out here? He kidnapped Cindy and she managed to escape?"

"Or she ran away to live with him and changed her mind. This guy, what do you think the chances are he's had a woman in the last ten years? Suddenly there's this pretty young thing paying attention to him. Forget vision quests; here's his spirit animal standing right in front of him, ripe as an August cantaloupe. Men don't think with their brains—use your head, Stranny."

Ettinger flexed her inner thigh and the horse turned north and clopped up the trail. The snow was deeper than they'd expected, the rivulets iced over—winter still had a few teeth in its head this high. The trail snaked through forest to ford a jump-across feeder creek, then left the bottom to follow that creek, climbing through solid timber as the afternoon waned. Columns of steam blew from the horses' nostrils. A few flakes of snow sifted out of a leaden sky.

"Whoa there." Ettinger drew her mount to a halt and leaned over the saddle. "What do we have here? Is this your bear hunter?"

The track, or rather the line of tracks, approached from the west and turned along the trail. Stranahan dismounted and put his boot inside one of the prints. It was a mite bigger than Sean's size ten hiking boot, which meant it was a mite smaller; the tracks looked to have thawed and refrozen several times over the past few days, growing a shoe size in the process.

Ettinger said. "That's not much of a foot for a man called Bear Paw."

Sean grudgingly agreed. "Just because someone else was hunting here doesn't mean the shot Katie and I heard wasn't our man's."

"No, but I think we're going to have to call it a day. By the time we get back to the junction it's going to be dark and anyone as green in the saddle as you are is a paraplegic waiting to happen. We'll come back up here another time."

Stranahan's nod was glum. Another time meant never.

"Buck up," Martha said. She dismounted to stand beside him. "Let's eat a sandwich before we turn around." She rummaged through a saddlebag and cut a sandwich in half with her knife. It was elk meatloaf with ketchup and American cheese. They wiped snow from a log and sat down, chewing in silence.

"Damn that's good," Martha said, wiping at her mouth. "You know why there's all those cooking shows on TV now, Stranny? Everybody polishing their knives?" She had just started calling him Stranny. It was meant affectionately, but Sean knew it was also a way of keeping him at arm's length.

"No, Martha, enlighten me."

"It's because food's the new sex. It's just as good but without the mess. You don't wake up the next morning smelling some Neanderthal lying next to you, thinking, 'What the hell was I thinking?' Nobody knocks on your door to tell you she's pregnant. Nobody calls a month down the road to say, 'I hate you.' You just brush your teeth and go to bed."

"Yeah, but nobody calls to say, 'I love you,' either."

Martha muttered, "Hopeless romantic," and washed her sandwich down with a swig of water.

"Do you smell that?"

Martha replaced the cap of her water bottle. "I smell our horses." Her nostrils flared.

"No, it's smoke. The wind shifted, it's gone now." Stranahan pulled a tuft of old man's beard hanging from a spruce bough and let it fall, the dried moss sifting down the hill. Again, he smelled the smoke. "What's up there?"

Ettinger brought up the map screen on her GPS. "There's a bench of timber about six hundred feet above us. The trail switchbacks to the north of it."

"Bench sounds like a place for a camp."

Martha nodded.

"But if we ride any closer, he'll be able to hear the horses whinny."

Ettinger nodded again. "We'll tie them off." She unholstered her radio and turned the volume knob down before transmitting. Got Walt, waited while he punched in the coordinates. "We're all the way to the headwall, Marth. We can be there but it's going to be at least an hour."

"We can't wait that long."

"I don't like you going in alone."

"I'm not alone."

"No offense to Sean, but he doesn't have the experience. Remember what happened with old man Nichols? The guy he shot didn't make it. Let's not have any déjà vu."

Ettinger said she'd be careful and signed off.

"Nichols?" Sean said.

"Self-described mountain man, abducted a girl to make a wife for his son. Things went sideways. I'll tell you another time." She tried to raise Harold, but got no answer. "On the other side of the divide," she said. "They couldn't get here before dark anyway."

She tied off the horses, marked the waypoint, and drew her .30-06 from the scabbard. Raised one eyebrow. *Here we go.*

It took thirty minutes to climb to the bench, the snow patchy where the sun had its way, the smoke scent faint and intermittent, then heavy in their nostrils. Stranahan pointed a finger into the flanking pines, where smoke hung like a layer of fog over a thicket of second-growth lodgepoles. No flames visible, but he could see a shifting column of gray where a fire had burned out. Ettinger brought up her binoculars. "I can see a rifle leaning against a tree."

"Is it a muzzle-loader?"

"It's got a long barrel. I think so."

"He has to be close."

Martha nodded. She unsnapped the strap over the hammer of her revolver and handed Stranahan the Ruger .357. "Only if he goes for the weapon. Stay three paces behind, step right in my tracks."

Stranahan felt blood hammering at his left temple. He rubbed at it and nodded. Thirty yards into the thicket. Forty. A blur of wings as two jays fluttered into a tree. A shelter inched into view. It was a lean-to, the roof constructed from branches tilted against a ridgepole and thatched with pine boughs, the fire built in front, the fire out but the coals still had color. A sooty coffee can was suspended on a stick angled into the ground. Granite boulders the size of medicine balls had been piled up behind the fire to reflect heat. Martha and Sean exchanged a glance. Only someone of enormous strength could have moved such rocks.

The brass of the patch box on the rifle glinted dully in the evening gloom. Stranahan immediately recognized it as the muzzle-loader Cinderella had shot in the video. He joined Ettinger before the open front of the shelter, which was about twelve feet long and had elevated sleeping platforms, one twice the size of the other. A modicum of privacy was provided by an elk hide suspended from the roof, separating the bedrooms, if that's what you could call them. The beds were quilted with layers of pine boughs for cushioning. Animal skins draped over them, mostly deer, but one white skin from a mountain goat, presumably the one the eagle had knocked off the cliff. Another hide had once clothed a cinnamon black bear.

Against the side wall of the larger room was a crude bench made from a slab of pine. There was a draw knife for working hides. Bits of leather and a lot of shaved wood curls about. Stranahan examined a box of various feathers, together with some small hooks and coarse thread that looked like it had been unwoven from a red sweater. Fly-tying materials? He looked up, saw half a dozen crudely tied flies with their hooks sticking into the underside of the roof thatching. Bear Paw Bill was a fly fisherman.

"It doesn't appear that they were sleeping together," Sean said.

"Maybe not, but that doesn't mean he didn't have her when the mood struck."

"What now?"

"We wait. I don't see him wandering very far without his rifle."

Stranahan walked to the muzzle-loader and thumbed the hammer to half cock. He pried off the percussion cap. "Let me have your Swiss Army knife and a ChapStick," he said.

Martha handed the knife over and he used the head of the small screwdriver to dig out the explosive material inside the cap. Then he smeared the ChapStick into the priming hole of the nipple. He replaced the cap and lowered the hammer. The rifle was nothing but a club now, but McKutchen wouldn't know that, even if he cocked the hammer. He'd see the reassuring glint of the cap.

Stranahan noted Martha's look of mild surprise. "Sam builds these things, I've shot them a bit," he said.

They retreated thirty yards and took cover behind a jumble of downfall. The minutes ticked by in uncomfortable silence, their sense of anticipation blunted by the awkward position, their butts cold against damp ground. The jays that had perched in the tree flew back down to the ground. They hopped about, pulling at something in the brush. Stranahan watched their antics, his mind on Bear Paw Bill. But his eyes kept coming back to the birds. Gray jays—the old-timers called them whiskey jacks—were scavengers. They weren't pecking for bugs as he'd initially assumed. Probably they had something dead in there. It could be the carcass of a rabbit that McKutchen had skinned, or whatever other animal he'd collected when Sean and Katie had heard the shot. He glanced at Martha, drew a question mark with his index finger.

Ettinger peered through her rifle scope. "It looks like a piece of tack, something leather," she whispered.

Stranahan nodded and they stood up, the jays flitting away. As they approached, it became clear that the birds had been pecking at a boot, or rather a moccasin made of tanned elkskin. The moccasin was as big as a small beaver tail and it wasn't until they were standing over it that they saw what the birds had been eating. Martha slung her rifle over her shoulder and bit at the knuckles of her right hand.

"Jesus, Stranny."

They were looking at a foot. It was a left foot, severed a few inches above the collar of the moccasin. Flesh around the bone had been dug out by the sharp bills of the jays, so that the bone stub protruded. The bone wasn't splintered but appeared to have been cut clean, as if by a heavy cleaver.

Grim-faced, Martha walked to the shelter. Before, they had given it no more than a cursory going-over, expecting McKutchen's imminent return. Now there was no hurry—if he did come back, they'd have plenty of warning. Sean found a long peeled stick with twists of snare wire at regular intervals and puzzled over them only a moment before realizing it was a crude fly rod.

Ettinger crooked a finger. She pulled back the skins on the larger bed to show Sean where they were stained with blood. Her eyes ran over a King James Bible on a shelf affixed to the back wall of the lean-to. A pair of scratched reading glasses rested beside it. She looked under the framework of the sleeping platform and drew out a drawstring leather bag and a metal canister with a screw lid. The label read FFG BLACK POWDER. She shook it. About half full. She opened the bag and rolled half a dozen lead balls into the palm of her hand. "What do you figure, fifty caliber?"

"Or fifty-eight."

"You find anything on the girl's side?"

"There's a couple cans with dried clay in them. No food, though. No clothes. No personal items. I'm guessing she came up here with nothing but the clothes on her back and left the same way."

"Except for the elkskin jacket Harold found," Martha said.

"Except for that."

Ettinger shook her head. "You're still thinking this is platonic, him giving her her own quarters, but what I'm seeing is that she waits for him to fall asleep and brings the ax down on his ankle."

"Where do you suppose they keep their food?"

"Probably hanging in a tree. Bears get hungry after the winter nap. Only a fool leaves his food in camp."

"I didn't see anything hanging."

"It would be over by the creek. They can get food and water on the same trip."

"You have an answer for everything but where he is, Martha."

"We'll see about that. He's minus one of his paws now. He can't have gone far."

They walked the perimeter of the camp, looking for a drag mark where the man might have crawled. Most of the snow had melted under the thin tree cover, making the job harder. Martha muttered something about Harold never being around when you needed him. They made a second circle, wider than the first. They were on their fourth circle, about a hundred yards to the south of the camp, where the bench ended and the ridge sloped sharply down toward the canyon bottom, when Sean saw a gouge in the earth and puzzled over it. Ettinger stepped ahead and pointed with the muzzle of her rifle to a pair of deep pockmarks in the ground. And another set, farther along.

"He's made crutches," she said.

The trail led onto a shaded slope where a dirty sheet of snow clung like gauze. Now it was no longer necessary to connect the dots, for the single boot that the man wore had pressed through the rotting snowpack and the stump of his left leg had dribbled blood. Here on the steeper slope he'd fallen, then floundered getting back to his feet. A few feet farther along he'd gone down a second time, opening his wound and marking the snow with clots of black blood. On the ground were the crudely made crutches he had discarded. From this point he had crawled, the bloody trough of his progress reminding Stranahan of trails where hunters' horses dragged gutted elk. The skid headed straight down toward inky stands of lodgepole and spruce that marked the creek bottom.

"It's nothing but a shintangle down there," Stranahan said.

Martha nodded. McKutchen would never be able to climb through the downed timber. The distance he was ahead of them would be measured in feet now, not miles. She removed the cartridge from the chamber of her rifle to sidestep down the slope. Progress was slow, as Ettinger stopped every few yards to glass the forest coming into view below them. Only a few smears of rose and purple marked the twilight. In ten more minutes it would be too dark to see anything beyond the beam of a flashlight. As they reached the skirt of the ridge, an odor invaded Stranahan's nostrils, a dark scent with a taint of sour dog. He heard the subtle click as Martha eased the bolt to rechamber a cartridge.

Ahead, where the trunks of the trees formed a wall, a bearlike figure bulked against a crust of snow. It was making a low moaning sound. The moaning stopped and the figure jerked. They heard a thud, then a crack like a branch breaking. The moaning began again, a lament that reminded Stranahan of the dying note of a wolf's howl. Ettinger tapped the headlamp on her forehead. "When I flick it on, that's when we take him."

CHAPTER TWENTY

Hollywood Hero

Later, it would occur to Stranahan that his first impression of Bear Paw Bill had been on the mark. The man had the broad taut stomach and humped shoulders of a bear, and he breathed like one, his exhalations stentorian, his breath as rank as a grizzly scavenging winter kill. It had been like closing in on a dying bear, too, cautiously approaching from behind, Ettinger's rifle at the ready. The man was on his knees facing the thicket, but as they neared he swiveled his head and opened his mouth as if to roar his agony, an ax brandished in his right fist. But no words came out and he fell forward in parts, the ax falling from his hand, the shoulders slumping, and finally the body losing its battle with gravity. He fell with a soft grunt, facedown, his hair fanned onto the snow.

It took ten minutes to wrestle the body to a tree trunk broad enough to support his back. He was wearing a canvas rucksack, and after they got it off him and lifted him to a sitting position, the man's breathing seemed less labored. For a brief few moments he opened his eyes, the pale orbs swimming and uncomprehending. Ettinger makeshifted a tourniquet from her belt and tore her fleece vest into strips to bandage the stump, while Stranahan gathered up the wood the man had been cutting and built the fire that he had obviously intended to light.

They raised Walt on the VHF and informed him of their position. He and Katie were about an hour away, about how long it would take Martha to bring in the horses.

"I'll do it," Stranahan offered.

"Do what? Charm them like your sexy librarian and expect that they'll follow? No, you just make sure Bill here doesn't start leaking while I'm gone."

Ettinger started climbing back the way they'd come, her light bobbing out of sight. Stranahan heard the radio crackle. It was Walt, saying he'd raised Harold and Etta. They'd join up and come in together. "Don't let your guard down," he cautioned.

Stranahan assured him that the man was hardly a danger.

"It's the hardly dangerous ones kill you," the ex–Chicago cop said.

Stranahan signed off and sat down on the far side of the fire, watching the flames lick gold and green fingers up and down the mountain man's beard and lion's mane of hair. The image reminded him of waterfalls of color he'd witnessed during displays of the aurora borealis.

"We're going to get help for your leg," he said. "You're going to make it." They were just words; he didn't expect the man to hear them.

Stranahan heard a cough. Slowly, the right arm of the man lifted and the hand rubbed at the spittle on his mouth.

"Hin." The word blew out with his breath. "Aappen . . . S-s Sin-er."

Stranahan walked around the fire to hear better, but the man seemed exhausted by the effort and tilted his head back against the trunk. Stranahan saw that his eyes, fully open, were the same watercolor blue as his brother's. He bent close to speak, ignoring the pungent zoo smell in his nostrils.

"Are you saying 'Cindy'? Is 'Sin' 'Cindy'?

"Cin-her." He pulled his hand toward his chest. *Move closer.* Stranahan remembered Walt's caution. "I can hear you," he said, without moving forward. The thick fingers beckoned. *Only a few inches,* Stranahan told himself, and then, with a sudden movement, the snapping of a shadow, a hand clamped on his throat and he began to reel toward unconsciousness, seemed to swim upward into the swirl of stars and then, abruptly, he was back, felt the snow cold underneath him as he stared into the wavering, upside-down image of the face looming over him. The icicles on the man's beard melted from the fire to drip onto Sean's forehead and sting his eyes.

"Where's my kick . . . a . . . dee?"

Sean tried to speak, but couldn't form the words.

"Lost . . . my kicka . . . dee."

"Let go," Sean managed. But the heavy hand wasn't clasped around his throat. It had relaxed and was merely a weight, the knuckles resting against his cheek. The man had gathered him up, like a silverback gorilla pulling one of his sons to his immense chest.

"My kick-a-dee."

Sean peered up. Bill's head was haloed by his cascade of ringlets, blotting out the handful of stars that challenged the overcast sky. He remembered the moonlike visage captured on the potter's video, the bearlike creature that had run from the cabin where the couple were clasped in their embrace.

"Did . . . Cindy . . . cut off your foot?"

"Proud . . . I'm proud . . . of her."

"Was . . . she your lover?"

Bill sat back against the tree trunk. "Car-coal. She tell you . . . in car-coal. I made her . . . color." He shook his head. "Have to . . . find her." His chest heaved. His breath rattled with the inhalation, caught, then shuddered out. His head tilted back against the trunk of the tree. Gradually, the breaths became regular. Stranahan kneed back to his side of the fire, where he sat heavily. He felt his own chest draw oxygen in a counterpoint rhythm to the mountain man's, then they were breathing as one and the firelight colored behind his eyes as he closed them. The color darkened to the wine of the horizon and his world went black.

———

Looks like Papa and Baby Bear are in for their long winter's nap." Martha loomed over him, her hands on her hips.

"I fell asleep," he said.

"Uh-huh. How's the patient?"

Sean got to his knees and fed a branch to the fire from the stack. "Do you have any water? I could use it."

Ettinger got a bottle from one of the saddlebags and unscrewed the lid. Sean swallowed, feeling the burn where Bill's fingers had closed on his throat. He tried not to let the pain show on his face.

"We had a conversation," he said, handing the bottle back.

"About what?"

"His chickadee. I think he meant Cindy. He wanted to know where she was."

"Let's just hope he can hold on until morning when we can get a chopper in here. Meantime our job is to keep him breathing. Here, hold the flashlight while I check that dressing."

Ettinger switched on her headlamp, the beam glancing off Sean's face before illuminating the slumbering giant. She brought the light back to Stranahan.

"Turn your head. No, the other way."

"My good side?"

"You've got blood on your clothes."

Stranahan reached for his right shoulder, his hand coming away wet. "It must have happened when we were putting the dressing on."

"Bullshit. What the hell happened when I was gone?"

She listened, her face impassive. "And you weren't going to tell me," she said. He began to protest. "No," she cut him off. "Is it because you're embarrassed he got the drop, or are you trying to protect him?"

"I think you have the wrong idea. He could have been trying to help that girl and—"

"That's not the way you get your point across. You don't leave me out of the loop. Ever. How can I work with you if I can't trust you?"

"I'm working for Etta Huntington."

"Not up here you're not. And that's not the issue and you know it. Jesus, Sean. This is cowboy shit. You've got to trust me."

"I'm sorry, Martha. It won't happen again."

She blew out a breath. "Go rustle up his rucksack," she said. "We might as well have a gander."

Sean brought the rucksack back to firelight and unlaced the drawstring. Chips of obsidian for sparking fire, along with charred strips of cloth for catching the spark, were in a small leather pouch inside the bag. He rummaged further. "This is weird." He drew out the companion moccasin to the one they'd found with the man's foot inside. Strips of leather had been cut from the top of the moccasin. Several were floating around at the bottom of the rucksack.

"He's wearing a boot," Stranahan said. "Why would he be carrying the moccasin?"

"A better question is why would he be cutting it up?"

They had to wait another half hour for Harold to arrive and offer a credible explanation.

"I've seen this before on the reservation," he said. "He's eating his clothes. The man must be starving."

———

As soon as she dismounted from her horse, Katie Sparrow checked the unconscious man's respirations and heart rate, then began undoing the bone section buttons of his elkskin greatcoat.

"It's his leg that's hurt," Martha said. But she chastised herself even as Katie continued to peel back layers. How could she have been so negligent? It had never occurred to her that the mountain man's injuries might extend beyond the obvious.

Bear Paw Bill gave credence to the term "dyed in the wool." The green-and-black stag shirt he wore under the coat had stained his chest and abdomen in a checkerboard pattern and was difficult to remove; the grizzled hairs of his chest were caught in the open weave of the fabric and cemented with dried blood. Katie shone her light on a black button under the ribs that looked like a seeping blister. She wrinkled up her nose.

"This is a puncture wound," she said.

"It looks like he was stabbed," Martha said.

"Look at these," Katie said. She pointed to several pink dots of raised scar tissue. "Like he was shot with a shotgun, but the wounds healed over. The smell is from the puncture wound. His body's being poisoned from a ruptured intestine and he's burning up trying to fight the infection. We've got to get the fever down. Get me the medical kit in the whatchamacallit, the saddlebag."

Martha hooked her thumbs in her utility belt as Katie cleaned and dressed the wound. It was snowing again and she lifted her eyes to the occluded sky, goddamning the situation in general.

"Can he hold on until daylight?" she asked Katie. "The chopper's not going up in this shit."

"I'm a wilderness first responder, not an EMT," Katie said. "But the sooner we get him out, the better."

"What about Josh?" Walt said. "His heli's got infrared, AP, he can fly that grasshopper on a night as black as bin Laden's heart."

"Joshua Byrne, the actor?"

"I told you. He shotgunned with me in Chicago when I had the shield. Wanted to get my speech patterns down for a part." Five blank stares. He elaborated. Joshua Byrne was a former Navy SEAL who had parlayed his shoulders and square jaw into a civilian career fighting bad guys on the big screen. He owned a working cattle ranch with a helipad in the Boulder River Valley.

"I heard his place is up out of McLeod." Martha said.

Walt was nodding. "Eighteen hunnerd acres. I saw a muley buck with a rack like a candelabra last day of rifle season. You want to hunt that property, I can get permission."

"And he can fly on instrument flight rules?"

"That's what I'm saying. He could hoist an elephant off this mountain as the clock strikes midnight, we had mountain elephants, that is. You go back in the fossil record—"

"Walt!"

"I'm just saying it's possible."

"Has he filed the paperwork with the department?"

"He's good to go."

"Then for Chrise sakes use the sat phone. Let's make him a real hero."

CHAPTER TWENTY-ONE

The Star of Pegasus

Many years ago, at a birthday party, a sweat bee had walked into Sean Stranahan's ear and set up residence for thirty maddening minutes. Once or twice a year something out of the blue would remind him of that buzzing drone. Or in this case from the black. The helicopter sounded underwater, then became a deafening roar as it dropped over the shoulder of a mountain. The searchlight swept the field of snow that Sean and Walt had marked off with strobes. When the chopper kissed the snow, it was enveloped in the whiteout caused by its rotor.

It took them all, hero and nonheroes alike, to get Bill McKutchen onto the stretcher and carry him to the panel door. Joshua Byrne was craggy and affable and said it was like setting down in Afghanistan, except for the shooting-at-you part. His teeth shone, even in moonlight. He said there was room for one more passenger, and Martha was persuaded to board; she could facilitate the paperwork at the other end. She told Sean she'd pick him up in the morning and drive him to Law and Justice, where he'd left his rig.

Katie Sparrow sidled up to Sean, licking at the snow melting on her upper lip.

"Be still my heart," she said.

Stranahan said he wasn't *that* good-looking.

"You're just jealous."

They saddled up, and the rest of it was riding out in a sifting, fairytale snow.

───────

Do you really live in a tipi?" Etta Huntington said.

"It's an eighteen-pole Sioux design. Harold Little Feather lent it to me until I get the house up. I'll give you the tour."

After loading the horses into the trailers and seeing them off, Etta had offered to drive Sean home, during which they had talked of little else but Bear Paw Bill. Sean assured her that they would swab his cheek for a possible DNA match with the fetus her daughter had carried, that the test would take a few days and beyond that they just had to hope he lived until he was able to talk.

"If he's the one who got her pregnant," Etta had said, staring through the half moon of windowpane cleared by the windshield wipers, "the thought of that giant and my Cindy . . . I wanted to hate him. I thought if I was alone with him I would kill him. But watching him just trying to breathe and remembering the video, how she'd reached out to him. And him on that awful stump and me with my arm, both of us being in that club. I don't know what to think."

Sean admitted he didn't either. "This is the turn," he said.

When he undid the sticks that closed the front flap, Choti bounded out and began to run in circles. Sean ducked inside and lit the lantern, filling the tipi with golden light. He held the flap for Etta to enter, then sat cross-legged behind the fire ring of stones, facing the flap. "Tipis are pitched with the door to the East," he explained. "Custom dictates that a woman enters to the left and takes her seat on the south side of the lodge, to my right. That is because the south side represents life, the growing of life on the earth." He patted a folded blanket. "Please sit. Do you want me to make you coffee for the road?"

She remained standing. He watched her make a heart with her lips, considering.

"For the road," she said, looking at her shadow against the tipi wall.

"Or you could stay here. You can have the cot. I have plenty of blankets, and with a center fire this place warms right up."

"Aren't you afraid Martha will see my truck? I wouldn't want to put you in an awkward position tomorrow morning."

"It's not her business."

"No, but you care what she thinks of you, I know you do."

"I'm offering."

She didn't seem to be listening. "And what must she think of me, a heathen who stares at stars?" She was looking at the triangle of sky showing through the vent. Snowflakes swarmed at the opening, snapping out like fireflies. Etta caught a survivor on her tongue. It brought a flicker of smile. Then the shoulders fell as her face worked into the heartrending expression of her grief.

"I was just so sure it was Landon," she said. "And a part of me thought, 'Young love,' you know. At least she would have known young love. If they had run away together and met some . . . fate . . . at least they were together. Now, tonight, that man. It could have been my daughter who cut off his foot. Could she really do that? Could she have shot him? She must have gone through something so terrible."

"Etta—"

"Don't 'Etta' me. They say the worst thing is the not knowing. But it isn't. The worst thing is that she was in trouble and I wasn't there. I was giving that stupid clinic, teaching teeny-bopper cowgirls how to wear their hats so they wouldn't fall off when they turned the barrel . . . Why didn't I just drive back? If I'd been home earlier, maybe she would have come to me. Maybe"—she gestured with her good arm—"maybe none of this would have happened."

"You couldn't have known, Etta. You can't beat yourself up over that."

"Oh, but I can." She sighed. "Who am I kidding? Cindy didn't share her life with me, not what mattered. Maybe if we could have found her diary. When Jasper discovered that powder horn hidden in Snapdragon's stall, I thought Cindy's diary could be there and he just hadn't looked hard enough. You two were looking at me like I was crazy when I tore out the wall, but I really thought that's where it could be."

"Why is that?"

"Because that's where I found it before, in a wall in her room. She'd pulled the nails out of the baseboard so she could hide it between the bottom of the wall and the floor. The floors had settled, so there was a gap. I found her on her knees one day and it just seemed an odd place to be. She said she was looking for an earring. Up there, I was hoping maybe that man had it with him, but he didn't."

A wall. Sean and Martha had searched the forest cabin, but a recess in the wall might have escaped their attention. Or perhaps in the thatching of the lean-to?

"I suppose you know I'm a wreck," she said, turning her face away. "They say when women overdose, what they're asking for is attention. But women in Montana, in Alaska, strong independent women, we're more likely to man up and pull the trigger. It's a statistical fact. When I get up in the night, I'm not just searching the universe to find Cindy. I'm trying to find a reason to keep living. I think if I can fixate on a star and convince myself she's watching, that's my tether to the earth. I'm not telling you this to gain your sympathy. It's just a way of saying that the other night, you were an escape for me. I told myself it's okay, Etta, making love is life affirming, he's a gentle man, I can escape from myself for a little while. He won't think less of me, and if he does, he's just the vehicle. I'm being honest with you."

"You used me. I'm hurt." Stranahan tried to keep a light note in his voice.

"Yeah. I guess dropping my arm on the floor did the trick. Made me irresistible."

"Stay here tonight, Etta. Nobody has to use anyone. But I don't want any more of this talk about suicide."

"That's what people say, don't they? 'I don't want to hear any more of this talk.' What's that supposed to mean? You don't want to hear the truth?"

"You had to deal with a lot tonight." Stranahan reached up to take her hand. "We'll figure out how to get through tomorrow, tomorrow."

She sat beside him and rested her head against his shoulder.

Stranahan could feel her tears against his cheek. After a while he built a fire and she lay beside him on the blankets, burrowing against him for warmth. When he woke up, cramped and stiff, the cold deep in his bones, he saw her staring up through the flap. The snow had stopped to reveal the crystal pepper of the stars. She pointed out two of the four stars that formed the body of Pegasus, the winged horse.

"See that one on the right that pulses in and out? That's Beta Pegasi. It glows when it's hot, then it gets fainter as its surface cools. I lied to you before, when I said that the star I see Cindy in changes every night. It does change, but this is the star I see most often, because it beats like a heart."

"Why lie?"

"Because it would have revealed too much of me and I didn't know you. Because it was our secret. It was Cindy showing me she was in heaven."

She rolled onto her side facing away from him, positioned his hand so that it cupped her breast. She was wearing a jacket but it was Etta underneath, and Sean doubted he could fall back asleep but did, breathing to her rhythm, and the next time he awoke he was hearing a droning sound like the helicopter in the distance, and hoped it was a dream, knowing it wasn't.

———

Get in, keep your tongue in your mouth, I'm not in the mood for conversation."

Martha turned the Jeep around, its headlights flaring past the dawn silhouette of Etta Huntington's truck.

"How's the puma this morning? Licking her paws?"

"I thought you weren't in the mood to talk."

She shook her head. "I shouldn't have said that. I don't want it to be like before. We're friends. We need to be open with each other, even if there are things I don't want to hear. Or see."

"It was two in the morning. I told her she could sleep in the tipi, 'sleep' being the operative word."

"Then sleep it was. I thought we'd swing by the hospital on the way, see if the Hulk's awake. When I called, the doctor was prepping to operate."

———

Sean, always a pleasure."

Arjun Anand had an oily forehead, liquid eyes the color of cocoa, and a close shave on a beard that would make a razor surrender after a dozen strokes. His voice rattled like pebbles in a tin can. He took in the others with a glance, bowed his head curtly, and said he'd be only a minute.

When he disappeared behind the curtain, Walt rolled his eyes.

"What?" Martha said. "You exercising your corneal muscles?"

"Just recalling there was a time you said Indian people in Montana knew who you were talking about. It's an observation."

"Uh-huh. Like referring to him as Sabu a minute ago." She frowned at Sean. "How do you two know each other?"

"Arjun is a fellow fly tier. He consulted on Patrick Willoughby's knee last summer, you know, from the Liars and Fly Tiers Club."

"Humpff."

The doctor was back. He placed his hands, one crossed over the other, on his slight potbelly.

"This man is very grave," he said. "He has had a perforation of his small intestine for days, maybe weeks. It is a miracle he lives."

"What was it caused by?" Martha moved her hand to her throat.

"A blade. I extracted six shotgun pellets as well. Four point five seven millimeter."

"That's BB shot," Walt said, nodding. "Goose load."

Martha frowned. "Are you saying he had lead poisoning?"

"No." Anand shook his head. "Lead poisoning from shotgun pellets is rare, in this case impossible. It is steel shot."

"So what happened? He was trying to remove the shot and accidentally punctured his intestine?"

"Using a knife, it is possible."

"Or he was stabbed," Walt said.

"That is also possible."

"What about the foot?" Martha tapped her foot.

"The stump was cauterized. I was told he was camping, so by a burning stick, perhaps? But he has lost very much blood, more than five pints. So much that in a person of ordinary size he would be dead."

"Can you tell me anything about the amputation?"

"The leg was severed cleanly, perhaps an ax, or a maketti."

"Machete," Walt corrected.

"Perhaps that. A week ago, two weeks, by the progress of the encrustation. I'm told the foot was transported with the victim and is in a refrigeration unit. The medic told me it looked gangrenous and had a puncture wound under the arch. Surgical reattachments are difficult in the best scenario. In this case, too much time has passed even if the tissues were healthy. And the load-bearing requirements on the tibia . . ."

"I'll send someone from the department for it," Martha said. "Dr. Anand, we need to talk to this man."

"That is not possible. He is very heavily sedated. Not out of the woods, as one says."

"But he'll live?"

"The body is an enormously powerful engine. This morning, he squeezed my hand. This hand." He held his right hand up. "This hand is my occupation, yes?" He spread his fingers. "I must be careful not to let it happen again. So yes, with transfusion, antibiotics, I think he lives."

He nodded. "Sean, please give my salaams to Patrick. Someday you will travel to Kumaon as my guest and we will resolve this issue of the mahseer."

The liquid eyes moved to Martha. "Sean and I have an argument about the greatest fish for the fly rod. I say the golden mahseer of the Himalaya. He insists it is the Pacific steelhead. As I have not caught a steelhead and he has not caught the mahseer, our disagreement is specious."

It was time to continue his rounds.

"You'll let us know when he can speak?" She handed him her card.

———

Let's stop for coffee and kick this thing around," Martha said.

Ten minutes later she switched the engine off and opened the window to drink in the sound of the Gallatin River. "I'm seeing two scenarios." She held up one finger. "First possibility. Cinderella Huntington experienced something so horrible that rather than go to her mother or stepfather, she ran away into the mountains to be with Bear Paw Bill. Or"—she held up a second finger—"Bear Paw Bill was so intoxicated by her visit that he went down into the valley and kidnapped her."

"We've been over this ground before."

"Hear me out. I'm one of those people who thinks better when they think out loud."

Stranahan blew steam from his coffee cup. Outside the window, a red-winged blackbird perched on a cattail, flashing his epaulets. "I'm listening," he said.

Martha continued her train of thought. "According to Doc, Cinderella Huntington became pregnant either shortly before or after her disappearance. The only person we've ruled out for paternity is Anker."

"We'll know whether Bear Paw Bill was the father inside a week," Sean said. "This isn't like you, Martha. Speculating before—"

"Will you let me finish? I'm speculating because if it turns out our mountain man is *not* the father, we need to consider the consequences of that now, not wait for DNA corroboration. Say that Bear Paw Bill was acting as her protector, that she fled the valley of evil for the sanctity of the mountain, to use his own words. What else was he to her besides a refuge, a shield? Think about what she revealed in the documentary. She talked about brain damage from the accident, about her mother's drinking and her stepfather's disappointment in her, about her dreams of going to college. I'm waiting for the shoe to drop."

"He was her confessor."

"Exactly. And if I was that someone from the valley who made her take flight, I wouldn't be getting much sleep tonight. I'd be wondering what Cinderella told Bear Paw Bill. I'd be more than a little concerned about what he'd say when he came around, or what he might have told authorities already."

"Do you think he's in danger?"

"McKutchen?" She shrugged. "Ten years ago I would have said that stuff's only in movies. But who knows? I'm going to have a deputy posted at the hospital at least through today and tonight. In the meantime, we release an official version of what happened up there and an unofficial one. The official version presents the facts of the rescue, including Joshua Byrne's involvement, but the department isn't releasing details because it relates to the ongoing investigation into the death of Cinderella Huntington. The unofficial version is that McKutchen talked to at least one of his rescuers, and that as a result, the investigation has taken a turn, focusing on the paternity of the child Cinderella was carrying. That should flush out the real father, if McKutchen isn't our man."

"Why not release that publicly?"

"Because it would look like I'm fishing and it could scare somebody away. It's best to come from another source."

Sean brought his finger to his chest.

"That's what I'm thinking. I'll drop a word here and there while you start knocking on doors, asking questions, stirring the voice of doubt in someone's head. Then we sit back and wait for that someone to do something stupid."

"We can't keep eyes on everyone."

"No, you're going to prioritize. You found the mountain man for us. I don't have to tell you how to do your job. In the meantime, let's hope Bill comes around and points the finger for us."

"What if he points it at himself?"

"Best-case scenario. Case closed."

"About Bill." Stranahan reached into the pocket of his jeans. They were the same jeans he'd worn when he'd gone to the cabin with Katie. He handed Martha the shotgun pellet and told her the story behind finding it. "It's a BB pellet. It's steel," he said.

"So he's a Peeping Tom, like the lovers thought."

"Or he was looking to take something from the cabin."

"I don't see where it gets us, either way."

"Neither do I."

"Still, curiouser and curiouser." Martha turned the key in the ignition.

At the Law and Justice lot, Martha idled to a stop behind Stranahan's Land Cruiser and peered in the rearview mirror. She ran a ChapStick across her lips, the closest she'd come to applying makeup since, well, since the dance the summer before at her cousin Bucky's wedding reception. It was the first time Sean had kissed her. No, she was the one who'd started the kissing. What should have been, what could have been. She shook her head at the memory. Now it was as if none of it had happened.

"You okay, Martha?"

"I'm just off to the wolves and not looking forward to it." She snapped the cap onto the ChapStick. "That Gail Stocker at the *Star*, she'd eat her husband for a story, and she isn't married. After I read my statement, every reporter in the state's going to be ringing my number. I told you before I underestimated this thing, but I *really* underestimated it. You'll think it's me who's the movie star, not Joshua Byrne."

"People already think you're, who's that actress?"

"I know who you mean, but that's just because she played a sheriff. I get Marg Helgenberger, I even got Connie Britton once but I don't know what they were smoking. I don't see the similarities. I'm tall, I'm . . . I don't know."

"You're Martha. You don't need to be anybody else."

"That's what mothers tell daughters who inherit the unfortunate half of the genes."

CHAPTER TWENTY-TWO

The Birth of a Foal, the Death of an Iguana

Sean ran his eyes around the walls. One unsold painting after another stared at him reprovingly, eliciting a clicking of his tongue over his tenuous financial situation, Etta Huntington's contract notwithstanding. He focused on the half-completed canvas on his easel, an impressionist piece of pointillism titled *Sunrise—Sawyer Key*. A sea of golden wafers was shattered by a tarpon at the height of its jump, its gill rakers beads of crimson. He prepared his palette but then failed to work himself into the mood of the painting. He put his paints away, found a legal pad, and had penned in a dozen names to plant the seed of doubt with when the phone rang.

"Kemosabe."

"Sam! Where are you?"

"I'm at the fucking airport."

"You're not supposed to be back until Memorial Day."

"Well what do you know? I am. Let's say I've had health concerns. Get your ass over here and pick up your buddy. My flights got fucked and I spent all night in the Salt Lake airport surrounded by snoring Mormons."

Stranahan tore the list of names from the pad and folded it into his pocket. The big man was waiting outside the sliding doors to the baggage claim, carrying four rod cases taped together and wearing a hoodie with the hood up over a ball cap.

"Traveling incognito?" Sean said.

Sam pitched his duffel bag into the way back and settled his bulk into the passenger seat. He pulled off the hood and removed his wraparounds, revealing the ovals of pale skin around his eyes. The rest of his face, under a billed fishing cap that read CRAIG, MONTANA: A QUIET LITTLE DRINKING TOWN WITH A FISHING PROBLEM, was burned the color of a pig turned on a spit. He removed the hat and shook out his hair. "Just drive me to Peachy's so I can pick up my dog."

They were nearly to Four Corners before he spoke again.

"You know where I tie up my skiff at Garrison Bight, well, yesterday morning, no, day before, I'm supposed to be fishing Stephen Dunn, you been out with him."

Sean nodded. "Trophy Man." Dunn was a fund-raiser for nonprofits who sunk his profits into the pursuit of saltwater game fish. He affected a Belizian accent whenever he hooked up, saying, "The Trophy Mon's got a beeg one on."

"Yeah, he's decent people," Sam said. "Anyway, I'm late to the dock and Trophy's standing there and says, 'What do you got under the tarp?' And I think, 'What tarp?' Sure enough, there's a tarp on the bottom of my Maverick. I pull it back and there's an iguana, one of those red-head males looks like the Creature from the Black Lagoon. Four fucking footer. Gutted like a deer, blood and God knows what all over the bottom of my boat. It's got its iguana tongue sticking out and get this, the tongue is wrapped around a cigar somebody's been smoking. Yeah, half smoked. I jumped right back onto the dock. I mean, it's your basic wake up with a horse's head in your lap. And Trophy, you got to hand it to him, he says, 'Is this somebody's idea of a joke or should I start looking for another tarpon guide?'"

"Jesus," Sean said.

"Yeah."

"Did you tell him to find another guide?"

"I told *all* my clients to find another guide. They were referrals anyway. I only had to deal away a few dates."

"So who did it?"

"Carolina's got this brother, Raimundo, the fuckin' little prawn.

She tells her mother about me, next thing you know this guy's on a plane. Turns out he's got a friend and Carolina's been promised to this friend, it's like it's already happened in the eyes of the family. Anyway, Raimundo takes us out to dinner at Louie's. Carolina excuses herself to go to the ladies' and he leans across the table and tells me she's spoken for, says Montana's supposed to be nice weather this time of year. I say what the fuck does that mean, and all he does is give a contented little belch. Next morning—iguana."

"And you left, just like that?"

"No, I hunted the dude up to brace him, and he's talking with this other guy's got about six chin hairs, looks like Roberto Durán, the fighter. Raimundo hands the guy something, wraps his fist over it. I'm thinking bills. Understand, they don't see me, we're on Duval and there's a lot of fucking tourists, and the guy walks right by me. Then he stops, turns his head over his shoulder. Eyes as dead as a shark's. Pulls a cigar from his pocket and lights it. It's a Maduro Robusto with the yellow band. Same fucking cigar the iguana had in its mouth. Walks away. *That's* when I decided to look at a plane schedule. I mean, I could see things getting pear-shaped in a hurry."

"Where's your boat?"

"Julio says he'll tarp it in his backyard, no charge." Sam looked out the window and shook his head. "Raimundo doesn't know jackshit about Montana."

"How so?"

"This is a fucked time of year to come to Montana."

After dropping Sam, Stranahan fed his Land Cruiser regular at the Sinclair station in Norris, eyeballing the green dinosaur in order to avoid watching the numbers flipping on the pump. At least this tank was being expensed to Etta Huntington, and thinking of her, wondering if she was still at the tipi, he pulled the list of names from his shirt pocket. He glanced down it, men to a man with one exception, Donna Anker, Landon's mother. Prioritizing, he circled her name, as well as

Earl Hightower, the Bar-4 ranch manager, and the horse trainer, Charles Watt. Hightower and Watt had been interviewed at length by Harold Little Feather at the time of Cinderella's disappearance. But Stranahan's acquaintance with them went no further than shaking hands, and Watt, at least, had been one of the last people to have seen Cinderella the evening before she disappeared. Stranahan tore the receipt from the pump and decided to pay a visit to the ranch. But first he'd have to pick up Choti.

Turning into his drive, he saw that Etta's truck was gone. She'd scraped a heart into the hard-packed earth of the tipi's floor, had etched a star inside it.

The Sheltie, curled at the foot of the cot, regarded him with her mismatched eyes.

———

Etta answered Stranahan's knock sans arm, sans smile, wearing the same clothes she'd worn on the manhunt.

"Why are you here?" she said. "My husband's driving in tonight and it would be awkward for you to be here."

So now he's her husband, Stranahan thought.

"I thought you preferred calling him 'that bastard.'"

"You think you know me, but you don't."

Using her good hand, she pulled the empty sleeve on her right arm around her left forearm so that she stood, leaning back from her hips, with her arms crossed in a keep-your-distance posture. "That star in the heart wasn't you, it was Cindy."

"I know it was. I'm not here for you, I'm here to talk to Earl Hightower and Charles Watt about the night she disappeared. And to give you this." He handed her the elkskin jacket that they had found outside the cabin. As it was not evidence in a crime, Ettinger had released it to him and he had simply not got around to giving it to Etta.

"We believe McKutchen sewed it for Cinderella. I thought you'd like to have it."

She took the coat without comment.

"I'm just doing the job you paid me to do."

"Earl thought the world of her."

"I'm sure he did. But the way I work is, you ask questions until you find answers."

"You found Bear Paw Bill."

"And that may be the end of it, but until he talks I'm working on the assumption that something else could have happened that night that caused her to run away."

She nodded, and the guarded expression on her face was replaced with resignation. "I'm sorry. I've always been a person that people want something from and it's hard to open up the way I did with you. So I step back. It's just my instinct." She looked past Stranahan toward the mountains.

"Did you tell your husband about what happened?"

"Between you and me?" She shook her head. "Of course not—oh, you mean about Bill. I called him an hour ago. He'd find out anyway and just get mad at me if I didn't. It's hard to stay civil as it is."

"How did he react?"

"He said he'd never heard anything about a mountain man, but he'd kill him with no questions asked. That's just Jasper being Jasper."

"How do you mean?"

"Jumping to conclusions, threatening to kill somebody. He's a hothead. You saw that side of him in the Pony Bar. But I've never known him to be calculating. Jasper's not a cold-blooded bastard, just a bastard." She let go of the empty sleeve and turned to go into the house. "I'll call Earl and let him know you're coming. Then if you still want to see Charlie, drive around to the stables. The vet's here and we've got a mare ready to foal at a civilized hour for once."

———

Earl Hightower's house was built on three acres of floodplain he'd purchased from Etta Huntington five years previously. Stranahan took the turn, the Land Cruiser's tires lifting a sheet of water at the creek ford, then climbing out of the choked bottom through greening cottonwoods to reveal a split-level ranch/rambler-style home, the roof topped with a weather vane shaped like a rooster. A border collie charged out, nipping at the tires. Hightower opened the door of his house, windmilling his arms.

"Keep a-coming. Don't pay her no mind."

They shook hands as Stranahan read the map of the man's past in the broken capillaries of Hightower's cheeks and nose. He remembered what Jasper Fey had said about him being a sponsor in AA. But the eyes were clear and the smile was ear to ear over teeth that looked to have had a recent whitening. He led Stranahan into a living room dominated by elk mounts with glassy eyes and indicated a chair at a table with turquoise inlays. The place was ranch decor from ceiling beams to red oak floors, except for a painting of a seaside golf hole, breakers hitting the bluffs. The obligatory weak coffee came in cups with painted horses on them. Hightower's palms made a smacking sound as he placed them on the table.

"Etta said to tell you all I know, which isn't much. The night you're asking about I was parked right here, Lorraine my wife where you're sitting. I had the laptop, looking at vacation rentals on the north shore of Kauai. The missus and I go every spring after calving. Hell, it was just a month ago we were there. With everything that's happened since, it seems a long time." He shook his head, then raised his eyes to Stranahan. "Life takes a hell of a turn, doesn't it?"

"It does."

"Well, like I said, an ordinary night. The next morning Etta came roaring down in her truck all worked up about Cindy, asked if she was here. We're standing on the porch and I look off and there's a truck parked out by the blacktop direction of Wilsall. Just a speck till I put binoculars on it. We drove down there and it was Landon's truck. I said, 'Etta, a dime takes a dollar they were driving down to the kid's folks' place for breakfast.' I thought they had hitched or hiked into town 'cause the spare was a flat, and we'd find them tucking into Donna's buckwheat pancakes. But they weren't there. You know all this if I'm not mistaken."

Stranahan nodded. "Was Landon working that last evening Cindy was seen? Etta said your arrangement was loose."

Hightower nodded. "Charlie or I gave him chores and he'd come over once or twice a week after school and on weekends, keep his own hours. He was a good kid. Used to be they was all good kids, but now you got no-accounts smoking weed and plinking gophers, pass it off as a day's labor."

"Did you know he was gay?"

"He wasn't swishy, but I wasn't surprised when it came out. It wasn't my business. But to answer your question, he did drive past that day. Onto the property, I mean. I assumed he was going up to the south end to put a new H brace on the fenceline, something I'd told him needed doing. I was driving back here at the same time and he tipped his hat, I tipped mine. That would have been about seven-thirty, give or take."

Stranahan had read about the brief encounter in Harold's report, but not if Hightower had heard the ranch hand drive back out later in the evening.

Hightower said he hadn't. "But you have to recall this was November, we had the place shut up and a fire going. About all I'd hear is snap, crackle, pop."

"And you don't remember any headlights coming back?"

"No, there's a rise in the road where you see lights, but we had the curtains drawn. The way I calculate it, he could have driven back out anytime between say eight or eight-thirty and seven in the a.m., and the only one would have known would be Patches here." He bent down to pat the head of a spaniel with liver-colored saddles that had materialized from some further recess of the house.

"Does Patches bark when a vehicle passes on the ranch road?"

"Only if she doesn't know the engine. This old girl can tell the difference between a 2.6-liter Mercury and the 3.1 at half a mile."

"What about someone on foot?"

He nodded. "If she was sitting in the window where she can see out, and that's something she does most nights, why she'd let us know."

"Did she bark that night?"

"She surely did. Woke me up." He rubbed the dog's ears. "Didn't you, girl?"

"Do you remember when?"

"Actually I do. It was two in the a.m. or thereabouts. I couldn't get back to sleep so I came out here and slipped in a DVD of Jack winning the Masters back in eighty-six. I could watch him play Amen Corner a hundred times over. But you're asking if it was a vehicle, and I can't say it was. It could have been a person. Or a bear. Or a cat more likely. We got a bobcat with two kits. Patches and that cat got a pissing match going on, spraying trees all up and down the creek."

He tucked his hands under his arms. "Isn't this sort of beside the point now? You got the one can answer your questions up at Deaconess. I heard it directly from Etta."

"It's a guess whether he'll come around again, at least in this world."

"What did he say when you found him?"

"Not much. He called Cinderella his chickadee."

"His chickadee." Hightower's voice had a bite of sarcasm. He smiled, but his eyes didn't smile, and Stranahan watched as the mask of hospitality dropped away, the jaw finding a set, the lips pursing out as the cheeks hollowed. The pupils were black as obsidian, a hard glitter from deep folds of flesh.

"I'm trying to read between the lines here and figure just what you're getting at. That I had something to do with what happened to Cindy, or I'm covering for somebody? 'Cause I'd sure consider that an insult. After all I done for Jasper and Etta."

"I know this isn't pleasant to talk about."

Hightower didn't appear to have heard. "I'm talking to you in my own house as a courtesy to Etta and because it would be a good thing all around to put some closure on this thing. I loved that girl of hers. She could make the sun come up in the morning."

"I understand."

"I'm not sure you do."

"Mr. Hightower, sometimes you can't find out who is behind someone's death until you eliminate who isn't. If you're so certain no one at the ranch knows anything that could help, then who does?"

"You don't think I haven't asked myself that? I'm watching a good woman go to pieces and there isn't a damned thing I can do about it. No sir." He blinked and Stranahan saw that his eyes were shiny. The hard jaw began to crumble. "Go on now. I'm sorry getting hot like that. You keep asking your questions. You find out who done this."

Stranahan rose, then stopped himself as he caught sight of the dog lying under the table. "Mr. Hightower—"

"It's Earl."

"Earl. On the night that someone cut the tails off the horses, did Patches bark?"

"No, she didn't. I asked myself that, and I'm pretty darned sure she didn't. Etta said the dogs up there didn't bark, either. That's what got that detective thinking it was an inside job, and I see the logic, only there wasn't anybody inside, myself and Charlie excepted, and we'd both left the stables by seven o'clock. It really doesn't matter anymore. You have to wonder, what does?"

Stranahan left a half a cup of coffee on the table and Hightower shaking his head about what mattered, looked up from the porch to see the rooster spinning, the wind having picked up as it does as the day warms, and drove to the stables to see a horse born at a civilized hour.

Etta waved to Sean from the entrance to the stables and led him to an empty stall, where she sat on clean straw with her back to the wall, her head tipped back, hat brim hiding her eyes, a stick of straw in her teeth. Her jeans were pulled down over the cowboy boots with the rose stitching.

"You look like the woman who kicked out the stars," Stranahan said.

A halfhearted smile. "Was Earl any help?" She breathed deeply. "God, I'm tired."

"I'm not sure. Probably not."

"I could have told you that. Charlie won't be, either."

"I'd still like to talk to him."

"This isn't a good time. The mare won't accept anyone she doesn't know in the stall. Plus she's a maiden, so it's new to her. She doesn't really even want Charlie there."

"What about the vet?"

"He'll stay hunched in the corner. The only way he'll come out from under his hat is if it's absolutely necessary."

"How will you know when it's time?"

She pulled the walkie-talkie from her belt holster as it crackled. A low voice: "She just broke." Etta stood up and dusted the straw off her pants. "You can watch. But you have to be quiet."

She led the way to a stall where a stepladder was unfolded. "Just high enough to peek over," she whispered.

"What about you?"

"I've seen a lot of horses born. I'll sit this one out."

Climbing the ladder and peering over the divider, Sean saw a chestnut mare lying on a bed of hay. Her tail was wrapped and her rear legs were shiny with amniotic fluid from the rupture of the placental sac. The mare nickered. After a few minutes, she rolled onto her belly and struggled up, standing with her head down. The two men who were sitting with their backs to the foaling stall didn't move. The mare looked back at her side and nipped at it. Time passed and she lay back down. Her eyes were large and brown and, to Stranahan, seemed surprisingly calm. Charles Watt lifted his chin and met Stranahan's eyes in a tacit acknowledgment of his presence. Stranahan pumped his feet on the rungs of the ladder to keep the blood circulating. A whitish sac began to protrude from the mare's vulva. Inside the sac, Stranahan could see a hoof with a few inches of leg behind it. A second hoof showed, the sac elongating as more of the legs emerged. Each time the mare pushed, her ribs collapsed and there was a shiver of her hindquarters. Minutes passed, the mare occasionally lifting her head off the straw to look back along the spine of her body.

Stranahan saw the vet nod. Charles Watt unsnapped his shirt and peeled it off. Dewlaps of flesh hung over the waist of his jeans, but the rest of his upper body was muscle and sinew. A ruff of reddish hair whorled around his pectoral muscles and hung in a wispy thatch under each arm. A stripe of light gray hair ran up between the pectorals to flower at his throat. He washed his arms in a liquid poured from a plastic bottle, then toweled them dry.

Moving slowly, Watt knelt behind the mare and used scissors to cut through the viscous sac covering the foal's forelegs. He reached behind him for a towel the vet extended. He wrapped the towel around the two hooves, then pulled the legs down toward the mare's hooves. The foal's head emerged, then, with gentle but firm coaxing, the shoulders. Watt let the mare rest, then pulled again, the hindquarters emerging with a soft plopping sound. With only the rear legs of the foal still inside the mare's body, Watt crabbed backwards and sat beside the vet. Stranahan watched the foal turn so that its chest was against the straw. The rest of the saclike material broke, spilling more clear liquid. The foal's ears flopped like limp rags as it struggled to breathe. Sean saw the vet tap his watch. Watt moved forward again. He pinched one of the foal's nostrils, took a deep breath, and exhaled into the other nostril. The foal jerked its head and started breathing.

Stranahan felt a tapping on the ladder. It was Etta motioning him down. She asked what was happening and he told her, matching her whisper.

"They'll rest like that a while," she said. "It's important that the umbilical's intact because it's still bringing blood into the foal. When the mare stands up, the umbilical will break and it will be over. We'll have had a successful birth."

But when Stranahan climbed back up the ladder, it was neither over nor was it beginning. The sensation of standing without being connected to earth, and which was not a function of the ladder but of his own excitement, that had started when Charles Watt shrugged his shirt off, was unchanged. It remained unchanged even after the foal staggered to its knees, lurched, and crumpled back to the ground. It was only after Watt had painted the raw navel of the foal in an iodine solution and put his shirt back on, covering up the tattoo of a face on his upper right arm, that Sean felt the swimming sensation in his veins abate and his body settle slowly to earth.

CHAPTER TWENTY-THREE

Seven Crows a Secret

The trainer was cordial enough after the birth. Stranahan trailed him as he walked with the veterinarian the length of the stables. Watt said, "Phew," doffing his railroader's cap and wiping it over his brow, shook hands with the older man, whose crow's feet made a pattern like a river delta at each temple, and then, after the vet had driven away, offered Stranahan a smile and a wink.

"Anytime you have to go mouth to nose, it makes the ticker skip a beat," he said, patting his pocket for a cigarette. He lit the cigarette, his cupped hand shaking as he held the match, and dragged deeply.

"What happens now?"

"When the colt stands up, Etta will guide him to the teat. Me, I'm going to hit the hay. I've been in that stall all day and half of last night, ever since Trudy's nipples waxed up." He flicked the ash of his cigarette. "I heard about that mountain man fella. Wouldn't want to be in his position, no sir." He drew on the cigarette and the smoke snaked out of his mouth with a hissing sound. "No, I would not want to be that man in this valley. That was a beloved young woman."

He faced away from Stranahan as he spoke, and Sean didn't know what to make of it. Was he trying to deflect attention from himself? But then why would he think he needed to? He was difficult to read.

The tattoo wasn't. That the inked face on Charles Watt's arm was the same tattoo he'd seen on the masked man in the Mile and a Half High Club video, he had no doubt. Not because of its detail. The image in the video had been too blurred to identify, and in the birthing stall he'd been too far away for Sean to identify his tattoo as a match, even if the resolution had been sharp. But it was a similar size and in the same location as that tattoo, and the skunk stripe of chest hair was all Sean needed for confirmation. To this point the coincidence of Cinderella's death occurring in the cabin where members of a sex club held their lurid "assignations" was just that, a coincidence. Strange but true, but then that was life. And Charles Watt being a member of the Mile and a Half High Club? It really wasn't any stranger than anyone else being in the club.

No, what had raised the hair on Sean's forearms was the tattoo. Even from ten feet away, it was clear to Sean that the face was that of a clown. A painted face with sad fat lips and carroty patches of hair. There had been letters inked in a banner underneath the face, perhaps a name, though the script was too small to read from Sean's vantage on the ladder.

THE CLOWNS ARE HERE

Sean said the words to himself, the words that had been scrawled in dying ink on the open page of the guestbook at the cabin. Cinderella's words, as he had assumed when he'd shown the page to Martha.

THE CLOWNS ARE HERE

Had she meant Charles Watt? And if so, who else? He decided to take a shot in the dark.

"We'll have the paternity test back in a couple days. If it turns out the mountain man didn't get Cinderella pregnant, the focus will shift to finding who did."

The information about Cinderella's pregnancy had not been made public, and Stranahan watched as Watt brought the cigarette to his lips. The hand was steady enough but his lips tremored. Watt spat the cigarette and ground it out with his heel.

"I didn't think that whippersnapper had it in him," he said under his breath.

"If you're speaking of Anker, he didn't. His sister provided DNA for a paternity test. It wasn't him."

"Then I'm afraid I can't help you." When he spoke again his voice had lost its drawl. "That girl wasn't herself since Casper. She had a scratch to itch she might have itched it with anyone swung a dick. I'd be looking at her schoolmates, that rodeo crowd she hung with. I'm sure Etta could draw you a list."

"That's an idea. I'll do that."

"So correct me if I'm wrong, but if it isn't this McKutchen fella and you come up with someone you suspect, you can't just ask him to spit in a cup, or can you?"

"You can ask anything you want, but no, you can't force him to provide a sample unless there's corroborating evidence. Then you can get a court order." Stranahan was talking off the top of his head. He had no idea if you could obtain a court order for genetic testing without first making an arrest. "But if someone says no," he continued, "that's as good as an admission of guilt. The next step is to try to tie that person to Cinderella or to the location of her death. If the sex wasn't consensual, it's reasonable to assume that Cinderella was running from the responsible party. That's the sheriff's thinking and I agree. If that led to her getting stuck in the chimney, even though months passed between the two events, then there could be serious charges."

Watt's eyes had become remote. "Mebbe she knew she was knocked up and didn't want to face the music. That's why she skedaddled." Again he patted at his shirt pocket, but it was a nervous gesture and he wasn't reaching for a cigarette.

Stranahan let the moment stretch, watched the man not meet his eyes. "Cinderella kept a journal," he said. "It wasn't on her when she died. We're going to go back up tomorrow and look through the cabin for it, and who knows what we'll find. Did you ever see her writing, maybe when she was in Snapdragon's stall?"

"No, I can't say I did."

Stranahan handed Watt one of his cards. "Call if you remember anything that could help."

Watt accepted the card without comment.

"Thanks for your time," Sean said. "It was fascinating, watching that colt be born."

Watt nodded. "That was an easy one, you don't mind blowing the snot out of a horse's nose."

They had shaken hands and Sean, having put the worm on the hook as he would tell Ettinger an hour and a half later, turned away, feeling the whisperer's eyes on his back. It took him twenty minutes to drive into Wilsall and pick up a bar of reception to leave Martha a message. It took another twenty before she returned his call and a few more to sketch in his suspicions. The sun was two fingers from the horizon when she drove to the rendezvous point at the Shields River bridge, a grudging smile on her lips as Sean's sheltie bounded to greet her, the shadow of its tail slicing like a scythe through the gold of the grasses.

"Why the suspense?" she said.

"Because if I tried to explain it over the phone, you'd just raise your eyebrows like you are now."

"I drove my truck. I brought my gun case. I've got the geocache like you said. Talk."

She stood with her hips cocked, sliding her lips over each other as he related the events of the past couple hours. When he wound down, she brought out her ChapStick. "Goddamned dry air," she said. "You'd think I've been necking with my paramour, and the only loving I get is from a dog." She gave Stranahan a reproving look. Making light to ease the discomfort.

"You didn't get the DNA workup on McKutchen yet, did you?"

She shook her head. "Wilkerson says tonight, tomorrow for sure—that's if it's not a match. If the graphs show similarities, it will require more tests to confirm. So what makes you sure Charles Watt fathered the child?"

"I'm not. But he was alone with her in the stables on a regular basis. He was in a sex club whose members met in the cabin where she died. '*THE CLOWNS ARE HERE.*' It seems pretty likely to me that he's the clown, one of them. Did you find that pen to see if her fingerprints are on it?"

"No pen. And we checked Watt out last fall. He has an arrest record for assault, but that was in his rodeo days. No marks on his permanent record, certainly no sexual offenses."

"Even so. If he goes back up there, he's trying to cover something up. You can catch him in the act."

"Of what, crossing a Caution ribbon?"

"Removing evidence from the scene of a suspicious death. I figure the least he'll do is take the camera card in the geocache. As far as he knows, he and the woman he was with were the last couple from the club to have been there."

"But we took the card."

"He won't know that. I have one just like it in my camera."

"That's entrapment."

"All I told him was I was going back to the cabin to look for Cinderella's diary. It's the truth."

"Are you going to tell me your plan, or do I have to guess?"

———

By nightfall the pieces were in place. Ettinger's unmarked truck was parked at the access a hundred yards from the forest cabin. Her unzipped gun case was in plain sight on the passenger seat. The note on the windshield was penned in felt marker.

> *To Whom It Concerns (that means you, Jen),*
> *I'm backpacked up the South Fork, back on Saturday. If not, then I have a bear down and will be packing hide and meat.* <u>*DO NOT*</u> *call Search and Rescue like you did last time!*
> *Love, Dan*

The note had been Ettinger's contribution. It was just quirky enough to read true and ought to satisfy Watt if he was alarmed to find a truck at the trailhead. The empty gun case added authenticity as well.

They had mulled over the idea of removing the combination lock to the cabin door, finally deciding that it would be more damning if Watt broke in through a window. Watt had been exhausted after staying up with the mare and Sean thought it likely he would do as he'd said he'd do, drive home to his place first to get a few hours' sleep. But there was also the possibility that he would be too anxious to sleep. In the one case, their wait would be long, in the other, short. But if he was coming at all it would have to be tonight, under the cover of darkness. He couldn't take the chance that Sean would search the cabin when it grew light.

"We should have picked up a pizza," Sean said. He hugged the arms of his heavy wool shirt.

"We should have our heads examined, is what we should do." Martha had brought a horse blanket and spread it over their thighs. She nudged her shoulder against Sean for the extra warmth and then seemed to think better of it, patting the blanket for the dog to lie down between them.

From the forest's edge they had a clear view of the cabin, the pond below it mirroring the clouds and the sweep of escarpment falling away toward the blacktop of the Shields River Road. Ettinger offered Stranahan a piece of gum and they chewed in silence. Sean watched a crow with a stick in its beak fly to the roof of the cabin. It disappeared with the stick into the flue. A moment later a flock of crows alighted on the gnarled branches of an aspen snag, jockeying for position amid a flurry of curses. Their hierarchy sorted, the crows brooded silently, as black as ebony statuettes. Sean glanced at Martha, who raised her eyes. Then, as if by common consent, the crows took wing, the one that had disappeared in the chimney cawing after them, taking the day with them, leaving only the funereal smear of the twilight.

"In England they call it a murder of crows," Martha said.

"Do you figure that's the same crow that pecked out her eyes?"

Martha chewed. "When I interviewed the guy who found the body, your buddy Smither, or Gallagher, or whoever he is, he told me this counting crows rhyme. I hadn't cleared him at that point, so I looked it up to see if he was messing with me. It's Old English, goes, give me a second." She spit her gum into a tissue and folded it into her pocket. " 'One crow sorrow, two crows mirth, three crows a wedding, four crows a birth. Five crows silver, six crows gold, seven crows a secret never to be told.' How many crows did you count?"

"I didn't."

"There were six in the tree, the one in the chimney makes seven. That's what I'm afraid this is"—she waved her hand—"this poor girl's tragedy. It's a story that will never be told."

Another piece of gum and an hour later, any pretense of physical autonomy had dissolved. Stranahan had his arm around Martha's shoulder and Martha's head was buried against his neck. Sean remembered the first time they had become entwined to keep from shivering. It had been during a manhunt in the Madison Range, a hundred or more miles to the south.

"Remember when we sat under a tree like this, up Beaver Creek?"

"I remember."

"That's the first time I wanted to kiss you."

"Yeah, right."

"No. I'm telling the truth. Makes me want to kiss you right now."

"Be serious."

"We could make out. Stay warm and help pass the time."

"Forty-year-old women don't make out. And you're involved with that one-armed truck salesman anyway, aren't you?"

"If you mean Etta Huntington, not really."

"What kind of answer is that?"

"The only one you're going to get. You left me, it wasn't the other way around, if you remember."

"Yes, I did."

She sighed, her shoulders slumping as Stranahan worked his fingers into the muscles at the back of her neck.

"Come on, one for old time's sake."

"No." But she was looking at him, their faces a foot apart.

He lifted her chin and she turned her head away.

"All right, just one."

"You can do better than that."

She did, her lips warm and her mouth tasting of mint, then abruptly broke it off.

"This is not happening. It's ridiculous. I'm the sheriff of Hyalite County."

"Hold that thought, Martha. We have company."

The headlights that had veered from the river road swept rows of wheat, then ghost snarls of sage as the access road dipped and rose. Where the road turned along the foot of a hill, the cones disappeared and only a milky haze betrayed the rig's progress. Sean felt Martha's hand tighten on his arm.

The truck—they could identify its silhouette when it appeared beside the pond—ground in a lower gear. It drew alongside Ettinger's T100 and stopped, the motor idling. A figure stepped out. In the lens of Stranahan's binoculars, the figure was discernibly that of a man wearing a Kromer-style cap, tall or perhaps only angular and spare. The man was holding a flashlight and moved to Ettinger's truck, shining the beam.

"What's he doing?" Martha said.

"He has his hand on the hood, probably checking to see if it's warm. We've been here how long, a couple hours, it should be cold."

"That V6 block is cast iron. It stays warm a long time."

"You're a pessimist, Martha."

"Now what's he up to?"

"He's got the light on the note."

The figure moved back to the truck and the truck crawled up the road and stopped with the headlights illuminating the cabin. The man walked to the door. A pause. The door opened and a light shone inside. Then he walked back and shut off the truck. He let himself into the cabin.

"I thought you said they changed the combination," Sean said.

"That's what the woman I spoke to at the office told me. Once a month."

"I wonder how he got the new combination?"

She ignored the question. "Ready?"

Sean patted the bear spray on his belt holster.

"I can sign off on a concealed-carry permit for you," Martha said.

"I don't want to wear a gun."

"Just don't spray that thing in my direction. Will Choti stay here?"

"If I tell her to."

Angling toward the cabin, they kept to the treeline, then strode quickly across the open ground, the patchy snow crunching but not a thing to do about it. They were at the east wall, where the ladder stood against the roof shingles. Martha's breath made puffs that ascended the rungs. She held up a finger as a light appeared in the window of the cabin, then moved away. A glance at the truck. Martha raised her eyes. Sean shook his head. He didn't recognize it. Martha made a fist. Sean nodded and stepped onto the porch, making as little noise as possible. He was cocking his hand to bang on the door when they heard the voice.

"From where the sun now stands, I will fight no more forever. I surrender."

Sean opened the door and saw Harold Little Feather sitting in one of the cabin's four chairs. He raised his palms. His revolver rested on the scarred wood of the tabletop.

"Jesus, Harold, what the hell?" Martha replaced her Ruger in the holster.

"The note was a nice touch," Harold said.

"That isn't your truck outside."

"My sister's. Mine's up on the blocks, got to swap out a U-joint."

"Walt tell you where to find us?"

"Walt told me."

"Then you know why we're here."

He nodded. "The man I believe you're waiting for isn't coming." He struck a match on his thumbnail. "Not tonight." He moved the match to a candle sticking out of a Mateus wine bottle. "Not unless he starts breathing again."

CHAPTER TWENTY-FOUR

The Dog in the Nighttime

Charles Watt's house was a ramshackle affair, ranch style if you had to put a name to it, with a clapboard addition thrown up and smoke curling out of a masonry chimney. About a mile off the Brackett Creek Road on a two-track, tucked into the pines.

"House smells like a den of dead snakes," Walter Hess said by way of greeting. "Inside is a sty."

"That's the XY chromosome working for you," Martha said. "Harold, why don't you see what's to be seen on the premises." She inclined her head toward Walt. "Let's have a look at the body."

"What about me?" Sean said.

"You can do the sketch. Harold ought to have forms in his truck."

Martha tapped her foot for the minute it took him to find the pad, and then Walt led them around the house to a woodshed made of bleached-out boards.

"What the hell's it roofed with, license plates?" Martha said.

"Yup. I saw one dating to '47. He's tucked back in the corner there, behind the cordwood."

Martha put her hands on her knees to get a perspective. "I'd say he's dead all right." The body looked misshapen, the mouth an obscene oval with the tongue protruding. The loose jowls and the upper part of the exposed neck were a blotchy purple-brown.

"Dog was guarding the body when I got here, lifting his hackles at me. Two fingers to the carotid and called it in. Hanson's on his way. I roused Wilkerson. She's going to hitch in with Doc."

"Doc, huh? Doc hasn't been to a crime scene in over a year, now that we got a pathologist on call."

"Didn't you hear? Our dutifully elected death pronouncer had a near-death experience. Ash branch came down when he was backing out of his driveway. Sardined him in his Prius."

"Is he okay?"

"They had to use the Jaws of Life to pry off the lid. But he'll be fine. Don't you read the police reports?"

"That comic strip? No."

"I thought we needed a medical examiner. It was my call. I called it."

"You did good, Walt."

"I got the kids sitting in my truck, the little lying sacks of shit. You want to talk to them?"

"If we're done here, and I think we are. Harold's lead investigator. That's my call. I don't want to disturb the scene until we can put some better light on it and he can do his thing."

Walt nodded.

"Sean, you can stay, but no walking around. Got it?" She didn't wait for an answer.

The kids, brothers named Dumpfy, Paul the older, Peter the younger, had been staying with an aunt while their parents were back in Nebraska for a funeral. They'd told Walt they had been horn hunting.

"Like for sheds?" Martha said, after summoning them from the truck.

"Dropped antlers," the older brother said. He looked to be twelve or so, a rangy-looking kid with stringy black hair and a meager mustache. "You can get six dollars a pound when the Koreans come to town. They prop up their peckers with the soup."

Where do they learn to talk like that? Martha thought. Boys grew up so fast now, they scarcely had childhoods. "Straight from the tit to the whorehouse," as Walt put it. It made her think of David, who would arrive now in less than two weeks. So many regrets from her past, but not her sons, only the little she saw of them.

"So." She came back to the present. "Find any?"

"We found a mossy mule deer antler, but you can't get no money for it."

"How did you come across the body? Were you snooping around the house?"

"No, we never," the younger boy piped up. "We followed the dog."

"That's right," chimed in Paul. "He was nipping at our pants and running toward the house, and then when we didn't follow him, he did it again."

"Where did this happen?"

Both boys pointed to the crest of a ridge behind the house.

"Where's your aunt's place?"

"You got to hike down the road. You can't see it from here."

"So it was like Timmy and Lassie."

The boys looked at each other. "We don't know no Timmy or Lassie."

"Of course you don't."

There wasn't much more to get out of them. They'd seen the body from twenty feet and had never stepped a foot closer.

"I called out, 'Are you dead?' and he didn't answer," Paul said.

"And that's when you went into the house and used the phone to dial 911?"

"Yeah."

"Was the door opened or closed?"

"It was closed but it weren't locked."

"Didn't call your aunt first?"

"No. It's after dinner."

Paul the older looked at Peter the younger. Peter said, "She's in her cups after dinner."

Paul clarified. "That's what she calls being a pass-out drunk."

Martha cocked a finger at Stranahan's Land Cruiser and told the boys to wait there. She led Sean aside. "Like hell they were horn hunting. It was past dark when they called it in. They were looking for stuff to steal. Still, you got to give them credit for making up the story. Used to be you'd badge them and they'd pee their pants. Now they've all got attitude from watching TV." She told him to take their boot impressions and drive them home.

By the time Stranahan returned, the aunt having greeted him at the door with eyes as hard as shooter marbles—"the fuck you say" the first words out of her mouth, even before the slurred "whoareyou"—the crew was waiting for him to sketch the body. He fished the charcoal pencil from his shirt pocket and worked while Martha held a flashlight on the pad.

"I never could understand why they still want in-situ sketches," she said. "We have photos from every angle imaginable."

"It's because sketches are more accurate, especially with regard to dimension."

"Humpff."

When he'd finished, they carried the body to a bit of flat ground. Sean took the legs, Harold the arms, while Martha held the head from sagging. It wasn't much different than carrying a gutted deer from a pickup bed to hang it in a barn. That same dead slack weight. Walt had found a more or less clean sheet in the house and they laid the body on it, face up, then studiously avoided looking at it.

"Okay, while we're waiting you might as well tell us what you got?" Martha said.

"Contrary to popular opinion," Harold said, "I'm not one of those trackers who can follow a housecat over slide rock. There are some scuff marks, made with a rubber heel or maybe a cane with a rubber tip, but I didn't find a cane inside the house. Footprints"—he shook his head—"maybe when it's daylight, but the floorboards of the porch are a poor surface for impression and the ground is hard."

"Walt says there's blood on the porch."

"I was getting to that. You turn off your flashlights, I'll show you."

He flicked a Carnivore tracking light to its tracking mode, activating the red and blue LEDs that would highlight spots of blood, making them appear to levitate.

The crimson trail of blood drops led from the front door, down the steps of the porch, and then around the house toward the woodshed.

"I'm guessing the victim was inside and our perpetrator waited for him to open the door. The tails of the drops mark the direction of travel. Since there isn't any blood leaking from the vic, it's got to be from who grabbed him. He overpowered Watt on the porch and carried him back to the woodshed."

"Carried him?" Martha said. "Watt's not a small man."

"I would have noticed if he'd been dragged."

"How do you know he waited for Watt to come outside? Why couldn't he have been lying in wait before Watt drove up the drive and took him on the way in?"

"Because Watt had fired up the woodstove."

Martha mentally slapped herself for the question. She hated appearing dumb in front of Harold.

"So where was he killed?"

"There are three or four clusters of blood drops, indicating the person carrying Watt stopped. The one by the door I showed you, and there are other places en route to the shed. Hard to say exactly when the man expired."

"How about inside the house?"

"I'll let you see for yourself."

Walt's description of the place was an understatement. The floor was not a space so much as a network of trails between piles of refuse—magazines, pizza boxes, discarded clothing. Half a dozen ashtrays overflowed with butts. The dog, a sad-eyed beast of indiscriminate heritage, was cowering under the footrest of a recliner in front of a TV set.

"You don't look like Lassie to me," Martha said. She extended a hand and the dog let her scratch his ears.

Harold pointed to a pile of blankets near the fireplace. "You'll understand why he slept here when you see the bedroom. It's just feces and piss. He must lock the poor mutt up when he's gone."

Ettinger wrinkled her nose in response.

"Strange thing is," Harold said, "I was here twice last fall, first when I got the call for the horsehair thief and then when Cinderella disappeared. House was in order first visit. Man presented himself like a human being. Second time, the place was okay, him not so much. Seemed distracted. Jumpy eyes. In retrospect, maybe he was high."

"So what do you have to show us? I don't want to spend any more time in here than necessary."

"A couple things." He led them to a rolltop desk that looked incongruously patrician amid the chaos. One drawer was open and Harold stepped aside so they could see. Inside were a dozen corner-cut plastic bags, three secured by twist ties with what looked like sugar crystals inside. There were crumpled balls of tinfoil and what Walt identified as an insulin needle with the needle broken off.

"Meth head," Walt said. "A newbie. Only newbies smoke. Give him a couple more months and we'd find spoons and a syringe."

"If he isn't shooting, what's the needle for?" Martha said.

"It's called a keister feast'r. You dilute the crystals and use the insulin needle to inject the meth into your rectum. Mark my word, you'll find some lube in the bathroom."

"That's disgusting. I don't understand how people operate using this shit. Watt trained horses for half a dozen ranches." She shook her head. "How could a woman ever let a man like that touch her?" She was thinking of the video of the tryst in the cabin.

"Junkies wear ties to offices every day, Martha. Every day." Walt nodded.

"You said two things, Harold."

"It's in the addition."

He was turning that direction when Stranahan said, "He's the horsehair thief. That's what you found. Watt's the one who cut the tails off the horses."

Harold had stopped and now all eyes were turned to Sean.

"How did you know?" Harold said. "He's got a footlocker filled with it."

"Because the dog didn't bark in the nighttime."

"Say what?"

"It doesn't matter. Watt knew people who showed horses. They pay money for extensions. It was an inside job, just like you thought it was."

Walt tapped the back of his neck. "Man had to feed the monkey. It's your classic escalation. You go through your money, you steal the stuff close to home first, the safe stuff, then you park behind the 7-Eleven and pull on the ski mask."

"Well I'll be damned," Martha said.

A light swept across the windows, illuminating ceiling cobwebs.

"Here's Doc. That's Wilkerson's Subaru coming up the track."

———

First thing I'll make clear," Hanson said, "is that this isn't a proper surface for an examination. The body's been contaminated by direct transfer from the sheet. Couldn't you have found anything cleaner? We're going to need to run an extension from the house and hook up any lamps you can find that work. I'm not going to conduct an examination in the dark." He hadn't made eye contact with Ettinger since his arrival and she shook her head, a gesture he caught.

"Be a pro, Bob."

"What's that supposed to mean?"

"Help us out here. Please."

Harold had a bemused smile. "Worse than a couple nanas squabbling at a Lame Deer basketball game."

Georgeanne Wilkerson put on a cheerful face, helping with the positioning of the lighting—they found a stand-up lamp with a 60-watt bulb in the living room—and showing how the helpers were to hold their flashlights while Hanson conducted his examination. Hanson stood in resolute displeasure of the situation, then sighed and pulled on his latex gloves. He squatted, catcher-like, and began to pass his hands over the victim's limbs while speaking into a recorder. "Onset of rigor in the small muscles of the neck. Subpericardial petechiae in the eyelids, in the sclerae, and other parts of the face due to ruptures of the microvasculature."

"Tardieu spots," Wilkerson explained. "They can indicate death by asphyxiation."

"He was strangled?" Martha said.

She shook her head. "You would see ligature marks or contusions where the thumbs pressed. Palpation of the tissues might reveal crushing of the larynx or hyoid bone."

The medical examiner cleared his throat. "May I continue? I really don't appreciate you talking over the recording."

Wilkerson faced her hands in an *I back off* gesture.

Hanson continued his examination. "Intensive hypostatic congestion of the lower face and neck." He paused his recorder. "That's the purpling effect. It's caused by postmortem pooling of the blood, also indicative of asphyxia. I'm"—his mustache began to quiver—"I'm just an emotional old fart. I'm sorry, Gigi. Martha." He regarded them with watery eyes. "My only frustration is with myself."

He started to unbutton Watt's shirt, exposing the skunk stripe of chest hair. He pulled the shirttails out of the pants.

"Hell and tarnation," Walt said. "What's all that?"

"The ribs of the upper left quadrant are separated from the sternum. Evidence of compression with the left rib cage folded over the right upper chest quadrant, creating a linear bulge in the dermis. There's a scar of roughly three centimeters diameter on the lower right quadrant." He started to say something else and stopped. He turned off the recorder.

"I've never seen anything like this. Have you ever seen anything like this, Gigi?"

They all stared. The chest looked to have been cracked into two parts, with the left rib cage detached from the sternum and overlapping the right rib cage. In addition to this grotesque disfigurement, the abdomen was bulged and there was a ropy-looking lumping of the tissues.

"Looks like there's an alien under there." Walt gave a shudder. "I never did get over that movie. When that creature come a-poppin' out of that guy's stomach, I—"

"Walt, that's enough." Martha held up her hand.

"I'm just saying I per near lost the lunch."

"I saw something similar when I was in CSI school," Wilkerson said in her breathy voice. "A man was constricted by a Burmese python when he was trying to feed it a rabbit. It looked like he'd been sandwiched in a car crusher. Both shoulders separated, cracked rib cage, and so many Tardieu spots you'd think he had the chicken pox. Give you the heebie-jeebies."

"How big was the snake?" Walt said.

"Thirteen feet. It weighed about two hundred pounds."

Martha caught her lower lip in her teeth. "Not too many of them in these parts. If Bear Paw Bill wasn't in the hospital, I'd say this has his name written all over it. Who else could crush somebody like this?" She paused, the shoe dropping. "He *is* in the hospital. Walt, tell me he's in the hospital."

Walt walked back into the house to use the landline.

"Hey Hunt," they heard him say. "How's the mountain man doing tonight?" A long pause.

Martha lifted her eyes to the stars.

"No, I was out of the office . . . no, Judy didn't transfer. You should have called me directly."

"This is what you call the 'Oh shit' moment," Wilkerson said.

CHAPTER TWENTY-FIVE

Cowboy Poetry

What I want to know is how a three-hundred-pound man with half a leg walks out of a hospital and nobody notices? I'd like to ask Huntsinger to explain that to me."

"He's pretty embarrassed about it, Marth. He's got a touch of the stomach flu—"

"Don't they have cameras in those rooms?"

"Only in the emergency ward and ICU. McKutchen was moved to a standard room this afternoon. Like I was saying, Hunt had to drop a deuce but couldn't find the *Field & Stream* in the magazine rack. So he went up to the second floor to look and that's where he hit the head. Said he was gone fifteen minutes tops. When he came back, he took his seat outside the door. Didn't think anything of it for an hour or so when I guess it crept up on him he couldn't hear the man snoring. A nurse was coming by to change the drip and they went into the room together. Man had pulled out his IV and his catheter and just plain vamoosed."

"Vamoosed?"

"They had crutches in the closet and they're gone. Hunt said all he'd have to do was hop about fifty feet of hall and turn into the fire escape staircase. Door's always unlocked. I wouldn't be too hard on Hunt. When he went off shift tonight we weren't going to have a guard posted, anyway."

"What did he do, hobble away?"

"Looks like he stole a vehicle. Hunt said an ER doc reported his

Explorer gone. Had a tricky ignition, so he just left his key in it twenty-four seven. Hunting rig. Locks were shot."

"You gotta love Montana," Martha said under her breath.

"Man was missing his left foot. I figure he drove with his crutch on the clutch. Yep, that'd be the way, all right." Walt kneaded his Adam's apple.

They had moved away from the body and Martha called over to Wilkerson.

"Gigi, you didn't by chance get the DNA results on McKutchen?" She raised her eyebrows to make the question.

"I just finished that up. The graphs aren't a match, not even close. He isn't the father."

"We seem to be having a lack of communication around here. Why didn't you tell me?"

"You had a full plate and I didn't see how it related to this. You guys don't keep me in the loop enough. I'm not trying to hijack your investigations."

"You're right. That's my fault."

"I had a look at the severed foot." Wilkerson widened her eyes, which were already magnified by the lenses of her glasses. "Like a size twenty-five. The puncture wound under the arch was through and through. That's where the gangrene spread from. I found iron particles inside the foot. I can't say if they're from the same source as the nail that broke off in Cindy Huntington's foot, but it's a very good chance."

Martha looked up to catch Sean's eyes. He met her expression, acknowledging the coincidence.

"What's up with all this?" Wilkerson said.

"I wish I knew. Go ahead back and help Doc. Make sure you swab the bastard."

"He's the one who did it to her, didn't he? This Watt guy," Wilkerson said.

"Yeah, he raped her." Martha's voice was flat. "Either that or he had leverage to make her do what he wanted."

When she was gone, Martha turned to Walt and Sean. "Harold, I want you to hear this, too." Harold switched off his tracking light.

"I think we all know what happened here. Bill McKutchen knew Charles Watt fathered Cinderella's baby. It doesn't matter how he knew but my guess is she told him. He stole a vehicle, drove up here, and revenged her. In his mind it was justifiable homicide. But this isn't case closed by a long shot, because we still don't know how she wound up in that chimney. Remember the story about the crows? Everybody recall that?"

She waited until they had nodded.

"Earlier tonight, Sean and I saw some crows at the cabin. It started me thinking about how the crow takes the eyes of the dead to heaven. And then the other part of it, when something so bad has happened the gods can't restore the soul and the crow has to fly back to earth to set matters straight. Well, I took a vow up there I was going to set matters straight. I'm going to be that crow. Harold, you're going to be that crow. You too, Sean. And you, Walt. We're all going to be that crow and we're going to find out what happened, so her soul can rest. Now let's help load the body for the morgue and get some sleep. Walt, why don't you run the crime tape while we're waiting for Doc's okay."

"Okay, Marth, but aren't we going to put out a BOLO on the vehicle?"

"Sure, Walt. Why don't you do that when you get back to the office."

"That won't be until nine in the morning."

"That's all right."

She looked from one face to the other.

Walt shook his head. "You start going down that road you never come back. He might be able to tell us what happened to her, you think of that? No, we gotta call it in. What he done might be jakey with the big guy up there, but we got to follow the law."

"Sure, Walt, you do what you have to. And while you're at it, you can take the dog home and drop it at animal services tomorrow." She turned and walked away.

"She's mighty loquacious tonight," he muttered.

"What's that, Walt?" Harold picked at his teeth with a stem of grass. "You learn a new word?"

"Yeah, it means voluble or garrulous. I'm thinking about becoming a cowboy poet and you got to know a lot of words to rhyme with things."

"But you're not a cowboy."

"That's what would give me the edge. You got to set yourself apart from the pack."

Sean left Walt and Harold to their discussion of poetry and rejoined Hanson. "Doc, can you cut the shirt on the upper right arm? He's got a tattoo I'd like to take a look at."

It was a sad clown, as he had remembered. Tears tracked down its cheeks. The banner read *Sarabell*.

Sarabell?

"Sounds like a clown name," Wilkerson said. "Does it have a meaning for you?"

"Some, not enough. How about a wallet?"

"I bagged it," Wilkerson said.

"What's the name?"

She looked through her notebook. "Charles Angus Watt. Age forty-seven. Hair brown. Eyes brown."

"How long will the DNA match take?"

"Three days."

"What about the blood?"

"You mean to determine if this is McKutchen's blood on the porch?"

Sean nodded.

"Two, if I push it."

He thanked her and found Martha standing by herself, away from the lights.

"I didn't intend to do that," she said without turning to face him. "I don't know what got into me."

"If you were trying to rally the troops, you did a good job of it."

"I meant it. Even the stuff about the crows. But who am I kidding? There's two people know what happened up there, and Cinderella's dead and Bill's in the wind. What do you make of the wounds, the both of them having iron in their feet? You think they both stepped on that bear window with the nails that Katie found? Cindy's wound hadn't turned to gangrene."

"Maybe they stepped on the same window, but her at a later time." Martha shook her head. "Still a lot of questions."

"We're going to solve this thing, Martha." Sean looked at the haloed moon. "So when you kissed me up there, you were thinking about crows, huh?"

"No." She crossed her arms over her chest. "Fool that I am, I was thinking about us."

CHAPTER TWENTY-SIX

The Kiss of Death

People fish for different reasons. They fish to shed the cataracts of age, to relive the thrill that was the dancing of a bobber as a sunfish nipped the worm and that thirty years later is harkened by the rising of a trout to a mayfly. They fish because a cast is a prayer for the believer and a hope for the heathen, and the more casts you make, the more likely your prayer will be answered or your hope be realized. And they fish because a fish is a miracle of nature, its fins as wondrous as the wings of a bird, and because you can touch the one but not the other.

Though he could not have expressed it if asked the question—and there was no one around to ask along the stretch of the Madison he drove to the next morning—what Sean Stranahan fished for were a series of moments. The wings of caddis flies pulsed over the river like dust motes in shafts of sunlight when Stranahan's imitation vanished in a swirl. That was one moment. Another came when the trout leapt, and a third when the leader tippet snapped. Stranahan waded to the bank and sat down, consoling himself with the thought that a fish lost is still a moment caught, for the hollow feeling that is counterpoint to the elation upon netting a fish remains an essential touchstone of the sport.

Or so he told himself. A trout will make a philosopher out of you, especially a big one.

Sarabell?

He whistled up Choti and said the name aloud as he dug his fingers into the fur of the dog's neck. "Sarabell." What he'd told Wilkerson was true. The name held no meaning and had given pause only because of its association with another word that rang in his memory—what was it? *Sherry?* No, not Sherry. *Shirley,* that was it. Shirley was the name that Charles Watt had told the librarian, Ariana, to call him on the night of their "assignation." When she'd said Shirley was a silly name, he'd said call me Gus. Gus made sense. The name on his driver's license read Charles Angus Watt.

But why tell her Shirley at all? Why not Sarabell, the name on his arm? Ari had said the members chose their own club names. Sarabell would have come to mind immediately, so why not choose it? For several days Sean had meant to stop in at the newspaper to have a look at the assignations as they appeared in the classifieds, if for no other reason than to satisfy a prurient curiosity. But perhaps they could shed some light.

He whistled again for Choti, who had strayed from his side and had her head down a gopher hole. Forty minutes later he pulled into the lot for the *Bridger Mountain Star,* which was housed in a brick building that had once served as a slaughterhouse. *"Where News Goes to Be Butchered,"* someone had tagged on the side of the building, and the *Star* had endured as the butt of the joke ever since. He found the receptionist painting her nails and said he wanted to look in the archives. The woman indicated the only other person Sean could see in the building.

"Talk to Gail Stocker."

Stocker, a petite woman with straight hair the color of brown sugar, had a phone to her ear, or rather a foot from her ear, when Stranahan stopped at her desk. She held up a pencil—*one minute*—as Stranahan listened to a muted tirade. The reporter rolled her eyes. "Anger issues." She mouthed the words, and brought the phone to her ear.

"With due respect, Congressman," she said, "I didn't say you were an asshole. I said that was something an asshole would say."

Sean heard the click as the party hung up.

"Asshole," the woman said. And looked up at him with slate-blue eyes. "What?"

She twirled the pencil in her fingers and shook her head. "We have a computerized databank, but only news and sports. We don't archive the classifieds. How far back are you interested?"

"February."

"Then we might still have the newspapers. We keep them for one year, but sometimes people want to buy back issues, so it isn't a complete set."

Ettinger had likened Stocker to a black widow spider, but, standing up, five feet no change, she didn't seem particularly black widowy. She shrugged into a double-breasted trench coat, belted it, put the pencil behind her ear, and led him to a room at the back of the building. The room was uninsulated, cold and dank. Metal files of newspapers stood against three walls. A fold-up table was unfolded against the fourth.

She switched on overhead track lights. "Do you know the date?"

"Ballpark."

"Do you know what part of the classifieds?"

"Personals."

"Still looking for that blonde who waved out the car window?"

"Something like that." Stranahan smiled.

"You're the private detective. It's Sean, isn't it? I interviewed you on the phone after Weldon Crawford got his brains splattered on Sphinx Mountain. I never heard back after the story came out."

"That's because you quoted me correctly."

"Is this about the mountain man? I tried to get to Ettinger after the press statement, but she won't return my calls."

"What makes you think I'd know anything about that?"

"She released the list of people on the search. You were named. So was Etta Huntington. She won't take my calls, either."

"They must have their reasons."

"Come on," Stocker said. "Just between you and me."

"Right."

"You're shaking your head. Does that mean yes?"

"No."

"This could be the start of a beautiful friendship."

Stranahan had to smile. "Tell you what. When the time comes, you're the first person I'll tell."

"You're as noncommittal as my almost ex-boyfriend."

"Best you're going to get."

When she'd left, Stranahan pulled out his notebook and found the notes he'd scribbled down after meeting Ariana. Her assignation with the masked man had been on Valentine's Day, February 14. She'd got the information from a classified ad, she'd told him, at the beginning of the month. Did that mean the first?

It did. The ad was in small type, no boldfaced letters or numbers.

> Love In Thin Air
> Shirley and Book Girl 41/2
> N" 74'6—64
> W" 71'82—011
> 2574
> Trapdoor

Stranahan penciled the information into his notebook, reversing the numbers to break the simple code for the GPS coordinates, the date of the assignation, and the lock combination to the door. He circled "Shirley" and put a question mark after it.

Ari had said that the man was physically "not as advertised," had called him a creep. That didn't sound like someone who would be admitted for membership in a club with the standards Ari had touted. It raised a question. Had Charles Watt stepped in for someone else, someone who called himself Shirley? If so, who was Shirley? He reshelved the newspaper, knowing, if nothing else, his next destination. Stocker was on the phone and spun the pencil around her ear. *Call me.* He gave her an agreeable smile, but his mind was down the road.

———

The detective's here. I'd almost lost faith in him."

Ariana Dimitri looked up from the checkout desk in the library.

Her hair was tied back in a ponytail, revealing earrings in the shape of handcuffs. Today's lips were pink, the eye shadow lavender, her scent rosewater. She made her mouth a heart and crossed her arms, lifting to deepen her cleavage.

"I had a few more questions."

"You're not here because you want to see me?" She looked down and away, then raised her eyes demurely.

"As much as I'd like—"

"As much as you'd like . . . what?"

"Ari, you're incorrigible."

"The man remembers my name."

A boy approached the desk, extending a book called *Slim Green*, with a green snake on the cover.

"Ooh," Ari said. "That's a classic. Do you have your library card?"

"You can't get one until you're twelve."

"Silly me." Her voice dropped to a whisper. "You just look so mature I forgot."

The boy's mother advanced with a stern look and Ari checked out the book to her.

"He has a crush on me but his mother doesn't approve." She looked after them. "Story of my life."

"Ari, he was eight."

"But he was so cute."

"Can we talk outside?"

"Okay, but it's your turn. I usually give Henry a couple dollars."

Stranahan fed the yawning guitar case as the homeless man looked up with rheumy eyes. "God bless," he said. They stopped at the same picnic table where they'd talked before.

"We've got to stop meeting like this." But the lilt was gone and she held his eyes, bracing for the unwanted question.

"Ari, that man you were with was Charles Watt. He was a horse trainer who worked at the Bar-4, where Cinderella Huntington lived. She's the girl who was found in the chimney."

Ari looked away. "You knew that when you came before and you didn't tell me. I had to find out on the TV. Shame on you."

"It was police business and I wasn't at liberty to say. Watt's middle name was Angus, that's why he told you to call him Gus. He was killed last night."

"Don't tell me you found him in a chimney."

"No. He was murdered at his home. Somebody squeezed the breath out of him."

She crossed her arms, but this time it was a defensive gesture. "God. My mother always told me I was the kiss of death."

"Ari, I need to know more about that night. You said the man wasn't 'as advertised.' What did you mean?"

She shuddered. "Okay, the deal is we all submit profiles. Amoretta mails out a list to everybody, your profile with your club name. She uses the profiles to match us up. So when she makes an assignation, you can link the name in the ad with your list and get an idea of the person you're supposed to meet—physical appearance, fetishes, that kind of stuff. That way you can back out if something about your partner isn't your cup of tea. You can put an ad in the paper saying you can't make it and she'll set up another assignation."

"So who was Shirley supposed to be?"

She curled tendrils of her hair around a forefinger. "It said he was a rancher and had worked on movies. Handsome, broad shoulders. Short, but 'not short where it counts.' That you take with a grain of salt, every man says he's well endowed." She unwound the hair. "What was important was he wasn't into anything rough, no BDSM for me, no thank you. But then this guy shows up and he's tall and he smokes. It's in my profile that I don't want to be with anybody who smokes. Amoretta's meticulous about that stuff. I mean a joint, okay. But she'd never set me up with a smoker. This guy . . ." She shook her head. "After we turned the camera off, he got rough. I don't mind rough when it's a kid who's so excited he wants to be everywhere at once, but it wasn't that kind of rough. It was holding you down so you can't move while he rams himself into you. He kept calling me 'a bad little girl,' telling me if I didn't want it why did I come on to him. I got scared, and I don't scare, but then afterwards it was okay, it was like he was contrite without exactly apologizing. He said he'd sleep in the main room and I could have the bunk room to myself. Told me he'd cook me breakfast, make eggs on the woodstove. I was trying to think how to get out of having sex again because it's sort of the point of being there, but after we had coffee the next morning he said he had to go work. He actually shook my hand. That's a first."

"Did you complain to Amoretta?"

She hesitated.

"Ari, if you know who Amoretta is, I really need to talk to her. Because that man you were with, we believe he raped Cinderella Huntington last fall and she ran away from him, that's why she was missing. I want to know whose place he took for your 'assignation,' who you were really supposed to meet."

"I told you, all I know is his club name. But why does that matter who it was supposed to be, if this other guy's the one responsible?"

It was a good question, one that he'd been turning over ever since he'd lost the trout. He thought he knew, and it wasn't a pleasant thought.

"Oh all right, I'll tell you who Amoretta is," Ari said. "Just don't tell her where you got it."

When she confessed the name, Stranahan shook his head. He ought to have known, or at least suspected.

"Now you owe me that 'or something' we talked about before," she said.

Stranahan was turning to go when she caught his arm and moved her face up to his, her lips pooching out, *I'm sad, aren't you going to kiss me?*—then lifting into a smile, *You will kiss me, you will.* She touched noses with him. "You don't get away with an Eskimo kiss, mister detective." It was as she brought her smile closer yet that he thought of a question.

"Ari," he murmured.

"Mm-hmm." She kissed his upper lip.

"Ari."

"Mm-hmm." She kissed his lower lip. "My you taste good."

"Ari." Firmly.

"Okay."

"Charles Watt had a tattoo of a clown. It said 'Sarabell.' Did he say what it meant?"

She took a deep breath and let her shoulders fall. *Poor unwanted me.* "It was his clown name. Back when he was in the rodeo. He told me he'd saved his friend's life by jumping in front of a bull and the bull got him in the stomach with its horn. He showed me the scar. When he got out of the hospital, his friend took him to a tattoo artist and they both got one, to make them blood brothers or something. I think he was trying to impress me, but I was on the side of the poor bull."

This time it was Stranahan who kissed her. She looked at him with drowning eyes and pressed against him. For a slight-looking thing, she was a lot of girl in his arms. It was with some reluctance that he extracted himself from the embrace.

"My my, it took awhile but I do think the man is coming around to my charms."

It wasn't that, but he left her with the victory.

CHAPTER TWENTY-SEVEN

Dom by Day, Sub by Night

Like many Montanans who live alone, Sean Stranahan did as much talking to his dog as to his fellow man. If Choti had had the faculty to understand English, she would have heard him say, "Jasper Fey, you son of a bitch," as he gunned the motor and drove away from the library. By the time he idled down to cross the bridge over the East Fork of the Gallatin River, Choti would have known her master's mind to the following extent.

That Jasper Fey was the man with the code name Shirley, Sean had no doubt. Fey was short and powerfully built, as his profile for the club had advertised, with bowed legs and broad shoulders; for that matter, he also had worked in film. If he rolled up his sleeve, Sean knew it would reveal a tattoo similar to the one on Watt's arm, only with *Shirley* in the banner. Why Charles Watt had taken Fey's place for his assignation with Ariana puzzled Sean, but there was a more disturbing question, having to do with the scribble found in the cabin's guest log. "THE CLOWNS ARE HERE." Could one of the men Cinderella was hiding from have been her stepfather?

"Happy families are all alike; every unhappy family is unhappy in its own way," Stranahan muttered. He told Choti to stay in the rig and prepared to do battle with the geese. This visit, he didn't bother knocking on the door of the house, but went around to the prefab building, scattering guinea fowl along the way. Under a low sky, the chimney puffed like a dragon.

He knocked, heard an unfamiliar voice say, "Come in," and went in. The woman standing before a brick furnace acknowledged his presence with upslanted eyes that had an obsidian, piercing quality, and were obscured several moments later when she brought her glasses to the bridge of her nose. She had pixie cut hair that was the dull, dry black of craft fur, wore heavy gloves and a canvas apron over khaki shorts and a T-shirt. She could not have been much taller than the iron pipe that she picked up from a rack of tools. For a second Sean braced himself—he had seen the rusted Suburban in the drive and knew the woman wielding the pipe was Eileen Barnes's lover, whose antipathy toward men Barnes had mentioned more than once. But the woman ignored Stranahan, and, turning her back to him, she extended one end of the pipe into a tunnel-shaped orifice in the furnace. The sleeves of her shirt were rolled up and the fine muscles of her shoulders squirmed as she dipped the pipe. Stranahan felt beads of sweat pop out on his forehead. It must have been a hundred degrees in the room.

"I know who you are," she said, when he offered his name. Her voice had a low register and an unplaceable, eastern European flavor, neither of which were congruous with her appearance. "Eileen will be here in a few minutes, yes. In the meantime you can make yourself useful. Put on those glasses on the bench." She waited until he had. "When I pull the pipe out of the glory hole, the end I'm holding will be hot, very hot. I want you to pick up that pail of water so I can dip it before the glassblowing commences." Stranahan followed her orders as she extracted the pipe, which was pregnant with a blob of substance that resembled molten lava.

"This is silicon oxide," she explained. "It's called the 'gather' and is heated at two thousand degrees Fahrenheit. Hot, yes?"

She cooled the end of the pipe in the water and brought her lips to it. A translucent bubble shivered to life at the end of the pipe. As the bubble enlarged, she took the pipe from her lips and waved it across her body in perpendicular arcs. The bubble elongated like a balloon. Again she brought her lips to the pipe, blew, and then, as she started to swing the pipe, swiveled sharply. Stranahan, recoiling, found himself on his back, pinned against the floor by a searing heat. He instinctively rolled his head to the side and heard a sizzling sound that, with horror, he realized was his hair singeing against his skull.

"You . . . fucking . . . pervert."

The woman hovering over him took on a monstrous shape, her hair a lion's black mane, her face shrinking, the features pulling together until Sean was seeing the head of a cobra. The slit of her mouth appeared to breathe with the very fire that she held against his head. The chimera began to waver, the blob of molten glass blinding Stranahan. He felt a searing pain, as if the safety glasses were melting against his temple.

"I'll cook the tongue out of your mouth first."

"Maria Teresa Vanaga!" The name was shouted.

The black mane shook. The heat still pulsed against Sean's head.

"Maria, don't." The voice was stern, measured. At the periphery of his vision, Stranahan could see a rectangle of light at the door, could feel more than see another person's presence.

"I told you he wouldn't be satisfied just to look. I said he'd be back. Didn't I? His eyes don't deserve to see." But even as the woman spoke, the heat was pulling away. A clang as the pipe was cast aside. Stranahan could see her clearly now, the reptilian intensity of her stare seeming to vibrate, then shrink away, leaving her face passive, her hair just hair. When she spoke next, it was a pleading in a much younger voice.

"Oh, I did wrong. I should have asked permission. But you wouldn't have said yes."

"Maria, we've had this conversation before. Go to the house."

As soon as the woman had gone, Stranahan stumbled out the door.

"There's mud in the tire ruts around back," he heard Eileen Barnes say.

Stranahan dropped to his knees and dug, bringing a cool handful of muck to the side of his head. The relief was almost instantaneous. By the time Barnes knelt at his side, his heart rate had subsided and he could no longer feel the artery pulsing in his neck.

"It feels worse than it looks," she said. "You lost some hair and got a bit of sunburn. We'll make a punk of you yet."

"I didn't see that coming."

"If it's a consolation, you're not the first to say that about Maria. Please don't press charges. You won't, will you? Maria's anger is not directed at you personally. She married a man from Latvia, where domestic violence toward women is common and condoned. He kicked her until she lost the child she was carrying, because that child was a girl. I don't want you to think—"

"I won't press charges." Stranahan sat back, holding the mud to his temple. "I thought you were the submissive," he said, and winced.

"I'm a dom by day, sub by night. It's not uncommon. A lot of career women who have responsibility can't just flip a switch at five o'clock. The only way to alleviate their stress is to submit. It's a form of release, letting someone else make the decisions. It's healthy, like meditation. A lot better than alcohol, which is the alternative. You can recharge the engines to face the next day."

"Well thank God for that . . . I guess." Stranahan's smile was thin, but he managed it.

"You were about a half minute from having your tongue burned out and already you can smile about it. Facing life with a sense of humor is an attractive quality in a man, or a woman. But why did you come without calling? Why are you here at all? I showed you the video, I told you all I know."

"I'm here . . . *Amoretta* . . . because you didn't."

He watched her expression segue from concern to hostility to embarrassment, and finally to resignation. She sat heavily beside him.

"It means 'little love.' But that's not why I chose it. My first lover said I smelled like almonds. I was her drink of Amoretto. I just changed the last letter." She brought a forefinger to the center of her chest. "Me, the farm girl who wore husky jeans. I would have told you if I thought it meant anything, but our club has nothing to do with what you were asking about. How did you know?"

"That the Mile and a Half High Club was your project? Call it an inspiration. You struck me as a leader, not a follower. I suspected. It was confirmed."

"By who?"

"By someone who realizes truth can be important. I'm not interested in revealing your secret. I'm here because you've got mixed up in something that goes beyond matching sex partners. Why did Jasper Fey have someone stand in for him for his date with Ariana Dimitri?"

"So it was Book Girl who told you. I thought she was more trustworthy."

"She was, she trusted you. But you set her up with a violent man, a man who probably raped a young woman. Last night, that man was murdered."

Barnes's face sagged. "How was I to know that? I'm very conscientious about assignations. I thought Jasper would be a good fit. I didn't know he'd send someone else. There's no room for abusive people in our club."

"You call her Book Girl, but you call him Jasper. Did you two know each other outside the club?"

"No. Well, yes. We met at a party. I'd been setting up assignations for a year or so, but location was always a problem until Jasper suggested the cabin. It was on forest land at the edge of his property and he knew the man who did the bookings. He'd reserve us the dates in advance, make sure we got Christmas and Valentine's Day, for special assignations. So the coordinates of the cabin and the geocache became an inside joke, because we always used the same place. Did he, Jasper . . . was he the one who killed that man?"

"No. We think we know who, but the name hasn't been released. I *will* tell you that it is related to Cinderella Huntington's death. Forgive me for asking an insulting question, but was she connected to your club in any way?"

"No. A thousand times no. Anybody who joins our club does so of free will. It's adults only. Book Girl's actually one of our younger members."

"I had to ask." He'd never glanced from her eyes and believed her. "Is there anything else you need? I do want to help."

"You have." He got to his feet, still holding the mud against the side of his head. "I must look like a zombie," he said.

"If you need to talk, I'll be here. But call first, okay?"

Stranahan lurched toward the Land Cruiser. "Tell Maria the lesson was very instructive." He stopped. "Satisfy my curiosity, Eileen. Why did you start the club? I understand someone like Ari joining up, but you don't strike me as being quite so . . . hormonal."

"Based on what, our long friendship?"

"Wasn't it you who said, 'What's time?' That you can look into the eyes of someone you've just met and read a story that person has never shared before. Isn't that just another way of looking for love?"

"Then you've answered your question. I was looking for, at least, affection. People think sex is a crude form of introduction. But I'd sooner start a relationship based on human touch than join an online dating service, which is what passes for intimacy today. You're right. I was hoping affection would lead to love, though I'm skeptical of the word. I think recognition is what we're looking for, our reflection in someone's eyes, someone who gets us. It's why some of us are in the club. Not most, but some. You'd be welcome to join us."

"I could be Scarface," he said.

She didn't offer a comeback and he climbed into the rig, the first drops of the rain splatting against the window, their tears streaking the dusty glass. "Time to see the unhappy family," he told Choti.

CHAPTER TWENTY-EIGHT

If Words Were Silver and Sentences Gold

What happened to your head?"

"I got too close to a glassblower's pipe. Is your husband home? There's something you need to sit down for."

"Oh no." She covered her mouth with her hand. "I . . . you found out." Her jaw began to quiver. "What happened that—"

"Part of the puzzle, Etta. I found out only part of it." He slapped his jacket against a rail to shake off the beads of rainwater.

"Jasper," he heard her call into the dark of the house.

They sat on the sofa facing Charlie Russell's sunset, a foot of tension between their bodies as Stranahan told them straight out that Charles Watt had been murdered, that the mountain man who had harbored their daughter over the winter was suspected, and that his probable motive was to revenge Cinderella by killing the man who sexually molested her. He said the crime lab would provide a DNA comparison with tissue taken from the fetus. They would know for certain if Watt was the father in three days.

"Have they caught him, this so-called mountain man?" Jasper Fey's voice was controlled, but his face had undergone a remarkable transformation since Stranahan's arrival. His smiling mask, firmly in place for the handshake, had vanished as he stepped back to minimize the height differential, the blood boiling to the surface, reddening his skin. At the mention of Charles Watt, his visage had turned to one of stunned disbelief. Then—it could not have taken a second—the blood drained, leaving a map of broken capillaries to color the right cheek. Stranahan had audited a class on reading faces at the police academy in Billings, and remembered that the reaction was a fight-or-flight response. When the body felt it was under threat or suffered great stress, the surface blood vessels constricted, reducing circulation to the skin as it pumped blood into the internal organs and heavy muscles, to prepare them for survival. Stranahan understood that Fey would be shocked to learn that his lifelong friend had violated his daughter, but even so, the reaction seemed extreme.

Fey broke the silence. "You think you know a person," he said. He started to speak again and then didn't, just sat shaking his head.

"He's also your horsehair thief," Stranahan said. "At least the horsehair was found in his house. And drug paraphernalia. We think he sold the hair to buy methamphetamine."

"That bastard." They were the first words Etta Huntington had uttered since sitting. "That fucking bastard. I wish I'd killed him myself."

"Now Etta—"

"Fuck you, Jasper Fey. Fuck you. I told you a hundred times there was something about him . . ."

She turned to Sean. "You never knew who he really was," she said. "He hid behind that leather face, give you a wink and that bullshit drawl, a fucking homily a minute. Sit through a dozen dinners but you didn't know him. But Jasper did. Drinking buddies, fighting buddies. *Whoring* buddies." She exhaled the words. "Yeah, they had rodeo groupies. Little cokehead cowgirls."

"Etta, the man saved my life."

"I wish he hadn't."

When Fey reached to touch her shoulder, she jumped to her feet. Her left hand grappled for a cup on the coffee table and she hurled it at the mantel. It bounced off the rock and fell to the Indian print rug, intact.

"Fucking worthless arm. I can't even break goddamned china." She stalked to the front door and slammed it behind her.

Fey sat with his head bowed. When he looked up, the color had returned to his face but he seemed to be very far away.

"I want to be mad at you," he said, his voice barely a whisper. "For bringing this calamity into my home I ought to just kick the shit out of you, but I'm all wrung out."

"It isn't me who's brought the calamity. It's you and it's your old butt buddy. I know about the club, Jasper."

Fey started to voice his objection, then just shook his head.

"What I don't know is why you had Charles Watt take your place. He was rough on that girl in the cabin. Or did you know that? But then why should he be any different with her than anyone else? Did he have some kind of hold over you, is that what it was, you paying him off in sex?"

"You don't know what you're talking about." He was looking at the picture on the wall, narrowing his eyes, as if assessing it at auction. "Old Charlie sure knew a sunset." He spoke softly, to himself, as if Stranahan wasn't in the room. "Back east, they have no idea."

Finally he looked over. "I'd ask you not to tell Etta. The club doesn't have a damned thing to do with Cinderella and all it will do is disturb her to no purpose. I loved my daughter. Whatever happens, happens. I'll let God be the judge of me. But I loved her." He looked at Stranahan. "Just get the hell out of my house before I shoot you for trespass."

———

She was standing at the side of the road, her hair stringing in the rain. Stranahan was at least a quarter mile from the house and he had only been a few minutes behind her; she must have run the entire distance. He stopped and pushed open the door and she climbed in, bringing in the cold, pulling Choti onto her lap and hugging the dog until she whimpered.

He let out the clutch. "Where to?"

"Go to the stables."

He started to turn the wheel, but she gripped his hand. "No, the second right." A hundred yards farther down she had him turn onto a two-track. She got the gate and they followed a road that headed north, then curled around to the back of the stables. "Park behind the tractor," she told him. She stepped out of the Land Cruiser. "I want to show you—"

She stopped. There was silence. Choti cocked her ears.

"That's Jasper's truck. He knows I go riding, that it's how I deal with stress. If he tries to stop me—he won't, but if he does—don't get all protective or anything. I'm my own woman. I can handle him." But the growl that drew even with the elevation of the stables began to fade.

"He's leaving," she said. "Wherever he's off to, he won't be back until midnight anyway. He'll just drive and talk to that little mutt of his. I'd say he'd go all the way to Pony if he hadn't been kicked out of the bar. He'll probably end up at the Cottonwood, playing poker. No, that's only on Tuesdays." She made a dismissive gesture. "Why am I even thinking about it? I don't care where he goes."

"He seemed pretty upset about Charles Watt."

"Yeah, more upset than hearing what he did to my daughter. That's Jasper all over." She turned her head toward the mountain backdrop behind the property, the peaks drowned in clouds.

"It will be turning to snow in the high country," she said. "We'll have to wear chaps."

———

If words were silver and sentences gold, Stranahan was still a poor man at eight thousand feet. He told Etta as much when they stopped to let the horses blow, having been climbing for more than an hour.

"What's that mean?" It was only the second time she'd spoken since helping him with a stirrup adjustment at the stables.

"Something my mother used to say about my father. He never met a stranger, but at home he could go hours between words. She called him the 'man of little comment.'"

Etta responded by clucking to her horse and another half hour passed and Stranahan was no richer.

The country they'd been climbing into was new country yet familiar, the trail following a creek bottom behind the stables into the upper acreage of the ranch, passing a graveyard of farm machinery, the rusty tines of a defunct rotary tiller looking like a dinosaur's spinal column, before entering Forest Service land and switchbacking up the sidewall of a canyon. Topping out, they stopped again, the ribs of the horses expanding like accordions as they blew great plumes of breath. A vista spread before them, its features blurred by the haze of snowfall, but showing peaks ahead and to the south. A dark crease marked the South Fork of the Shields River. Stranahan's eyes followed the crease to the feeder creek up which he and Martha had climbed to discover Bear Paw Bill's camp. Farther to the west was the bald ridge, at the foot of which, facing the valley, stood the cabin. Because the foothills fanned out between the ranch house and the cabin, the distance between the two points seemed considerable. But it was no more than a couple miles or so, at least as measured by the wing beats of an eagle.

Etta tied her horse to a stunted pine and shrugged into the straps of a daypack. From this point they followed a path made by mountain goats, where their hooves had chipped the rock a lighter color than the surrounding obsidian. To either side, the ridge fell away in a shoulder of scree, then into nothing at all. "Just keep your eyes on your boots," Etta said. "This isn't as bad as it looks. If you fell here, you wouldn't die."

"Oh? Which part of me wouldn't be dead?" Stranahan felt lightheaded and had the sensation that the ground was shifting under his feet.

He counted steps until they had crested out onto a windswept expanse of rock, from which they could look east all the way to the prairie. Directly in front and about six hundred feet below was a small lake, dropped like a pearl from heaven, with a thread of silver creek running from the outlet. Stranahan knew where they were now but decided to let Etta tell him her way, in her time. They switchbacked down to the shore, where they sat down after scraping the snow skiff off a flat rock. Choti had negotiated the precipitous terrain without a whimper or false step and started chasing after a marmot that scolded from a rock. Sean called her back.

"I recognized this place when I saw the documentary," Etta said. "Or at least I knew that I'd seen it before, but I didn't put it together with the lake until the night you found Bear Paw Bill. It's the closest lake to his camp; it wouldn't have taken them more than an hour to climb to the ridge behind us."

Stranahan nodded. "Cindy must have shot the video from the headwall." His eyes swept the semicircle of exposed rock that cupped the basin. The cliff faces were sheer, with a band of rock scree near the top, and pocked with caves. "Have you climbed up there?"

"No, it would be pretty hard with one arm. Anyway, I'm more interested in what she contemplated—I guess that's the word. I've never been on a vision quest, but I've read about them. They say that when you focus on country for a long time, it releases endorphins. You become euphoric. My feeling is that no matter what Charlie did to her, she found a kind of bliss looking down at this lake. I hope she thought of me when she was up here. I know in my heart she would have returned to me, that that's what she was doing when . . . when it happened. Now, at least, I've found a place to scatter her ashes."

"Is that what's in your pack?"

"Yes. It's all that remains of her except what's in here." She fingered a silver and turquoise locket from the front of her shirt. "I have the ashes of all my children in this locket."

"Why did you bring me here, Etta?"

"Because I shared her star with you." She was silent a beat. "People have always made up their minds before meeting me. It's been a curse, like the curse of being betrayed by your body when you think you're bringing life into the world. But at least I had Cinderella for a little while. I'm sure you were warned about me, the madwoman of the Crazies, the second coming of that particular legend. But I'm just a mother who lost her children. All I ever wanted to do was ride horses and be a mother. That's all I ever wanted to do."

Stranahan didn't know what to say and they sat in silence, watching the riffles skate in the breeze. His sweat had dried and he buttoned his jacket.

"Would you mind terribly if I was alone?" Etta said. "I have some things to say to my daughter before I let her go." She took a plastic bag out of her pack and walked the shoreline toward the outlet of the lake. Sean turned his head the other way to respect her privacy.

When she returned, Stranahan was examining the caves in the headwall with a pair of binoculars.

"What part of me would be alive if I fell trying to climb up there?" He said it to coax a smile, but she took the question seriously.

"Only your soul," she said.

PART FOUR

THE FLIGHT OF THE CHICKADEE

CHAPTER TWENTY-NINE

The Cave

Rainbow Sam didn't like the look of it.

"If you took a piss off here it would evaporate before hitting the ground," he said. "You'd have time to say the Lord's Prayer before Saint Peter sent you to hell. Explain to me again why I agreed to haul my ass up here."

"Because you're going to hold the rope while I climb down to the cave."

"Why does it have to be this cave?"

"Like I told you, Cinderella said she wanted to go on a vision quest in a cave, and I'm about ninety percent sure this is where she was standing when she said it. Unless this fire ring was made by someone else"—he pointed to a ring of blackened stones—"this is the spot. There's a cave below the lip of the cliff. We can't see it but it's there, I saw it from the lake. It's the only one on the rock face that looked big enough to sit in. Ergo, as you like to say, vision quest."

"So what if it is? What do you expect to find?"

"Last night you said you'd help, no need for explanation."

"Me and my big fucking mouth. All right, buckle your ass into the harness."

It was the harness that had made Stranahan think of Sam in the first place. Sean had noticed it once—it hung in Sam's mudroom—and inquired about the straps, which looked like something you'd shackle onto a prisoner. Sam had told him the harness was for tree stand hunters. It was designed to distribute the weight if the hunter fell. "It's so you can dangle without your nuts turning blue." The remark was pure Sam, and Sean had remembered it when riding out of the mountains with Etta Huntington.

Sean buckled into the harness while Sam attached one end of a climbing rope to a tree growing on the crest of the headwall. He made two loops around a second tree and knotted the other end to a carabiner on the back of the harness. He'd pay out rope as Sean needed it, keeping the rope no longer than necessary by adjusting the turns on the second tree.

Sean stepped into a rift in the cliff. The vertical fissure in the rock was what he'd heard mountaineers call a chimney, and the irony of the word brought a grim smile to his lips. But the descent, while terrifying, was not as arduous as he'd expected, as he pressed his back against one side of the rock cleft and his boots against the other, inching down by alternating points of pressure. Twenty feet below, the chimney ended in a cul-de-sac, and from this point a ledge worked around toward the mouth of the cave, which he could now see was splattered white with bird droppings. The ledge was a couple feet wide and would have offered secure footing if it hadn't been for patches of old snow in the shaded depressions. Stranahan had started to edge along it when the rope tugged at his back.

"Pay me out a little more," he called up to Sam.

"You got it," he heard Sam say, but the rope remained taut. Sean realized that it must have wedged in the chimney. He could go back and try to free it, or he could unbuckle the harness and proceed without it. The cave looked to be only another twenty feet or so along the ledge.

"Is that enough?" he heard Sam call.

"The rope's caught. I'm unbuckling the harness. Tell Mother I died game."

"You sure?"

"Just stand by." Sean unbuckled the harness and took a step, then another. He began to breathe easier. It really wasn't so bad, as long as you didn't place too high a value on your life. Then he saw the track in the snow patch. There was only one, the pad and toes forming a circular impression the size of a tea saucer. The track was slightly distorted by the thawing and refreezing of the snow. Stranahan guessed it was a couple days old, though that was small comfort. A mountain lion might well rest up for several days after making a kill, and what better retreat than a cave on the face of a cliff? *If it isn't one thing . . .*

"Nice kitty," he said.

From above, he heard Sam's faint voice and ignored it.

"Good kittycat."

It occurred to him that if the lion really was in the cave, he was blocking its only line of retreat. This wasn't going to end well.

"Do you hear me?"

But there was only the wind for an answer, and a few moments later he'd reached the cave and ducked inside. The cave was not quite tall enough to stand in and he instinctively scuttled toward the back of the recess and sat down with his back to the rock wall. For several minutes he did nothing but listen to his breathing, amplified by the cave's acoustics, while waiting for his heart rate to dial down and his eyes to adjust to the darkness. Spread before the cave mouth were the wind-bleached teeth of the Crazy Mountains, with mantles of spring snow and crooked rivers of evergreens running under the peaks.

Stranahan kneed forward until he could look down at the lake. Yes, this must have been where she sat, with the splendor of nature's creation as counterpoint to the terrors in the valley. He turned to face the interior of the cave, which appeared to be about ten feet wide at the mouth and nearly as deep. He felt the hard barrel of the Maglite in his pocket and rotated the head to turn it on.

And caught his breath.

Along both sides of the cave as well as the back wall Stranahan saw pictographs, stylized rock paintings that remained startlingly vivid after perhaps hundreds of years of weather. The rock face at the back of the cave was black granite, veined by white quartz. The side walls were sedimentary extrusions that had worn away into a smooth brick-red surface. Sticklike figures were outlined in black on the reddish surface. The pictographs on the black rock were different colors—brick, green, and an off-white he couldn't place on his palette. Partly because the flashlight needed a fresh pair of double A's, Sean did not yet see them as individual pieces of art, but rather as a choreography of shapes and colors. His knowledge of the art form was basic, but the artist in him had no doubt that these were particularly fine examples of Native American rock art, in fact superlative.

There was nothing to confirm Cinderella's presence, though someone had certainly been here, for in a corner of the cave, stacked upright, were what appeared to be primitive torches made by bundling and binding sticks together. The ends were bushed to form cavities that held pieces of bark, dried grasses, and caked tree sap that was as varnished as peanut brittle. Near the torches were several cans that held traces of a substance that looked similar to caked clay in the can he'd seen back at Bill's camp. He also saw sticks with whittled points, their ends charred. A small pile of coals at first perplexed him, for his light revealed no fire ring or ashes. Sean realized that the charcoal must have been carried down from the top of the headwall, where they'd found the fire ring.

His light abruptly went out. Working by feel, he unwrapped the fresh batteries he'd taped to the barrel of the flashlight, knowing in advance he might need them, unscrewed the cap and made the switch. No cigar. It was the bulb that was shot, not the juice. If he was the kind of man who was prone to self-chastisement, he'd have given himself a verbal lashing for not bringing a backup light. Instead, he felt around for one of the torches he'd seen earlier, found a pack of matches in his pants pocket, and struck one on the chemical strip. It flared. He dipped the head of the torch while he rotated the match under it. The match burned down and went out. He struck three matches at once. This time the dried grass tinder in the head of the torch crinkled up, winking like a cigarette, before dying back down. He thought a few moments, then pulled a cotton bandana from his pocket. He tore it in half and wrapped one half around the tinder bundle at the head of the torch. The bandana went up in flame, there was a secondary flare-up as the sap crackled, and he had light, brilliant light that caught the colors of the paintings and made the figures appear to dance on their rock canvas.

Sean felt icicles of breeze as the hairs lifted on the nape of his neck. He'd suspected, at a gut level, that these were not pictographs of Native American hunts and pagan sun worship, had known the moment he saw the cans and charred sticks that the paintings, far from writing a bygone chapter of Rocky Mountain history, told of a more recent struggle in pigments that probably were still in the act of curing. The figures on horseback were not carrying Shoshone flat bows, chasing herds of bison, but were twirling lariats, roping short-horned cattle. Stranahan brought the torch closer to the figure of a woman who was standing inside a circle studded with stars. It was the largest of the pictographs, in the very center of the back wall, the ochre figure nearly three feet tall. The woman was holding her palm out toward the stars, with two red hearts trailing dust as they soared from her hand toward the heavens, while another heart remained in her palm. The woman in the pictograph was missing one arm.

When Sean had glassed the cave through binoculars the day before, he'd held out hope that if it was the place where Cinderella had conducted a vision quest, he might find a clue to her death here, perhaps even the missing journal her mother had mentioned. What Sean was looking at was the story of her life, told in a language that was nearly as old as the mountains.

"Kemosabe."

Startled, Stranahan jerked his head around to see Sam backlit at the mouth of the cave.

"What are you doing here, Sam?"

"What am I doing here? I'm only trying to see if my bud's breathing oxygen. I've been hollerin' for twenty minutes."

"I think the cave deadens the sound."

Sam brought the smell of the wind and his own sweat inside with him. He said, "Then I saw the fuckin' cat track. I thought you'd be gurgling in the corner and I'd be facing a lion licking the blood off his whiskers." He brandished the knife held in his right fist.

"You climbed down without the harness?" Stranahan was having a hard time believing Sam would or could have descended the rock chimney.

"Yeah, no net. And I thought it was scary finding an iguana in my boat. So what's so fucking interesting you couldn't bother to tell me you're alive?"

Sean reached for the one of the torches standing against the cave wall. He held the head of it over the flame still flickering from the old torch, the fire flaring up, flooding the cave in light.

For the first time since Sean had known him, Sam Meslik was speechless.

———

Climbing up the chimney proved a lot easier than descending it, the "Oh shit" factor notwithstanding. Sean found his backpack where he'd left it on the headwall, rummaged through it, made a face, and then removed a pocket-size Moleskine sketchpad and an artist's soft lead pencil. Fifteen minutes later he was back in the cave.

"No camera, huh?" Sam said.

"No, I thought I'd packed it. Do you have your cell phone?"

"There's no reception up here so I left it in my truck. I didn't think about taking a picture with it."

"Then we'll have to do this the old-fashioned way."

With Sam holding the torch, Sean began sketching the pictographs, concentrating on detail while consciously trying to avoid reading too much into individual pieces of art. There would be plenty of time for that later, and he needed to get it all down before they ran through the stack of torches. Ignoring Sam's occasional "What the fuck?" he worked for an hour and a half, four torches burning to ash, before folding the pad back into his shirt pocket.

"You want me to light the last one?" Sam said. "Try to make some sense of this before we leave? I mean, there's some weird shit going on."

Stranahan was tempted. It often proved more enlightening to examine evidence at the scene than in a laboratory, or in this case Sean's studio, but the torches themselves were evidence and he wanted to leave at least one intact.

They were back to the trailhead by late afternoon. Sean dropped Sam at his truck on the outskirts of Bridger.

"Gotta change the U-trou after that little escapade," the big man said, and hitched his pants, walking away bowlegged like a cowboy in a western. The image struck a memory and Sean called him back.

"You have a DVD player, right?"

Sam nodded.

"Then I've got some more work if you want it. Jasper Fey gave me a disk of the western series he works on. I never got around to booting it up."

"What would I be looking for?"

"I don't know. A man with a sign on his chest that says I did it. Anything strikes a chord."

"Will there be good-looking chicks who take off their clothes?"

"It's cable, I wouldn't be surprised." Sean found the DVD in the glove compartment and forked it over with a twenty. "Beer's on me."

"What about Killer? Guard dog needs his kibble."

Sean reached for his wallet and Sam stopped him with a beefy hand on the forearm. He dug down with his thumb until the arm tingled. "Just playing with you, Kemosabe."

———

Back in his studio, Stranahan decided on chalk pastels, largely because he already had sheets of sanded art paper that had a good nap to hold the color. Also, pastels would provide the most accurate representation of the pictographs, and though that was neither here nor there with respect to their interpretation, Sean was an artist first. He unfolded several sheets of newspaper over his drawing board to provide cushion, then clamped on a salmon-tinted sheet of pastel paper that closely matched the color of the sandstone. He placed the board on his easel and got to work copying the pictographs on the left wall of the cave, bringing his pocket-pad sketches to life. Working with a charcoal stick reminded him of the charred sticks. Sean supposed that the artist had used the points to make the initial sketches, then went over top of them with chunks of charcoal. He used the same technique, first tracing the outlines of the pictographs with a fine-tipped vine charcoal stick, which could be erased if he made a mistake, then using a broader, compressed charcoal stick for his final application.

He unclamped the paper and replaced it with another sheet to represent the exposure on the right wall of the cave. This panel had fewer pictographs and he completed his work quickly. To represent the granite at the back of the cave, he selected a sheet of black pastel paper that was four feet wide and nearly as tall, the largest one he had. The pictographs here involved a more tedious process of transference, being in color, and Sean worked long into the night. He saved the pictograph of the mother releasing the hearts of her children for last, and then arranged his three easels side by side. He brought the wings of the side panels in at an angle to simulate the depth of the cave. He found that his hands had a tremor. He knew he ought to try to get some sleep, but even when he shut his eyes standing up, the pictographs whirled in his head.

"Snap out of it," he told himself, which elicited a dog yawn from Choti, who was curled on the futon. Sean brewed a cup of tea and pulled his stool to a position in front of the easels. The panel representing the left-hand wall drew his attention first, as it had in the cave. These were the most simply executed pictographs, consisting, with one exception, of black line drawings on the salmon background. Stranahan guessed that they had been made first, and therefore could well be the most important. Starting at the top and scanning from left to right, he saw the stick profile of a girl or woman with scallops to represent breasts, drawn with long hair trailing from a cowboy hat.

The figure, who Sean supposed was Cinderella, was galloping on horseback and twirling a lariat. In front of her horse ran a short-haired figure—Landon Anker? The second pictograph showed the rope settling over the shoulders of the second figure, the next, drawing it close. To the right was a pictograph of the girl facing out, a tear under each eye, her torso a heart with a line cleaving it.

Sean faced the panel with his hands on his hips. "Girl gets boy, girl loses boy. Humpff. Tell me something I don't know." His impression of Martha Ettinger left something to be desired, but her sentiment would have been on the money. They already knew that Landon Anker had broken Cinderella's heart.

The pictographs underneath the top row initially puzzled him until he realized they were meant to be sequenced from right to left, in the direction that the profiles pointed. The first showed the girl riding away from a tunnel-like structure—the stables came to mind—then the same figure, on foot, standing under an inverted V, which Sean took to be a mountain. Now she was being pursued, for trailing her silhouette was a horseback figure wearing a cowboy hat. The simple A-frame design of what Sean took to be the Forest Service cabin loomed in the foredistance.

Below these pictographs was one more drawing that completed the panel, and it had haunted him since he'd sketched it in the cave. The image was a chimney with a quarter moon above the opening. The horseback figure wearing the hat had dismounted to stand beside the chimney, where he was joined by a second person, this one wearing a ball cap. Cones of yellow light extended from the hands of the figures. With one exception, the cones were the only color on the entire panel, and Sean would later suspect the color had been added at a later date, when Cinderella had access to pigments. But it wasn't the lights that drew his attention. It was the face that stared from within the chimney, as if looking out through an invisible wall.

The face was the shape of a balloon, the eyes large and round, and below them the mouth was an elongated oval. Tendrils of golden hair spun around the lower part of the face.

The pictograph sent chills through Sean's body. Here was Cinderella's death, painted in her hand or with Bear Paw Bill's help, and yet how could that be? Was it possible that the pictograph had been painted by the mountain man as a record of her death? That seemed unlikely. As far as Sean knew, no one had spoken to Bill of Cinderella's demise before he fled the hospital, and even had he known about the chimney, how could he have climbed from his camp to the headwall and from there to the cave? On one leg? No, Cinderella had painted herself into her grave weeks or months before her demise, and her face, with the mouth open as if to scream, was the image Sean finally fell asleep to sometime after midnight.

CHAPTER THIRTY

Getting Along

What is it?"

Martha sat up in her bed, Sheba stretching her legs to come up beside her head and run a sandpaper tongue across her chin.

"Stop licking me."

"If you say so."

"I mean the cat."

"Are you still in bed?"

"Of course not."

"I wanted to catch you before you drove to Law and Justice. I'm in my studio. There's something you'll want to see."

"Give me thirty minutes. No, forty. I got to feed the critters."

———

Martha ran her tongue over her lips. "And you did this from memory?" She inched up her chin.

"No. I had a sketchpad and made notes on colors and backgrounds. Each panel is scaled down, but the pictographs are accurate."

"I believe you. I just don't recall mention that Cinderella was an artist."

"Bill McKutchen was, though. The artwork on the powder horn has the same aboriginal quality. Perhaps he helped her, but I don't think there's any doubt that this is her life."

Martha nodded. "They're extraordinary. Have you drawn any conclusions?"

"I thought maybe you'd want to draw your own, then we could compare."

"You thought wrong." She glanced at her watch. "I've got a meeting with the DA at nine. I can give you twenty minutes, so shoot. Start with that one." She tapped the pictograph of the face in the chimney.

"Well, it raises the obvious question. I've had a day and a night to think about it, and the more I do, the more I'm convinced that it's meant to be taken literally. The pictographs leading up to it"—he pointed to the sequence on the opposing panel—"tell the story of Cinderella running from the stables and being pursued. They're straightforward. And when you look at this panel, which I think is the second she completed—"

"What makes you think it's the second?"

"Because it tells the continuation of the story. And I don't think she worked on the back wall until later because it was black and the charcoal wouldn't show up. She had to wait until Bill made the pigments. That night I was with him, he said, 'She tell you in car-coal. I made her color.'"

"How do you make colors?"

"You can make pigments from gumbo clay, hematite, mix in blood to tint it, use saliva as a binding agent—"

Martha spread her fingers. "I'm on board."

"Okay. On the right-hand panel, the next pictograph in the sequence, she's standing on top of the roof. That tells me the two men didn't find her; she got out of the chimney and escaped. Then here, she's walking on top of the mountains, and in the next she's joined by a giant with wild hair. We know who that is. Here's the lean-to, and here they are hunting deer. She's even stroked in smoke billowing from the muzzle-loader. You aren't convinced?"

"I'm saying it's a lot to, ah, intuit. These are stick figures."

"Granted, but they make sense. Regardless of what made her flee from the stables, if she was heading to McKutchen's camp, she only had two routes to choose from. She could ride out in back like Etta and I did yesterday, or she could strike out south, which is what I think she did, which puts the forest cabin right on her way. From there the trail takes her where it took us when we found Bill, up the bald ridge and down into the South Fork. That's the way I would go if I had to travel at night."

Martha pinched her lower lip. "She's on foot in this one." Martha pointed. "Why did she leave her horse?"

"If she knew she was being tracked, she did it to put her followers on the wrong trail."

"Then what were they doing at the cabin, shining flashlights?"

"I don't know. Maybe they only knew the direction she'd taken and the cabin was in that direction."

"There's a lot you don't know."

"Thanks for pointing that out."

Martha nodded to herself. "So who are they?"

"Charles Watt was a railroad man, he wears a cap with pinstripes. So I think he's this guy. The one wearing the cowboy hat is Jasper Fey."

"And they were in cahoots?"

"They did everything else together. 'Controlled hell inside the arena and raised it on the outside,' as Jasper put it. Remember what Cindy wrote over top of that entry in the guest log? 'THE CLOWNS ARE HERE.' Charles Watt had a clown tattoo. I'd bet money Jasper Fey has one, too."

"You're painting a picture of monsters."

"Cinderella dying where she'd hidden from them last fall, there's a tragic logic to it. If she had hidden in the chimney once and managed to climb back out, she'd have a false sense of security about doing it again."

"Only the second time she wasn't so lucky."

"Or maybe it was the third time, or the tenth. She was up there all winter and they survived on what, a couple deer Bill shot? People who rent out the cabin don't pack out their food sometimes. The place could be empty a lot during the middle of the week. Maybe she knew that, or Bill did, and they raided it on a regular basis. My guess is either she was trying to break in to find food when she died, or she was heading out to try to get help for Bill's leg and got stuck in a snow-storm. I looked up the weather for the time frame of her death and there were two storms, back to back. She decided to shelter in the cabin. Start a fire and warm up."

Martha shook her head. "You're forgetting something."

Sean waited. "By the way," he said. "I let you get away with touch-ing the paper once. If you do it again, I'll have to kill you. I haven't applied a fixative yet."

But she didn't respond and he knew the look, Martha staring into the middle distance of her own world, oblivious to the sundry mut-terings of the planet.

"What is it I'm forgetting?" he said.

She turned to him. "You're forgetting that she wasn't a little girl anymore. She was a young woman who was pregnant. She felt an obligation to the life inside her." She pointed to one of the color pic-tographs. "Don't worry, I'm not going to touch it. But look, that pea-nut inside her belly is her baby. No, she was going home. All these pictographs on the back wall"—she swept her hand—"almost all of them, the horses, the house, the figures here, they're her friends. This is a longing for home. Home and her mother who held her heart in her hand. She was going home even if it meant facing her rapist *and* her stepfather."

"What makes you think these figures are her friends?"

"Because that one is my son. That's David." She pointed to a paint-ing of a boy wearing light-colored chaps, who was holding his hat upside down while a horse dipped his head to eat out of the crown. "David wore chaps that were made from sheepskin. When you put somebody you haven't seen for six or seven years into a piece of art, it means you long for the past."

"Is your son still coming up this summer? I was looking forward to taking him fishing."

"He's flying in at the end of the month."

She turned away and produced her cell phone. "Yeah, Hunt, call

Bowers and tell him I'll run a little late . . . No, Hunt, you're not in trouble, but next time you're watching a potential runner and you got to hit the john, pucker up." She holstered the phone. "Where were we?"

"Talking about your son."

"Yeah, well, we'll see how it goes. Anything else? You really did good work here."

"Thanks. There's a few of the pictographs I can't decipher. One I keep coming back to is here, on the back wall. I think the figure is Landon Anker, but I don't know how to explain it."

Martha peered. The pictograph was a cluster of horses, perhaps a dozen. Half of the horses were lying on their backs with their legs in the air, while others were in the act of jumping over a sickle moon. Only one of the leaping horses carried a rider, and a similar figure was lying on the ground among the supine horses. She looked over at Sean.

"Landon, huh?"

"He's riding a painted horse with a white mane and tail. Etta Huntington gave me some old photos of Cinderella and he's in a couple of them, sitting on a paint with a white mane and tail."

"So this is him what—dead?" She pointed to the figure with the supine horses. "And this is him ascending to heaven?" She pointed to the figure on horseback.

She drummed her thumb against the grips of her revolver. "I gotta go," she said. "I'm going to ask you not to show this to Etta."

"Why? She's the only one who might be able to see something we missed."

"I know that, and I'm still asking. Remember Asena Martinelli? That guy she shot, she knew where to find him, or how to lure him to her. You told her, you didn't tell her, at this point I don't want to know. The fact of the matter is she got information she shouldn't have and somebody got dead on my watch. I don't want Etta going dark angel, do something like shoot her husband."

"She's the one who's buying my gas, not the county."

"I don't care."

He returned her stare. A centimeter nod. "Okay, I won't say anything. For now. But if this doesn't take us anywhere, I will."

"Then make sure it takes us somewhere." She found her jacket where she'd hung it on a chair. "You know," she said, "we're getting along. I like it better when we get along."

"I liked it better when you left the light on."

CHAPTER THIRTY-ONE

Montana Double Date

Boot Hill, Jasper Fey's western TV series, was better than its premise, a twenty-first-century pipe dream of a West that wasn't, complete with a sheriff who had to duck under doorframes, a deputy who doubled as a tribal elder on the nearby reservation, and a fallen angel who flashed turquoise rings and had quite the time of it keeping her body under wraps for a full sixty minutes.

"They're all so good-looking I wouldn't know who to screw first," Sam said. "Be like hunting water with a divining rod. Shut your eyes and start drilling where the stick hits the ground." He popped the cap off a bottle of Arrogant Bastard Ale. The horned devil on the label reminded Sean of the mask Charles Watt wore in the Mile and a Half High Club video, which reminded him of why he was here, sitting in the littered living room of Sam's house-slash-fly-shack on a bench overlooking the Madison River, halfway through season one.

The truth was he'd been without direction or morning coffee when Martha Ettinger left his studio, and after brewing a cup and adding wings made from a crow feather to a half-tied wet fly clamped into his vise, he'd called Sam, who said he hadn't got around to watching the video yet. Sean had invited himself over just to be doing something while he considered his next move.

———

Sam hit the pause button. "I got to water the garden," he said. Sean followed him outside and walked to the edge of the property while Sam unzipped. The Madison had come up ten inches in twenty-four hours and looked like chocolate milk. He heard Sam say, "Shaking it, boss," then the big man hitched up beside him, spinning underarm hair around his forefinger through a hole in a Rodriguez T-shirt that read I WONDER on the front, and on the back of which Sam had penned BUT I REALLY DON'T GIVE A SHIT. in magic marker.

"You'd have better luck catching snakes in Ireland than trout in this soup." Sam shook his head. "I'm so fuckin' depressed I couldn't get excited about pulled pork."

For a man without an appetite, Sam managed to get interested enough in the pizza Sean had picked up on the drive down. He put away half of it in the time it took the sheriff to kill a good man gone wrong, the deputy to mutter Native American wisdom about the meaning of life, and the love interest to pop peyote and run topless through a field of lupine.

Sam flipped a bottle cap. "I like six-guns and sweater venison as much as the next fella, but I don't see what any of this has to do with that." He jutted his chin toward the pictograph panels that Sean had set up near the television set.

"Let's take a look at the extra features," Sean said.

Sam reached a hand to pat Killer's broad forehead. The two men were sitting on Sam's couch with the stuffing coming out, two dogs between them with their heads on their masters' laps.

"You know what this is, Kemosabe? Couple bros watching the tube with man's best friends? It's a Montana double date."

Sean grunted his acknowledgment, his mind elsewhere. He clicked on deleted scenes. Nothing there. He clicked on "The Making of *Boot Hill*," still not knowing what he was looking for and not finding it. The last of the features was a running commentary with the director and lead actor, who bantered in film school shorthand as they dissected the pilot episode. The opening shot was Boot Hill, a treeless burial ground outside the fictional town of Malice, Montana, where a nineteenth-century gunslinger named Pinky "Fast Finger" Stubbs was said to be buried. In the opening scene a young couple with a bottle of hooch for fortification decided to make love among the dead, in a grave slated for tenancy the next day. The young woman had insisted on lining the grave with a blanket, which the man objected to on principle but didn't argue too hard about. The sex was off camera, and the scream didn't have anything to do with ecstasy. The camera zoomed into the grave, the girl cowering under the blanket in her lover's arms, the focus shifting to a finger that protruded from the wall of the grave. The finger beckoned, then a hand appeared to reach out of the grave, spreading against a red sunset as the credits rolled.

"What a great opening shot, mate," the actor said in his Aussie accent. Upon which the director, who had written the pilot, said, "Credit where credit due. The hand was suggested by Jasper Fey, he's our western expert. Jasper had all kinds of ideas for unearthing bodies. One was by erosion where the Musselshell River ate away the bank; we used that in episode five. Another was to have a body in a pit grave where ranchers bury livestock. Jasper said if you buried a body underneath a horse or a cow carcass, then if a cadaver dog sniffed it, the CSIs would find the animal and decide it was a false positive and quit digging. Perfect crime. I liked it, but you'd have to mock up the carcass, and that's ten grand for maybe five seconds' screen time. We don't have the budget. Now this next scene, this is shot with that new tracking dolly . . ."

Sean hit the pause button. He turned to Sam. Sam's side of the couch was next to a fly rod rack, and he reached a hirsute hand for the longest, an eleven-foot-seven-inch Meiser, and tapped the tip against the pictograph in the lower left corner of the back panel, where the horses lay on their backs with their hooves in the air.

"Do I have to say 'burial pit,' or are you thinking along the same lines as Uncle Sam?"

Sean didn't say anything. He couldn't believe what he'd just seen. Could Jasper Fey have described the very crime he would later commit? Would he be that careless? But then he remembered that Jasper claimed he hadn't watched the DVD. He may not have known anything about the director's comments in the special features.

"If you know where the pit is, I got the shovels," Sam said.

Sean scratched at the stubble on his jaw. "Maybe later, Sam. I better think this over. Would you mind taking Choti till tomorrow?"

"Be that way. Leave Sam out of it. All he did was step off a fucking cliff for you."

"I knew you'd understand." Sean scratched Choti's ears and stood up.

"Hey, that fly on your hat, you name it?" Sam said.

"I just tied it this morning. I was thinking Crazy Mountain Special, but then I remembered this secret kiss Etta Huntington had with her daughter. So I'm going to call it the Crazy Mountain Kiss."

Sam grunted his approval. "Has a ring," he said. "I like the red throat."

CHAPTER THIRTY-TWO

Spadework

You sure we aren't trespassing?" Katie Sparrow raised her eyebrows.

Stranahan used the cheater stick to open the gate and dragged the barbed-wire fencing to the side so she could enter. The shepherd had already wriggled under.

"This is Bar-4 property," he said. "I have permission."

"Then why did you park back in the trees?"

"Like I said when I called, I'm following a hunch. If it turns out I'm right, then I'll tell you everything."

Katie nodded as Sean struggled to reclose the gate.

"So you got three guys in a truck," Katie said, picking burrs off her pants cuffs. "How do you know who's the real cowboy?"

"The one in the middle," Sean said. "He never has to get the gates." He grunted with satisfaction as the wire loop dropped over the post.

"We're looking for a body or I wouldn't be here with Lothar." It was a statement.

"We're looking for a body."

"Why don't you just say it's Landon Anker?"

"Okay, Katie. It's Landon Anker."

"What makes you think he's here?"

"The ranch manager said something about burying the deadstock in the northeast corner. It would be someplace they could get to with a tractor and backhoe attachment. My guess is these tread marks are going to lead to it."

"What makes you think the body is with dead animals?"

"Something somebody said."

"That doesn't sound like a hunch." Katie blew at a strand of hair that had fallen across the bridge of her nose. "I just don't want to be overstepping Martha. Last time we did that, I caught hell."

"We aren't. But if it turns out I'm right, she'll be the first to know."

Katie, who spent most of her time in the company of dogs, kept up a running commentary as they hiked. For a while it was about a guy she'd gone out with, a fellow park ranger who raised Lothar's hackles each time he stepped out of his car, which meant the relationship was pretty much a nonstarter. She was thinking of putting an ad in the personals and had written her profile, which she pulled out of her breast pocket and handed over.

> SWF, 28, AL, NS, SOH seeking SM, 25–40,
> NS, NBG, FST, EMP for long walks, singing in
> the rain, dancing in the dark. No beards, PBR
> breath, MOM tats, or caps worn backwards.
> RU out there?

"I'll need a translation," Sean said.

"Single white female, animal lover, nonsmoker . . ." She jerked the paper from his hand. "SOH is sense of humor. Seeking single male, nonsmoker, no beer gut, full set of teeth, employed, ta-da ta-da. No beards, no Pabst Blue Ribbon breath, 'Mom' tattoos or caps worn backwards. I was going to add no cowboy hats and shitkicker boots, but then I would have eliminated every man in Montana."

Sean had to laugh. "You didn't mention your sex move."

She strode ahead of him. "I'm saving it for you."

For a mile or more the tracks rose gradually, then dropped into a fold of the hills. Metal glinted in the low angle of the sun. They were standing before the farm machinery graveyard Sean had seen with Etta on their ride to the high country—tires that would never roll, coils of barbed wire that would never make a fence, an old square hay baler that would never bale hay.

"We called it a John Deere graveyard on the sugarbeet farm," Katie said.

Sean picked up a bag of golf clubs. Wilson Ultras. He remembered seeing the photograph of the golf hole on Earl Hightower's wall.

"I guess somebody hit into the water too many times," Katie said. "If there's a putter around here, it'll be bent like a pretzel."

"This doesn't look like a burial ground," Sean said. He set down the bag. "Let's keep following the tread."

They followed the tire tracks over another rise, a pair of vultures circling high, and there it was, though burial pit was an optimistic definition for the acre of mounded earth grown up in sage and sedge. The spadework, or rather backhoe, had been slipshod, cavernous rib cages visible among assorted bones, a cow skull with bits of hide clinging, a calf, the region of its anus eaten away, eyes and gums carried off in bird bills. In one corner of the burial ground, the earth was recently disturbed, the tracks of the tractor frozen in the mud. Stranahan thought it must be where Hightower had buried the colt that had died of colic.

Katie told Sean to stand back and spoke quietly to Lothar. She unsnapped his leash and he began to range back and forth with his nose to the ground.

Katie said, "He doesn't turn back to look at me, did you pick up on that? That's a criterion for a good search dog, he knows what he's supposed to do. Some dogs, they have a good nose but you have to babysit them. Really, the nose is overrated. You can have a dog with a fantastic nose who has no gift for the work and vice versa. You really can't train for interest."

Sean looked up as shadows striped the ground. Blackbirds passing in a flock, the angle of the sun casting their shadows on the face of the slope.

"He's got it," Katie said. "That's his alert."

Sean watched as Lothar stood stiffly, his tail curled. He circled himself, then lay down where a horse hoof attached to a string of cannon bone stuck above the ground. Lothar extended his head along his forepaws, showing his soulful eyes as they approached.

"You're a good dog, yes you are," Katie said, her voice rising an octave. She dug her fingers into Lothar's heavy coat. He looked up expectantly as she pulled a biscuit from her pocket and broke it into three pieces. "One for you"—she fed Lothar's eager canines—"one for you"—she handed a piece to Sean—"and one for me." She sat down and patted the ground beside her. "Come on, you can do it. It's a tradition."

Sean sat down and chewed the biscuit. It wasn't the first of hers he'd tasted, and it wasn't the worst. He washed it down with water from the bottle in his pack and replaced the cap, finding that his hands trembled with excitement. *You bastard,* he thought, *you followed through.*

"Katie, what are the chances that Lothar made a mistake, that he's just reacting to the horse carcass?"

"No way. Decomposing human remains carry a signature scent."

"Could anything else draw a false positive?"

"Hunch-uh. Lothar tested at ninety-six of a hundred in the SAR trials in Pocatello. That means he could identify carpet squares as marked or unmarked with only four mistakes. It was his fifth straight blue ribbon."

"So even if the human body is buried beneath the horse, Lothar would alert just to the body."

"You betcha."

So much for Jasper's perfect crime, Sean thought.

"It's an old burial from the look of it." Katie stroked Lothar's head. "I'll never have another dog like you, no I won't."

Sean did the math. More than five months had passed since Anker disappeared.

"Okay, give," Katie said.

He decided to level with her. It took a while, long enough for the sweat to dry on his clothes and a chill to take its place.

"So what are you going to do? Call Martha and get a warrant to exhume?"

"The ranch is in Etta Huntington's name. I'm sure she'll give permission, but they might want the warrant to be safe. If this goes to trial, you need the I's dotted."

Katie nodded, her jaw working.

"What I'm wondering," Sean said, "is will there be evidence to link Jasper Fey to the body. He's too smart to have kept the clothes he wore that night, so there goes fiber, and I don't know what else there could be."

"Well blood, duh," Katie said. "Maybe he was cut. But you'd need to talk to Wilkerson, she's the one who'd know about transfer."

"Even if they lifted Jasper's blood, I don't think it's enough to build a case."

"What about the show? He's on record suggesting this as a good place to ditch a body. Seems incriminating to me."

"I still think we'd need something solid."

"You have the pictographs."

"We can't even prove Cinderella was the one who painted them. And they're subject to a broad interpretation. Maybe if we had the testimony of the mountain man, if Cinderella had talked to him . . ."

He was thinking out loud now, the way Martha did, and remembering something she'd said. Perps got caught either because they talked or they got nervous and did something stupid. Jasper Fey wasn't a career criminal. He'd be nervous, all right. And he'd already committed one act of stupidity by burying the body in a place he'd suggested to the director of a television show. The question was, could he be persuaded to do something else, something that stamped his ticket to the state prison in Deer Lodge.

"Katie, what do you know about entrapment?"

"I know poachers claim it when we trick them into shooting at animal decoys." She shrugged. "It's on the books as a defense in Montana. I had to look it up when a guy shot at an elk deke, but then his lawyer said the deke was across the state border, like by ten feet. So the lawyer said Montana law didn't apply, that it didn't matter that he was inside the park when he fired. But the judge convicted his ass anyway. Why? What are you thinking?"

"I'm thinking that if Jasper Fey was caught digging up this body, it would be pretty damning. But would it be entrapment if he was doing it because someone let it slip that we were on to him?"

"I don't know, but if a judge says that falls under the legal definition, then any evidence brought to light by the action could be suppressed."

"How do you suppress a body?"

"Well, maybe not the body, but evidence on the body could be suppressed as having been produced during the entrapment. You could get the DA's case thrown out."

There was another side to that coin and Sean thought about it. If he pulled Martha in and they exhumed the body, but found no forensic evidence to point a finger, Jasper Fey would skate. He might be suspected in the cover-up, from his suggestion about the burial pit, but a good lawyer could provide an alternative explanation. The simplest was that Fey had told Watt about his idea and Watt had taken his old buddy's suggestion as his own. Watt was the murderer. Fey was guilty of nothing more than giving voice to an idea.

He thought aloud. "If a concerned citizen was to see suspicious behavior and called it in, and law enforcement caught said person in the act . . ."

Katie shook her head. "That would be different. Only an agent for law enforcement can entrap somebody. But don't quote me."

Sean took a shallow breath. He'd been breathing through his mouth since they'd found the burial pit, probably the stench from the calf was getting to him, though he wasn't eager to test the theory. Katie wrinkled up her nose.

"Let's back off," she said.

There was nothing more to learn anyway, not without a shovel, and as they hiked to the road their shadows elongated and crept up into the higher ground, as if they were giants stalking the earth with a prehistoric wolf following, the grasses gone gold and the clock ticking down like the beating of a heart.

CHAPTER THIRTY-THREE

The Praying Mantis

When Stranahan returned, the last of the light had drained from the slopes. He sat in the John Deere graveyard, a discarded truck tire for cover, feeling the gloom settle around his shoulders and thinking about what could go wrong.

When he'd dropped Katie at her rig, his first call had been to Sam, who had readily fallen in with the plan Sean outlined. It was sixty minutes from Sam's fly shack on the Madison to the Cottonwood Inn, where, according to Etta Huntington, Jasper Fey was a regular at the Tuesday poker table. It was a house game, the dealer from the Inn skimming a percentage of the pot. Anyone with forty dollars could buy in, even a fishing guide who'd worn grooves in his teeth from biting monofilament tippets. Sam ought to be settling his bulk into the chair at the green felt table any minute now. But would Fey be there? And if he was, how would he react when Sam mentioned that he'd heard something about the disappearance of Landon Anker, that the body was buried up around the Crazies and he knew a fella who knew a fella who knew where?

"I wouldn't want to be the one letting the ghost out of the ground," Sean could hear Sam saying. "A man would need two hookers and a fifth of Jack to get through the night after seeing something like that." And he could see Sam brushing off questions about how he knew, though everyone would know how, the fact that Sean guided for him common knowledge in the valley. And that would give the rumor credence, because they'd heard his name in association with Martha Ettinger's. It was three degrees of Sean Stranahan.

He drew the SPOT Messenger from his pants pocket and stared at its face. The personal locator beacon, the size of a flip phone, had been a gift from Martha Ettinger, who said she was tired of relying on intuition to know when he was in trouble somewhere off the grid. Popular among elk hunters, the SPOT pinpointed location using satellite telemetry. At the press of a button, the unit would send a "Help" signal, along with GPS coordinates, to a central data-gathering facility, where the alarm would be relayed to the relevant search-and-rescue agency. It also had an "I'm Okay" button that sent an email with GPS coordinates imprinted on a Google map to the four addresses registered with the subscription service—in Sean's case, that was Ettinger, Harold Little Feather, Katie Sparrow, and Sam Meslik. When Katie received the "I'm Okay," which Sean would send when and if Fey arrived at the scene, she would phone Martha and Harold and tell them to saddle up, metaphorically speaking.

Not lost on Sean was that this was the second night in four days that he'd staked out a location, hoping for someone to incriminate himself. On the prior occasion Martha had chided him about packing nothing more potent than pepper spray, and he had nothing more lethal with him now. He wouldn't need it, not as long as he stayed out of sight, but still, it worried him. Lots of things worry you when the night sucks the light out of the sky, coyotes howl from a canyon in the Crazies, and you've been shivering for an hour.

He switched on his headlamp and ran it across the debris, looking for a weapon. He thought about the bag of golf clubs and cursed himself for having toted it to his truck earlier. Sean didn't play golf, but Sam was threatening to take up the game and Sean thought he'd appreciate the clubs. "What I wouldn't give for a two-iron," he said aloud, and thought he heard something in the tailing silence of the words. An echo? No, it was no echo.

There—a staccato, rattling sound. It grew louder before fading, then was louder again; it was as if someone had rotated the volume knob of a radio, one way, then the other. Now it had dialed down. Stranahan put his ear to the ground. Silence. He rose to a crouch, and as he reached up to flip off his headlamp, already worrying that it could have been spotted from the distance, the beam glinted off a curved piece of metal. It was an old iron hay hook, partly buried and as long as his forearm. The wooden handle had been eaten into an hourglass shape, possibly by a porcupine, but the hook was still a hook, hard and sharp and curved like an eagle's talon. Sean pried it from the earth. Better than nothing. He switched the light off and waited.

When he heard the rattling start up again, there was a throaty quality beneath it and Sean knew it was the rumbling of an engine. It was to his north, along the route he'd hiked in with Katie, probably following the same tracks. He guessed it would be the tractor with the backhoe attachment he'd seen outside the stables. The one he'd heard Jasper call the Praying Mantis.

At first it was just a shadow on a shadowed land, a difference only of darkness. Then, the steady creeping of a silhouette. Stranahan told himself he had nothing to worry about. There was no reason for the tractor to turn into the graveyard of machinery; there was no body buried here. But it would pass within stone-throwing distance on its way to the burial pit, some fifty yards farther along the side slope.

He looked at the SPOT, knowing he should have sent the signal as soon as he heard the rattle. But he had wanted to make sure. The unit didn't have an LCD screen like a GPS, just an orange plastic face with buttons, and in the darkness he couldn't see the buttons. If he was more familiar with it, he could have sent a message with his eyes closed, but he'd tested the unit only once, the day after Martha gave it to him. Now he'd have to wait until the tractor rattled out of sight before risking his headlamp.

The tractor crept inexorably along the tracks, complaining about its age, it drew abreast—and passed by. Sean let out a held breath as it climbed a rise where it imprinted against the sky, the backhoe attachment arched, its articulated neck and toothy head in silhouette. The cloud cover had dissipated and for a moment Sean saw the figure of a person in the tractor seat, or rather a shadow wearing a hat, before the tractor dipped out of sight into the burial pit.

Sean flicked on his headlamp and pressed the "I'm Okay" button of the SPOT. Now it was a matter of waiting until the unit acquired satellites to triangulate his position. It was a clear enough night, what was taking so long?

"Come on."

There it was, the blinking green light that meant the message had sent.

When he switched off his headlamp, he could see a milky glow over the burial pit. Fey must have switched on the tractor's headlights. It was making a different sound now, a mechanical, waterfall-like sound that he supposed was the engagement of the backhoe. The bucket should be scooping up the horse carcass, cracking bones, its hungry maw digging deeper to unearth Anker's body. Then what? Would the steel beast carry off the body to bury it somewhere else? Probably. Fey would just have to hope no one noticed the disturbed ground until it grew up in sage and spring grasses. But it couldn't carry away all traces of the decomposition, or could it? Sean tried to picture Fey's hands working the levers. Gruesome work. Two hookers and a fifth of Jack work.

The waterfall sound stopped and there was an undertone of the tractor at idle. Sean heard a scurrying sound, a patter of feet. He jerked his head around, straining his eyes in the darkness. A fox? One of the coyotes he'd heard? And something else, a sharp note from the direction of the burial pit. Could it have been a shout? No, probably just a clutch disk slipping. Whatever it was, it wasn't repeated, the waterfall sound resumed, and Sean heard no more pattering of feet.

He got up and stretched his legs. He'd seen what he'd come to see. Now it was a matter of waiting for the cavalry. He looked down toward the valley, trying to conjure headlights out of the blackness. But it had been less than half an hour since he'd sent the signal. Martha was thirty-five miles away, Harold another thirty to the west. It could be a while. In the meantime, he'd remain out of sight and follow the Mantis from a safe distance. He'd been holding the hay hook in his right hand and slipped it over his shoulder—the gap was just wide enough to do so—and shrugged his jacket on over it. Now he'd have both hands free. He took a step and felt the point dig into his scapula. He began to unbutton the jacket. It was a stupid idea. If he fell, he'd gaff himself like a fish.

He looked toward the pit; the pool of milk cast by the tractor headlights was steady. Once more the motor was at idle. He'd unbuttoned three buttons when again he heard the scurry of feet.

"Stop it. Don't turn around."

CHAPTER THIRTY-FOUR

The Carrion Beetle

Is that you, Jasper?"

Sean felt his heart rate jacking up.

"Is that you, Jasper?" A mocking tone. "Well now, I found someone trespassing on Bar-4 property. What do you think we should do with him, Poupette?"

Sean heard the scurry of the feet behind him. It was the dog he'd seen in the mudroom, the one Etta referred to as Jasper's ten-gallon-hat dog.

"She smelt you when we passed by in the tractor, but I didn't think too much of it till she took off looking. Not a good idea to let a dog roam at night, this many coyotes on the premises. I called her in and danged if she didn't go right back. 'Jasper,' I says to myself, 'I'm beginning to wonder if we're alone up here.' I had what in the business we call a micro-expression, when the character suddenly knows. Overdo it, you look like you're opening wide for the dentist. That Sam Meslik talking about a body, you put him up to that. Made me feel I'd got your coffee thrown on my face all over again."

Keep him talking, Stranahan thought. "Why did you kill Landon Anker? Or was it Charlie and you just helped him dig?"

"No sir. Hunch-uh. The way it works is, I ask the questions. Here's one. Do you know what happens to a head when a bullet going three thousand six hundred feet per second hits it? I'm talking any caliber bullet now, any number you pull out of a hat."

"I guess not."

"Well that head detonates, that's the best way to describe it."

"Is that how Landon was killed?"

"No. That's how you could die. I'm telling you because I read you as a man who has too much sense to do something stupid, like run. I put this Leopold scope on you, it gathers a hell of a lot of light. Kill you at a hundred yards just as surely as I kill you at twenty. You understand what I'm saying?"

"Don't get itchy feet."

"Yeah. That's one way of putting it. Now listen up. Rule number two, do not turn around. I catch you peeking, I shoot. You got that?"

Sean got it.

"Three, you're going to walk slow toward the pit, hands over your head. You lower them, I don't have to tell you what happens."

Sean understood.

"You have something on your hip. What is it?"

"It's a bear spray."

"That's right. You're the detective who doesn't carry a gun. Drop it on the ground."

Sean did, managing to fumble open another button of his jacket before unbuckling his belt. He felt the hay hook dig into the back of his shoulder, but it was small comfort. He was a dead man walking and knew it. There was no other way this could end, not unless he could give Fey a reason to let him live. He had two cards, and he played one of them.

"You're going to see headlights any minute now. That will be Sheriff Ettinger. She knows where I am. But if you let me live, there's still a way you can walk away from this."

Fey snorted his derision.

"Listen to me. All you have to say is that you gave a copy of the DVD to Charlie Watt. Charlie killed Landon and used your idea to bury his body."

"I don't know what you're talking about."

"Yes you do. The director talks about hiding a body in a livestock burial pit. He gives you credit. It's in the DVD."

"You're talking about the director's commentary?"

"Yes, you haven't seen it? Nobody told you you were mentioned?"

"No, nobody told me. And like I said, I don't watch shows I'm hired onto. Anyway, it's a little after the fact, isn't it? That body was cold in the ground before any DVD came out."

"In that case, you told Charlie that you'd suggested the idea for the show. The director will back you up. Watt doesn't have to have seen the DVD because he got it from the horse's mouth."

Fey didn't respond. *He's thinking it over,* Sean thought. He felt a glimmer of hope.

"Then what am I doing here?"

"You discovered that Charles Watt raped your daughter. It made you think he'd killed Landon, that Landon had tried to rescue her. You remembered telling him about the burial pit. So you came up here to check it out. The worst you'll get is a slap on the wrist for not telling somebody first."

All the time they talked, Sean walked, the growl of the tractor growing louder. He crested the rise of land. There was the tractor, its backhoe imprinted against the stars. The pit was illuminated by the gauzy glow of the headlights, moons of earth risen from shadows. Parts of animals were strewn, staring with eye sockets. It was a scene from a horror movie.

"Walk under the bucket. Get into the hole."

Sean found himself standing on the edge of a deep trench.

"Don't do this, Jasper. If you kill me, then nothing can save you. They'll be here any minute."

"Bullshit."

Sean played his last card. "I have a personal locator beacon. I sent the SOS. Here, I'll show you."

Sean felt the eye of Fey's flashlight on his back. He reached the SPOT from his jacket pocket.

"Toss it backwards. Okay. I see it. So that's what they look like."

"Remember, all you're guilty of is planting the idea."

Silence. When Fey spoke it was the voice of someone who had come to the edge of something and stepped past it. "I really wish that was true. I truly do."

"Listen to me."

"No, I'm done listening. Get in the hole."

The tone said the finger on the trigger was looking for an excuse. Sean stepped down into the hole, or rather he dropped. The hook jabbed him sharply as he hit bottom and felt the squishing of tissue under his boots. The remains of the horse, he guessed, maybe the rumen, not that it was a major concern. He stood, the sides of the hole coming up to his armpits.

"Face away from the tractor."

One last try. "They're coming, Jasper. You can explain everything else, you can't explain killing me. If you kill me—"

The words froze in Sean's throat as he heard the waterfall engagement of the backhoe. Instinctively, he jerked his head to see Jasper in the tractor seat. Pressing his palms on the ground, he tried to scramble out of the pit, but was pounded back into it as a bucket of earth and debris thudded onto his head and shoulders. As the tractor backed away and the Mantis curled its head to dig another load, he grappled the hay hook free from under his jacket. Something—a piece of horse hide?—had fallen onto his right arm and he jerked the hook back underneath it, out of sight, his hand gripping the handle. As the headlights swept past him he saw a rack of ribs joined by rotting fascia. It was a horse all right, the ribs were as thick as baseball bats. The bucket bulked against the sky and there came another crushing weight. Sean squeezed his eyes shut against the grit. He heard the beast move, gather itself, the bucket climbing. This time the thunder of the impact was muted by the dirt already covering him. He strained for breath, managing to draw a thin reed of air. He tried to move, felt his right hand flex, the hand that held the hook. It seemed to be the only part of his body not entombed in the earth.

Footsteps approached. They were on top of him, muffled impacts. As a boy he'd had nightmares of being buried alive, listening to people talk and trying to scream, and no sound coming out. He knew there would be no awakening from this dream. Desperate for breath, he jerked his head back and forth to create air space. Already his chest was squeezing in. Another attempt at breath. Another, feeling an oddly exquisite agony. Then the pain abated, replaced by a dreamy, flowing feeling. Images began to flicker behind his eyes. There were the faces of his father and mother, his sister. The image of a girl jumping rope, somebody he'd once known. Becky somebody. Martinique flickered into focus, so did Vareda Beaudreux, the loves of a more recent past. He saw Martha Ettinger, hands akimbo, talking without sound.

Something was moving. It was scratching at his face, like claws. Sean swam out of his reverie. The dog? He felt air on his face and heaved. Swallowing grit, he breathed again, feeling his ribs expand against the constriction of the earth.

"You going to live on me?"

Sean spit and hacked. Gradually, he felt his breathing steady. But he was still buried; only his head and right hand were above the level of the ground. His right hand tightened on the hay hook. But Fey had backed away from the trench and was squatting on his heels, out of striking range. The butt of his rifle rested on the ground, his hand on the barrel. Behind him, Sean could see the darting shadow of the dog.

"Did you see God?" Jasper's backlit face was cratered with shadows.

"I saw . . . people." Sean tried to move his legs. It was like kicking through sludge.

"The earth's disturbed now," he heard Jasper saying. "It will harden up like snowpack. You'll be here until the worms crawl in your ears."

"The locator beacon, they're—"

"I don't believe you. Oh, you were thinking about it. But you hadn't sent a message, and even if you did, I don't care. I asked a serious question. You saw people. What people?"

"From the past. I saw . . . my family, other people."

"But not God."

"No, no God. Do you have water? It's hard to talk with this dirt in my mouth." Sean squeezed the handle of the hay hook, exercising his fingers.

"You're talking just fine. Tell me, Sean, are you in love with my wife?"

"Etta?"

"Don't take me wrong. I wouldn't blame you. Her heat. You get within the radius, I've seen it time after time. And I've been around attractive women, professionally attractive women. But even actresses, they can turn down the heat. With Etta, there's no switch. That's why she doesn't have women friends. Women know they can't trust their men around her."

"I'm not in love with your wife."

"Are you sure?"

"I'm not in love with her."

"Because I was wondering. When I saw her this evening, before I left for town, she had an expression on her face, it was like she possessed a secret knowledge. Like maybe she knew what I was going to do before I knew what I was going to do. Like maybe she even knew you'd be here. I could have sworn she said your name under her breath, but I guess I was being paranoid. You see, paranoia, it's not a feeling, it's a creature, an animal. It has a scent. You go from one room into another, the scent follows you. Sometimes you get busy so you don't notice it as much, and sometimes it goes away, never far, just for a while. But at night, that's different. It hops up on your chest. It has a face, it has sharp teeth, like a wolf. You smell its breath."

"Why are you paranoid?"

Sean heard a low laugh.

"You want to keep me talking. So maybe you did send a signal. But okay, I'll talk. It's hard, keeping it in. Living with the uncertainty. You want to tell someone but you can't, so you talk to God. That's why I asked if you saw God, because I want to believe. Now Etta, she's lost three children. She's turned to Indian mysticism, liquor, anything to try to make sense of a world that would let something like that happen. I used to tell her to be a man, get a grip. That was a compliment. Etta's more man than almost any man I know."

He paused. Sean could hear a sound like masticating. In Montana, men chewed on nothing all the time, it helped pick their words.

"Why I had the truck window down that night, I do not know. It was November, not cold, but still, November." He opened his hand. "Why do we do anything? But then, if I'd had it up, I wouldn't have heard the screaming. I'd have driven past the stables and on up to the house, gone to bed like any other night. But I had the window down and I heard her. It was godawful, just on and on.

"By the time I got to the door the screaming's stopped. Now it's a whimpering, like a hurt puppy. It's coming from a stall. There's my girl, not a stitch on. That Anker kid's got her all wrapped up in his arms. I just lost it. I got my hands on his throat, he doesn't say a word. He *can't* say a word. Cindy's trying to peel me off. I never gave a thought that it could be anything but what it looked like. Not then, not till way later. Then I'm holding on the way you got your hand wrapped holding on to the bull rope. Digging down like you're going to press your hand right into the hide. It must have stopped the blood going up to his brain. And Cindy, she's screaming and now I can hear, she's saying, 'He didn't do it,' and I'm thinking the hell he didn't. All that adrenaline behind my hands, I couldn't release the grip if I wanted to. I can feel his chest heaving under me, and then it just stops. 'Cindy,' I say, but she's gone. I didn't even see her go out. Time passes, I don't know. I got this kid on my lap, all bug-eyed. It's like somebody put him there.

"I yell out for Cindy and hear Charlie hollering, like an echo. I didn't even know he was at the ranch. I was in such a hurry driving up that I didn't see his truck. He finds me and says, 'Where's that god-damned kid, I'm going to kill him.' He's got buttons ripped off his shirt. He takes one look in the stall, me and Landon, he says, 'You killed him.' Had this strange, taken-aback expression. Then it's like you see the gears turning, like something dawns on him. And I'm thinking he's just trying to comprehend what's happened, not that he's thinking up a story, because now I know that's what he was do-ing. He says he caught the kid raping Cindy down in another stall, and when he tried to stop him, they wrestled, and the kid got free and cold-cocked him. That he'd just come to and started looking for him. He says 'J.P.'—he's the only one in the world calls me by my initials—he says, 'We got to get rid of the body, J.P.'

"But I'm just thinking about Cindy. I look in Snapdragon's stall, door wide open, she's gone. I told Charlie the hell with the body, we got to find my girl. I don't know what I was thinking, that maybe if I talked sense to her she'd forgive me. That it wasn't broken so it couldn't be fixed, that maybe the kid wasn't even dead. Just lunacy. So we mount up. There's snow to follow the horse's tracks a little ways, but it's a goddamned pasture, so a bunch of horses have it tracked up, and we finally get up into the timber and we lose the track, but by then it might have been the wrong horse we were following.

"I said, 'Charlie, let's check the cabin.' It's only another mile or so along, thinking maybe that's where she'd gone. Back when I caretaked the place, I'd pay Cindy to do things like sweep up after people, reset mousetraps, chop wood. Tomboy chores. She liked to play house in it with her friends. But she wasn't there and Charlie keeps harping on we got to bury the body, that there's no blood so all we have to do is straighten up the stalls and it's like it never happened. People will think he ran away with Cindy. Charlie's got his .30-30 in the scabbard and I realize now that if we actually had found Cindy, he was going to have to kill both of us."

Fey stopped. The small dog had come up to him and Fey rubbed his forehead against the top of its head. "What I'd give for the life of a dog," he said. His hat had fallen off and he left it on the ground, the inside of the crown up. The little dog curled into it, spilling over the sides. "Where was I?" Fey said.

"Charlie was going to have to kill both of you."

"And he would have. I almost wish he had. But of course we didn't find her, my girl was gone. That ride back to the stables, I didn't even feel the horse under me. It was almost morning by then, I could see Snapdragon in the meadow, she returned before we did. I knew if we went through with Charlie's plan I'd be beholden to him the rest of my life, but I couldn't see a way out of it. Not any way that didn't mean prison. So that's what we done, buried him right where your feet are settin'. That's him over there, what's left, that pile of earth. And I got the blood on my hands and it's never going to wash off. But all these months, I never once thought Charlie did what he done to Cindy. My best friend, a man who took a horn for me . . . I never dreamed . . ."

He fell silent. After a minute he set the rifle down and raised his hands over his head, as if imploring the heavens, then let them drop to his sides. He sat back on his heels.

"I gave him money. I even let him take my place in the club. But not once did I think he'd hurt my girl."

"It's voluntary manslaughter, Jasper. You believed you were protecting your daughter from rape; to a judge that's a powerful mitigating circumstance. You might not even do time."

"No, there's where you're wrong. I've been doing time ever since that night. I don't know what I'm doing now. Since they found her, time doesn't seem an adequate description. Penance, I guess. Maybe I could have lived with killing that boy. Maybe I can live with losing Etta, too. But I can't live knowing what I did killed my little girl."

"Jasper, you didn't put her in that chimney."

"But if that night never happened, she wouldn't have run away. So you see, I did kill her. I had just as much hand in it as Charlie."

"How does killing me make it better?"

"It doesn't. But you start down a path, it gets so what happens along it doesn't matter. It isn't a justification. It's an explanation. You take the path, the path takes you."

A note of finality had crept into Fey's voice.

Where the hell is Martha?

Sean's cheek flexed, an involuntary contraction. He felt a prickling sensation. Insect legs were crawling from the dirt onto his face, the feelers light as feathers. Now the legs were tickling the corner of his mouth. He blew at the creature, sticking out his lower lip.

"It's a carrion beetle. He's just a little ahead of schedule. I'll get it."

Fey picked up the rifle and kneed forward. He jabbed the muzzle against Sean's mouth. As the foresight slid across his cheek, Sean released his grip on the hay hook and shot out his hand, grabbing for the rifle barrel and jerking it from Fey's grasp. Even as Fey scrabbled for it, Sean knew that there was no way to win a tug-of-war, not with one hand. As Fey's hand closed over the wrist of the stock, Sean abruptly let go his hold on the barrel, then reached his hand back under the hide of the horse and felt the smooth handle of the hook. With every ounce of his strength, he swung it. The point hit home and Jasper, the rifle in his hand, recoiled violently, yanking the hook from Sean's grasp. He lifted his left arm to look down at his side. Fey's right hand, the lobster hand that was half again as large as his left, pinched tentatively at the handle. He inched his face up to look at Stranahan, his expression incredulous. Then he looked back at the handle. Deliberately he set the rifle down and grasped the handle. He clenched his facial muscles and jerked at it, not to dislodge it, but as if trying to bury it deeper. It crossed Sean's mind that Fey didn't really know what had happened, or what he'd been hit with. An expression of air grunted from Fey's body. He jerked the handle again, his body lurching in spasm.

Slowly then, as if he was moving independently of thought, he rose to his knees, got to one leg, then the other. He stood, teetering. "I'll be back," he said in a matter-of-fact voice. He turned and walked, hitching to the side of his injury, to the tractor. He tried to pull himself up onto the seat and fell back. He stood, waited, and tried again, swinging up onto the tractor saddle. Sean heard the engagement of the gears and the tractor began to move, the bucket scraping at the small mound of earth, then lifting its grisly burden. *He's going to dump it on me*, Sean thought, and clenched the muscles in his neck to take the impact. But the tractor had turned and was lurching away. It tilted back and forth where the ground was uneven, like a drunk stumbling from a bar. The gears ground as the headlights rose, the tractor climbing a rise in the land. Then it pitched forward and to the side, out of sight, and as Sean heard it tip over, the milky eyes of the headlights careened across the universe.

Sean tried to move, but except for his right arm, he might as well have been encased in cement. He clawed at the dirt with his fingernails, then stopped, overcome by exhaustion. It was cold in the earth, but the air was colder still. *Just lie here awhile, get your strength back. It's over now.*

But was it? Sean kept his eyes on the silhouette of the hill that the tractor had climbed, half expecting Fey to appear, brandishing the bloody hook.

He didn't appear. After what Sean thought must be an hour, the tractor idled unevenly, coughed, and died. The smear of the headlights gradually faded, then died abruptly, leaving him in darkness that was total. He felt drops of rain on his face. It stopped. Then started again. The dog had run away in the melee and came back from the direction of the tractor. Sean could hear the patter of its feet. Finally it lay down again on the hat. He spoke to it, a dog in the rain, whimpering.

When the headlights came searching, Sean recognized the motor as being the truck Harold Little Feather had borrowed from his sister. He heard the door open, the lights switched off, then nothing.

"I'm here, Harold."

The beam of Harold's flashlight played over the pit, crossed Stranahan's face, then came back. Harold walked up for a better look and squatted down, the butt of his Winchester lever-action on the ground, in much the same position Jasper Fey had assumed. Sean realized how he must look, buried to his neck in earth and worse.

Harold turned to call back toward the truck. "It's all right, Katie. You can come on over."

Then, to Stranahan: "Not what I expected to find. Are you okay?" His face moved to Fey's bolt-action rifle lying a few feet away.

"Sure," Sean said. "There's a fine horse under me."

CHAPTER THIRTY-FIVE

False Dawn

Later, Stranahan would see the chain of events leading to that moment as a manifestation of Murphy's law. When Katie Sparrow received the SPOT message on her cell phone, she'd called Martha's number and, not receiving an answer, had tried Harold, who heard the ringtone but ignored it, as he was busy winching a Datsun sedan out of a barrow pit, which the driver had veered into when he was, quote, "arranging my junk in my BVDs." Harold's eyes had traveled to the sullen bottle blonde smoking a cigarette by the side of the road. He had arrested her once for solicitation and shook his head. He was still shaking his head when he got back to his sister's house and remembered the missed call. He hit the redial and told Katie to slow down while mouthing to Janice to make him a cup of instant.

"Where are you so I can pick you up?" Then to Janice: "I'm going to need to borrow your truck again," and a muttered "only white people dig up bodies" as he headed for the door.

———

How long have you been in the hole?" Harold said.

"Maybe a couple hours."

"What do you think, Sparrow? Will it take that long to get him out?"

It didn't, but they were stripped to T-shirts, sweating in forty-degree weather, before digging the last shovelfuls to set Sean free.

"Do you think you can walk?" Katie said.

Sean nodded.

"Stay three paces behind, the both of you," Harold said.

The tractor had tipped onto its side, the backhoe curled in an attitude of supplication. Something was half spilled out of the bucket. Rotting clothes, a slime of tissue over bone, a face, or what was once. A few wisps of the hair that Cinderella had longed to twirl in her fingers. Harold shone his light over the tractor. No one in the saddle, but a snail trail of blood led down the hillside. Jasper Fey had made it as far as a ditch, where he had curled into himself like a kitten. The hay hook was still buried in his side.

"He's all bled out," Harold noted. "Like you make a heart shot on a buck. Deer takes off and dies in stride, you open him up, the body cavity's a pool of blood. You don't even need to stick him in the neck."

He reached for his radio as Sean unfolded his knife and cut the sleeve of Fey's shirt. He wanted to see the tattoo. It was there. *Shirley* in the banner, a tear on each painted cheek.

"Ettinger's on the way," Harold said. Finally, a smile. "Fine horse, huh?"

Sean nodded. "I think it was a bay."

———

Martha didn't see the humor. She had climbed out of the Cherokee to award Sean her patented headshake, hands on her utility belt, elbows cocked. It was the Martha who had flashed behind Sean's eyes when the dirt covered him and his blood was starved for oxygen.

"I'm glad it's dark so I don't have to look at you," she said. "That goes for you, too, Katie. What were you thinking? No, you weren't thinking. How naive of me to think you'd be thinking."

"If it hadn't been for the dog—"

"Wake up, Stranny. You're in Montana. There's *always* a dog."

She had a point, and two hours later, having given his statement for Harold's digital recorder and with the beast in question sitting shotgun in the Land Cruiser, he drove to the Bar-4 to break the news.

Etta Huntington was already up, sitting down to coffee in her kitchen.

"What you're smelling is a livestock burial pit," he told her. "It might be better to talk on the porch."

The clouds that fed the intermittent rain had broken up and she hugged herself with her good arm. "It's the starless mornings that are hardest," she said, setting her coffee on the rail. "Sometimes I think if I can't see Pegasus, Cinderella will be gone forever. I'll no longer be able to remember her."

She didn't seem alarmed by anything he told her, starting with the death of Jasper Fey and going back to Sean's discovery of the pictographs. He was reminded of Fey's comment about a knowing expression, as if she possessed a secret knowledge. He was too tired to come at the question obliquely.

"What aren't you telling me, Etta?"

She ignored the question in favor of her own, asking if he was all right.

"I'm just tired."

"No, I mean, will there be consequences? Will they say you killed him?"

"The sheriff says I'll get what's coming to me. But I don't think I'll be charged, if that's what you're getting at. Jasper had me buried up to my neck. He swore he would kill me. I suppose the Board of Security could suspend my investigator's license. I'm guessing they frown at PIs wielding hay hooks."

"But was it you who really killed him?"

Sean saw what she was getting at. "You mean did the initial penetration tear the artery, or did Jasper kill himself by setting the hook deeper?"

"Can an autopsy determine that?"

"Maybe. But it's a technicality. I intended to hurt him as badly as I could. And I've had a while to think about it. He might have been trying to take it out. I'm not sure he knew what he was hit with."

"I'm sorry I got you into this," she said. "I don't want you to have to bear a burden."

Her voice seemed to carry from a distance. Sean felt the space between them growing.

"Don't do this to yourself, Etta."

"I'm not doing anything."

"There's something you're holding back. I just about lost my life trying to find out what happened to your daughter. I want to . . ." He stopped. He was thinking about the day when she'd led him to the lake.

"You know because you've seen the pictographs," he said. "That talk about how you couldn't get up there because of your arm. You climbed there, and you went down that rock chimney and found the cave. Did the pictures tell you something I missed?"

"No, you're wrong. I didn't know. I know now, I mean yesterday I found out about the pictures and . . . other things."

He waited.

"I tried to call you, but you must have already been up there at the pit, you and your friend with the dog. It wasn't something you put in a message."

She turned her face to him. He could see the artery pulsing in her neck. "He was standing right where we are. Sean, he was the one who made the paint for the pictures."

"Bear Paw Bill?"

"He drove up here in an SUV, an old rattley one. Jasper was gone by then, thank God."

"Was it an Explorer? That's what he stole from the hospital lot."

"I guessed it was stolen. I knew the police were looking for him, so I parked it around back. You should have seen him. All he had on was a hospital gown with a blanket wrapped over the top of it. Even on crutches he could hardly walk. I asked when was the last time he'd eaten. He said he had no idea."

"Did he say he'd killed Charles Watt?"

"He knew everything. He told me everything."

Sean waited for her to continue, but she seemed to have gone somewhere else and just stared at the sky, the wafer of light that was false dawn losing its lie.

Finally she spoke.

"Charlie found her diary, that's how he got to her. Bill said it had happened in the stables, that Charlie had seen where Cindy hid the diary between the walls and threatened to give it to her stepfather, unless she would take off her clothes for him. He told her that was all he wanted. So she did it. The next day, or night I guess, when I was in Helena and Jasper was gone, when Charlie was alone with her, he wanted, you know, more. He told her that a body like that was too fine to be throwing at a boy who wouldn't know what to do with it. He could give her what she wanted a lot better, that if she did she'd get the diary back. He set it on the stall divider, just higher than she could reach. Then he . . . did what he did."

She stopped, and again she contemplated the sky.

"Bill said Charlie laughed in his face when he confronted him about it, said the bitch begged for it. He didn't seem to be afraid of Bill showing up on his doorstep. Bill hugged him, that's the word he used. 'I hugged him until his chest broke, the Lord have mercy on my soul.'"

"What happened that night, afterwards?"

"You mean after my daughter was raped? You can say the word."

"Then."

"Then Landon showed up. Charlie hadn't expected him that night. He decked Charlie and she ran with him to another stall, and then Jasper came, and, well, I guess you know what happened then."

"Did Bill say she hid in the chimney, at the cabin?"

"Yes, like in the pictographs. He said she made it up to his camp later that night, but it was a week before she spoke a word. She didn't tell him about the rape until she was getting sick every morning and she began to suspect she was pregnant. He tried to convince her to go home, but how could she come back here when she'd been raped by her father's best friend, when she'd fought against Jasper while he strangled the boy she was in love with? All along I thought she was running from me, but it wasn't me, it was them."

She stopped, and Sean could hear her breathing.

"That bastard," she said. "All goddamned winter he plays along like Cinderella's disappearance is never going to be solved, and it's time to stop grieving and get on with life, and he knew what happened and didn't have the courage to tell the truth."

"Etta, when he told me he didn't know it was Charlie who raped her, I believed him."

"Maybe he didn't, but he knew why she ran away. He knew she could be alive and he didn't tell anyone. He let me fall to pieces so he could stay out of jail and keep being Jasper Fey."

"Etta . . ." He reached out, but she batted his hand away. Then, shutting her eyes, her shoulders falling, she came into his arms, blood and guts and all.

After a time he heard her murmur.

"Etta?"

"You're going to have to burn these clothes."

CHAPTER THIRTY-SIX

Crazy Mountain Kiss

As a man who'd done his share of sleeping in cars, Sean Stranahan always had a change of clothes, a bar of soap, and a toothbrush. He stripped down outside and walked to Etta's bathroom wearing little more than a weary smile. Twenty minutes later she put down a plate of scrambled eggs for him and began painting in the spaces on the cave walls, telling him what the pictographs hadn't.

———

For the first month, Bear Paw Bill McKutchen and Cinderella Huntington had been on the run, traveling underneath the spine of the range from south to north, trying to stay ahead of a manhunt that never materialized. Several times he spotted a single-engine aircraft sweeping the peaks, but was the pilot looking for Cinderella or trying to spot the fire of a lost hunter, he didn't know. As cold nights set in, he shot an elk with his muzzle-loader and brain-tanned the leather to make Cinderella a coat. Meat wasn't a problem, but nutrition was, and with winter's first heavy snowfall, Bear Paw Bill led Cinderella back to the south in a circuitous route, arriving at the shelter he'd built weeks earlier up the South Fork of the Shields River.

The arrangement with his brother, Myron, was similar to those they'd made in past years. About once a month, depending on road conditions, Myron would place a bag of lentils, dried beans, salt, rice and a half-gallon jug of hard apple cider in a five-gallon bucket with a snap-on lid that had a permanent home in a hole in the ground, and over which he rolled an immense boulder. The boulder was along the trail to the bald ridge, about a quarter mile beyond the Forest Service cabin and accessed by the same road.

Supplemented with venison and the occasional trout Bill caught with his crudely tied flies, the food cache was a hedge against starvation, though hardly an inspiring diet. Bill told Etta that he was ashamed to admit that he'd also scavenged food from the forest cabin, when renters had failed to lock the door upon their departure. It was Cinderella who suggested the chimney. When taking refuge on the night of her rape, she had discovered that she could not only descend it easily, but shimmy back up. If Bill would take her along on his monthly trek to the food cache, she could check the cabin. A locked door wouldn't matter.

As McKutchen told Etta a story of survival in the Crazy Mountains, storms that dropped three feet of snow and temperatures that plunged to thirty below zero, blood from the stump of his leg was slowly dripping onto the floor tiles of her kitchen. Bill said he was sorry for the mess and frowned down at it. It reminded him of the deer blood he used to color the clay with which they had painted the cave walls. Because they didn't want to blacken the cave with soot, they built their fires on the headwall, where Cinderella had filmed him for her documentary. He said that Cinderella was a quick study and did all of the rock art without his guidance, as she was as nimble as a goat and could climb down to the cave, whereas he could not.

At this point in her narration, Etta paused. "I asked him about his foot," she told Sean. "I wanted to know whether Cinderella had cut it off."

This was a question Sean had been asking himself since they had found the mountain man, doubting Ettinger's theory that Cinderella had severed it in order to flee from his camp.

McKutchen told Etta that he'd stepped on a nail protruding from a bear door buried in the snow behind the cabin. It had happened when he was trying to break in for food and had not realized it was occupied. He'd stepped on the nails while running away, and over the next few weeks the infection had spread until it was clear that without a tetanus shot and a course of antibiotics he would not only lose the foot to gangrene, but also his life. To make matters worse, a bear, ravenous after emerging from hibernation, had flipped over the boulder and dug out the last food cache. Bill and Cinderella were surviving on pemmican made from dried squirrel meat, berries, and the rendered fat from a deer, and it had started to turn rancid.

Where before he had taken care of Cinderella's needs, she now attended to him. Using the blade of a Swede saw, she painstakingly sawed a section of log to make a hard surface for the impact of the ax. She placed Bill's leg across the stump. With the ax buried in campfire coals, the only sterilization available, she coaxed Bill to drink the dregs of hard cider left in the jug. The mountain man then bit down on a scrap of elk hide. He had coached Cinderella in ax craft since the beginning of winter, and she raised the head with its thin glowing bevel, and brought it down with all her strength. It took two chops, the second in the gash of the first, before the blade stuck into the wood.

Bill bit all the way through the elk hide, but never passed out. He directed Cinderella to knot a rawhide tourniquet, and she had applied the entire tube of antibiotic ointment they'd found in a medicine kit in the forest cabin. That night Bill fell into a delirium. He dreamed, as the Crow warrior Plenty Coups had dreamed more than one hundred fifty years before, of the chickadee, the tree in which it perched the sole survivor of the four great winds. In Bill's mind the chickadee was Cinderella, and to him the dream meant she must return home, for the tree was trembling now and mountains no longer afforded her sanctity.

He called Cinderella to his side and explained what was to be done. She would hike out of the mountains while she still had her strength and find her way to Myron's house in the Bangtails. The season for the cabin rental had ended, so she could climb down the chimney and spend the first night there and build a fire to warm up. With an early start the next morning, avoiding roads and cutting cross country, she could make it to Myron's by nightfall. Bill stressed the importance of having Myron notify the sheriff before trying to get in touch with her mother. Under no circumstance was she to see her stepfather until her story was told. That was for her own protection.

Cinderella had argued. He'd been there for her; now she would stay at his side until he recovered. You must go for the sake of the baby, he told her. It must not be punished for the sins of the father, and there was no longer any food. Still, she was intractable. Finally, Bill had unbuttoned his greatcoat and pulled up his shirt. On his left side were several circular pink scars and a seeping wound. Bill told Cinderella that he had been shot with buckshot the same night he stepped on the nail. He hadn't mentioned it then because the wounds seemed minor and he didn't want to frighten her. But now he had become sick to his stomach and wondered if he'd got lead poisoning. He'd tried to pry out the pellets with his knife and just made things worse. The pain had become excruciating. *You would not want to see me die, would you?*

And so he prevailed over her objections, and it was as much to save Bill's life as the life of her child that she agreed to the plan. She left the next day in a light snowfall, and Bill, watching after her, had seen several magpies, those cousins of the crow that dress in black tie, their starched white shirtfronts sewn of breast feathers, and worried it was a bad omen. She had turned then and said the last words he would ever hear her say.

"Don't worry, Bill. I can fly."

Two weeks later, starving and in excruciating pain, he had spotted a coyote lingering at the edge of his camp, and thought perhaps it was Cinderella come to lead him to heaven. He had spoken to the coyote, and, getting no response, had begun to doubt its existence. *Maybe I'm hallucinating,* he thought. So he shot his muzzle-loader into the air. It was the shot that Sean and Katie Sparrow had heard when they found the bear window at the cabin. The coyote had lifted its head at the shot, then in a fluid movement melted into the trees. So it was simply an animal. He would live, perhaps, a little longer. The next day he began to crawl out of the mountains, and had made it a quarter of a mile before Ettinger and Stranahan picked up his track and found him.

———

Sean had not moved so much as a hand in the hour Etta recited Bill's story, and he found the coffee in his cup to be cold.

"It still doesn't explain how Cinderella got stuck," he said, placing a hand over the cup to indicate he didn't want any more.

She set down the pot and he watched a tear track down her right cheek. She rubbed it away.

"I have a theory, if you want to hear it." He waited for her to nod.

"When I heard Bill had the same type of foot injury, I thought it probably happened when they were together at the cabin. But her injury was minor and had only started to become infected. Did he say anything about her being injured to you?"

She shook her head.

"Then it must have happened the night she left his camp. It was dark. There was a storm coming and she was in a hurry to get the ladder up. Probably she wasn't paying attention to where she was stepping. If you drove a nail through your foot, it would have been more than painful, it would be debilitating. She would have to favor that foot when she climbed down the chimney. Maybe it happened as she was stepping down with her other foot. Maybe that foot slipped and she shot down the chimney and the other knee got wedged up under her."

Etta pressed her lips together. "Or maybe it was because she was five and a half months pregnant and she was bigger, did you think of that? That's what I thought of. But it doesn't matter. It doesn't change anything at all."

There was nothing to say to that, and they sat quietly, listening to the early birds. Something was coming to an end. Maybe it already had.

"I guess I better go see Ettinger," Sean said. "She's not done giving me the third degree." He got to his feet. "I'm going to have to tell her about Bill. He's still a fugitive from justice. My advice is to co-operate and give her a full statement. That will probably be the end of it."

"I gave him money," Etta said. "And I gave him food, a care package."

"I might not mention that part. Did he say what his plans were?"

"He said he'd go on a vision quest somewhere, he hadn't decided what range, anywhere but the Crazies."

She walked him to the door. "I owe you some money. You worked beyond the date of our contract."

"You don't have to—"

"No, you earned it."

"Then I'll come back for it." But he knew he wouldn't, that these mountains had become as haunted for him as they must have become for Bear Paw Bill and for Cinderella Huntington.

"Will you?" Etta said. "Something tells me I might not see you again."

"You'll see me." He kissed her forehead, and that's the way they left it, with Sean feeling the weight of her eyes as he walked away, knowing she saw right through him.

———

When the headlights faded down the road, Etta climbed to her bedroom and pulled the diary from the drawer of her nightstand. It was Bear Paw Bill who had told her where to find it. He said that Cinderella had grabbed it from the stall as she fled the stables, and, knowing how she treasured it, he had made an inside pocket in the elkskin coat he'd sewn for her. In this way, Cinderella had worn her diary next to her heart for several months, working on it with pens found in the cabin. Only days before she left, Bill had helped her unravel the binding and separate the book into sections of a few pages each, before sewing it between the layers of hide that made the coat. Thus it was undetectable, and Cinderella took comfort that no matter what happened, no one would ever find it.

Etta had hung the coat in Cinderella's room after Sean gave it to her, and when Bill had left the ranch, she cut the threads at the hem, her hand shaking. When she shook the coat, the pages sifted out onto the floor. The writing was legible but the reading tedious, for the diary had been written in pen and pencil over a period of eighteen months, and the ink had smeared here, or had run out there, only to be taken up in another color, and some of the pages were stuck together from moisture. Etta had stayed up all of one night ordering them as best she could, and then had bound them together with a ribbon.

The diary offered a glimpse of Cinderella's thoughts before and after the accident. After the accident the handwriting had become more expressive and artistic as the brain compensated for its injury, and the entries, especially those about Landon, were more romantic and poignant in their tenor. Reading them had made Etta weep.

Perhaps thankfully, no entries recorded Cinderella's rape and flight to the mountains. Bear Paw Bill, upon handing Etta the jacket, had prepared her for the omissions, as Cinderella had confessed to him that the night was too painful to write about. It was her suffering in those first weeks that had led to the pictographs. Bill had suggested writing her story on rock as Indians had, hoping that it would prove a form of therapy. He told Etta that the happiest days of his life were those he had spent with her daughter, mixing vegetable and animal blood pigments and teaching her the art form, for they had practiced on rocks for many days before he led her to the cave.

Untying the ribbon, Etta once again read the last entry, dated April 2.

> *Last night I felt the baby kick. Bill tells me I must think*
> *of it now with everything I do, even though I have not*
> *worked up the courage to do some of the things he wants me*
> *to. It is scary to watch him hone the ax, knowing what I*

must do with it. But it is even scarier to think about leaving and what I must do when I reach the valley. He knows my head is fuzzy and doesn't want me to do anything that would put me in danger. So I will find his brother and tell him about the evil in the valley of men, as he calls it, even though it means I can't go to mother for a few more days. I know she will love the baby and help me to raise it. Bill has made me promise I will raise it to believe in God. He says when I did the vision quest, God was in the wings of the birds flying on the warm air that flows up the mountains. Bill thinks I am a bird too, a chickadee. I do sometimes feel like I am flying, so maybe he is right. But most of the time I am just a girl who wants her mother. When I see her, I will give her a Crazy Mountain kiss.

Etta tied the ribbon around the book and set it on the nightstand. Slowly, she spread her fingers along the invisible face of the daughter who lived now only in the stars, and drew her fingers back until the tips touched her chin. She brought her forefinger to her lips and pressed. Then she pressed the finger against the lips of her daughter, before placing her hand on her heart.

CHAPTER THIRTY-SEVEN

Mothers and Sons

Three weeks after Bear Paw Bill visited Etta Huntington, the Explorer he'd stolen was found abandoned in Livingston. A kid had looked through the window to see money tucked into the folds of the gearshift and decided to help himself with the help of a rock. He was caught with two twenties stuffed down his underpants. A citizen's arrest, the citizen the kid's father. The cop who caught the call found the keys in the glove compartment, along with a note.

> *As much as I can spare for the gas. I'm truly sorry about the blood.*

"You wouldn't guess where he's headed?" Martha rolled a dart between her fingers as she held Stranahan's eyes. On the wall of her office a new page of the calendar, a leopard on an acacia branch with his tail dropping down.

"My guess is he hitched a ride to a road end somewhere. Maybe got his brother to drop him off. If it was me, I wouldn't look too hard."

"Yeah, but it's not you, is it? Some of us are paid to uphold the law."

Still, they were on speaking terms, an improvement since the night in the burial pit and largely the result of the arrival of Martha's son. David had grown into his body over the winter, had his mother's square shoulders now to go with her blue eyes and strong chin. He'd introduced himself to Sean with two unhesitating strides and a firm handshake, saying he was looking forward to the fishing trip and thanking him for the invitation. Three nights, four days, floating and camping between Divide and Melrose on the Big Hole River. A guys-only trip—David, Sean, and Sam Meslik, the latter included over Martha's objection, uttered under her breath with one eyebrow lifted. "That man would be a bad influence on a prairie rattlesnake."

But she'd known the trip would be good for David. She had gotten on with her son far better than she could have hoped for, including two late-night heart-to-hearts about his future, as they worked a crossword puzzle of a beargrass meadow. Still, he was a young man and he needed to do young man things, and the fishing trip would be a fitting send-off to the badlands, where'd he'd live in a tent for the next six weeks, chipping away at green siltstone rock to expose dinosaur bones.

"Just bring him back in one piece," she'd told Stranahan when he'd suggested the float, and told him the same thing again as their conversation about Bear Paw Bill wound down and she jerked her arm, sending the dart into the forehead of a fugitive on one of the Wanted posters pinned to the wall.

CHAPTER THIRTY-EIGHT

The Wooly Bugger Waltz

Doc Hanson heard the steps on the porch seconds before the knock. He looked over the top of his glasses, then set them down on the table where he'd been dealing cards from a pack he'd found in the drawer. It was Martha Ettinger who'd suggested the Forest Service cabin, when they'd bumped into each other in the lot of Law and Justice. Doc had promised himself the next time he saw her there would be no awkwardness, and there wasn't. She asked how he was doing and he'd said, "I'm so good I better hurry up before something goes wrong." He said he was thinking of taking a few days for himself to outline a book he intended to write, a field guide to Montana's reptiles and amphibians. The only one he'd seen on bookshelves was poorly illustrated and too big to pocket.

He'd watched Martha think, pinching her chin, before saying why not the cabin. That is, if he could get past the history. The last writer to go there wished he hadn't. Doc had reminded her that dead people were his profession. Well then, how many days was he thinking about? They'd firmed up the dates on the phone that night and she'd given him the combination to the lock.

He opened the door.

A woman stood before him. She was wearing a string backpack. She had dark curly hair and looked like a gypsy.

"How may I help you?"

"You must be Doc," she said, and held out a hand, rings on every finger.

He noticed the canvas duffel sitting on the floorboards. His expression was guarded.

"From the club," she said. "I'm Book Girl. Are you really a doctor?"

"Yes, but there must be some mistake. We must have our dates crossed."

"Oh, I don't think so." She breezed past him into the dark room, a light jasmine scent lingering in the air. Doc couldn't just let the bag sit there. He picked it up and set it inside.

"I brought candles," she said. The bracelets on her wrist jangled as she dug into her backpack. She placed a transparent gel candle with pink suspended hearts on the table and flourished a pack of matches. "Voilà."

"I'm sorry, but—"

"It's okay, Doc. This is your first time, it's natural to be a little scared." She frowned down at the cards. Solitaire. "Well, there won't be any more of that," she said brightly. She scraped the cards into the drawer and lit the candle.

"Who sent you?" Doc managed. All the air seemed to have gone up the chimney and he heard his voice as if from a distance.

"Amoretta, silly. The assignation was in the classifieds. Don't you know anything?"

She stepped closer to him and laced her hands behind his neck. "We have to have faith in our fellow human beings, I always say. You have to step out onto that branch. You're shaking, Doc. Oh, you are a dear. But that's okay." She kissed one corner of his quivering mustache, then the other. "I know the cure."

———

Martha lit the fire in the woodstove, leaving the door open so she could watch the flames. On Valentine's evening, when she'd opened *Gone with the Wind* for her annual sojourn to Tara, she'd pictured herself sitting before crackling embers as she turned the last page. Only twenty now to go, she'd draw them out, savor every word. She padded to the kitchen to make chamomile tea, another part of the ritual. Sheba on her lap, Goldie with her chin on Martha's slippered feet, that would complete the evening's preparations.

She opened the front door to call Goldie inside, listening to the vesper song of this bird and that one. Soon it would be dark and the crows that sat in a solemn row on a bare branch of the old dead cottonwood, that had perched there for the past three evenings, would assimilate into the night.

Had they come to tell her that their work was done and Cinderella was made whole in heaven? The daytime Martha would have shaken her head, said it was romantic foolishness to think so. But with the sun down anything was possible, even lore, even love, and having that thought she wondered about Doc, if the woman had shown up at the cabin. If she had, Doc would either never forgive her, or already had. Well, everybody needed what he was looking for—how had he put it, "a shudder in the bloodstream before the hands reach midnight"?

She could use some of that, too. But tonight she'd settle for the literary equivalent.

"I won't think about him," she said aloud.

But of course she had been, ever since he'd swung by to pick up David. They'd have floated into the heart of the canyon today. The tents would be up, Sean's raft pulled onto the bank. They'd have polished off their antelope steaks and would be sitting with cups of whiskey, their thoughts drawn by the catalyst of the campfire. Or so she envisioned.

But what did men left to themselves do? What did they talk about? She'd belonged to the boys' club of law enforcement for so long that all her friends were men, and yet what did she really know about them? That good ones like Sean and Harold meant well, but hadn't a clue. As for the Jasper Feys of the world, the Sam Mesliks? She shook her head. Scarlett hadn't understood men, either.

But when she turned to follow Goldie inside, she flicked the porch light on. She'd screwed in a new bulb, one of those spiral ones that lasted forever. She'd turn it off after Rhett didn't give a damn. Tonight was only a trial run. But tomorrow, and the day after, when David was gone and she was alone in the house? One could always reconsider. Tomorrow *was* another day.

———

Pay attention now," Sam said. "This is your basic salsa side step."

He shuffled to his right, his thick arms pumping to the rhythm of his steps, then to his left. "Quick-quick slow. Quick-quick slow. It's one of your basic Zumba moves. You want to peel down some of that Latina spandex, you got to have your moves." Dancing behind the flames, his mane of hair glowing in the firelight, sparks shooting past his face, he looked like a radioactive Smokey the Bear.

"Now, when you're working your minnow fly"—Sam pantomimed fly casting—"it's the same rhythm. You make your cast, let it swing, then pulse it. Quick-quick slow. Or you can go slow quick-quick, like the bolero, or a three count with the emphasis on the first pull. I call that last retrieve the wooly bugger waltz, but you can do it with any pattern, even the Crazy Mountain Kiss that Sean had you fishing today. Biggest trout I ever caught was waltzing a sculpin streamer, right here in the Big Hole. Eight-pound brown. Come on, get on your feet, show me your stuff."

Sean and David leaned back in their camp chairs and rocked with laughter.

"You did real good today," Sean said, still laughing. "I mean it, David, you were solid on the oars, made some decent throws, that last bow . . . a very nice fish. I almost wish your mother had been here to see it."

"She wouldn't like the pissing on the campfire part. She'd put her hands on her hips and say, 'Humpff.'" He mimicked his mother, his gestures expansive after three fingers of Wild Turkey. "She's in love with you, you know. She'd shag you in a heartbeat."

"Hey," Sam said sharply. "There's no talk of love on a trout stream. Give the river some respect. Come on now, shake that thing."

So they circled the fire as their forebears had, a blue moon above and the first stars as witness, conjuring trout from the flames, dancing the wooly bugger waltz.

**Keith McCafferty's fifth novel
in the Sean Stranahan mystery series
is now available from Viking.**

Read on for the first two chapters of . . .

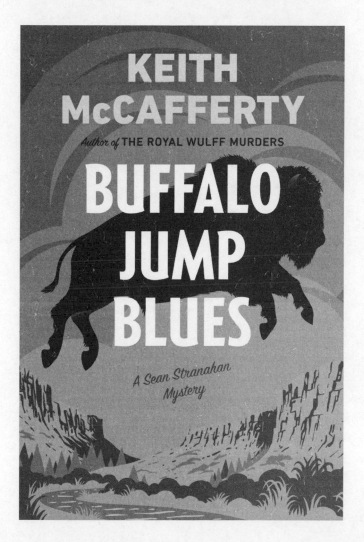

KEITH
McCAFFERTY

Author of THE ROYAL WULFF MURDERS

BUFFALO
JUMP
BLUES

A Sean Stranahan
Mystery

CHAPTER ONE

Kettle of Blood

"I suppose a gun would be too much to ask for."

Harold Little Feather stared across the river. A small group of gawkers, two fishing guides and the couples who were their clients, gathered at his back. Moaning sounds emanating from the tree and willow tangle at the base of the cliffs were spaced farther apart now, just in the thirty minutes since he'd driven up from Ennis. He'd been sitting down to breakfast when he got the call. His day off, a date to meet Martha and cast a fly in the braids of the Madison, hence unarmed.

"I mean, this being Montana and all, land of free men and open carry, I'd think somebody would be packin'."

If Martha was here she'd have her Ruger, day off or not. Strapping up was part of her a.m. ritual, like turning Goldie out for a run while she steeped her tea, running a ChapStick across her lips and looking at her face critically in the mirror before squaring her hat. On nights when Harold slept over he'd step up behind her, bring his big hands to her face, chestnut against white, lift the corners of her mouth so she saw herself smile.

"I got a two-two."

Harold turned around. He'd heard the crunch of gravel a few minutes before as another truck pulled up. It was Peachy Morris hauling his ClackaCraft, the one with the pink ribbon on the hull to show his support for breast cancer research, though anyone who knew Peachy knew the only breast research he was interested in was the hands-on kind. The lanky fishing guide crinkled up his eyes, a *What do we have here?* look on his face. Harold's glance took in Peachy's clients, a tall, sandy-haired man he recognized as a member of the Madison River Liars and Fly Tiers Club, though he had forgotten the name, and a small girl who looked maybe seven.

"And what's your name?" Harold asked the girl.

The girl hid her face behind a wing of straw-colored hair. *It's because I'm Indian,* he thought. When she'd boldly pronounced her armament, he'd been facing away from her.

The sandy-haired man extended his hand. "Robin Hurt Cowdry. We've met."

"Sure. You're from Zimbabwe, you import the African artifacts."

"Botswana," the man corrected. "Mugabe redistributed my keister all the way to Botswana. This is Doris, my niece." And to the girl, "Mind your manners."

She shyly faced Harold. "You can have my two-two," she said, "but it's back at the house."

"I might need something bigger than that," Harold said. His eyes turned to the cliffs as the moaning picked up in volume.

"Sounds like a bloody pride of lions," Cowdry said.

Harold's nod was half an inch. "It's bison. Guy on the Tenderfoot Creek game range saw them on the escarpment last night, maybe a part of the herd that came out of Yellowstone onto the Hebgen Plateau, reported it to Fish, Wildlife, and Parks this morning. A guide putting in heard the ruckus"—Harold jerked his head to indicate the group standing at the boat ramp—"so he called the county and here I am with my hands in my pockets."

"So you figure they fell over the cliffs?" Peachy Morris was tugging on his rowing gloves. "Fourth of July. All that racket down in the valley, people setting off fireworks. They could have panicked."

"That's what I'm thinking."

"Then let me see what I can come up with."

Harold crossed his arms against the bite of morning chill, caught the girl staring at his tattoos, the weasel tracks hunting around his left upper biceps, the hooves of elk following each other around his right.

"Are you an Indian?" she said, pushing the hair out of her face. "I've never seen an Indian."

"Absolutely," Harold said.

"I saw a Zulu warrior dance. They're fiercer than you."

"That's because I didn't put on my paint this morning."

Peachy was back, handing over a revolver in a leather holster.

"It's a .454 Casull. The loads are just snake shot, but there's some hard cast rounds floating around in my boat bag. Shoot through thirty inches of wet phone books."

The girl's eyes widened. "Jah, you could right donner them with that. Couldn't he, Uncle Robin?"

"Speak American, Dorry," Cowdry said.

Morris produced five hard cast loads with the comment that they might not be enough. "How many you think there are?" he said.

"Sounds like a few." Harold tipped out the cylinder to eject the snake loads and fed in the full-power rounds. He turned to Cowdry. "I left a message with the sheriff. She comes, she'll have donuts. Tell her to save me one of the glazed. Make sure your niece gets one."

He raised his chin to the guide. "Peachy, you think you could row me across?"

He spoke briefly to the group who'd been standing on the bank, telling them to wait until he'd crossed before launching and to stay in their boats until they were through the cliffs. He left them stringing fly rods and pushed off with Peachy at the oars of the driftboat, making for a backwater on the far bank.

"You want me to come with you?" Peachy dropped the anchor.

"No, I got it."

Harold ran his eyes to the tops of the cliffs, which were known as the Palisades and stood sentinel for a solid mile over the river's west bank. The moaning sounds were louder here and sounded more like growling, though the reverberation on the rock walls made them hard to place. He drew the Casull from the holster to double-check the loads. "I won't be needing this," he said, and tossed the holster to Peachy. He started hiking up the bank, holding the heavy handgun at his side.

The first buffalo was dead, a jagged edge of cannon bone sticking through the skin of its foreleg, its bowels evacuated, its enormous eye glazed over. A cow, fingers of shaggy winter coat hanging off it like brown moss. The cow had rolled after falling off the cliff, carving a wide swale through the brush. Twenty yards farther up, where willows choked the river bottom, was a second cow. Its cavernous rib cage expanded, then collapsed like an accordion. With each exhalation, a ragged gurgling sound blew bubbles in the blood covering its nose and mouth. Its eye followed Harold as he walked around it, but it lacked the strength to turn its head. Harold clenched his jaw. He extended his right arm and shot it in the back of its skull.

At the shot, Harold's arm jerked up and back, spinning him halfway around. He brought the barrel down out of recoil, feeling a sharp pain in his shoulder from the wrenching of his arm. Jesus, the thing was a cannon. His ears ringing, he sat down beside the dead bison. The roaring of other bison had become an undertone, dull and muted from the concussion. Eventually the underwater sensation subsided and the sounds of the dying animals came back.

Harold tucked his braid under the back of his shirt and fought through brush. He climbed until he reached the base of the cliffs, which was scree rock and sagebrush studded about with giant slabs of stone that had broken away from the cliff face. The rattling, guttural sighs seemed to surround him. He found another dead cow and then three bison still clinging to life, two of them lying down, one on its knees, feebly pushing its short horns against the withers of one of the fallen animals. Harold tore strips from his bandana and wadded them into his ears. He looked away for a few moments, putting off the inevitable. Then he grasped the rubberized grips of the revolver with both hands, extending his arms, and shot the bison that was on its knees. It rolled over and was still. He moved a few feet, sat down, and shot the next one, and then the third. The great heads rocked with the impacts and the moaning stopped.

Harold got to his feet. He pulled the cotton out of his ears. Except for the river running, he heard nothing, and the relative silence seemed oppressive. That must be the lot, he thought. He had gone a long way inside himself to find that still place where the hunter went when he killed, had gone so far as to regard the bison as "it" rather than he or she, something no Indian would do without conscious decision for they were his brothers, his sisters, and only now did he take in a bigger picture. Harold was Blackfeet, his people were buffalo people, nomads who had followed the herds until there were no more herds to follow. For thousands of years his ancestors had driven bison over cliffs similar to those above him. In fact, Harold thought, it was entirely likely that they had driven bison over these very cliffs, for this had been a Blackfeet hunting ground and the cliffs formed what was called a *pishkun* in the tribal language, a "deep blood kettle." But that was before the white man came with his seeds and his cattle, before the Sharps rifles spoke and the Sun Dances held on the reservation became only ceremony.

Harold squatted on his heels, facing the river. He watched the occasional car pass by on the highway, a quarter mile to the east. If you lifted your eyes it was Eden as his grandfather's grandfathers had seen it, the mountains uncolored by time. The irony of what he had done, killing the first bison to have returned to these ancient hunting grounds in one hundred and fifty years, was not lost on him, and the tears that hung on the high bones of his cheeks were the tears of his people. He ignored them as a white, boxy-looking vehicle slowed and turned onto the access road. That would be Martha's Cherokee. Well, he'd better get back across and give her the news.

The slope he'd climbed earlier was choked with willow and alder, and he looked for an easier route down to the river. To his right the gradient eased, and he'd descended a few yards when he saw the bushes above him bulging and heard a sound like rocks clashing. The head of a bison emerged from the brush, strings of bloody mucus hanging from its nostrils. It was striking its hooves against the stone scree, pawing it. The bison was thirty feet away and it came in a stumbling charge. A bull, its great hump standing taller than Harold's head, coming on three good legs, one rear leg flopping. Harold cocked the hammer on the last round in the Casull and held his fire. Twenty feet, ten, the bison's head dropping to toss him with its thick, incurved horns. Harold brought the muzzle level with its forehead and pulled the trigger, then jumped to the side as the bull fell heavily, its nose plowing into the scree. For a moment it lay still. Then, slowly, it began to slide down the hill. It picked up speed, rolled over once, and came to rest against the trunk of a limber pine tree.

Harold had felt the earth shake as the bison fell, and now he couldn't feel his feet underneath him. Where he'd been standing, blood painted the stones. He worked his way down to where the beast lay dead, into the envelope of its heavy odor, into their collective past. The underwater sensation was back and he shook his head. Such a magnificent animal. Such a waste of life.

That's when he heard the bleating. It was not loud, but higher-pitched than the moaning he'd heard earlier. He knew it must be a calf. He thought about going back to the landing, waiting for Martha, borrowing her .357 to finish it off.

No, do it now. Get it over with. He reached for the bone-handled knife on his hip.

CHAPTER TWO

Facts of Nature

Martha Ettinger stood on the riverbank, looking across to the cliffs where she'd heard the last shot.

"That's all he had with him, five rounds," Robin Cowdry said.

Martha placed her hands on her hips and drummed the grips of her revolver. Harold should have waited for her, but if he'd waited, he wouldn't be Harold.

"I can't hear anything," she said.

"He must have got them all."

Martha shook her head. This was going to make news. Bison were a hot-button issue in Montana, had been ever since the herds started migrating out of Yellowstone Park more than two decades before, hazed back by cowboys and helicopters, or shot after crossing the border. To a degree the animals were pawns in a controversy that went beyond animal control and was in fact cultural warfare, everyone in on the act, from the cattle ranchers who couldn't say the word "bison" without spitting to buffalo hippies who'd take a bullet for them, from Native Americans who wanted to bring herds back to the reservations to the urban electorate who'd like to see them roam freely on public lands. Even the governor was caught between the rock that was the livestock industry and the hard place that was public sentiment for this icon of the West that only a century ago had stood at the brink of extinction.

"Harold thought this was part of that Hebgen herd," Cowdry said. "The ones that came out of the park."

"Mmm."

He might as well have been talking to a river stone.

"Here they come," Martha said.

She'd seen the skiff pull out of the cove, Peachy hard at the oars. Harold wasn't sitting in the bow seat from which a fisherman would cast, but looked to be kneeling on the boat's bottom. Caught in the current, the skiff swept downriver at an angle, Peachy working it into the near bank some forty yards below the landing. He hopped out in his waders, taking the bow line to haul it upstream. Harold stayed where he was, Martha now seeing that he was bending over and his head was down. She felt a flutter in her blood and subconsciously brought two fingers to the artery in her throat.

"What's that in the bottom of the boat?" Cowdry had pulled on his waders and was stepping into the river to help Peachy with the skiff. The girl, Dorry, stepped up beside Martha and reached for her hand. Her mouth was white with powdered sugar from the donut Martha had given her.

"Look," she said. "Look." She let go of Martha's hand and jumped on a rock to gain a higher vantage. "Look, Sheriff, he's got a buffalo!"

Harold had stepped out of the boat into thigh-deep water, his back to the bank. When he turned around, the bison calf was bleating against his chest. The veins on his biceps stood out from the strain of lifting it. He sloshed to shore and stepped onto the bank.

Martha started to speak, but there was something behind Harold's half smile that gave her pause.

"Did that snakebit calf pull through?" he said. He set the bison down so that the girl could pet it with her sticky fingers.

Martha gave him a look. "No, I gave her mouth-to-nose until Jeff Svenson showed, but she was too far gone."

"What happened to the carcass?"

"Skinned and hanging. Why, do you want some veal? Personally, I'm a little put off by meat pumped with poison."

"When did this happen?"

"Last night." *Last night when you didn't come over.* That part went unsaid.

Martha caught the amused look Peachy Morris was giving them. The last time Peachy had heard Martha talking with Harold about something and what they were really talking about was something else, he'd told them to get a room.

She looked hard at the fishing guide. He rolled up a stick of gum and put it in his mouth, wiped the grin off his face.

"What did you do with the skin?" Harold asked.

The shoe dropped as Martha shook her head.

"Hun-ah," she said. "It isn't going to happen."

Harold knelt down beside the little red bison, which had quieted down while the girl had her arm around it, but was now bleating incessantly.

"Hey, little fella," Harold said. He lifted his eyes to Martha, who mouthed the word "No."

"Meet your new mother," Harold said.

———

It took some finagling. You couldn't just put a bison into the bed of a truck unattended. Somebody would have to hold it while the other drove, and Harold took the honor, climbing into the bed. After introducing the bison to the Angus cow that had lost her calf, presuming that went smoothly and there was no guarantee it would, they'd drive back to pick up the Cherokee, which Peachy Morris and Robin Cowdry agreed to shuttle downriver to Ennis after their float.

Martha looked at the girl, sitting under a frayed straw hat on the stern seat of the skiff. They'd had to pry her arms from the bison's neck and tears had tracked down her cheeks, beading up on top of her sunscreen. But she'd bucked up when Martha told her she could visit the calf, a lie of a certain color.

"Don't let her play with the siren," Martha said, as she pushed the driftboat off the ramp. "You know how birds attack a boat when you hit the siren."

"I won't let her touch it." Peachy pulled at the oars, winking at Martha, going along.

"And remember the ejector seat. Whatever you do, don't touch the red button."

Peachy curled his fingers underneath the rowing platform. "It's right under my thumb here."

"Ejector seat!" the girl said. Her eyes grew big. "You don't have no ejector seat. Do you?"

"Pitch you right into the water if you don't behave," Peachy said.

"Nah. He doesn't have an ejector seat, does he, Uncle Robin?"

Martha waved good-bye as the driftboat swept away down the river, Robin Cowdry already false casting his fly line.

She turned back to the truck. Harold had climbed into the bed and was sitting with his arms around the little bison. "Ejector seat, huh? I didn't know you were so good with kids."

"You forget I raised two of them."

Harold jabbed his chin, a *Look over my shoulder* gesture. "I knew we waited around, they'd finally show," he said.

"Who?"

"Drake. I can smell him from here."

Martha looked up the access road. Harold was right. A truck was coming, it rattled down the grade, a horse-and-cattle emblem identifying as a DOL vehicle—Montana Department of Livestock.

"Harold, this doesn't have to get personal."

"Maybe if your eyes are blue."

"Well, my eyes are blue, so just let me do the talking. Okay?"

It was Drake, Francis Lucien Drake, though everyone just called him Drake. He stepped out of the truck in parts, everything about him big, pushing his hat back on a high forehead, hitching his jeans, shaking his head when he saw the bison calf. He stuck a hand-rolled cigarette into the corner of his mouth and worked it without lighting it.

"You cavorting with livestock now, Harold? Getting yourself some of that barn candy?" A smile on his face, or rather a deliberate pulling back of his lips, exposing tombstone teeth stained by nicotine. He had a whorl of creases in his chin that constantly shifted, as if worms churned under the stubble.

Another man, shorter, swarthy, had climbed from the cab. He kicked caked mud from his boots against a big truck tire with a dragon-tooth tread. Carhartts head to cuff, old cracked boots. A gunfighter mustache gone salt-and-pepper. Martha knew him, had to wait a second to recall the name.

"Calvin," she said.

"Sheriff."

She made the introduction to Harold, who knew Calvin Barr only by his reputation as a wolfer for Animal Damage Control. Barr spoke out of the side of his mouth to say hello, his eyebrows, wiry and black, running together as he frowned at the calf. He came forward in a bowlegged walk and rubbed the head of the bison.

"Little red bull calf," he said. His voice had sandpaper in it.

"I see somebody's been crawling the stock of his rifle," Harold said.

"You'd think I learned the lesson." Barr tapped the upper arch of his right orbital bone, where dozens of half-moon scars, caused by the steel rim of a rifle scope, showed white through a forest of eyebrow hair.

"What kind of gun recoils so hard the scope cuts you?"

"Forty-five ninety Sharps original with a Malcolm's six-power. But it's my own durned fault. If I kept my cheek back where it belongs, the scope wouldn't jump back far enough to kiss me."

Martha had led Drake away from the truck. Harold could see them standing by the river, Martha with her hands on her hips, Drake shaking his head.

"Just so we're clear," Harold said. "He points the finger, you pull the trigger?"

Barr tilted his head as if considering. "That would be the job description," he said.

"I heard the wolf lovers called you Killer Barr."

The man nodded. "That wasn't fair. I made it my business to know if I was shooting a guilty party. A lot of livestock deaths are blamed on predators when it's rancher neglect, blue tongue . . ." He shrugged. "Teeth don't have a thing to do with it sometimes."

"No, it wasn't fair. You're just a man caught in the middle, doing his job. My problem's with the law that has you do it. 'Bout an hour ago I shot five bison that fell off the cliff. That's where I found this little fella. Don't know how he survived the fall."

"Must have fallen on top of one of the others, reduced the impact."

"Maybe."

"Had to be hard, what you did."

"Shooting them was an act of mercy. Seeing them suffer, that was hard. How many have you killed?"

"Bison?" The man took the question seriously, ran his eyebrows together as he considered. "I'd say three hundred plus since I contracted to DOL. They stray out of the park, out of the buffer zone, I get the call."

"You ever think about not answering the phone?"

Barr seemed to think about that question, too. "There's a way I look at it," he said. "If it isn't me, then they get somebody else. Then maybe the bullets don't go where they're supposed to and somebody has to clean up the mess, like you did yonder."

"You're the reluctant executioner who makes sure the job is done humanely."

"Buffalo take a lot of killing." Barr rubbed the hairy back of his hand against the bison calf's forehead.

"Those bison this morning," Harold prompted. "If they hadn't fallen off the cliff, you were going to kill them anyway, am I right?"

"I won't lie to you. As soon as they crossed onto the public land, the department had the green light."

"You'd have shot this calf along with the rest."

"That's the policy. You want to get all of them. You don't want to leave one that has the unacceptable behavior ingrained, because it will lead others back to the same place."

"Unweaned calf do that?"

"It's policy to cull them all."

"'Cull.' That's an interesting word. I saw some cowboys cull a herd of thirty up out of Gardiner once, enough blood to cover a football field. One cow was dragging her guts on the ground, little calf like this one following her."

The calf was bawling again and Harold rubbed its head.

"What are you thinking to do?" Barr said.

"Sheriff has a cow lost its calf. We'll wrap this little guy in the skin and hope she accepts him."

Barr nodded. "I heard of that being done, but never heard of it take. Worth a shot. I say good luck to you."

Martha and Drake were coming back, Drake making a tisking sound with his tongue as he shook his head.

"Harold, you know I can't let you have that calf."

"Not my calf to give. This is a wild, free-ranging bison," Harold said.

"There ain't no such animal, no sir."

"Times are changing, Drake. The buffalo are coming back, just like the wolf did. It's people like you the clock's ticking down on."

"You're wrong about that, but that's not the issue. This calf hasn't gone through quarantine and it could be spreading disease to cattle."

"You mean brucellosis. That's bullshit and you know it."

"My job is to remove bison that have strayed beyond the zone of tolerance, which this herd clearly had. Plus you're violating state law pertaining to possession of wildlife."

Harold looked at Martha, who didn't return his glance. He looked at Barr, who had stepped away from the truck. It had become an old-fashioned western, two men in a dusty street.

"'Pertaining,' huh? You must have learned a new word, Drake."

Drake pulled at his cigarette. "We'll wait until you're gone to do our duty, that makes a difference to you."

"No, I'll be taking him with me."

The man nodded, showed his teeth in a gray smile, as if that was the response he'd expected.

"Then I'll have to write you up to the supervisor. Someone will be knocking. Probably be me."

"We'll have the TV crew on call. World can see you for what you are. Tell you what, though, it comes to that, I'll rub your smile in buffalo manure for the camera. Rest of your life, first thing people will think when they see your face is how an Indian stuffed your mouth with shit."

Drake stared at him, his eyes squinted up in folds of flesh. The worms in his chin crawled and crawled. He spat the butt and ground it under his heel.

"We're done here, Calvin. Let's go before I do something I regret."

"Anytime, anywhere," Harold said.

Drake took a half step forward to find Ettinger blocking the way.

"You want to do something about this, go through your channels," she said to Drake. "But once the calf is on private property, you'll have to get a court order to have it removed."

"Not according to interagency statute, not if I deem it an imminent threat to livestock or property." He shrugged. "But maybe I won't have to take him. Sometimes, animals just disappear. It's a fact of nature."

"Anything happens to this calf," Harold said, "you'll answer to me."

"Is that a threat?" He was looking at Ettinger. "This man has threatened physical violence upon my person and all I'm doing is trying to execute my job. I want it duly noted."

"Not a threat." Harold rearranged his grip on the struggling bison calf. "Like you said, Drake, some things are just a fact of nature."

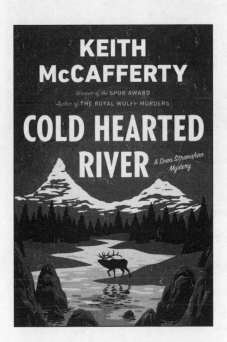

ALSO AVAILABLE

THE ROYAL WULFF MURDERS

THE GRAY GHOST MURDERS

DEAD MAN'S FANCY

CRAZY MOUNTAIN KISS

BUFFALO JUMP BLUES

COLD HEARTED RIVER